A Woman Born of Might and Magic . . .
A Love Forged from Passion and Prophecy . . .

As foretold by a Druid priestess, Gwendolyn grew into golden womanhood, luminous in grace and power. When England's mightiest knight taught her the arts of war, she taught him the art of passion, and their love burst into flame. But a jealous knight to whom she had been promised vowed to destroy them both. Only their deaths would quell his rage . . . only their union, destined by the gods, would forge the lifeblood of a new and timeless age.

"*QUEEN OF KNIGHTS* is an unusual fantasy in which history as well as fiction dances to the author's piping."

—Roberta Gellis,
author of the *Roselynde Chronicles*

Books by David Wind writing as Monica Barrie

Gentle Fury
Turquoise Sky

Published by TAPESTRY BOOKS

PUBLISHED BY POCKET BOOKS NEW YORK

Distributed in Canada by PaperJacks Ltd., a Licensee
of the trademarks of Simon & Schuster, Inc.

This novel is a work of fiction. Names, characters, places and incidents are either the product of the author's imagination or are used fictitiously. Any resemblance to actual events or locales or persons, living or dead, is entirely coincidental.

Another *Original* publication of POCKET BOOKS

POCKET BOOKS, a division of Simon & Schuster, Inc.
1230 Avenue of the Americas, New York, N.Y. 10020
In Canada distributed by PaperJacks Ltd.,
330 Steelcase Road, Markham, Ontario

For information address Pocket Books, 1230 Avenue of the Americas, New York, N.Y. 10020

ISBN: 0-671-46973-8

First Pocket Books printing March, 1985

10 9 8 7 6 5 4 3 2 1

Printed in Canada

THIS NOVEL IS DEDICATED WITH LOVE TO
Bonnie Marilyn Wind,

For always being there,
for her unending belief,
for her unswerving faith.

ACKNOWLEDGMENTS

To K. McCabe—for the trust to let me free my mind.

To Tony Chilton—resident expert in arms and armor for the BBC—for sharing his devastating wealth of knowledge with me in Hay-on-Wye, Wales.

To Roberta Gellis—the first lady of historical fiction—for allowing me not only to pick her brain, but her extensive research library as well.

To Leslie O'Gwin Rivers—for her invaluable aid as my researcher.

To Frank Yerby, Rafael Sabatini, Edgar Rice Burroughs, and Andre (Mary Alice) Norton, to name but a few—who through their novels taught me the meanings of adventure, speculation, history, and fantasy.

To Julia Coopersmith—who believed when others did not.

And to all the wonderful people in England and Wales who helped me with my research and aided me in my travels.

From the Author

Entwined throughout the roots of history lies legend. For, what else is early history but the remembrances of men's thoughts? Within those early memories, those early thoughts, lay the old tales of superstition and legend; for is it not truth that history and legend are born within the minds of people, and the only distinction between them, is in the eye of the witnesses to those bygone events?

Who among us actually looks to discredit the tale of Robin Hood? Who seeks to destroy the legend of King Arthur? Who would challenge the might and power of Odin? Who would dare say the Druid circles were but randomly placed stones?

And who of you, when turning the pages of this legend, will be unwilling to free yourself from the binding restraints of recorded history and journey into a realm that could have been, and for all we know, might have been—for legend and history are inexorably linked by the random joining of truth, need, and thought.

Know you, who read on, that Richard the Lion-Heart and Saladin lived in the past, and, with Gwendolyn Kildrake and Miles Delong, they live again in the legend of the *Queen of Knights*.

David Wind

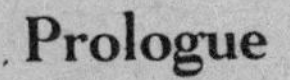

Prologue

On the Estate of Sir Hughes Kildrake, Duke of Devonshire, at the Pool of Pendragon

THE SUN GLANCED DARINGLY across the calm waters of the forest pool as a young woman stood near its edge. The cool water beckoned to her and, as if in a trance, she disrobed and entered.

She was a maiden of beauty, a true daughter of the land of England. Her complexion was fair, with sapphire-blue jewels for eyes, and raven hair that gleamed boldly against the milky whiteness of porcelain skin. The birds who sat upon the branches of the forest trees sang sweet tunes whilst they watched Gwyneth, daughter of Sir Hughes Kildrake, barely ten and six years, welcome the first warmth of summer by entering the pool.

This part of the forest, since earliest memory, had always been called the Pool of Pendragon. Here, it is said, King Arthur and his queen rested and played in the days of the first Lord of Devonshire (Sir Hughes's great ancestor, Byron of Kildrake, first Duke of Devonshire), who had been granted these lands by his Majesty Arthur, and dubbed by the sword Excalibur.

And now, centuries later, in the almost mystical pool, the youngest of the line of Kildrake, Gwyneth, daughter of Hughes, lay on the shallow rock bottom, her eyelids half shuttered and her mind in a dreamlike state while she remembered the words of the old seeress.

It had happened the night before when they had finished the evening meal and she and her mother, Ariel, had gone to the women's chambers to work on their tapestries. As they worked and talked, an old woman had entered and come toward them. Gwyneth had seen her many times about the castle, but had never spoken with her. Yet her mother, Gwyneth knew, had spoken frequently with the strange old woman. The woman's eyes, like the small black berries found in the farthest corner of her father's lands, burned intensely into Gwyneth's.

The woman's name was unknown, but everyone called her the *old one* and whispered of ancient powers. They said she was a Druid priestess.

The old woman had come directly to them, and Gwyneth remembered clearly what had transpired, as if it were happening now, in the Pool of Pendragon.

"Through a mist of many-colored bands will come the father of your child. A giant among men, the last of his earthbound race. Gold will spill from his head and flow past his shoulders. His muscles will ripple with the strength of the mightiest bear, yet he will move with the grace of a running stag.

"His eyes will be the color of the early morning sky, and he will come to you, as if in a dream, and beget by you the lifeblood of a new race. Greatness will follow the issue of this union, greatness unknown ever before. Kings will bow low before the power and might and strength of this child when the child grows to adulthood.

"This child will be among the tallest in the land, with fair hair and a mind that grasps the unthinkable, and will turn the impossible into reality. Across the breadth of the world, valor and strength will be known of the issue of Kildrake, and the legend will grow."

Last night, Gwyneth had tried to understand the meaning of the crone's words, but had been unable to. Today brought no enlightenment. Her hand was promised to Malcome of Kingsgrove, but he was short, wide, and of a dark, ruddy complexion. No child of golden hair and sky-blue eyes could be foretold. No child of stature and strength would come of that union.

In just three cycles of the moon she would wed. To leave this forest, this glade, this pool, and her home forever.

Gwyneth's body floated to the surface of the glassy pool, making the water swirl when her full breasts broke its calm surface. She felt a sudden chill rush by, carried upon the early summer air.

The sun was almost at its zenith, sending shimmering rays of light through the forest. In the near distance a small dark cloud released its water to the earth. When the rain stopped, the reflection of the sun upon the newly wet trees produced a rainbow that held all the colors of creation. Gwyneth's heart stirred with its beauty.

She gazed at the rainbow, again in a trancelike state, feeling herself afloat as if she were riding a cloud, until suddenly the beginning of a dark shape formed behind the rainbow. The shape was hidden by distance, but, slowly, the form took substance.

Gwyneth could not move, not even when the birds of the forest fell silent and the insects stopped their calling. Growing taller within her vision came a man. *She must get out of the water! She must dress,* Gwyneth told herself, but her body would not obey her commands. Slowly, the form came closer.

When she finally saw him, emerging through the rainbow, she became even more powerless to move. His long blonde hair, falling in thick waves, was lost behind his shoulders. The rainbow was at his back, and his size was larger than life. With his every step, muscles rippled. About his waist was a girdle of dark pelt; upon his feet, boots of shimmering silver skins; at his side, a longsword glistened when a shaft of sunlight struck its handle.

And then Gwyneth saw him clearly. His eyes pierced her with bright morning blueness. He was the tallest man she had ever seen, a giant among men. His thighs quivered powerfully as he walked, the muscles standing out with every stride. His chest was broad, his shoulders massive, but Gwyneth could only look at his face.

No scar marred his skin. High cheekbones stood out against a strong, straight nose. His hair was the color of golden wheat and silver moonlight; his teeth were flashes of white against a thick golden beard.

And then Gwyneth knew who he was. She had heard the stories of the fearsome Norse people—the Viking raiders of old. But the race had died out. It existed now only in legend.

Yet he was real, alive, and here at the Pool of Pendragon.

Finally, after an eternity of watching and waiting, the Norseman stood above her. His head was framed by the sun, and his coppery skin shone like armor. Gwyneth could do nothing but gaze at him, unafraid.

Gwyneth watched as his large hand reached out and blocked the sun. His palm was upraised and waiting. She could not help herself from extending her hand and letting it become encased within his. He lifted her gently from the pool and pulled her to his chest. The water conducted his heat across her body, and Gwyneth felt herself begin to burn. She smelled the forest scents clinging to him, mixed with the aura of his power and sex. His lips went to hers, and in her dreamlike state, she did not protest. Ever so slowly, he lifted her with his mighty arms as if she weighed no more than a feather. Gently, the Norse giant, who stood three heads taller than Gwyneth, placed her on a bed of soft, grassy moss. Gwyneth could not summon the power to force her body to movement. Yet she was still unafraid of the blonde giant who stood above her.

She was unafraid even when he removed the pelt girdle, and placed that, with his glinting longsword, upon a rock shaped like an altar. He stood above her, letting the sun pour over his nakedness, and Gwyneth felt her body come alive. Her deeply drawn breath echoed like thunder in the stillness of the forest.

Slowly, the giant lowered himself until he covered her body with his. His head came down, and his lips gently tasted hers. A rush of heat again flowed along the length of Gwyneth's body until she grew lightheaded. With their mouths together, the Norseman moved between her thighs and, for one instant of time, Gwyneth remembered who and what she was.

This could not happen, she told herself silently, even as she felt the heat of his loins burn against her tender flesh. She tried to fight, to push against his great strength with her pitifully small hands. He paused at this resistance, lifting himself on outstretched arms. His blue eyes gazed down at her until all resistance fled. He kissed her again, and Gwyneth's world dissolved as the blonde giant took her.

He filled her, lancing deep within her. She cried out, but did not know she had, as she was carried to a place she had never dreamed of, and knew instinctively she would never return to again. But this time of magic and power and mystery would not be denied. This one time would content her until she left the earth behind.

The rush of pain from his deep, piercing thrusts subsided, and soon her body joined his in its lithe movements. Their bodies, so different in size, blended; the smaller, doelike woman moved in harmony with the staglike giant above her. While they made love, Gwyneth's eyes remained open, watching the face that was only inches above hers.

The sun was like a fringe of golden light surrounding his head. His eyes of morning blue glowed as he gazed deeply into hers, until suddenly a haze clouded her vision and a wrenching tore through her soul to whisk her away from the mossy ground of the Pool of Pendragon, to float above herself and look down upon both her and the golden giant.

She heard again the echoing words of the old seeress, just as the Norseman's final thrust filled her with his molten fluid. "Across the breadth of the world, valor and strength will be known of the issue of Kildrake, and the legend will grow."

And Gwyneth knew the seed of the legend, the lifeblood of his family, had been planted deep within her.

Ever so slowly, Gwyneth returned to the earth and rejoined her body. The Norseman held her tightly, gently pressing her breasts against his chest. He held her like that until their breathing eased, before he slowly drew from within her.

When he stood, Gwyneth saw her blood smeared on his thighs, but felt nothing except the loss she would retain for the rest of her years. His eyes told her he felt the same, and when the time came, in another world, on a different plane, they would be joined, never to part.

Gwyneth stared at him, her eyes wide, unrelenting in her desire to capture his face forever within. He nodded slowly, then went to his pelt girdle and sword of silver.

When his girdle was secured he turned back to Gwyneth. He walked to her and stood above her. Slowly he knelt upon one knee and brought his palm to rest upon the softness of her belly.

Gwyneth felt a jolt pass from his palm and enter deep within her womb. The Norseman, the last of his true race, nodded again, solemnly, then stood. Swiftly, he lifted the sword from the altarlike rock with both hands and raised it to the sky. Gwyneth gasped at the ray of sunlight which raced from the sword's tip to its pommel. She watched the sword glow silver, radiating a warmth that encompassed the man, the woman, and the forest glade. Then, with his arms still upraised, he bowed his head and turned again to the raven-haired Gwyneth.

He stood with the sword raised above them both. If any were to have seen them at this moment, bathed in the silver-and-gold light that joined sword and sun, they would have trembled with fear for Gwyneth's life. But Gwyneth had no such fear. She knew.

The giant smiled tenderly, and with a movement that blurred light, the blade swiftly arched, ending its path at the tip of one swollen nipple.

Again, with a hairsbreadth of air separating blade and skin, Gwyneth knew no fear.

The giant Norseman knelt once more and, with bowed head, laid the hilt of his sword upon Gwyneth's abdomen. The tip of the blade reached past her ankles. He kissed its silver shaft and then the skin between the pommel of the sword and the tender, downy hair below it.

He stood, leaving the sword upon her, and as silently as he had come, walked back into the rainbow mist that had borne him.

Gwyneth did not immediately return to the castle when the Viking was gone, but rather, stayed by the pool, unmoving on the soft carpet of moss, her eyes remaining closed against his leaving while her hands caressed the hilt of the sword that remained. Finally, she opened her eyes and looked at the crystal sky above, then down at the sword.

Her hands grasped the hilt, and she knew he had left it for his son. She knew he had planted the seed, and the seed would grow strong within her. It was only when she lifted the sword that she realized its difference was not in its silvery glow alone. Although the sword was as wide as a broad-sword and the length of a longsword, she hefted it with surprising ease. Its weight was no more than the small wooden swords the soldiers made for little children to play with. But even when she lifted it high, catching more of the sun's rays along the length of the blade, the silvery sheen did not diminish. She knew also that the blade was coated with the purest of silver.

And with all the knowledge she had so suddenly gained came one more thought. Gwyneth realized she must hide this sword, keep it safe until her son was born and grew into manhood.

Unwilling to cleanse herself of the aftereffects of her lovemaking, Gwyneth stood, placed the sword upon the altarlike stone, and dressed herself. Carrying the sword in the crook of her arms, she began to walk along the path leading to her father's castle. Halfway there, she veered from the path to enter a deep area of the forest. Not a hundred feet from the narrow roadway was a special place she used to go as a child, a place known only to her and her mother, Ariel, who had once shown it to Gwyneth when the girl was only seven. It was a small cave, and her mother had whispered it was a place that had been inhabited by a sorcerer of bygone days. But Gwyneth knew her mother had only been teasing, and had taken this cave for her very own. It held two things that were important to her—pleasant memories and a strange, comforting warmth no matter what season was upon the land.

Bending low to gain entry, Gwyneth stepped into the cave. Once inside, she tore a strip from the hem of her skirts and carefully wrapped the sword within it. Reaching high, Gwyneth placed the cloth-bound sword on a ledge and left the cave.

She covered the remaining distance to the castle quickly, ignoring the startled glances of peasants, serfs, and men-at-arms, which were caused by her disheveled appearance. Once inside the castle, Gwyneth held her head high and ran quickly to her mother's chambers to quietly tell Ariel what had happened at the pool. When she was finished, she sat with her head pressed against her mother's breasts, and it was then that Sir Hughes entered the chamber.

He stood in the archway, staring at the close tableau. His raven hair, lightly veined with gray, fell to his shoulders. His tunic of burgundy was embroidered with the coat of arms of Kildrake. A long dagger hung at his waist, and leather boots of the finest quality covered his feet, encasing burgundy leggings that disappeared under the tunic's bottom.

"What has happened?" Sir Hughes roared, his face dark and accusatory. His eyes, the same sapphire-blue as his daughter's, flashed from woman to woman.

"It has come to pass," replied Ariel in a soft, clear voice, her arm drawing Gwyneth tighter to her breasts.

"What are you saying? What riddles do you speak today?" He was well used to his wife's strange ways and did not like her less for them.

"Last night, Husband, I told you of the old woman. I spoke the words she spoke to Gwyneth. She spoke truthfully. Our daughter has been ravaged."

"The old one? That toothless pagan hag you have been feeding at our tables?" bellowed Hughes, unable to contain his rage. He had heard of his daughter's trek through the inner ward and had become both worried and angry.

She was a maiden, and had been kept as such, never allowed in the company of men without at least three handmaidens to attend her. Her marriage was but a short time away, and he was not prepared for any change in plans. The marriage would make an alliance of two families who had feuded for a hundred years.

"What has that nameless woman done to you?" he shouted, spittle flying from his mouth as he pointed a stocky finger at Gwyneth.

"Do you not remember what I told you last night? Were you, Sir Hughes, so deep in your cups that you heard not?" challenged Ariel.

"Am I expected to believe that foolish prattle about a giant among men?" he asked defiantly.

"That foolish prattle has come true." Ariel flung the words back at him.

"Tell me!" Hughes, Duke of Devonshire, demanded of his daughter. A blend of love, fear, and total command emanated from him. Although his renown as a savage fighter had traveled the breadth of England, Sir Hughes had always been gentle to his only surviving child. He was a good father, kinder than most.

When Gwyneth spoke, her voice took on an ethereal quality that drew Hughes into the tale. She related everything that happened factually, omitting only the final gift of the sword. When she was done, she opened her tunic and bared her nakedness. Her thighs, caked with her own dried blood, bore testimony to her words. But what she had not seen before, and that which held her parents' gaze captive upon her unclad belly, proved every word she had spoken. Upon the soft skin of her abdomen was a shadow in the shape of the silver sword's hilt.

Slowly, Gwyneth lowered her eyes, following the gaze of her mother and father, and saw the shape emblazed there. She smiled when she lifted her eyes to theirs.

"I am with his child," she told them. Neither disputed her word. Not after what they had just witnessed.

And so it came to pass, that Gwyneth, daughter of Hughes, betrothed to Sir Malcome, entered into marriage not with Malcome, but rather with Sir Guy of Halsbred, a man twice the age of Gwyneth's father. The change had been accomplished diplomatically, with no loss of face on either side. And Sir Guy of Halsbred gained much more than a wife. He gained the pledge that his lands would be looked after and protected by the powerful Duke of Devonshire. Upon his death, Sir Guy's lands would go to the son of his brother, a monk, and be turned over to the church. Sir Hughes would then take back into his home his daughter Gwyneth and her child.

Seven months following the marriage came the winter solstice.

It was just as the sun dropped from the sky that Gwyneth was taken to the birthing bed. The day outside was angry, and the winter wind whistled through the cracks of the castle walls, which were poorly kept up by Sir Guy, who cared for little, not even the young wife he had married. Already in residence were Ariel and her servants.

Gwyneth's bedchamber had been made warmer by the women, who had hung large tapestries upon the walls to stop the cold winds from stealing through. A fire roared in the fireplace, and a large pot boiled above the flames. Almost to the minute of the setting sun, Gwyneth's first pains came.

When the head of the infant emerged, a sudden hush filled the chamber and all movement stopped. Then the door flew open to reveal an old woman in flowing black robes. She was a frail figure, stooped with age. Gwyneth did not see her through the haze of pain, but everyone else did. The woman moved slowly upon entering the chamber, and it seemed to all who watched her that she grew taller with each step.

When she reached the side of the bed she stood perfectly straight, her toothless mouth smiled, and her small black eyes danced with delight.

She raised old, gnarled hands into the air, and spoke guttural, unintelligible words. Suddenly the baby was free, and Ariel held it aloft.

There was a sudden intake of breath when Ariel stared at the child. A full head of blonde wispy hair, shimmering from the wetness of its mother's womb, glowed as if lit by the sun.

"The cord!" cried one of the servants. Another quickly grasped the cord and began to tie it.

Gwyneth gazed at the child for a moment, feeling a sudden ache within her swollen breasts. Then she saw her mother's face. Ariel's features were pinched, her skin the color of newly fallen snow as she looked at the baby. Gwyneth turned her head slightly and saw the old woman. She smiled, and the Druid smiled back.

"The legend begins. The golden-haired giant has been born! The knight who wields the silver sword has entered the world," she proclaimed in a barely audible whisper.

"No!" Ariel screamed, holding the blonde-haired baby high for all to see. "It cannot be as you have foreseen. Look you! Look old witch! Look Gwyneth! Look!" she cried, lowering the child.

"It will be," replied the old priestess who smiled and took the infant into her own arms. Slowly, gently, she transferred the child, the golden-haired one destined for greatness, into the arms of its mother, to suckle at the swollen breast which already held its life fluids.

"We know, Gwyneth and I, that it shall come to pass. It has been ordained," she said to everyone. Then, lowering her voice, she spoke only to Gwyneth. "When the child reaches the age of ten, you will tell the story, and give the sword to its rightful owner."

Gwyneth gazed languidly at the old woman, before she looked down to the child at her breast. Slowly, she raised her head to see her son, and when she did, the shock could not be hidden.

"But . . . ," she began, her eyes filling with tears as she looked from her mother to the old Druid priestess.

"It is as it should be. It has been foretold," repeated the seer, who walked to the door. Framed within the stone opening, she turned back to the people within the chamber. "The child's mate has already been born, eight years ago, on this very day. In seventeen years the child will marry, and from that time, destiny will flow, and the legend will continue."

Again, slowly, the Druid priestess changed into the stooped old woman, and by the time she was through the doorway and into the halls, she once again looked gnarled and small.

No ear heard the low sea of laughter that issued from her mouth. No eyes saw the merriment that filled the old one, making her face look for the briefest moment as it had seventy years before, when she was but ten and seven.

No one would believe the words she had spoken tonight, no one except Gwyneth, who would remember and would tell the child about its father. It was foretold that no one but its mother would. And when the girl child grew older, the world would be changed.

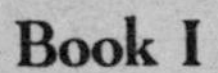

Book I

Of Gwendolyn and Miles, the Awakening of Power, and the Joining of Destiny

Chapter One

RAYS OF SUNLIGHT FILTERED through the branches of the large trees, creating shafts of light that formed bars of yellow sunshine. A lone rider astride a horse of jet black wove through the bars of light, following the pathway they illuminated through the forest.

The horse, a finely muscled mare, moved with the sure-footedness of youthful confidence that had to be shared to be understood. The rider, bending low against the horse's flowing mane, seemed to blend into the animal as a single entity. A long dark cape fell from the rider's shoulders, its hem flowing behind, evidence of the mare's speed. As the horse's thundering hooves rushed onward to the heart of the forest, a loud call sounded from high above.

Two hundred feet over the tree tops, a golden eagle raced the wind. It dived, skimming along the tops of the trees until it caught the current it searched for, and suddenly it rose, wings expanded, spiraling upward. On the ground, the rider looked up, smiling at the sight.

Far behind the lone rider was a group of riders trying in vain to find their leader. Eventually they slowed their mounts, but did not cease to call a name. Their voices, becoming more distant with each powerful stride of the mare, echoed through the forest. With another smile, one of satisfaction, the rider turned between two bars of sunlight and entered still deeper into the thickening woods.

Now only one voice, heavy with male coarseness, reached

the rider's ears. The rider reined the horse and waited to see if the man would follow his voice.

Shaking off the hood, the rider loosened a full head of blonde waves.

"Gwendolyn," came the faint echo, no closer than the last.

"Not today! Today is mine," she said with a smile to the eagle soaring above her. Gwendolyn, daughter of Gwyneth, Lady of Halsbred, granddaughter of Sir Hughes Kildrake, Duke of Devonshire, filled her lungs with the purity and clean scents of the unsullied Devon Forest.

Her eyes, the color of an early morning sky, danced happily as she patted the neck of the mare. Today was her day of freedom. It was early summer and she would have no restrictions placed upon her. Her friends, or so they thought themselves, and her servants, would spend the day looking for her. But today they would not find her. Today she would bathe in the Pool of Pendragon.

Ever since the tenth anniversary of her birth, she had visited the pool on this day. She had come the first time with her mother and had listened to the tale of her conception and been told of her father. For three more years, she and her mother had traveled here, but when she was in her fourteenth year, her mother had died.

Gwyneth had died with a smile on her lips, and Gwendolyn had not shed a tear. She knew her mother wanted to be free to join her father, to spend eternity within his arms. Gwendolyn felt the loss, but she also knew happiness, because her mother would finally be joined with her unnamed husband.

Dismounting, Gwendolyn led the mare through the last edge of the trees that surrounded the pool. When she entered the open glade, she dropped the reins, knowing her mount would not stray. Before letting her eyes drink in the surrounding beauty, she looked skyward until she spotted the dark shape circling high above, lazing on an upward draft of air.

Valkyrie, the giant eagle whom she had found in the fall season five years before, with an arrow shaft embedded in the joint of his wing. He had been lying in the grass, bravely defying one of the castle dogs.

She had chased the dog away and walked up to the eagle. She had not feared it as she knelt beside it. The eagle's yellow eyes had riveted her, unblinking as its long, curved beak opened. She had stretched out her hand and waited. The eagle had pressed its beak to her palm and slowly rubbed upward. Gwendolyn had known the bird would not hurt her. No animal feared her, just as she feared no animal. She had picked up the eagle and carried it back to her chambers. For all the long, cold months of winter, she had nursed the large bird, tending it faithfully, helping it to survive.

When the first warm breezes of spring arrived, Gwendolyn had grown to know the proud bird well, and had known also that he must be free. Without regret, but not without sadness, she had taken him to a large open field near the forest's edge. She had held him high, his large claws securely fastened on her well-covered wrist as it looked around.

Gwendolyn had thrown her arm upward, unaffected by the weight of so large a bird, and had watched as the eagle freed itself from its perch and tested its wounded wing. The eagle had dropped toward the ground and skimmed it, coasting above the grass as it worked its wide wings. Then the eagle's shattering scream had pierced the air and, before her eyes, the bird rose. Gwendolyn had smiled when it flew higher. She felt justified in saving it, even more so in freeing it.

With a wave of her hand to bid the proud eagle farewell, Gwendolyn had turned her horse toward the castle. Before she was halfway home, a swirling breeze had rushed across her head and she looked up as the eagle passed by. She had reined in her horse, puzzled, while she had watched the bird circle her and dive.

Then she knew.

She had held out her arm and watched. Her heart had raced when the eagle had descended from the sky and had come to rest on her wrist. From that day forward, the eagle had never flown without returning to Gwendolyn.

Gwendolyn drew her eyes from the swiftly flying bird and gazed about the pool. It was always the same as she remembered it—the calm, still surface, the slate-colored rocks that surrounded two sides, forming steps that led upward yet nowhere, and the lush carpet of green, grassy moss, so comforting to her back.

The area surrounding the pool was heated by the sun and caressed by gentle breezes. Sighing, Gwendolyn walked to the pool's edge. There, she took off the light cape and loosened the leather girdle that held her tunic closed, and, when that was done, opened and removed the soft burgundy cloth emblazoned with the crest of Kildrake, freeing her body to drink in the sun.

As she did every year, Gwendolyn looked down into the mirror-bright surface of Pendragon's pool and saw herself looking back. She could almost imagine it was her father that gazed upward; the vivid descriptions her mother had given her still lived strongly in her mind. His long golden hair was like hers, the color of wheat and moonlight. Gwendolyn ran her hands through her hair, lifting it and shaking it free. Her father's hair had reached to midback. Hers dipped below her waist.

She stood taller as she looked in the pool. Until three years ago she had been like all the other children. Then the sign of her womanhood had come, and the flow of blood had signaled a change. But unlike the others of her age, Gwendolyn grew until she was taller than any boy or girl she knew. It hadn't ended there; she continued to grow, as her mother had told her she would. And now, in her seventeenth year, she was the tallest person she had ever seen. She stood two inches above Morgan Dublaise, Sir Morgan of Guildswood, her betrothed. And Morgan was rumored to be taller than any knight except Miles of Radstock, whom she had only heard of, but had never met.

Gwendolyn looked at her reflection—tall, well-muscled—and was proud of her body. There was no feat she was afraid to attempt. Her hips were narrow, her waist small. Her breasts were full, firm, and rode high. Her shoulders were powerful, but well-proportioned to the rest of her body, complementing the smooth, rolling muscles of her arms, thighs, and abdomen.

Her neck was graceful, and held up a face that drew admiring glances. High cheekbones accented a straight, smooth nose. Her soft lips were shaped like a man-at-arms's bow. Her eyes were large, almond-shaped, and blue, and her skin was the same fair porcelain as her mother's.

At last, bathed in sunlight, Gwendolyn stepped into the pool, fighting off the urge to turn and walk naked through the forest to her cave, which had been her mother's secret place. Her hands and fingers itched to hold the silver handle of her father's sword. She wanted to feel the way her blood sang through her body, as it always did when she held the sword. She wanted to swing it, to use it, as she had for the past seven years while she secretly trained herself.

But not yet, she told herself; first she must complete her own ritual. First the bath in the pool, then to lie on the mossy carpet and dry in the sun. When that was done, and only then, she would go to the cave and unwrap the sword to daylight.

Lowering herself into the pool, Gwendolyn floated on her back. She enjoyed the cool, almost cold feel of water against her naked skin. The fresh water relaxed her, made her feel clean and whole. She swam for a few minutes, dipping her head beneath the water's surface, diving down to touch the rocky bottom, turning underwater to let her feet find purchase on the rock bottom before propelling herself upward with a powerful thrust. Her graceful body broke the water's surface as she reached high into the air.

Slowly, Gwendolyn turned on her back again, floating with the sun full on her face. She played for several more minutes before swimming to the pool's edge. Drawing herself onto dry land, she stood letting the water cascade from her body. Then she lay face down on the soft carpet of mossy grass, her head resting on one arm, to let the sun dry her completely.

Gwendolyn felt as one with the forest that surrounded her, and, although drowsy, she was fully aware of the sounds emanating from it. With a suddenness known to those who live with and love nature, Gwendolyn sensed something wrong. The forest had grown still. No birds called, no insects chirped, and the silence was deafening. An icy chill ran along her spine, ending with a tickling sensation of warning at the base of her neck. Slowly, Gwendolyn turned and sat.

Valkyrie, the golden eagle, saw them first, and his fierce cry rang to the heavens. Gwendolyn saw them next. Three men, dirty and evil-looking, emerged from the trees across the pool. Standing, she ran to her clothing, not to dress or cover herself, but to take her jeweled dagger from its sheath on the leather girdle. While she ran, her eyes took in every aspect of the men. Their mismatched clothing proclaimed them mercenary men-at-arms, their unshaven faces, filthy hair, and unfriendly eyes told of their desertion, or worse. Gwendolyn, who had never known fear before, trembled as she watched their menacing expressions.

The coolness of the dagger's handle calmed her as she stood to face the three. The men, seeing her unclad body and the weapon she held before her, smiled.

"Look, a forest nymph, just like the old tales," said the leader as his eyes narrowed to beady slits. He signaled his two men onward with an abrupt motion. Both men held shortswords, as did the leader, but these men said nothing. Only their eyes spoke, devouring Gwendolyn.

"Stop!" she ordered, standing straight and proud against them. She could feel the blood race in her body. Her muscles tensed dangerously as an energy built, unlike any she'd known before.

" 'Stop' she says." The leader of the ragged trio laughed. "We'll not stop until each of us is satisfied thrice over!" he snarled, advancing ahead of his two companions. Ten feet separated them when Valkyrie screamed again. The three looked skyward, but too late. The huge bird of prey dove, striking the leader full in the face. The giant eagle's claws sank deep into forehead and eyes. The man screamed in agony, dropping his sword as he fell to the ground, his hands beating futilely against his winged assailant.

Without thinking, Gwendolyn dove for the shortsword. As her fingers closed around its hilt, she rolled in a perfect somersault, landing lightly on her feet to face the remaining two men. She watched them shake themselves free of the haunting image of eagle and man fighting on the ground and saw their expressions turn fiercer as they advanced toward her.

She held the sword in front of her, moving it smoothly, loosening her wrists and preparing to fight. She knew she was outnumbered and inexperienced, but the singing in her blood bid her to challenge.

A slow smile spread on her lips as her gaze followed, instinctively, not the men's footsteps, but their eyes. Closer they moved, their swords raised above them, trying to frighten the tall, golden-haired woman. Then the first cried out and he lunged toward her.

Gwendolyn expected the attack and, as he came at her, she spun under the man's blade, her own sword's tip biting into his shoulder.

Sir Miles Delong, Earl of Radstock, Knight of the Realm, and military advisor to King Richard the First, stared at the ground, looking for signs of those he sought.

The filtered sun glinted from the dark chain maille covering his arms as he squinted in an effort to locate the trail. He, with his two squires, twin brothers named Arthur and James, had been riding since sunrise to catch the three men whom he had found to be thieves. Miles knew they were near; he could feel it with every sense he possessed.

"Here, Sir Miles! The trees are marked." Miles turned his charger and looked in the direction to which Arthur pointed. On the bole of one large oak was a gouge made by a man in passing. Miles rode to the tree and looked down. His eyes, the deep green of the ocean, examined the mark minutely. He bent and stretched a hand out to graze the scratch, and it came away with fresh sap between thumb and forefinger.

"Close," he said. His word was followed by the screeching of a large bird. Snapping his head up, Miles saw a golden eagle diving toward a not-too-distant spot in the forest. The eagle disappeared. Suddenly a horrible shrieking echoed. "Come," Miles ordered the two boys.

The squires jumped on their horses and followed their lord.

When Miles neared the spot he had fixed in his mind, the sounds of fighting came to his ears. Drawing his longsword, Miles spurred his mount onward. The trees flew by in a blurring of speed as he came nearer to the scene of battle. One moment he was deep in the forest, the next in an open glade. Reining in the horse, Miles looked about.

He froze in the saddle at the sight that greeted his eyes. Before him, on the ground, was one of the three men he hunted. The man was still. A golden eagle—its claws buried within his face—stood victor atop him. Then Miles's eyes flew toward the fighters. His breath exploded as he watched the tallest woman he had ever seen do battle with the two others he sought. She was naked, her long blonde hair flying wildly about as she parried and fought the renegade men-at-arms. Time seemed to come to a halt. Miles saw the woman perfectly—the satiny sheen of her skin and the muscular perfection of her body lent a magnificent gracefulness to her moves. She was doing well, his military mind noted, but she also showed signs of inexperience by failing to take advantage of openings.

With a cry of rage, Miles charged the three figures just as his two squires broke from the forest. Miles rode at one of the men, his sword circling his head as he closed in. From the corner of his eye, he saw the woman's startled expression when he cut down one of her foes.

Reining in the charger, Miles wheeled him around and bore down on the other man. The man, Arrant by name, saw his death coming and began to run. Miles smiled as the woman swung her sword at his retreating back, barely missing him, then laughed as the frightened thief ran into the knife point of James, twin brother of Arthur. The man stopped, and his shortsword fell from his fingers while James's knife held him at bay.

Quickly, Miles dismounted and went to where Gwendolyn had dropped her clothes to the ground. He picked them up and walked to her; admiration reflected in his eyes. She stood proudly, unheeding of her nakedness as her full breasts rose and fell from her labors. She gazed directly into his eyes, and as he came closer he could only think of the beauty of a morning sky. Looking into her eyes, Miles held up the burgundy tunic for the woman to step into.

Dropping the sword, Gwendolyn took one step toward the knight and turned. He wrapped her in her tunic, and as her hands closed the material she turned to face him. Their eyes locked again, and Gwendolyn felt her blood begin to race anew. The depth of his eyes was bottomless, and the strong, angular cut of his chin was commanding. His prominent cheekbones added to the power that was in his face. Dark, almost black hair fell to his shoulders, framing his deeply tanned face. His full lips held only a faint trace of smile, and a flash of white teeth showed between them

Miles turned from the woman to face his squires. "Take him and fetch the men. I will await you here." A moment later the twins, along with the sole survivor of the trio, disappeared from the grass that surrounded the Pool of Pendragon.

Gwendolyn willed her heart to slow and her breath to

return to normal as she faced the knight. She had yet to take her eyes from him, and from the fact that this man was the first she did not look down upon, he must be at least three inches taller than she.

"Thank you, Sir Knight, for your gallantry. I daresay, if you had not arrived when you did, it would have taken me a bit longer to finish the two."

Miles could not believe his ears as he listened to the words she spoke, but in his heart, he heard not the words, but the bravery and the spirit which filled them.

"Perhaps, yet I think you lack the experience to have finished them. But we shall never know, and for that I am grateful. I would not want to have seen you, if your valiant effort had failed."

"I would not have failed, but again, Sir Knight, you have my thanks, and my debt," she said as she curtsied to him. "And whom do I have the honor of being saved by?" Gwendolyn asked with a smile.

"Forgive me, but my manners have always been a poor second to my sword. Permit me, I am Miles Delong," he said with a slight bow.

"Sir Miles? Earl of Radstock?"

"The same, I fear," he replied with a smile.

"From the tales I have heard, Sir Miles, you fear little."

"And you?"

"Forgive me. I am Gwendolyn Kildrake."

"Sir Hughes's daughter?" asked Miles, a frown creasing his forehead. Word had reached Miles, several years ago, that Hughes's daughter had died.

"His granddaughter, Sir Miles. Daughter of Gwyneth, who was wife to Guy of Halsbred," she explained.

"Of course!" Miles exclaimed, a smile erasing his frown as he looked at her. Her height should have told him who she was. Miles had heard of Gwendolyn Kildrake; his mother had told him the tale ten years ago, when he was fifteen, and word of Sir Guy's death had reached their lands. Rumors had flown, and Miles had heard of the strange affair of Lady Halsbred's return to her father's lands. When he asked about it at the table one night, a gale of laughter had followed his question, and many explanations had flown across the boards. But later, his mother had told him that Gwyneth, her distant, fourth cousin, had given birth to a daughter, eight years to the day of Miles's own birth, and that the child was not the daughter of Sir Guy. His mother, gentle soul that she had been, spoke only good of Gwyneth, and advised him not to listen to unfounded rumors. Then, almost four years ago, when Miles was fighting with Richard in Normandy, word had come of Gwyneth's death, followed by other tales of her strange daughter, a blonde-haired girl, beautiful but overly tall.

While Miles recalled these facts, his eyes continued to trace the lines of Gwendolyn's face until she turned and moved to the rest of her discarded clothing. Silently he watched as she completed dressing. When the leather girdle had been buckled, securing her tunic, and her jeweled knife returned to its sheath, Gwendolyn moved toward the eagle which now stood alongside its conquered victim.

He watched the tall, golden-haired woman kneel and extend her arm. It was then he noticed a leather binding covering her right wrist. *And she flies an eagle,* he thought when the bird climbed onto her arm.

Gwendolyn felt a surge of warmth when Valkyrie stepped onto his leather perch, grasping her wrist in a light, but secure hold. She looked into the eagle's amber eyes and smiled. "Thank you, my friend," she said to him as she stroked his chest. She turned and, with a deep breath, lowered her arm. With a fluid, graceful, and practiced motion, Gwendolyn swung her arm upward. The eagle left its perch, arched down and, as its wide feathered wings spread, began to lift toward the treetops.

Gwendolyn watched her friend, which was how she thought of the eagle, fly skyward. Behind her, she heard Miles's voice.

"You've trained him well. I've never seen an eagle that is gentler than a hawk." Gwendolyn spun to face the knight.

"I've not trained him at all. He comes with me by his own choice," she informed him.

"I would expect nothing else from one such as you," he said. "My men will be here shortly. I would see you safely home."

"My thanks, Sir Miles, but I would see myself home. I have many things to do today, and returning to Kildrake Castle before the sun is down, is not one of them," she said as she bent and retrieved her cape.

Miles watched her carefully. He had never met a woman who carried herself so well, who emanated such strength and power, yet did so without conscious effort. He knew she spoke truthfully, and was not trying to hide anything. Suddenly Miles knew something else also. Now that he had met her, he knew he would never be satisfied with another woman. In that moment, Miles Delong made up his mind to marry Gwendolyn Kildrake.

Gwendolyn watched as Miles accepted her words and moved closer to her. She saw his eyes change and noted the tightening around his mouth. She realized her heart was beating madly within her chest as his gaze swept across her face.

"Gwendolyn Kildrake, granddaughter of Hughes, are you betrothed?"

"Yes," she whispered through the knot that had suddenly formed in her throat. She turned from him and walked to the black mare that had stood so patiently waiting. Before reaching the mare, she felt Miles's hand stopping her and pulling her around to face him. She tried to ignore the hot throbbing just beneath her skin as she faced him.

"Do you have feelings for your betrothed?" he asked, his green eyes boring relentlessly into her lighter blue ones.

She tried to form some evasive answer, but the words would not leave her tongue. Slowly, she shook her head.

"I have no choice. The bargain was made shortly after my mother's death. I am to marry Morgan of Guildswood, by summer's end."

"After your mother's death? She would not have approved the match?" he asked, searching her face for the answer. Then he smiled. "I would give you your choice!" he stated boldly. "Would you have me for your husband?" Gwendolyn knew with a strange certainty that life with this man would be everything she could want. Even the one thing which she knew was impossible, but was her most cherished dream.

"I would," Gwendolyn whispered, her heart stopping for an instant.

"Then I will speak of this to Sir Hughes. I will strike a bargain he will be agreeable to."

"But . . ." Gwendolyn began, taking a deep breath as she lifted her hand and gently stroked his cheek. The sensation of his skin on hers sent tremors along her arm. Her thoughts swirled with the possibilities of the future, and she knew she must voice them before anything further could come of this meeting. "I would ask one boon if you are to marry me."

Miles's eyes were unblinking as he looked at her. Then he nodded. "When I saw you, I knew you were no ordinary woman. Your boon, or as many as you ask, shall be granted! One, or a hundred, it matters not."

Her heart swelled at his words. She wondered for a moment if this was just his passion speaking. Then he smiled again, his face softening.

"You have a strong chin, Sir Miles, and intelligent eyes. I could fare worse. There is one, and only one, boon I would ask."

"Then speak it, for it is granted."

"Not yet. If you succeed in winning my hand, you will hear my boon on our wedding day."

"And why not now?" Miles asked, puzzled by her secrecy, yet at the same time feeling an intense anticipation.

"Because, my gallant knight, until we are actually betrothed, and until the words of the marriage ceremony are to be a reality and not a dream, I will trust no one with what I must ask."

Hearing the passionate depths of her words, Miles tightened his grip on her hand. "You will always be able to trust me, my lady, always. Now, up with you," he said as his hands went around her waist and he lifted her effortlessly onto the mare's back. Gwendolyn closed her eyes at the pleasure of finally having someone who could make her feel like a woman.

"Soon, my Lady Gwendolyn, I will come to claim you."

"I know," Gwendolyn whispered. Then she sat straight on the horse's back and, using her heels, urged the mare into the trees. She rode smoothly, not giving in to the impulse to glance back. She had no need. Miles's features were indelibly printed in her mind: his strong face, his deep, but gentle eyes, the strength in his hands, and the aura of his power.

Gwendolyn knew that now she must go to the cave. She must feel the sword of her father in her hands, and with it, she must think over everything that had happened to her this day.

Chapter Two

GWENDOLYN RODE DEEP into the forest, her mind confused, yet peaceful at the same time. Over and over, she forced herself to replay the encounter at the pool. She analyzed every moment now that she had the time to do so. She remembered all her mistakes clearly, but at the same time she realized she could have done no better. All her training-in-arms and the ways of fighting had been learned by observation of the squires and knights when they practiced; and her own practice had been limited by necessity to the times when she was alone. And then she could only fight imaginary foes with her sword.

She reviewed what had happened and again saw Miles charging forward on his mount, his head bared, his halberd hanging on its thong, and his sword held high, reflecting sunlight and gleaming its intent as he whipped it downward against the others. But there was his handsome face . . . shivering, even in the warmth, Gwendolyn wondered what the fates had in store for her.

Why had she spoken so boldly? *Because I have waited a lifetime for him! Because he is the only man I have ever seen that I could allow myself to be with! Because I see within him a vast good.*

Without realizing it, Gwendolyn had arrived at her destination. She slid from her mount's back and dropped the reins. Pausing as she looked at the obscured opening in the face of the moss-covered hill, she felt her heart beat faster.

Breathing deeply, Gwendolyn started forward. As always,

a tingling began in the balls of her feet, and by the time she reached the entrance, it spread through her entire body. It was a far-from-unpleasant feeling and one she always looked forward to.

Ducking her head, Gwendolyn entered the darkened cave. Inside, she walked unerringly toward the deep niche in the far wall. Reaching up, Gwendolyn's fingers searched, and within a moment brushed against soft chamois. She sighed in relief. It was always so, every time she returned to the cave: she feared that she would never find it. Her fingers grasped the object and she drew it down.

With the chamois-wrapped blade secure in her hand, Gwendolyn walked toward the entrance of the cave. Halfway there she reached the daylight filtering inward in a misty flow. At the first edge of light upon the cave's floor, she stopped.

Sinking gracefully to her knees, Gwendolyn placed the chamois on the ground and gently unfolded it. She gasped as she always did when the light struck the blade. The silver shimmered, and Gwendolyn felt warmth emanating from it.

She gazed at it for long moments, her eyes reacquainting themselves with her treasure—her inheritance. The pommel, a perfect oval with a round silver ball on top, and a tapering and simple quillons cross bar beneath it, was crisscrossed with fine lines, and Gwendolyn knew the design was not for beauty, but for traction on the skin.

The blade was several inches longer than most longswords, yet so thin it was almost invisible when turned sideways. Its gleaming length was unmarked, showing not one nick from battle. But instinctively, Gwendolyn knew this sword had seen more battle than any sword in England or Normandy.

Reverently, she grasped the hilt and lifted the sword. Although it should weigh so much that both hands of the strongest knight would be needed to lift it, the sword floated upward featherlike, within her one-handed grasp.

The tingling that rippled through her increased when she stood, and she could feel her blood begin to sing. The sword of her father always spoke to her thus, always gave to her a feeling of belonging, knowledge, and courage.

The longer she gazed at this most wondrous of instruments, the faster her blood coursed through her body.

Unexpectedly, a low glow rose from the sword. Yet, no fear entered her mind; rather did she gaze on it with wonder.

Soon the ethereal glow increased, and the interior of the cave was illuminated with a shimmering silvery light. Gwendolyn was bathed within it and warmed by it. The walls of the cave were luminous, sparkling with the sheen of moss. All the while, the sword hummed in her hand, joining the singing of her blood until she could not distinguish her body from the sword.

And then she saw a darkened shape appear in the rear of the cave. At first it was a wavering coalescence of shadows, but it grew steadily, at pace with the sword's light. Finally the misty wavering figure solidified, and a robed figure with long flowing hair stood before Gwendolyn's wide-eyed inspection.

Gwendolyn held her breath as the apparition appeared, and when the figure had become steady, she released it with a long sigh. Gwendolyn was bathed with a feeling of tranquility at the appearance of this ghostly stranger. She watched the robed figure step toward her and saw clearly the other's face.

It was old and deeply lined, older than she had ever seen before. But it was not hideous. In the instant it took for Gwendolyn to gaze into the strange woman's face, she saw kindness, concern, and love. Then, as her mother's stories flowed through her mind, Gwendolyn knew who it was.

"You are dead," she whispered to the apparition of the Druid priestess.

"What know you of death, my child? You who are the very essence of life itself—the blood of thunder and lightning flows through your veins. You are the chosen! You are the daughter of the giant Norse warrior, he who is the right hand to the god of thunder, he who rides the myriad skies with his bride, the fair Gwyneth, your mother!

"They look down upon you as they traverse the heavens and smile when they see what they have created. Know you, Gwendolyn the chosen, whose blood is of the purest, unsullied blood of Britain and Wales, that you were born to fulfill a destiny. You must live for it, and with it!"

"Why have you come now?" Gwendolyn asked, accepting the priestess's words without knowing why, but understanding that she must.

"Because it is time. Because today you have taken the first step on the road toward your destiny." As the old Druid stopped speaking, the silver sword began to vibrate in Gwendolyn's hand, and she was hard pressed to hold it. "Release it!" the old one commanded, pointing one knobby finger at the sword.

Gwendolyn stared at her, but refused to loosen her fingers.

"Release it," she repeated, this time in a husky whisper.

Gwendolyn's eyes were riveted to the priestess's as she slowly unlocked her fingers. When she opened her hand fully, the sword's hilt rested on her palm, yet the sword did not dip toward the earth. Hesitantly, Gwendolyn drew back her hand a fraction.

The sword floated a hairsbreadth above her palm, burning even whiter as it wavered in the air. "You speak the truth," she whispered to the priestess.

"None can lie when they envoke the power of your father's sword. Listen, my beautiful child, for it will not be often that we talk. This sword was cast untold eons ago, when the earth had not yet cooled. It is of the purest metal, forged by the powers of those whom you call the northern gods. It was made for only one purpose, to fulfill the destiny ordained by its makers, a destiny that must yet come to pass."

Gwendolyn, held by the dark orbs of the priestess's eyes, felt as if she were being drawn within a vortex that was the other's mind, pulled from her very body. Swirling colors assaulted her senses, a sensation of separating, and a fleeting impression of floating above the world sought to claim her, but even as it did she still found no fear within her.

As the old one spoke, Gwendolyn could see the silver sword being cast, she could see the northern gods, bearded, blonde, and powerful, their bulging muscles aglisten with sweat as they worked the sword, shaping and testing the blade until it glowed with unearthly perfection.

"Thousands of years ago it was ordained that mortal man should fight mortal man, for they lost the way of the earth when they ignored the teachings of the ancient ones and desecrated the place they lived upon. They fought and killed each other, and called upon whatever gods they had created in their minds to justify this need for blood. And today it grows even worse. The people have turned their back on the way of light, and chosen, instead, a path of evil whom those you call the gods refuse to witness.

"But, it has also been ordained that this path may be broken; however, the ancient powers will not interfere bodily. This road must be traveled, not by the blood of those who have chosen to follow desecration in error, but by those who have remained pure. Who, although they have no knowledge of what has happened before them, and what will happen after, have kept themselves unsullied by the powers of deceit."

Gwendolyn listened, entranced by the priestess's words, yet all the while wondering if this were not but a dream.

"'Tis no dream you stand within, Gwendolyn. 'Tis but the reality denied to a mortal," she whispered as lightning danced around them, and carried them to the top of a floating mountain.

Gwendolyn knew she was still in her cave, but she also saw that she was rising above the boiling tip of a mountain. Suddenly the volcano exploded, and blood-red lava rose to engulf them.

"But I am mortal!" she cried, defending herself against this awesome vision, never once realizing she had spoken aloud.

"Yes, but you have been chosen."

"Why?" Gwendolyn asked, fighting to regain her sense of reality while challenging the old one as boldly as she had the three men-at-arms a bare hour ago.

"When the time comes for you to know, you shall. Now listen to me, my child, for my time here is almost gone and there is much to tell." The priestess made a swirling motion with her hand, and they were again in the confines of the cave. The silver sword floated gently downward, until it rested upon the chamois that was its home.

"Today you met the man who was chosen, when the sword was cast, to be your mate. You will marry him, as custom decrees. Your life will be devoted to protecting him, for it will be his seed within you which will produce the race that, in a thousand years, will inherit the earth."

A chill raced through Gwendolyn as she listened to the old one's prophesy. She lifted her head to gaze into the ancient eyes of the priestess, but instead of the old lined face, she saw the sea-green eyes and jet hair of Miles of Radstock.

"Yes!" the priestess cried. The visage of Miles dissolved and the ancient face of the Druid returned. "Yes, he is the one. He was born for you, as were you for him."

It was then that Gwendolyn knew completely that the old one had told her the truth; the priestess had reached into her mind and had seen what was there. Slowly, Gwendolyn nodded her head.

"Good," said the priestess, a smile curving the edges of her lips. "You must remember that you are different from all the others. You are special. The oldest powers of creation flow through you. You must use your mind, because it is your richest possession. For through it, the world may become yours. Remember, my child, the silver sword of your father is but a channel. Your mind and heart control the channel as do your hands control the paths of the sword. Use them both well and you will become supreme. Your children will be the inheritors of the earth, and a new world in the far distant future will be created by them. Fear nothing and no one, for the powers of thunder, of lightning, and of light ride above your shoulders. They will protect you, and guide you to where you are needed."

As Gwendolyn stared at the Druid, the unearthly force of the old one's words filled her body. Then she saw the shimmering light begin to diminish, and the ancient priestess wavered before her eyes.

"Wait!" she cried, stepping forward with her hands outstretched in entreatment. "I must know more. . . ."

"You will, child," came a thin whisper from the shadow that the old one had become. "You will teach yourself. Use your mind and the sword," she said. Her shadow dissolved, and the cave was once again dark.

Gwendolyn sank to her knees, staring at the spot the priestess had once occupied. Her mind erupted in turmoil. Everything the old one had said echoed within its chambers, and she had to force herself to gain some calm in order to understand it all.

She sat on the floor for hours, until finally she put everything in order. She had thought of Miles, handsome, tall, and gallant. She had thought of the old one's words—that she would marry him, for he had been chosen.

"Use your mind, the sword is its channel," whispered the voice in her ear. Haltingly, Gwendolyn reached out and grasped the hilt of her father's sword and lifted it above her. Its tip almost grazed the rounded curve of the cave's ceiling as she closed her eyes and concentrated. The sword began to vibrate within her hand, and her blood once more sang. Her mind blossomed with light, and on light's wings came confidence.

Gwendolyn opened her eyes.

The cave was filled with light, and she stood in the center of the purest white she had ever known. She lowered the sword slowly until it was at eye level and grasped it with both hands.

Using her mind, she concentrated on the light, and it was magnified. Then she stopped, and the cave was plunged into sudden darkness.

With tears tracing paths downward on her cheeks, Gwendolyn brought the blade to her lips and kissed it. A moment later she folded the sword in the chamois and placed it on its shelf. She found this leavetaking from the cave was to be harder than any of her past partings, but it was time to return to the castle and face her grandfather's wrath for leaving the others.

Gwendolyn stepped into the cool dusk air and walked to her horse. When she sat astride the black mare, Valkyrie's cry tore through the trees. The golden eagle dove low, and Gwendolyn stretched out her arm for the giant bird to settle upon.

A group of horsemen broke through the woods and, moments later, crested a low hill. In the murky distance, set within the confluence of two small rivers, was the imposing form of Kildrake Castle standing proudly upon high earthworks. Because of its high perch, the castle had no moat: its defense was in the very height it occupied. The triangular shape of the stone castle was unusual in this area, but ten-foot-thick walls and high battlements told all approachers that an attack would be foolish.

The two knights riding in the lead reined in their mounts. The entourage behind them did the same. "Kildrake is more impressive than I remembered," said the knight who wore a polished hauberk covered with a simple surcoat bordered in purple.

"It *is* imposing, Sire. The duke has added much to it in the last few years, especially the new barbican. Look how the stone reflects even this poor light," ventured Miles. "But he has proved his loyalty to the crown many times over."

"You have no need to remind me of that. Miles, are you sure you want to do this . . . thing?" Richard fixed Miles with a riveting stare.

"Yes, my lord," Miles replied, meeting the king's probing stare with openness.

"I shall never understand this thing between a man and a woman."

"One day you shall, Sire."

"I think not. You know the stories they say about me. That I have no temperament for women. That I seek only the company of my knights. What is it that prevents my people from accepting the fact that I am not yet prepared to marry?"

"Your subjects want only to have an heir, Majesty." Miles's reply was tactful, yet at the same time he was reminding the King of England of his royal responsibility.

Richard laughed harshly when Miles spoke, his bearded face split by a half sneer. "You are a true statesman, Miles. But behind my back they call me a lover of boys!"

"What care you what they say, for it is truly behind your back. You are the king of the mightiest country in the world. You are Richard, King of England, Duke of Normandy, and the strongest knight the world has ever seen."

"And you have the gall to flatter me yet. . . . You must want her very badly."

Miles's face was suddenly drawn into tight lines. The two men were of equal height; both were strong figures looming almost larger than life as they sat on their horses, staring at each other in the last light of the day. After a moment, Miles slowly nodded. "As I have never wanted another," he admitted.

Richard lifted one large hand and placed it on Miles's shoulder. In the fast fading light, king and earl gazed into each other's eyes, and the friendship flowing between them was a thing that could be felt. "Then you shall have her, my friend. I must tell you that I envy you your feelings."

"Sire?"

"I wish I could please my people. I wish I could find a woman who would arouse my passions, but I cannot. I have known this since I was twelve. Women are too weak, too easy to overpower. I have no use for weakness, only strength. I have met only one woman who was strong, and the shame is that she is my mother."

Miles could say nothing to this. He had known Richard for years. He was as close to the new king as any man was and knew that England's king loved only one thing—had only one all-consuming passion—fighting.

"Come," ordered Richard. "It is time to meet this maiden of yours."

Together, the King of England and the Earl of Radstock led their men to the gates of Kildrake Castle.

Although it was still early spring, the weather was warm, and that evening a gentle breeze blew along the battlements and walkways high on the castle's walls.

Standing in a darkened corner, Roweena, Gwendolyn's servant, watched her mistress tread the stones. Only moments before she had helped bathe Gwendolyn, as she did every night, winter or summer. She smiled when she thought about the other servants and their foolish superstitions. They feared that to bathe oneself so often led to sickness and insanity. So had she, until she watched her mistress grow strong and healthy. Never once in the last nine years had Gwendolyn been ill. So even though the others made fun of her mistress, Roweena bathed her nightly, and after Gwendolyn retired for the night, Roweena herself bathed, with Gwendolyn's water and permission.

"My lady?" Roweena called.

Gwendolyn stopped walking and turned toward her servant. She gazed openly at the small, plain, yet pretty woman dressed in her servant's tunic.

"I am worried. Sir Morgan was in foul temper today when he left."

"That does not concern me," Gwendolyn said.

"I am afraid for our future," Roweena whispered.

"Because of Morgan?"

"Because he is a cruel man. He will hurt you if you do not obey him once you are married," Roweena whispered.

"Never!"

"He is unlike your grandfather. He is Norman not Saxon. He treats his people like dirt, taxing them beyond their abilities, leaving them half starved, and if they protest, he whips them."

"Peasants and serfs are always spreading lies about their lords," Gwendolyn protested half-heartedly, but she, too, had heard these tales, and not from the peasants.

"It is said that the men of Guildswood beat their women for sport," she added in a fear-filled voice.

Gwendolyn shook her head sadly. She would not deny Roweena's words; she could not. She knew all too well a woman's lot once she married and left the protection of her own family—she was her husband's servant. Her only use was to breed children, and male children at that. But she also knew that she would never tolerate being beaten. Never!

"It will not happen!" she swore to both herself and her maid. And as she did, the face of Miles Delong loomed before her. She felt the warmth of his sea-green eyes wash over her, and knew, somehow, she would never fear Morgan.

"I pray so daily," Roweena whispered. "But yesterday, when Sir Morgan returned to the castle without you, his temper was fierce. He beat the stable boy, and even today the lad has not recovered."

"My grandfather did nothing about this?" she asked in shocked disbelief.

"He did not know until after Sir Morgan had gone this morning."

"It will not happen again!" Before Gwendolyn could say more, the sound of horses and men in armor floated above the castle walls. Whirling, she went to the edge of the parapet and looked down.

Beneath her, in the outer bailey, were more than a dozen men. She tried to see through the darkness but could not. She watched the gates open and the men enter. A sudden flurry of activity erupted within the courtyard, and Gwendolyn turned to Roweena.

"We have guests. Help me dress." Moving quickly across the walkway, she returned to her bedchamber.

Inside, Gwendolyn shed the robe she'd worn and stepped into a long white tunic that Roweena held for her, securing the tunic tightly about her narrow waist with a maille girdle. Her golden hair hung freely down the length of her back. But when she turned to leave, Roweena stopped her.

"Your hair," she reminded Gwendolyn.

"We do not have the time."

"The coif-de-maille?"

Gwendolyn nodded, and Roweena lifted the long headpiece and brought it to her mistress. The coif itself, unlike the knight's protection after which it was named, was of the finest golden strands. Each strand was interconnected by a small unpolished jewel. Gwendolyn bent to let her servant place the headpiece over her hair. When Gwendolyn stood, the gold seemed to blend with the color of her hair, which made the gems, unpolished as they were, stand out in beautiful contrast. The only polished jewel, a teardrop ruby, fell to the exact center of her forehead. The maille covered her hair and draped down her back, ending in a staggered diamondlike pattern of jewels.

Gwendolyn reached the door and opened it, but was again stopped by Roweena. "Your mantle?" her servant called.

"Not tonight," Gwendolyn replied. She stepped out of her bedchamber and walked to the main staircase.

Halfway down the wide stone steps, Gwendolyn stopped. Below her a strange tableau unfolded. Within the flickering illumination of the taper-lit walls, she watched her grandfather take the extended hand of one knight and raise it to his lips. Instantly, Gwendolyn understood. Her eyes went to the other knight and her breath caught in her throat.

It was Miles. When she returned her gaze to the first knight, she saw the deep border of his surcoat. Slowly, her eyes traced the faded coat of arms emblazoned within its center.

The king! Even as she recognized Richard's trappings, her grandfather stood and began to shout orders to the servants, but she could not will her feet to move. Finally, after a long, agonizing moment, Gwendolyn forced her muscles to obey and she started to retreat up the stairs.

At that instant, Miles turned and looked at the staircase. His eyes bored into hers, and all thoughts of fleeing vanished. He smiled, showing strong white teeth, and Gwendolyn could do nothing but return the smile.

Drawing in a deep breath, Gwendolyn descended the remaining steps and walked toward the three men. When she was within proper distance of the king, she dropped to one knee and bowed her head low. Richard extended his hand,

and Gwendolyn took it. She lifted his rough-edged hand to her lips and kissed the large ring on his forefinger.

"Rise, Lady Gwendolyn," Richard commanded in a deep voice. Gwendolyn rose gracefully and gazed at her monarch.

Rather than trust her voice, she looked from the king to Miles. Their eyes locked, and the message that passed between them was clearly seen by Richard. He smiled as he turned to Sir Hughes.

"Your granddaughter is even lovelier than I had been led to believe. I congratulate you."

"Thank you, my lord," Hughes said in his gravelly voice. Gwendolyn realized her grandfather was staring at her with a strange expression. When her mind began to work again, she thought about what Richard had just said, and understood the look on her grandfather's face. She almost laughed, but stopped herself. The Duke of Devonshire was thinking of a match with the king!

"Your Majesty . . . Sir Miles, if you will excuse me, I will check on our servants' progress," she said as she looked pointedly at her grandfather.

"Yes," Hughes agreed. He guided Richard, Miles, and several other knights through the hall and into the great hall that was now being readied to receive them.

Gwendolyn watched the men leave. Her heart was racing, but she did not let her emotions show. When the knights passed from sight, she turned, her mind galvanizing her body to action. She went into the kitchen, issuing order after order. The smoke-filled room was a beehive of activity as the cooks tried valiantly to make a banquet fit for a king without any notice in advance. Everyone worked madly, and the only person who seemed relaxed was the tall, blonde woman who continually told everyone what to do.

When enough food was ready, Gwendolyn breathed a sigh of relief. The servants began to bring out tray after tray, and even at this late hour, the feast was begun.

Two hours later, Gwendolyn entered the hall. For the rest of her life, the memory of what she saw would live within her mind.

The stone walls were alive with glowing tapers. Servants streamed in and out, carrying cask after cask of mead and ale. Seated at the center of the high table was King Richard, looking every bit the majestic warrior of whom so many tales were told. To his right, in the position of honor, was her grandfather, and to Richard's left sat Miles. Along the tables set beneath theirs, was a mixture of Hughes's and Richard's knights, ten of them to each table. Behind the king stood his squire, and behind each of the knights stood theirs. Gwendolyn noticed that only one of the twin squires stood behind Miles. As was fitting, the squires were dressed in the colors of their lords.

Gwendolyn realized that the most powerful man in the world graced her grandfather's table. She knew it would be a night that would be spoken of in Kildrake for years to come.

Stepping completely into the room, Gwendolyn walked toward the table. Conversation froze when she neared the men. Finally, when she was within speaking distance of the king, she stopped.

"I pray everything was satisfactory, your Majesty," she said.

"Would that all my subjects feted me in this manner," he replied.

"Thank you." Gwendolyn bowed low before the king. "Chambers have been prepared for you and your knights, Sire, and pallets have been laid for your squires. I pray you enjoy our home. Good-night, your Majesty."

Rising, Gwendolyn nodded to Miles, turned, and started gracefully from the room, her heart pounding with each step. She sensed something important would happen tonight, and hoped it would happen before she left the room.

"Lady Gwendolyn," Richard called out.

Turning, Gwendolyn stared at her king.

"Please join us for a moment."

"Your Majesty." Gwendolyn blushed as she gazed at her grandfather and waited. Although the king had commanded her, it was still her grandfather's castle, and he, not Richard, was lord of the manor. Gwendolyn knew that Richard's request should be obeyed by both her and Sir Hughes, but the request itself was filled with impropriety. This was not a public feast where men and women sat together. She stood still for a moment, glancing at her grandfather.

Hughes, because of his expansive mood, nodded and smiled at Gwendolyn. She returned to the table and sat directly across from the king.

After she was seated, Richard exchanged a quick look

with Miles. He lifted his hand to tug at his beard for a moment before continuing. "I have been king only a short time, and in that time, I have fought more battles than I had thought possible. Soon I will have to return to the Holy Land and fulfill my commitment to the pope. Before that, I want to unite my kingdom."

Gwendolyn listened to Richard while she gazed at the knights sitting at the other tables. They all seemed entranced by their warrior-king, and listened to his every word.

"It is with this in mind that I have ridden here, to Kildrake."

"Sire, you wish me to renew my pledge to you?" Hughes asked. It was not unheard of for a king to seek out individual members of the nobility and ask for a renewal of their oaths.

"Nay, Hughes, we have no doubt of your loyalty to us. I am here for another purpose. I am here on behalf of Sir Miles."

"Sire!" Miles cut in, his voice hard as he looked at the king. Suddenly the smoky air of the hall grew tight with tension. Not even the sound of the squires' feet on the rush-covered floor could be heard as the boys themselves stood frozen. The knights stared at Miles and the king, and Gwendolyn's breath once again froze in her chest.

"Very well, Sir Miles Delong, speak your piece!" Richard ordered with a sardonic smile.

An uneasy silence lingered across the boards when Miles gazed directly at the old duke. He stared steadily at him for several seconds before glancing at Gwendolyn. When his eyes swept across her features, his face eased the harsh planes.

"Sir Hughes," Miles said in a clear voice for all to hear, "I have come to ask you for your granddaughter's hand in marriage."

Hughes stared at Miles silently for several seconds before looking at the king. Finally, Sir Hughes, Duke of Devonshire, understood the reason for this unexpected visit. He shook his head sadly. "I wish it could be. The uniting of Kildrake and Radstock would be of great benefit to England, but Gwendolyn is betrothed to Morgan of Guildswood. The contracts have been signed. I am powerless to stop it."

"We appreciate the lawfulness of what you say," Richard

interrupted as he lifted a cup and drank, "but I am your king, and I can order the betrothal ended."

"Your Majesty, I am an old man. I have fought with your father and have defended my country and my honor equally. I have never broken an oath, and will not willingly do so now!" Hughes declared, his eyes challenging the new king boldly.

Gwendolyn felt a swelling of pride within her as she listened to her grandfather stand against Richard. Although she wanted to be free of Morgan, she did not want this at the expense of her grandfather's honor.

"Hughes, I am your king, and Morgan of Guildswood's also. You are both honor-bound to accept what I order. I shall issue a royal decree, compelling this marriage for the best interest of England. Such an edict will absolve you from both your pledge and from any wrongdoing."

Gwendolyn's heart beat faster as she listened to the words. Miles had kept his promise! He had succeeded in gaining her hand. But uneasiness clouded her happiness. There would be trouble. Morgan would not give in readily. She knew what would happen in the years to come. She gazed at her grandfather's pained expression and knew she was right. He, too, saw the problems to be faced.

"Your Majesty, you cannot do that," Gwendolyn said.

Several gasps were heard, and Gwendolyn saw the look of fury her grandfather directed at her. But she knew she must speak. Her eyes remained fixed on the king's, and, ignoring the warning within them, she continued.

"To issue this decree would be wrong, and would hurt you in your efforts to rule England peacefully and totally."

Richard's face ran a gamut of expressions until finally there was only a tolerant smile on his lips. "Continue," he said with a disdainful wave of his hand.

"Sire, my grandfather's word as a knight is sacred, and thus it should not be put aside by royal decree. However, because of the code of chivalry, the very foundation that makes such oaths sacred, it would be possible to have this betrothal set aside." Ignoring the open-mouthed stares of the knights, she bravely continued. "It is possible by using the very code that has made England so strong."

"And what would you suggest, my lady?" Richard asked indulgently.

"A simple thing. If Sir Miles is of the ilk that he thinks himself, issue your command, my lord, but allow Sir Morgan the right to challenge. A joust would be fitting," Gwendolyn declared. She breathed deeply while she watched Richard, hoping that all she had heard of his love of fighting and ceremony was true. She had no doubts of Miles's ability, only of her own in manipulating a king who did not like women.

"So it is blood and death you seek," Richard commented as he favored her with a penetrating look.

Gwendolyn blushed again, not from embarrassment, but from anger. When she spoke, her voice betrayed no emotions. "No, my lord, even if that were so, I would not take a knight from you, nor would I have the death of either man upon my shoulders. A joust, with blunted lances and dull-edged swords only, would suffice to uphold both men's knightly honor."

The table erupted with laughter and cheers at her words, and Gwendolyn allowed herself to smile as her eyes locked with Miles's. She read a new respect in them, and her heartbeat slowed to normal.

"By damn!" Richard cried, looking from Miles to Hughes. "Do you agree?" he asked. Both men nodded. "Then it shall be as the Lady Gwendolyn has said. By damn!" he repeated, giving Gwendolyn a long, appraising look of respect.

A few minutes later Gwendolyn rose and bid everyone good-night, purposely avoiding a too long look into Miles's face. When she bowed before Richard again, she smiled. "Thank you, Sire," she whispered.

Richard cupped her chin with his calloused fingers and made her look him in the eye. "You have much faith in his ability."

"He is your knight, is he not?" she responded as she stood and raised herself to her full height and looked King Richard level in the eyes.

"Not since the moment he met you," Richard conceded with a barking laugh.

Chapter Three

THE BANQUET HALL WAS SIlent as Miles glanced around. It was after midnight and all but three of the knights had gone to their chambers; the three who remained were sleeping face down on the table, their squires asleep in a far corner. Richard had left the table an hour earlier, which allowed anyone who wanted sleep to depart.

Sir Hughes had stayed for another half hour, talking earnestly with Miles. Miles, in the short time he'd spent in conversation with Hughes, had found him a likable man. Although his mannerisms were refined, and he bore himself proudly, Miles also saw the old Duke's need to know his lands would go to the right heirs.

He had as much as admitted that he'd not wanted the match between Gwendolyn and Morgan, and had even let slip that he had, once Gwendolyn had grown to her full height, despaired of ever finding someone who would marry her.

Miles reasoned that that was the very reason for Gwendolyn's early betrothal to Morgan. This knowledge eased his mind even more. He knew of Morgan by reputation as a fierce, but uncouth fighter, and he did not foresee any problem with the joust.

"Sir Miles?" called Arthur. Miles turned to see the anxious face of his squire standing above him.

"You have found out?" he asked.

"I know her room."

"Take me there," Miles whispered. He watched his young squire glance at the sleeping knights. "They are in another world."

Arthur led Miles toward the stairs. Ascending the steps, Miles heard the varied sounds of the sleeping castle: breezes filtering through openings in the stoneworks, tapers sputtering, and, although it was still night, the faint sounds of the scullery servants preparing for the large morning meal.

When they reached the top of the stairs, Arthur turned down a torch-lit hallway and motioned for Miles to follow. Miles glanced at the walls and took in the tapestries covering the windows and door openings. They were all of fine workmanship, depicting many scenes of tourneys. He wondered if Gwendolyn's fingers had wrought any of these patterns.

The castle was not old by Saxon standards, perhaps a hundred years, if that. But the construction was solid, and the design of the castle denied its Norman heritage.

Until the Norman invasion, the homes of English nobility had been built of wood. Castles were no more than a large grouping of homes, defended by a high wooden fence. But, with the conquering of the Saxons came the Norman builders to show the English the benefits of stone.

No more did entire families die needlessly in the fires that had been as common as the deer in the forest. No more did each member of a family have to live in a separate dwelling within the compound. With stone buildings came security, security against fire, and security of sorts against attacks. But, Miles thought as he traversed the hallway in his squire's wake, although the Normans had given them stone engineering, the true Saxon within each of them refused to follow the designs of the Norman castles. Here, as in Radstock, they clung to the old Saxon ways. The lord and lady of the castle lived in one wing, and the other family members in another. Not everyone in England adhered to this, but Miles was glad that Kildrake followed the older traditions.

In Kildrake, the heart of the castle was its great hall, and from there, it spread outward. Some castles had as many as five separate wings for family and guests. Kildrake had two such wings, and the third for the Duke's men-at-arms and servants.

The castle was ringed by a stone wall, and Kildrake's

triangular design, with its three towers and three wings, was easily defended. From its high parapeted battlements, any enemy or visitor could be seen from a mile away.

"Here," whispered Arthur, stopping before an arched doorway. At this doorway no tapestry hung. Instead, a leather-hinged, hewn door was fitted. This alone told Miles it was a room belonging to a member of the family, rather than a guest chamber or servants' quarters.

"Wait here for me," Miles commanded the boy as he pushed the door inward. After a slight hesitation, the door opened, its hinges barely making a sound.

Entering slowly, Miles closed the door behind him and let his eyes adjust to the dark. On the far wall, above the fireplace, a single taper burned, sending low shimmering lances of light throughout the room.

The floor was covered with fresh rushes, and their sweet fragrance rose to assault his senses. There were no window openings, but several tapestries hung on the walls. As his eyes swept the room, he saw a small alcove covered by another tapestry and knew Gwendolyn's personal maid was sleeping within. Finally, Miles glanced at the bed. It was large, much larger than he would have expected, and framed with dark wood. Four posts rose, and thin curtains framed it, almost but not quite hiding its occupant from view.

Miles stepped toward the bed. When he did, he heard a flutter of wings behind him and a bird's low cry. He spun to face the large golden eagle called Valkyrie.

The eagle stared at him from its wooden perch, and Miles willed his breathing to return to normal.

"He will not harm you," Gwendolyn whispered.

Miles whirled again and saw she was sitting up, her bedcovers around her waist. In the instant before he spoke, he took in her entire countenance and reveled in the flowing blonde hair that framed her face, the proud carriage of her shoulders, and the full thrusting of her breasts beneath the bedclothes.

"Because he knows I will not harm you," Miles stated.

"Because he knows you from the forest," Gwendolyn corrected. "Why are you here?"

"To speak with you," he replied as he moved closer to her. Gwendolyn reached out and pushed aside the bed-curtain, allowing Miles an unrestricted view of her.

"It is improper," she whispered, but her voice held no reprimand.

"What I have to say cannot be said with others about."

"What if someone comes?" she asked with a smile.

"It is a chance I must take," he replied honestly.

"I have heard you are different than most. I am glad."

"What have you heard?" Miles asked as his eyes searched her face. Again, he realized her beauty was devastating. Her pale blue eyes sparkled in the subdued light, and her allure was something he had never before known.

"That you are kind, considerate, and, above all, a knight of honor."

Miles was no stranger to a woman's bedchambers, and the words he had heard before had been similar, but when he gazed into her eyes he knew she spoke openly and without guile. "Yet I stand in your bedchamber uninvited. . . ."

"Am I to be in fear of you?" she asked in reply.

"Why did you speak out to Richard? Why did you not let him issue his edict?" Miles asked, pointedly ignoring her question.

"Did I embarrass you? For if I did, I apologize."

"You could not embarrass me—frighten me, perhaps, because you do not understand Richard and his views on women. But you almost shamed your grandfather," Miles chided.

"My grandfather gets angry, not ashamed. He knows I would never do that to him! I speak my mind when it is necessary. It is something you should know if you are to take me as your wife."

"Do you have doubts about marrying me? Is that why you want a tourney?" Miles asked.

"Nay. I would not have you make Morgan a lifelong enemy because of the king's decree." Suddenly she reached out and took his hand. To Miles, it was as if his hand were encased by heated coals, so hot was her touch. "An order from Richard would make Morgan your enemy for life. I know this man," she said bitterly. "He is vain, vindictive, and filled with self-importance. He is a bitter man and would make an evil enemy. I do not want our life together to start in such a way."

As Miles listened to this beautiful woman, he realized she spoke to him as if she were his equal, a fellow knight rather than a woman. And while she spoke, he felt Gwendolyn's emotions as if they were his own.

"If you win my hand by tournament, it will make his loss more palatable. You are said to be the finest fighter in the land next to Richard, and Morgan can feel no shame at losing to you."

"You are so confident then?"

"You have already granted my boon. Would I chance its loss so easily?"

"It must be very important to you," Miles whispered and lifted her hand to his lips.

"Its importance is for both of us," she said as her eyes held his for a moment.

Slowly, Miles lowered her hand and then released it. At the same time, he stepped back from the bed. "We may still make an enemy of Morgan."

"I can only pray we will not," Gwendolyn said, throwing the bedcovers from her and arising. They faced each other at a distance of inches, she in the loose nightclothing that hung to the floor, he still dressed in maille.

"I still think it to be senseless when Richard can save us from needless fighting," Miles protested again.

"But it is the only way to allow my grandfather to be free from breaking his word. With Richard's decree, my grandfather would eventually have to face Morgan to defend his honor. My grandfather is over fifty. He cannot fight Morgan."

"You are right, my love," Miles admitted.

Suddenly Miles could not control himself. He pulled Gwendolyn against him. She did not resist his hands when he drew her to him, nor did she fight him as his mouth covered hers.

The kiss became an all-consuming fire that roared between the two, lasting for long minutes that felt like an eternity. Then, as suddenly as Miles had drawn her to him, he pushed her away. Both were breathing harshly.

"I must leave now," Miles declared, "or I will not leave at all."

Gwendolyn's breasts pushed against her night rail, and for the first time in her life she wanted to be held within a man's arms and never be released. Instead of admitting this desire that could not yet be satiated, she merely nodded.

Drawing a deep breath, Miles smiled gently. "I had always thought that I would marry to continue my line. I had never once thought to marry for love. I was wrong," Miles stated as he took her hand in his.

"From the moment I saw you, I loved you," Gwendolyn whispered.

"I . . ." Miles began but could not finish. How could he tell her of his emotions upon seeing her naked, a sword swirling in her hands. "I will see you in the morning."

"I ride before the morning meal. It is a beautiful time," she said as she searched his face, waiting for his reaction to her unspoken invitation.

"Alone?"

"I am never alone." She smiled as she pointed to Valkyrie.

"I will see you in the morning, my lady." Miles lifted her hand once again and kissed it gently before leaving the bedchamber.

In the hallway, Miles and Arthur returned to the walkway above the main hall and then continued on to the north wing. Inside the small chamber, James, Arthur's brother, woke instantly and rose from his pallet. Together, he and Arthur undressed Miles.

"I did not know if you wanted to bathe, but I have kept the water heated," James said.

Miles went to the wooden tub and stood at its side while James and Arthur poured steaming water into it. After he sank into the water, Arthur began to wash him, but Miles waved him away. "To sleep, both of you. We rise early. Have my horse ready an hour before the morning meal," he ordered. Then, with the hot water working its magic, he closed his eyes and thought about the golden-haired woman he would soon be fighting for.

"My lady?" Roweena called as she rushed out to the parapet that Gwendolyn was on. She stopped next to her mistress and gazed quickly out at the darkening sky.

"I see them," Gwendolyn replied, pointing to a line of mounted riders. The banner of the house of Guildswood fluttered at the column's head. "Prepare my clothing for the evening meal," she commanded.

"Yes, my lady," Roweena replied in a subdued voice,

leaving Gwendolyn alone once again. Roweena was deeply disturbed about her mistress, but would never let it show in her voice or face.

They shared a close relationship, almost a friendship, she thought quickly, but washed the errant thought from her mind. It was wrong. She was base born, the daughter of a scullery maid and blacksmith in the service of the Duke of Halsbred. When she had turned six, only two years younger than her mistress, she had been chosen by Lady Gwyneth to become the Lady Gwendolyn's personal maid. She began her training then, and in nine years had never willingly been far from her mistress's side.

Roweena loved Gwendolyn with a loyalty rare among servants. She had always been treated well and had served as best she could. She never challenged her mistress's strange ways, and always accepted whatever Gwendolyn required of her.

But tonight something seemed different to Roweena. Rarely had she seen Gwendolyn in as dark a mood as covered her mistress now. But she also knew the mood was caused by the imminent arrival of Sir Morgan, and the next day's tournament.

For the last three days, everything in Kildrake Castle had changed. The king and his men had stayed, and because of that, the servants worked five times as hard.

Roweena also noticed the change in Gwendolyn with each passing day. Although she knew nothing of love, she realized her mistress was in love with Sir Miles. They spent more time together than was proper, and not once had Gwendolyn left the castle without Miles. When she and her knight left, they always returned together. That, too, was different from the times she rode with Morgan, with whom she rarely returned to the castle.

And Sir Miles was as gentle a man as he was handsome, never raising his voice in anger to his squires or the other servants. Each night since his arrival, Roweena had prayed that Miles would defeat Morgan and gain her mistress's hand.

With the insight of one who sees all, and must live within the restrictions of a society she has no control over, Roweena knew her life would be a good one as the maid to the Lady of Radstock.

A sudden knocking at the chamber door startled Roweena. She put down the tunic she was holding and went to the door. When she opened it, one of Sir Miles's squires stood before her, an intricately carved leather box in his hands.

"Arthur?" she ventured. The boy, Roweena's age, smiled and shook his head.

"James."

"How does anyone tell you two apart?" she asked, her brows knitted together in perplexity.

"I'm the younger brother," James said dryly as he held out his hands. "This is from my lord, for the Lady Gwendolyn."

Roweena accepted the box and smiled. "I will see she gets it at once," she told him.

By the time she put the box down and lifted the long undertunic from the bed, Gwendolyn had entered through her private doorway on the other side of the room. "This one?" Roweena asked, holding up a brightly trimmed overgarment.

"Yes," Gwendolyn said absently. Because of her height she disliked the newer fashions; they restricted her movements. But tonight, as she had since Richard's arrival, she would wear the more uncomfortable, fashionable clothing.

"Sir Miles's squire brought you a gift," Roweena ventured and saw her mistress's eyes widen for a moment. "'Tis on the bed," she said.

"The white undergarment also," Gwendolyn ordered as she went to her bed. While Roweena prepared her clothing, Gwendolyn looked at the leather box. Lifting it slowly, she inspected the leather's intricately tooled handiwork.

When she opened the box she gasped. Inside, on a bed of velvet, rested a small, jewel-encrusted dagger, its blade encased within a tooled leather sheath. She set the box down and lifted the small curved blade in her hand. Then she saw the piece of parchment and took that from the box.

Unfolding it, she read the neatly scribed Latin, and a smile lit her face. Miles had written that he had purchased this Saracen-made blade in Italy, but had not known why at the time. When he met Gwendolyn, he had learned the reason.

Gwendolyn put down the note and gazed at the knife. It was beautifully crafted, and when she withdrew it from its scabbard, its barely curved length glinted dangerously. She had seen only one such dagger before, and that was years ago at Halsbred, in Sir Guy's armory.

"My lady?" Roweena called. Gwendolyn turned and smiled at her servant. The smile faded when she gazed at the clothing. She shrugged away the helpless feeling and nodded. Roweena undressed her and then began the process of dressing.

First she stepped into the slippers Roweena had set out for her, and then the undergarment went on. Not for the first time did Gwendolyn wish she had been born into the lower classes. If that were so, then she would not have had to wear anything more than this garment. Sighing, Gwendolyn allowed Roweena to attach the cloth girdle around her waist. Then she stood still while the servant fluffed out the skirt. When that was done, Roweena held up the outergarment.

Gwendolyn stepped into it and waited until Roweena adjusted the bodice for her breasts and clasped the five silver buckles together at each side. The bodice rose to the base of her neck in a perfect circle, emphasizing its grace and beauty. The outergarment was tucked in at her waist, and cut at her hips, where the material tapered to a point, centered midway to her knees in front and back. The sleeves belled downward, reaching almost to the floor, and Gwendolyn shook her arms to free their many folds.

The sleeves, and the border of the neck, were braided in a bright blue, and complemented both the garment and her complexion.

"This suits you well, my lady," Roweena said.

"I still dislike it."

"I think Sir Miles will like it."

"Enough!" Gwendolyn said in a loud voice, but failed to put any anger into it. She smiled when she saw Roweena trying not to. "My hair?"

"I can braid it and use the silver comb," Roweena suggested.

"Not tonight. I think a simple crown braid will do," she decided. Twenty minutes later Roweena finished her hair and Gwendolyn stood. "The mirror," she ordered.

Roweena brought out the polished-steel oval and held it for Gwendolyn. She studied herself critically until she nodded her approval. Her hair flowed in smooth waves down her back, but the sides had been braided in a tiara, and rested on the top of her head.

"Did you wish a necklace?"

Gwendolyn shook her head and turned away. "Wait," Gwendolyn called. "My long chain, I have a use for it," she said. Moments later she held the gold rope in her hand.

She took the small jeweled dagger from the box and, using the link that was on the sheath, attached it to the long golden rope. Then she had Roweena slide it over her head. The jeweled handle of the dagger fell in the exact center between her breasts, and Gwendolyn knew it was perfect.

"I think it is time I made my appearance," Gwendolyn whispered, speaking to herself as much as to Roweena.

Gwendolyn had already spent too much time preparing herself, and was, because of it, negligent in her duties. Tomorrow was the tournament, and tonight the center courtyard would hold the feast.

She had spent the entire afternoon involved in preparations for the feast, and instructing the servants on how to set up the courtyard for their guests.

Kildrake Castle was filled with guests. Since the moment the king's messengers had gone out to report of his decree to Guildswood, all the neighboring nobility had come to witness the fight between Morgan and Miles, and partake in the presence of the king. Tonight's feast would be a long one, and one that Gwendolyn knew would draw deeply on her reserves of composure.

Gwendolyn thought again of the Druid priestess, and her words in the cave. She turned from Roweena and closed her eyes. She pictured the silver sword in her hand, and the peaceful, pure white light that had been cast by it, and opened her mind to it. Warmth flowed through her, and the tension that held her prisoner began to drain. Slowly, she opened her eyes and turned back to her servant only to discover Roweena staring wide-eyed at her.

"What's wrong?" she asked.

"Did you see it?" Roweena whispered, genuflecting quickly.

"See what?" Gwendolyn asked.

"The light. You were surrounded by a light, my lady."

"A trick of the tapers," Gwendolyn said quickly, regretting the impulse which had made her call those strange powers when another person was present. She promised she would not do it again. "I saw nothing," she added. But she knew Roweena had seen it, she could still feel the warmth of the light, and the peacefulness flowing through her veins.

"Come, it is time." Striding purposefully toward the door, she prepared herself to face the long night ahead.

Chapter Four

MILES STOOD IN THE CENTER of his chamber; the tapers lighting the room aided him in the inspection of the equipment his squires had prepared for tomorrow's match. His hauberk had been cleaned, and glowed darkly. His helmet shone, and its nasal bar looked like an inverted cross.

On the floor next to the maille were his cuisses, the leather-padded leggings that protected his thighs. The heavy gamboise undergarments would add even more width to him, and the gambeson that would be between the maille and his surcoat had been freshly aired.

Because it was a tournament and not a fight to the death, Miles decided to not wear several of the heavier pieces that would slow him down. Blunted swords and flat-tipped lances were dangerous but rarely fatal, and in a joust such as this, no thought was given to killing or maiming, just winning.

Miles waved away greaves, hournskull, and breastplate, but nodded to the rerebraces that would protect the outer part of his upper arm.

"We think it best you wear the greaves and breastplate. We've been talking to some of the other squires," ventured Arthur.

Miles looked at the twins and nodded his head. He regarded them with love and caring, and knew they felt the same toward him. When they ventured an opinion, Miles had found it best to listen. "Go ahead," he ordered.

"It is said that Sir Morgan gives no quarter, even in tourney. He likes to beat his opponents badly, not merely win," whispered Arthur.

"He goes for the legs also," added James.

"Very well," Miles said. "Set up full armor then, but not the hournskull. I want my face free."

"Yes sir," the twins replied in unison, their blue eyes brightening and blonde heads bobbing with his words.

Miles was filled with a restless energy and decided to take a walk. He was not tired, and the sounds from those who still feasted echoed into his room. He needed a place to be alone, where he could think, undisturbed, about tomorrow.

After giving the twins further orders about his equipment, he left the room and went through the hall to a door on the far side that opened onto the parapet. There he walked by himself for a while, thinking about his life, and his future.

He was committed to Richard, even as his father had been committed to Richard's father, Henry. Miles had spent four years at Richard's side, fighting whomever Richard had chosen, and traveling through Normandy, Italy, and secretly visiting the Holy Land. He had sworn an oath with Richard, outside the walled city of Jerusalem, to come back with Richard and return the land to Christianity's embrace.

Miles knew that in a year Richard would have his army gathered, and they would debark on a crusade against the Saracens. He wanted to be at Richard's side when they rode through the gates of Jerusalem.

Miles stopped to gaze at the star-filled sky. He knew tomorrow marked an important day for him. It signaled a change in his life, a significant change, and he was eagerly looking forward to it. By winning tomorrow's joust he would gain a wife and complete the first part of his commitments to his family. And that commitment was a strong one. Miles of Radstock was the last male of his line. His only legitimate brother, Roger, had been killed fighting for King Henry the Second, and his bastard-born brother, Theodore, had chosen the life of the church.

Just as Richard took the crown upon his father's death, so did Miles draw on the mantle of the Earl of Radstock upon the news of Roger's death. Roger had died without leaving issue, and it was up to Miles to continue a line that was as old as Britain itself.

But it was more than the responsibilities of his name and rank that filled Miles's mind—much more. From the first time he had seen Gwendolyn of Kildrake he had known what love was. Watching her fight the two men had been a gift given to him, and he had seen a vision permitted to few. He also knew he would never allow Morgan to take her from him.

Miles thought himself to be a simple man, enjoying everything about life and devoting himself to the arts of being a knight. His desires were normal, and his vows sacred. It bothered him to some degree that Richard had to issue his edict for Miles to gain Gwendolyn's hand, but short of open warfare against Guildswood, there was no other way.

Yet with tomorrow's sun, Miles felt he would be absolved from the deceit which enabled him to take Gwendolyn from Morgan. Morgan . . .

Miles remembered Morgan's arrival this evening. Miles had been standing to one side in the great hall, talking with a knight he had not seen in some time when Morgan had entered with his entourage. Miles had carefully watched Morgan, studying his adversary closely as he approached the king.

Sir Morgan of Guildswood was taller than average height, but still a good four inches shorter than Miles. His lack of height was more than made up for by his powerful width. His neck, rising out of the light maille hauberk, was thick and powerful. His arms were massive, and his legs, encased within the padded riding hose, were like two tree trunks.

Before Morgan had reached the king, his head had turned and his eyes had found Miles's. Within their deep-set darkness, Miles had seen the man's hatred flare. A chill coursed through him when he sensed the rage contained within the knight's stare.

When Morgan had turned from him, Miles knew he had gazed into the eyes of a man who was destined to become his lifelong enemy, and a dangerous one at that. He had thought this even as Morgan reached Richard and made his obeisance to the king. When Morgan had lifted Richard's hand to his lips, Miles had left the hall to go to his room and dress for the evening's festivities.

A loud bark of laughter reached Miles on the parapet and he recognized Richard's laugh. The king would be among the last to finish tonight; he had to impress his new subjects with his presence, his stories, and his power.

Miles concentrated in an effort to see through the darkness, and was rewarded by glimpsing the shadowy shapes of tents on the flat tournament field. Even now his squires would be making their way toward his tent to lay out his armor and weapons—to sleep by them, to make certain everything would be ready for the morning.

It would be there, on the fields tomorrow, that he would meet Morgan. And, if everything went well, by the time the sun was setting tomorrow, the day of his wedding would be set.

For the last several days, Miles had wondered to himself if he were mad. He wondered if he saw more in Gwendolyn than there was. Her height alone was unequaled, and her beauty was made even more apparent by this height. It was this evening, at the feast, that had given Miles the answer to his unasked questions. When she had entered the courtyard he had seen the jeweled blade hanging on its golden rope. The handsbreadth-long dagger swayed gently between her breasts, and he had known that everything she had said to him had been true. She had been the first woman to capture his heart, and Miles was suddenly glad of this.

In an effort to pull his mind from Gwendolyn, he thought of the feast of which he himself had partaken so little. But throughout the long hours of revelry, he had been aware of everything happening around him. His mind had been as clear as the crystal night under which they had eaten. The lights from the torches added to the silvery sheen of the ten thousand stars that had shown down upon them. The night, like his mind, had been open and calm.

In the forefront of the courtyard, set five feet above the rest of the tables, was the High Table. At the table's center was King Richard, to his right, Hughes, and to his left, Gwendolyn. At the extreme ends of the table of honor, separated by Richard's advisors, sat the opponents, Miles and Morgan.

Below the table, and spread out across the wide courtyard were the tables of the Duke's guests. All the nobility from the surrounding countryside were in Devonshire to witness the fight between Miles and Morgan for the right to wed

Gwendolyn. With them were their families, their knights, and behind them, their personal servants and squires.

"She is a lovely morsel, Miles, but is she worth this folly?" Edward, Earl of Lydford asked.

Miles glanced at the earl, a man he had known for several years, and one whom he had shared battle with in Normandy. "Morsel?" he asked with a smile.

"Well, perhaps a healthy bite," the earl added jovially.

"Edward, my friend, I promise you this is not folly," he whispered.

"It had best not be. Morgan is no man to trifle with. My brother met him in tourney last year and felt the blows of his sword for almost two fortnights. He told me that fighting Morgan is like fighting the devil. The man has no mercy in him."

"He moves slowly, he does not worry me overmuch," Miles said confidently.

"He is built like a bull, and like a bull, when he is in full charge, he is a fearsome thing," Edward warned. "He flinches not in the fight, and he cares nothing for what happens to him. He seeks only one thing, victory!"

"I shall heed your warning and act accordingly," Miles promised. "I thank you for your concern."

Miles turned and glanced at Morgan. He studied him for the hundredth time since sitting down at the High Table. The other knight was dressed in the modern Norman manner. His overcoat was shorter than Miles's, barely reaching to his massive hose-covered thighs. The overcoat was trimmed boldly with a multitude of gold threads, and Morgan's coat of arms, a black-winged lion floating above a castle, was wrought carefully across his chest.

Miles smiled at him. Morgan met his stare but his lips did not move from their straight line. Then he saw Morgan turn toward Gwendolyn. Miles watched Morgan's eyes sweep across Gwendolyn's face, and then drop to the full swelling of her breasts.

Rather than be angered by this proprietary gesture, Miles kept his features emotionless. Between her breasts hung the Saracen dagger, which Morgan could not miss noticing. When Morgan looked back at Miles, Miles smiled fully at the knight—he knew Morgan had been told of his gift. Morgan's face darkened with anger, which Miles countered with his continued smile.

"Careful," Edward cautioned, "or you'll be fighting on top of this table."

"Which you would greatly love to see."

"I'll not deny that," Edward replied with a laugh.

But Edward's laughter was only an echo as he turned to Gwendolyn, and was ensnared by her blue eyes. She sat proudly at the king's side, her shoulders straight, her hands daintily picking at the food before her. He knew that somehow, tomorrow, he must beat Morgan and win Gwendolyn.

Throughout the meal, Miles had let his glance continually wander to Gwendolyn, and he had noticed that she barely ate from the array of platters on the table. Her silver cup sat untouched, and Miles knew she was as tense as he. Whenever their eyes met, unspoken messages passed between them, and Miles took refuge within these.

He too ate sparingly, just enough to satisfy his hunger, and when he lifted his cup of wine, he barely let the sweet liquid touch his lips. Tomorrow was too important to be slowed by drink or food. Yet, across the boards, he saw Morgan eat his fill. But he did notice that the knight drank very little.

Good, Miles thought, at least he has more brains than most. A fanfare of trumpets called, and Miles took a deep breath.

The cheers of the guests rang out as a long line of servants began to wind its way through the tables. Each servant carried a silver platter, and centered upon it was a dressed pheasant. The tenth course was being served.

By the end of the feast, twelve courses would be served, and as many wines and meads would accompany each course. A feast such as this held certain obligations to those who attended, and each person was expected to eat his fill, again and again. To do less would be to dishonor their host.

So Miles took a portion of pheasant and began to slowly cut at it with his knife, but in a few minutes, James, as he had been doing all evening, would take his platter and replace it with an empty one.

While the guests ate and talked loudly over the entertainment, he once again sought Gwendolyn's eyes. He watched her converse with Richard, and felt his heart swell. He had never met a more beautiful woman, nor one who held herself so proudly. He knew himself to be favored by what would soon be his, but at the same time he instinctively knew she would be his only on her own terms.

She was no meek daughter of nobility, bred to sew and breed. His one glimpse of her naked body when he'd first seen her, with its smoothly outlined muscles, had told him she was much more than that. Added to that was the quickness of her mind, and the fascinating mystery within her sky-blue eyes.

Miles reached for his cup and lifted it. As he did, Arthur bent to his ear. "It is time," he whispered.

Miles handed the silver cup to his squire before rising. He turned to Edward and smiled. "I leave you to enjoy yourself, and I pray that your head will not hurt overly much in the morning."

Edward grinned lopsidedly and struggled to his feet. "I care not whether my head aches in the morning, I shall be seated on wood watching you. I pray that God grant you victory," he said as he grabbed Miles's hand within both of his.

"My thanks," Miles replied as he left the knight and walked to the center of the High Table.

Suddenly the voices in the courtyard were stilled, and the only sounds were of the musicians. Miles knew every eye was on him as he walked. When he reached Richard, he faced him across the High Table and he waited until the king acknowledged him. Bowing his head, Miles spoke in a voice that carried to everyone's ears.

"With your permission, Sire, I would retire for the night to prepare for the 'morrow."

"Granted," Richard said.

"Sir Hughes, Lady Gwendolyn, good-night," Miles said, gazing deeply into Gwendolyn's eyes. Only then did he turn to face Morgan. He stared into the other's hate-filled eyes and bowed his head to the knight. "On the 'morrow," he said in a low voice. Without further words, Miles turned back to Richard, bowed, and left the courtyard. When he reached the archway leading to the south wing of the castle, he turned to see Morgan repeating his movements of moments ago. Miles smiled to himself. His purposely early departure had been more of a goad at his opponent than a courtesy to the king. Morgan's stiff formality was the sign he watched for and found. His being first to leave the feast had served to fuel even more anger in Morgan's mind. An angry opponent on a jousting field is less cautious. However, Miles studied his adversary's movements and saw that the knight was no slouch. Instinctively Miles saw Morgan was as much a fighter as he himself.

Footsteps intruded on Miles's thoughts of the banquet and drew him back to the reality of the parapet. He turned to see Roweena, Gwendolyn's servant approach him.

He waited patiently until the girl reached him and dipped her head. "Yes?"

"My lady sent me, Sir Miles. I have a message," she whispered as if afraid of being overheard.

"Go on," Miles instructed gently.

"It is written," she replied and handed him a rolled piece of vellum.

Miles accepted the paper and nodded his head. "Thank you," he said.

"Sir Miles?" Roweena asked.

"Yes?"

"I pray you win," she said before quickly disappearing through the archway.

Miles waited until she was gone before he opened the message. Stepping close to a torch, he read the neatly scripted Latin.

When he was finished, he smiled. The message was short and perfectly put. "Valkyrie shall watch over you on the fields tomorrow. On his wings will be my love; it, too, shall watch over you."

Miles folded the message and turned to the edge of the parapet wall. Once again he gazed out at the darkened field where he would be fighting tomorrow. His mind was strangely calm, and he made an oath to himself that tomorrow he would be victorious.

Gwendolyn had avoided any public meeting with Morgan, preferring to speak with him only at the feast. Then, after Miles and Morgan had departed, she too had asked the king's permission to withdraw. When it was granted, she had returned to her rooms. With Roweena's help, she had undressed and changed into the tunic she would sleep in.

She sat at her dressing table and gazed fondly at the dagger Miles had given her. Its jeweled pommel reflected the light in the room, and a myriad of sparks flew outward from the handle. Carefully, Gwendolyn slid the blade free from the sheath to look at it. The lightly curved blade bore several indentations, and as she studied them she realized the words were written in the Saracen language.

Suddenly there was a knocking at her door. As Roweena answered it, Gwendolyn placed the knife on the table and turned to see who was there. At that very instant, she saw her servant flung away and Morgan step inside.

"I have tried to speak with you since my arrival," he said in a growling voice. "Why have you been avoiding me?"

"I thought it improper," Gwendolyn replied, glancing at the frightened servant to make sure she was all right.

"Leave us," Morgan ordered.

Roweena looked at Gwendolyn, and Gwendolyn nodded. "Wait in your room," she said to the servant. Both she and Morgan remained silent until Roweena disappeared behind her tapestry. Then Gwendolyn rose to face Morgan.

"How dare you come into my rooms and give my servants orders. This is Kildrake Castle, not Guildswood."

"You left me no choice! You are betrothed to me!"

"I know," she replied as she stared into his eyes. Inwardly, Gwendolyn shivered, but nothing of her revulsion showed on her face. "But the king has made a decree, and there is nothing my grandfather can do."

"I care nothing for what that sodomist has decreed. It should have been John, not Richard, who sits on the throne of England! But it is not, yet! So, my lady, I will win you again, tomorrow. Gwendolyn, you will be my wife!"

Gwendolyn stayed silent; there were no words to be said.

"When the joust is done, and I have defeated this fool, I will take you to Guildswood."

Gwendolyn heard both the boast and the threat within his words as she held his eyes with hers. "There must be a marriage first," Gwendolyn reminded him.

"I have already spoken with the king's bishop. When the joust is over, I will wed you on the very field where I defeat this thief of a knight who would steal you from me. I will wait no longer to have you!" he swore.

Gwendolyn listened to his tirade, noticing that his voice grew huskier with each word he spoke. When he finished, he moved unexpectedly, and before Gwendolyn could evade him, his arms were around her, pulling her to him. As his mouth reached for hers, Gwendolyn slipped from his hold and stepped back.

"You have not won yet. Until you do, and we are married, I will not have you pawing me like your whores!"

She saw her words strike Morgan, and she saw his face stiffen even as his eyes widened. His face hardened and he stepped toward her. Gwendolyn retreated until she was against her dressing table.

"*You want him, not me!*" Morgan declared as he stared at her. "Don't try to deny it, you deceitful bitch! You planned this, didn't you? Answer me!" he demanded.

Gwendolyn silently stared at his angered face.

"No, I did not plan this," she protested, but even as she spoke, she knew her true emotions were visible on her face. Suddenly she no longer cared.

"I will have you," he whispered. "No man will stop me. And when I've had you, you'll want no other."

"You will never have me," Gwendolyn hissed as she put her hands on the table for support.

Morgan's face turned darker, and Gwendolyn knew he was about to enter one of his mindless rages. Morgan's lips turned ashen just as Gwendolyn's fingers touched something cool and hard—the Saracen dagger.

Then time slowed as Morgan drew his arm back. She saw his hand open, readying to strike her, but she had no fear of him as her hand closed around the dagger's handle.

Moving swiftly, before Morgan could react and bring his arm toward her, Gwendolyn brought the dagger out from behind her. With a blurring movement of her arm, the blade flashed in front of her and, as Morgan's eyes saw the glint of steel, she stepped forward and pressed the point to his throat, breaking the first layer of his skin.

"Leave! Now!" she commanded him.

Slowly, while Morgan's eyes remained locked on the dagger, his hand dropped. "You will regret this."

"Leave!" she repeated.

"I will leave your lover lying in a pool of his own blood

tomorrow. And tomorrow night, the blood of your virginity had best be on my bed!" Morgan spat the threat at her, turned and walked from the room.

When the door closed, Roweena emerged from behind the tapestry and gazed at Gwendolyn.

"Do not look so worried; Miles will win," she whispered, fighting hard to control her emotions. Everything had happened quickly, but the few seconds it had taken had seemed like an eternity.

"He must," Roweena said as her eyes traveled to the door, and then to the dagger, still clenched within Gwendolyn's fist.

Gwendolyn wiped the drop of blood from the dagger's tip before replacing it in its sheath. She sat at the table and, opening a small leather box, took out a single sheet of vellum. Then she opened a small jar, and dipped her quill. She wrote quickly and neatly and when she was finished, the dark ink blotted, she handed the paper to Roweena, instructing her to deliver it to Miles. After Roweena had gone, and Gwendolyn was alone, she walked to Valkyrie and gently stroked his head. She gazed into the eagle's amber eyes and drew a peace of sorts from them.

"We will win," she whispered to the bird. "We will win."

Chapter Five

An hour before dawn, Miles rose from his bed and strode across the room. The fire had died, but there were still a few glowing embers to point out its former might. Before he reached the tapestried guarderoom, James was at his side.

"I would be alone for a while," Miles told the boy, gently placing a strong hand upon his shoulder. "Go to your brother. I will be at the tent shortly."

James nodded once and left the room quickly. In the guarderoom, with its taper glowing low, Miles dipped his hand into the basin of water James had set out and washed the sleep from his eyes. Then he dressed himself in the waiting tunic, slipped on his sandals, and took a deep breath.

Five minutes later, Miles was walking along the battlements of the near tower. He paced casually, but inside he was anything but calm. He knew his future depended on the outcome of this day, and because of that, his nerves were stretched tautly. But, as he faced east, he paused. The sun was rising and casting a golden glow across the spring moors. Emerald green began to shimmer even as the pink clouds of dawn faded.

Miles was caught within the beauty of the Devonshire morning and let himself become one with it. By the time the sun floated above the moors, the sky was cloudless and crystal clear. He blinked twice and shook his head, realizing for the first time that the color of the morning sky was the exact color of Gwendolyn's eyes.

Moving only his eyes, Miles looked across the outer keep to gaze at the banners flying above the myriad of tents. Then he looked at the open tournament field, and the rows of tiered benches that had been built in the last two days. In a little while he would be out there on the greensward, fighting for his very life—not his physical life, but the life he knew he wanted.

A loud cry from above him wrenched his mind and drew his eyes aloft. High above Castle Kildrake, Miles saw the large golden eagle spiraling skyward. He watched the magnificent bird arching in the morning sky and wished that for once, he, too, could be freed from his earthly bonds to float above the world, uncaring of the machinations of men.

Valkyrie seemed to hang motionless in the air over Miles's gaze. Then the eagle turned once more, and Miles thought the giant bird had heard his wishes, because Valkyrie, his amber eyes locked upon Miles, dove to the very spot on which Miles stood.

As he had been caught by the beauty of the morning, Miles was also captured by the grace of the wide wings of the diving bird. Then Miles caught his breath, but did not flinch, when Valkyrie swept past him, barely a foot above his head and cried out once more. Miles followed the eagle's path while it circled the outer ward in slowly descending loops.

Still Miles's body would not relax while he stared at the eagle, who dropped to the height of the tent tops. Another loud cry echoed through the air as Valkyrie circled above his own mast and banner. Then the golden eagle descended once again, and came to rest upon the cross staff of the banner of Radstock.

All at once the tension which had held Miles drained, and he let go his breath in a gentle sigh. Gwendolyn had sent the eagle to him, it was her way of being with him during the morning. "Thank you, my love," he whispered to Gwendolyn. "And to you Valkyrie, I, too, grant a boon. When I win today, your form shall be added to my family's crest."

With his decision made, and his mind more at ease than it had been since waking, Miles left the battlements without returning to his room, and went down the three levels to the ground, crossed the inner ward, went through the barbican, and angled toward his tent.

"My lord," cried Arthur, when Miles entered the tent. James turned from polishing Miles's sword to bow toward his lord.

Miles smiled confidently at his squires, who were on the brink of manhood. "Do not look so sober, the tourney has yet to begin."

"I have prepared a light meal," Arthur said, knowing Miles's habits well. "Please," he said, pointing to the small table.

Miles went to the table, set with a platter of cold meat, a tankard of mead, and another of water. He pushed aside the mead and began to eat, watching the twins work over every inch of his maille, carefully inspecting it to make sure that there was nothing that could cause injury to their lord.

A half hour later, Miles rose from the table and removed his tunic. He stood naked before his squires, and, as they had so often in the past, they moved to him with fresh garments in their hands.

First, Arthur undraped a narrow sheet of material and wound one end around Miles's waist. Then he slipped the free end down his buttocks and through his thighs, capturing Miles's loins within it, and passing the end through the material at his waist. He reversed the order and repeated his movement once more, effectively protecting Miles and securing his organs within the confines of the uncolored loincloth.

Then James and Arthur together helped Miles into the padded-leather gamboise, the only protection his skin would have against the hardness of the maille. This particular gamboise was split, as was his hauberk, but was a good inch shorter than the maille itself. Next, the squires attached the cuisses, the vertically padded protection for his thighs, knees, and shins. When they were buckled, and Miles flexed his knees to test them, the squires nodded solemnly to each other and stepped to the armor.

First came the chausses, the maille leggings. While Arthur laced one, James did the other, carefully weaving the metal upward to his knees. At the knees, the squires manipulated the metal, leaving his joints free for movement. Then they laced the chausses to midthigh and secured them tightly before putting on the greaves, after which came the poleyn, the hard leather knee-protector. Now, Miles was protected from toe to midthigh.

They worked on his arms next. First came the rerebraces to protect his upper arm, then the vambraces for his forearm. When they were laced on, again, the squires stepped back.

Still working silently, the squires lifted the hauberk and carried it to their lord. Together, they held the heavy maille coat and draped it over his body. A moment later, they adjusted it properly.

Throughout this time, Miles maintained his silence. His squires had been trained by himself, and he trusted them implicitly. Although he was impatient to be done, the hour it took to dress him properly was necessary to bring his nerves to the fine edge he needed.

He closed his eyes when the boys placed the arming coif on his head, knowing the heavy leather piece would protect his scalp from the bite of the maille. Then came the coif-de-maille, the full head protection that no knight could do battle without and hope to return alive. The metal throat guard and chin protector was heavy, but not uncomfortable. The squires adjusted the coif, and secured it to the hauberk.

Next came his helmet, a simple curved cap with a nasal bar. When that was in place, the squires, acting as one, slipped on the maille gloves. Then, almost reverently, James and Arthur lifted Miles Delong's gipon, his armorial surcoat, and carried it to him. They slipped it on him and adjusted it smoothly. When the gipon was on and adjusted, the squires attached the waistchains for his weapons.

Miles knew exactly what he looked like. Although all that was visible of his skin was cheek and mouth, no one could possibly mistake him for another. The crest of Radstock was proudly displayed on both the front and back of his gipon: a scarlet shield with the Welsh dragon in one corner, the lion of Normandy opposite, and the chevrons of Radstock beneath. Miles Delong, in full battle armor, was a sight to behold, and one that few ever forgot.

"Weapons?" asked James, while he and his brother encased Miles's mailled hands within his tournament gauntlets. Then James placed the sword and its scabbard onto the waiting chain.

Miles flexed his gauntlet-covered fingers while eyeing the

weapons his squires had laid out. "The axe," he whispered.

"My lord, Morgan is a full Norman. He will use the mace . . ."

"I am counting on that. The axe!" Miles ordered sternly.

Without argument, James picked up the axe and attached it to yet another of the chains. "We have picked four lances," he said as he and Arthur brought the mighty wooden poles to Miles. Each lance was smoothly finished, with a tapering, but blunt tip. On each hung the pennant of Radstock.

"Good. It is time to go." But his words were almost drowned out by a loud cheering that washed through the tent. "Yes," he added, knowing that Richard had arrived.

Gwendolyn stepped from her room and took a deep breath of air. Trailing five feet behind her was Roweena. Gwendolyn was dressed in a style befitting King Richard's presence; however, her Norman dress still held signs of her proud Saxon heritage. The bodice was close to her skin, and the V of the neckline plunged to the valley of her breasts. The sleeves of the dress were tight until they reached her elbows where they began to grow wider. By the time the upper part of the sleeve reached her wrist, the lower part was a hairsbreadth above the floor. Around her waist was a girdle of silver. This was her Saxon heritage, and she displayed it proudly. Attached to the girdle was the Saracen dagger. The skirt billowed out from her hips in gentle folds, emphasizing both her elegant height, and her womanly figure. Upon her head rested yet another golden coif-de-maille, set with amethysts, rubies, and sapphires.

No matter what her outer trappings were, within Gwendolyn turmoil was rampant. Yet she knew that none of her thoughts must show on her face.

By the time she and Roweena reached the courtyard, her grandfather had appeared. At his side, standing almost a half head taller, was Richard.

Gwendolyn dropped to her knee gracefully before the king and rose at his touch upon her shoulder. When she was again standing, she gazed into his golden-flecked eyes, but remained silent.

"You are a worthy prize, Lady Gwendolyn. Would that I had found you first," he whispered.

"You are too kind, Sire," Gwendolyn responded quickly. "And an example of chivalry to all."

Richard's smile was hesitant yet gentle, and she saw a vague flicker within his eyes. "You remind me of my mother," he said absently. "Not in your looks, but in your carriage. She is a brave woman, too, a strong woman. There are so few of them . . ." Richard suddenly shook his head. "But, it is time, mamsell," he stated, offering his arm gallantly.

With Gwendolyn on one side of the king, and Hughes on the other, the entourage walked slowly from the inner ward toward the tournament site. With each step, Gwendolyn's heart beat faster, and she was hard pressed to keep her face free of emotion.

Within the sanctity of the seats set aside for Richard, Gwendolyn looked outward at the vast array of tents across from the joust arena. Her eyes skimmed across their tops until they came to rest upon the standard of Radstock, above which sat Valkyrie. Her heart speeded again for a moment when she saw her eagle, but she forced her eyes to move again when she heard Richard speak.

"Tell me, Marshall, who shall you wager on?" the king asked.

William Marshall, the burly knight and chief advisor to Richard, and before him, his father Henry, laughed loudly and shook his head. "To wager against one, is to be for the other. We cannot afford to lose either." When the older knight finished, he fixed Richard with a powerful stare. "And you, my lord?" he asked.

"I must agree in conscience, if not in fact."

"Then stop this foolishness," demanded the knight. "An injury to either man will hurt all of England."

"I cannot and will not stop it!" Richard replied in a steely voice.

"Very well," Marshall whispered and turned to stare out. But not before Gwendolyn saw the look of suppressed fury on his face. She had met William Marshall several times and had been impressed by his logical thinking and steadfast loyalty to England, rather than to Normandy.

Before anything further could be said, a fanfare rang loudly. Gwendolyn's breath caught as she watched the mounted knights ride forward, resplendent with all their weapons. The sun glinted off Miles's dark maille, and sparkled from the pointed tip of his helmet. She let her breath escape in a low hiss a bare second before both knights stopped in front of the king.

Suddenly, within Gwendolyn's racing mind, the words of the old priestess returned, and with them, her body relaxed. Miles will be triumphant, she told herself. He must be!

She gazed into Morgan's face and a shudder passed along her length. His dark eyes held hers, and she felt as though he were ravishing her before the world.

"Are you ready, my knights?" Richard called in a deep voice.

"I am," replied Miles.

"I am," echoed Morgan. But before Richard could continue, Morgan turned his charger and moved it a step closer to Gwendolyn. "As your rightfully betrothed, I ask a favor to carry into tournament."

Gwendolyn stared at Morgan for a long moment. She turned to look first at Richard, whose eyes were etched with amusement, and then she looked at her grandfather. When she spoke, her voice was flat and unemotional. "Because of the nature of this tourney, Morgan of Guildswood, I cannot give one man a favor without giving the same to the other."

In the silence that followed her words, Morgan's glare of hatred darkened, and within it, Gwendolyn glimpsed the empty, horrid future awaiting her if Morgan was victorious today.

Suddenly Morgan reined his charger back, and turned to face the king. "At your command!" he shouted, lifting a gauntlet-covered hand.

Richard stood, his arms extended, one hand toward Miles, the other toward Morgan. "I charge you both with the following rule. This is a tourney, not a battle. The winner and loser shall both walk from this field to do battle, in earnest, with the enemies of our country. Do you understand?"

"Yes, my lord," Miles called softly, before bowing his head to Richard.

"And you, Morgan of Guildswood?" Richard asked when the knight remained silent.

"Yes, my lord," Morgan said, but everyone, including Richard, heard the reluctance within his voice.

"Then let the tournament begin," Richard declared.

Gwendolyn breathed deeply at the words and watched the knights ride to their squires at the opposite ends of the jousting field. While the squires removed the weapons that would not yet be needed, she tried to calm her emotions.

Jousting was a relatively new part in the tourneys, and a part that Gwendolyn despised. It caused too much injury, and many times, even with the blunted tips of the lances, death was found.

She forced herself to think of other things as she waited for the first joust to begin. The morning sun was growing hotter overhead, and still no cloud had appeared in the skies above the moors of Devonshire.

The fanfare of trumpets called out, and with her lower lip caught between her teeth, she watched Miles and Morgan charge each other. The sound of eight hoofbeats echoed like thunder, and was the only sound to be heard. They met ferociously, and the loud splintering of wood upon shields crackled in the air. Both knights remained in their saddles, but their lances were splintered and broken. They turned their chargers about and rode to their squires.

Miles threw his shattered lance down and took the fresh one from James, as Arthur turned the heavy-boned charger around. "He's like a rock. It didn't even jar him," Miles said, more to himself than the squires. His arm still vibrated from Morgan's lance shattering on his curved tournament shield, and he willed away the trembling as he readied himself for the next charge.

Fitting the lance under his arm and resting it against his side, Miles spurred his charger to the gate. When the fanfare signaled loudly, Miles thought of nothing except the target charging toward him. The charger, for all its great weight, moved swiftly and surely along the path. Three seconds later they met amidst a jarring collision of wood and leather, and the snapping of lances sounded loudly.

Miles whirled his mount and started toward his squires. When he passed Morgan, the knight spat on the ground before him. "You will die today," Morgan called in a voice loud enough for Miles alone to hear.

Miles ignored both his words and gestures as he rode to receive his new lance. Again, when the trumpets sounded,

Miles charged forward, his eyes fixed only on Morgan's shield.

They met in the center of the outer ward, as they had twice before, and for the third time, the sounds of their meeting echoed. Miles shook the sweat from his eyes and rode back to his squires.

With his new lance in place, he waited for the next charge. But he was bothered by the last. He'd barely deflected Morgan's lance, which had grazed the inside edge of his own shield. Only his quick deflection upwards had stopped Morgan's lance from hitting his abdomen. And, Miles knew it had been intentional. Yet, because of that, Morgan had not splintered his lance and had lost points.

"His lance!" Arthur warned when the trumpets sounded. Miles's eyes left Morgan's shield and he saw what had caused Arthur's yell. Morgan had changed lances, and this new one had a sharp tip. It was not a metal head, but the wood was almost shaven to a point. Taking a deep, preparatory breath, Miles spurred the charger on.

He moved with the mount, sitting deep in the wooden saddle, his buttocks pressed tightly back, awaiting the impact of the lance. Suddenly, he spurred the charger harder, knowing that if he were to live, he must do the unexpected. The sharp tip of Morgan's lance was coming nearer and would soon penetrate through the heavy leather of the shield.

His horse moved faster, and when they were within five feet of each other and Miles saw the position of the lance, he bent forward, tilting his shield at the last second. This deflected Morgan's deadly intent, just as the blunted tip of his lance hit the exact center of Morgan's shield. A loud gasp rose above the sounds of combat. Miles's lance bent, but did not splinter. Suddenly the lance was free, and a loud cheer followed. Miles reined in the charger, turning the lumberous horse as quickly as he could and saw Morgan just beginning to stand. He had unseated him. He had won the first round of the tourney.

Miles, elation flowing through his body as fast as his blood pounded, rode to the squires and dismounted. On his feet, he turned to stare at Morgan, whose squire was running to him, his mace held forward.

"Axe," Miles called as he studied the mace, making sure that it was indeed a tournament mace, and not a spiked battle weapon.

When Morgan's squire reached the knight, Arthur handed Miles the heavy axe. Its blade was blunt, but even so, it could kill if necessary. Miles had no wish for that. A moment later, his regular shield on his left arm, he stepped forward to meet Morgan.

Morgan swung the mace in the air, the heavy lead ball whooshing loudly in Miles's ears as he stepped up to his foe. Then, with his shield held in ready, Miles hefted the battle-axe and charged.

Both knights' screams rose as their weapons descended on the other. The heavy ball thudded against Miles's shield, and the impact sent pain shooting through his arm. But he stood his ground, and even as Morgan drew back to let loose the mace again, Miles's axe descended.

Its flattened edge struck the outer umbo of Morgan's shield, bending the thick metal band and making the heavy-set knight stagger. But the mace's ball did not falter as it again struck Miles's shield, sending another wave of pain upward to his shoulder.

Miles spun, lifting his shield to cover his head, but he'd anticipated wrong, and the mace struck his side in a devastating blow. Miles stumbled, but his instincts came fully to life. He dropped his shield low, this time rightly anticipating Morgan's move. The ball hit his shield, and as it did, Miles flicked his wrist to send the ball ricocheting harmlessly away. In the same move, he swung the axe horizontally toward Morgan. The wide-set knight moved faster than Miles had thought he could, neatly deflecting the axe with his shield.

Then they stood apart for a moment, staring at each other and taking several deep breaths. Both men were conscious of the unusual silence that had fallen over the crowd. There were no strident calls, no cheers of encouragement, just a deadly silence that called for more fighting.

Slowly, Morgan lifted the mace and began to whirl it over his head. Miles watched his eyes, not the mace, as Morgan stepped closer. Then, before Morgan could take another step, Miles whirled in a circle, shouting out a battle cry and bringing the heavy battle-axe downward in a swift movement. Morgan's shield barely contained the surprise move. His mace glanced harmlessly off Miles's shoulder, yet the glancing blow was effective enough to stop Miles's attack.

Rivulets of sweat poured down both their faces as they fought on. Attack and defend, attack and defend, for endless and wearying minutes. Five minutes after the battle had been joined, Miles's shield was ripped and tattered, almost as badly as was Morgan's.

But neither knight would stop. When Miles charged yet again, his foot caught on a clump of grass and he tripped. Cries were heard from the crowd, amongst theirs, Gwendolyn's. Her knuckles turned white as her fists curled ineffectively and her eyes stayed locked to the combat.

She alone, among everyone else, was aware of the truth of this fight. Morgan would do whatever he could to win, and if he could at the same time kill Miles, he would not hesitate. Not even Richard's command would stop him.

"Bad," whispered Marshall behind her.

Morgan's mace whirled again as Miles rolled on the ground. Suddenly the deadly metal ball whisked downward, and a loud shout rose from the crowd, obliterating the sound of the ball hitting Miles's left shoulder. But even as the mace fell, Miles had freed his right arm and swung the axe upward. When the ball hit his shoulder, his axe met the wooden handle of the mace.

Then the unbelievable happened. A loud sound crackled in the air, and the round morningstar continued to arc harmlessly to the ground, followed by both the chain and half the wooden handle. In one swift movement, Miles rose to his feet, the axe held near Morgan's throat while he stared at the knight.

Morgan's enraged eyes did not blink as he released his hold upon the useless bottom half of the mace.

Slowly, Miles dropped his shield and lowered his axe. He stepped back a foot, and bowed to his opponent.

"It is not over yet," whispered Morgan.

Miles smiled, ignoring the pain in his side and shoulder from the mace's cruel blows. "Soon," he retorted in challenge.

"Upon your death," Morgan stated.

"So be it," Miles replied, grasping his pommel and drawing the longsword out smoothly.

He hefted it above his head, and brought it down slowly in salute to the other knight. Never once did his eyes leave the dark, rage-filled ones of his opponent.

Moving forward, Miles began to whirl the longsword in the air. Their swords met in a glinting clash above their heads, and Miles again felt in the jarring of his arms the animal strength of his opponent.

Morgan showed none of the effect of the axe, but Miles felt the mace's lingering caress in his shoulder. Spinning under the blades, Miles bent low, swinging toward Morgan's thighs.

Another loud clash echoed when Morgan parried the attack. Then, cautiously, both men fought. Each attacked in turn, learning about the other's weaknesses as the minutes dragged on and the spectators began to shout encouragement to their particular favorite.

"You can't win," Morgan whispered when they were close. Miles ignored this, and accented his silent reply with a devastating blow to Morgan's shoulder. The blunted edges of the sword would not cut through the maille, but the effect of the blows that fell was in their punishing pain.

Again, acting like the bull he resembled, Morgan took up the attack, slashing, striking, using his brute strength to weaken Miles and force him back.

Miles realized his danger while he retreated. He could not fight Morgan on the knight's terms; Morgan was too powerful. *Use your mind!* he ordered himself. Then, as Morgan unleashed yet another furious attack, Miles drew his sword back and stepped forward. He knew it was a risky move, weighted down by the maille and leather armor, but he had no choice. Calculating everything to the very inch, Miles somersaulted forward, a hairsbreadth beneath the flashing blade, and rose behind Morgan before the man could stop his forward rush. Moving with lightning speed, Miles swung the sword just as Morgan spun to face him.

As soon as his sword met Morgan's he knew! The sound of a blade breaking in battle was unmistakable, and the hollow cracking of metal reverberated loudly above them. Morgan stared at Miles, and then at his own broken blade. Suddenly, loud cheering erupted from everyone's mouths as they realized the end of the tournament had been reached.

Silently, still holding Morgan's maddened eyes with his

own, Miles bowed formally to the other knight. Then, he sheathed his sword and removed his helmet. Turning, he strode toward Richard, Gwendolyn, and Hughes. When he reached the place before them, he loosened his coif-de-maille, and dropped its hooded continence to his shoulders before bowing to his king.

"Rise, Sir Miles, victor," proclaimed Richard in a loud voice. Miles stood, but rather than look at Richard, his eyes locked with Gwendolyn's and he drank in the emotions pouring from them.

"Sir Morgan, step forward," Richard called loudly. He waited a moment until the knight, accompanied by his squire, stood next to Miles. "Today, two of my bravest knights fought for the hand of Lady Gwendolyn. But," Richard said, pausing to gaze at both knights for a moment before he continued, "but, what everyone here today witnessed was more than just a tournament. What they have witnessed is the power, and the might of England and Normandy, and what they have seen today is but an example of what the Saracens shall feel when we arrive in the Holy Land!"

The crowd cheered lustily with Richard's brave words, none noticing the strange look that passed between Gwendolyn and Miles when he spoke. Their eyes met again and held, until he finished his political speech.

"And now we declare this tournament ended. Sir Miles Delong, Earl of Radstock, champion of Lady Gwendolyn, granddaughter of Hughes, Duke of Devonshire, soon to be the Lady Gwendolyn Delong!"

Again the voices rang out, and none noticed that Morgan had stepped back. Miles's and Gwendolyn's eyes were locked upon each other's, until Miles saw Gwendolyn's blue eyes go wide. The crowd became hushed, and Miles, a tickling at the nape of his neck warning him, spun.

Morgan stood three feet from him, a shortsword raised high, his eyes mad and unseeing of anything except the target before him.

"Hold!" cried Richard as Morgan took a threatening step forward.

"No!" screamed Gwendolyn, vaulting the small barrier before her and stepping between Miles and Morgan. "Stop before you dishonor your family," she said in a low voice.

"The king has spoken. There is nothing that can be changed. It is over. Leave!"

Miles stared at Morgan, timing everything as his hands went to Gwendolyn's waist and readied himself to toss her from between them; then he saw the sword waver and slowly drop until it pointed at Miles's face.

"For as long as you live, Delong, you will have Guildswood for your enemy. As Christ is my witness, I shall not rest until I am avenged for what you have taken from me this day. Whenever you go to sleep at night, pray that you will wake in the morning!" With his oath done, Morgan threw his sword to the ground before Gwendolyn and Miles. Then he bowed elegantly to Richard, turned, and stalked from the field.

Gwendolyn turned to face Miles, her eyes still wide with the effects of Morgan's words, but before Miles could comfort her, Richard spoke again.

"Do not think overlong on his words. He was angered, both by his loss of you, my lady, and by his defeat on the field. He is a good knight; he meant not what he said."

But Gwendolyn knew the truth, as did Miles. Together, her smaller hand clasped in his tournament gauntlet, they turned to face the king and bow their understanding.

"But smile," Richard declared, "for the marriage you both desired will come to pass. I shall witness it myself, in two weeks' time. Sir Miles, send word to Radstock!" Everyone bowed when Richard started from the field, but he stopped and turned back to Miles and Gwendolyn once again.

"You are a brave woman, Lady Gwendolyn. I have never seen another step before a sword willingly, except for my mother. You are the first woman I could compare to Eleanore of Aquitaine, and she is a woman to look up to." With the shock of his words apparent on the faces of his closest advisors, Richard walked from the field, followed by Hughes and Marshall, and then Miles and Gwendolyn.

Behind them, the cheers of the people followed, but above that sound, forcing both Miles and Gwendolyn to pause and look up, was Valkyrie crying out his victory call.

Chapter Six

DUSK FELL OVER THE MOORS, subduing them in understated tones as was Devonshire's wont. Each day the moors affected a different view, from bold and beautiful, to a misty haze that none could penetrate. But there was no land that Gwendolyn could envision which would be able to compare to the beauty of Dartmoor. And none, she knew, would ever hold the lure and mystery that her home did.

Tomorrow she would be leaving her home. For the third time in her life, she would be entering a new place, a new home, but this time she looked forward to it.

Tomorrow, Miles would arrive in the early morning, as custom decreed, with his full retinue of knights and family. The king had returned yesterday from his tour of Cornwall and seemed impatient for the wedding to be over, so that he could return to London, and then onward to Normandy.

But these past two weeks had been very busy for Gwendolyn. Besides preparing her belongings to be moved to Radstock, she had taken many days to ride in the moors to go to the Pool of Pendragon, and her mother's cave. In the cave, she had done many things besides communing with the sword and helping her powers to grow stronger. She had also prepared the cave for her wedding.

Four times she had gone to the cave. She had sat on the strangely warm floor and held the sword in her hands. She'd opened her mind, accepting and receiving the soothing channel of energy and light within her. The first three times she had called out to the Druid priestess, seeking advice, but had received nothing for her efforts. On the fourth try, as she had sat amidst the pure silver light of the sword and formed her thoughts to call for the old woman, something within her had made her stop.

As hard as she had been trying, she'd suddenly understood it had not been necessary. Realization had flooded her mind, making her blood run warm through her body. She'd held the sword aloft and felt it begin to vibrate in her hands. There was a crackling in the air, and the cave had become filled with the scent of a summer thunderstorm. Slowly, she'd released her hold upon the silver hilt, and as she did, beams of light, combining all the colors of creation, sprang from everywhere along the sword's length to dance within the confines of the cave. The sword had floated above her, and all around her she sensed eyes watching her.

Taking a long, calming breath, she'd waited. Willing the tension in her mind to ease, she'd sensed a relaxing of those ethereal beings around her.

"I have been chosen," she'd whispered, knowing exactly what to say without knowing how she had.

"You have," a single voice had replied. Tears had welled within Gwendolyn's eyes when she'd heard her mother's voice.

"As were you," she had replied.

"As was Gwyneth," came another voice. Within the voice had been all the power of the heavens, and thunder vibrated within Gwendolyn's mind. But she'd been unafraid of this new voice.

"As were you, Father," she'd stated calmly.

"As we all were," he had replied. But Gwendolyn heard the approval in his voice, and her heart beat proudly.

"And Miles?" she'd whispered.

"He was chosen for you. Together you and your husband will rise to the greatness that is necessary for our survival."

"I understand," she'd said.

"No, not yet, but you will, my daughter," intoned the son of thunder. "Prepare yourself well," he had added in a gentler voice.

When the voices had gone, the light faded. Gwendolyn had closed her eyes and grasped the pommel of the silver sword. Her tears fell slowly along her cheeks, but went unheeded as she thought about her father's words.

"I will," she'd promised. Slowly Gwendolyn had wrapped the sword in its chamois, and had risen from the floor. She had only one thing left to do before returning to the castle. She went to the package she'd brought with her and slowly untied it. She spread out the newly made rush mat, and smoothed it carefully. Then she'd placed the sword within its niche and left the cave. The sun was still out when Gwendolyn had mounted her horse and headed back to Castle Kildrake.

"My lady?" called Roweena, forcing Gwendolyn's mind to return to the present. She glanced at her servant and waited. "Your bath is ready, and then I must finish your wedding mantle."

"Very well," Gwendolyn said in a low voice. She gazed once more at the darkening vista of the moors, before following Roweena back to her chamber.

Gwendolyn stood patiently upon the highest point of the near tower, waiting with Valkyrie perched upon her wrist, until the sun rose majestically over the moors. When it finally crested the tallest hill, and its rays glowed down upon the earth, Gwendolyn smiled. Light glimmered from the helmets of the approaching knights, and the pennants of Radstock flew high.

Valkyrie, uttering a low cry, arched his wings in anticipation of his coming flight. Sensing his impatience, Gwendolyn lowered her arm and drew it gracefully back. Then she moved it swiftly forward, lifting it high, until the large eagle left its leathery perch and entered its own territory. She watched the eagle drop from the tower and sighed when he caught the currents. Slowly, gracefully, Valkyrie rose in lazy circles.

Once he flew above her, the golden eagle called out. Turning, Valkyrie arched majestically above Castle Kildrake, until he dropped lower and flew toward the oncoming procession.

When he had passed over the long line of riders, he circled behind it, and returned to the front. Then a solitary arm reached skyward. The richly embroidered material fell away from the wrist, and sunlight glinted off silver cuffs. Valkyrie seemed to stop in the air above the rider and then float downward until he was perched on the man's shoulder.

Miles accepted the weight of the eagle when it came to rest on his shoulder. He gazed up into the bird's amber eyes and saw he was being regarded carefully.

"Hello, old man," he said.

Valkyrie stared at him unblinkingly.

Then Miles saw the chain around his neck, and the small piece of vellum attached to it. Gently, he drew the chain over the eagle's head and unclasped the paper. He opened it and read, in Gwendolyn's precise scripting, the message meant for him alone.

When he was finished, he replaced the chain on Valkyrie and looked upward at the high battlements of Kildrake, until he saw the form of Gwendolyn upon the parapet. He held out his arm for the eagle, and when the bird reached his wrist, he threw Valkyrie skyward.

Ten minutes later Miles was in the inner ward of Kildrake, kneeling before Sir Hughes, who pulled him roughly to his feet and pressed him close in welcome.

"The archbishop is with the king, the ceremony will start in two hours. I have had my own chamber prepared for you. Go to it," he advised. "I will see to your family."

"My thanks, my lord," Miles replied honestly.

"Do not thank me too soon. You may yet regret your hasty decisions."

"No, my lord, I shall not."

Hughes gazed into the deep green pools of Miles's eyes. "I think not either, Miles, though I can't for the life of me understand it."

"There is nothing to understand, my lord. You must do as I have; accept it."

"Well spoken. Miles, I am glad that Devonshire and Radstock will be allied. It will be beneficial in the future."

"Thank you," Miles replied, feeling the emotion of Sir Hughes's words strongly within his heart. Then, Hughes clasped Miles's shoulder in one of his large hands and squeezed gently.

"Go," he repeated.

Miles motioned to Arthur and James as he started toward the stone wall and the entrance leading within. Behind him, his twin squires carried a large chest and walked as fast as they could.

Inside, he turned to them. "Take that to the duke's chambers. I shall join you in a few minutes."

Silently, the squires started up the stone staircase in one direction, while Miles ran quickly to the staircase opposite. A few moments later he stood at Gwendolyn's door and knocked gently.

Roweena froze at the sound of the knock, the hem of Gwendolyn's skirt still clutched in her hand. She looked up at her mistress, who nodded her head. She released the material and went to the door, opening it slowly. She gasped when her eyes met Miles's, and instinctively bowed low.

"Your mistress summoned me," Miles said when he stepped inside and his eyes fell on Gwendolyn, taking in the image she projected. Her beauty was a picture he would never forget. She wore not the style of the Normans, but a traditional Saxon wedding dress. A sleeveless smooth tunic, dyed the palest of blues. It fit her perfectly, and although the bodice started almost at her chin, not a single part of her body was hidden. The full swell of her breasts rose and fell beneath the sheer material, and her slim waist was emphasized by a webbed girdle of pure gold, held together by buckles of gold with silver inlay. The skirt dropped smoothly to the ground and was edged with a triple band of woven white. Her bare feet were scarcely discernible through it. At her waist hung only one ornament, the jeweled Saracen blade he had given her.

Gwendolyn's face was only lightly made up, a picture of sublime comeliness. The rose tint of her cheeks stood out proudly, bringing even more attention to her pale-blue eyes. Her long silver-and-gold hair was brushed into luxurious waves that reached to her waist and glistened from the reflected light filtering through the window openings.

After another moment of inspection, Miles exhaled heavily and stepped closer. "You are truly beautiful," he whispered.

"As are you," she replied through her suddenly dry mouth. Then she glanced at Roweena, motioning her out. "Give us a few moments before you return." Once Roweena had gone, Gwendolyn stepped close to Miles. "It is time to talk about your promise," she said.

"My . . . yes," Miles said as he stared into her eyes. "The boon you requested."

"I would tell you of it now, before we are wed."

"But our agreement was after."

"No, my lord, I was to tell you on the day of our marriage, when everything was certain."

"I can wait."

"Can you? You see, my lord, it is no small thing that I would have, and if you cannot find it within you to accept what I ask, I will accede to your wishes, and if you would not marry me, I will understand."

Miles stared at her half in shock, half amused by her words. He smiled tolerantly and shook his head. But, when he spoke, his voice held a tinge of wariness.

"I have not done battle with Morgan, nor risked Richard's wrath to stop now. Speak what is on your mind, now if you wish, or later, after we are wed. I have already given my word."

Gwendolyn lifted her hand to caress his cheek. When she dropped her arm, she nodded. "It is simple, my lord, but the boon I ask you is unheard of, and never done before. I would have you make a knight of me."

"Make a . . ." Miles began, but stopped himself from saying anything else as he stared, shocked, into her eyes. Then, another smile formed on his lips, and a low laugh rumbled out. "I will still marry you, but what you ask is truly impossible. You are a woman, made to bring children into the world. You are not a warrior!"

Gwendolyn did not blink, did not retreat from his words; rather, she, too, smiled tolerantly while keeping her temper in check. "That day in the forest, when you found me fighting those men, you asked nothing of my boon before you granted it. You did not even wait until hearing it to agree, but gave it without hesitation or foreknowledge. Is this how I am to expect you to honor your vows and oaths? If so, my lord, I pray you not marry me!" she finished, defying him both in word and speech as she stared at him with disdain filling her eyes.

"Why?" he asked in a voice so low she could only read his lips.

"If I were to tell you now, you would not believe me. Affirm your oath to me so that we may marry. When our marriage vows have been sealed, not by the church, but by our bodies, you shall learn the reason for my request," she stated. "But affirm it you must, if you wish to marry. Do not forget that you leave within the year to fight in the Holy Land. Would you not have your wife able to see to your lands? Would you trust them to the likes of Richard's brother, John Lackland?"

Miles stared at her for a moment, her words ringing within his mind. Since the first moment he'd met Gwendolyn, the course of his life had been changed, and his destiny altered. And even now, with this latest madness unveiled before him, he sensed something stir within him. Slowly, he raised his hand to her chin, cupping it gently.

"I will see you at the altar," he stated. Quickly, he bent and brushed his lips across hers before leaving her.

When he was gone, and Roweena returned, Gwendolyn no longer cared what she looked like, or what the people would think. Her life was about to begin, and the path she would follow would start in a matter of hours.

Noon was almost upon Devonshire, and beneath the golden orb, Gwendolyn, escorted by Roweena, prepared to enter into the small anteroom of the chapel. Her veil was secured in place, and through it, everything had a misty, golden visage. The veil had been her mother's, and Gwyneth's mother's before. It was an intricate webbing of golden strands, attached to a golden coif-de-maille, which reached to the very ends of her hair. The frontal piece of the veil, a mesh of gold, covered her face and dropped to the top of her breasts. Taking a deep breath, Gwendolyn nodded for Roweena to open the door.

When the door opened, the voices within quieted. Every eye turned in expectation. When Gwendolyn stepped inside, a collective sigh issued from the waiting women, and smiles burst forth upon their faces.

"Magnificent!" cried Estelle Demarchier, wife of her grandfather's chief of arms. Three other women, dressed in flowing white Norman robes, rushed forward to embrace their friend. Through all of it, Gwendolyn felt as if she were in a dream, that she was an observer, and that this was happening to someone else.

The women cried and cooed and complimented Gwendolyn, forgetting for the moment all the whispered rumors of her birth, and treating her as their dearest friend.

"Turn! Show us everything!" cried Sanella Llewelyn, her cousin from Cardiff.

Gwendolyn gazed at her younger cousin for a moment before she smiled and spun once for them. But when she stopped and faced them all again, she heard a dissenting chord from William Marshall's daughter.

Gwendolyn fixed her with a withering stare as the room fell into silence. "Does it bother you that I wear the clothing of my heritage?" she asked in a low voice of challenge.

"Before a Norman king?"

"Before any man or woman, I am not ashamed of who I am!" Gwendolyn declared. "Nor do I seek to prove myself something I am not!" Marshall's daughter turned scarlet and drew her eyes from Gwendolyn's. It was well-known that William Marshall, although a gallant knight and the king's highest advisor, had been raised from humble beginnings, and given the Earldom of Pembroke through the combined mastery of military strategy and his prowess on the tournament fields. But, the Marshall family was English-born, and ruling a Welsh shire held a certain taint.

Before anything further could mar the wedding, the chapel door burst open and Hughes stepped in. Hughes, in his fifty-fifth year, was still a sight that could draw fear and admiration equally. Today, he was dressed in the finest of robes, his surcoat showing the proud insignia of Devonshire and Kildrake, and his fur-collared mantle billowing fully when he walked.

Hughes stopped when his eyes met his granddaughter's. He gazed at her, taking in her appearance, until a slow smile spread across his features. Stepping back, he raised his arm and the chamberlain entered, the long staff of his office held high before him. He rapped it three times on the stone floor before he spoke.

"It is the hour of the joining of Devonshire and Radstock. It is time for the vows to be sealed," he stated formally.

Gwendolyn took a deep breath and stepped forward. Her three handmaidens fell in behind her and lifted the hem of her long mantle as she walked to her grandfather. The duke turned when she reached him, and together, they entered the chapel, stepping onto the carpet of red wool laid out before them.

Suddenly, Gwendolyn's heart began to beat faster. Her eyes flickered to-and-fro as she looked at the people staring at her in the small chapel. The chapel was no larger than double her own chamber, and because of that, only fifty people were to witness her marriage. Gwendolyn was conscious of a hundred eyes upon her while she walked, but was unable to see or feel their expressions. Thankfully, reality departed and the strange feeling of being once again a spectator at her own wedding helped to ease her tense nerves.

When she saw Miles, her breath caught. He was dressed as befitted an earl and knight of England. A surcoat of forest-green contrasted perfectly with his long black hair. Leggings of the same color graced his calves, but his long, flowing mantle was of pure white, clasped together across his shoulders by a thick golden cord.

Endless moments later, Gwendolyn reached his side. She gazed into his sea-green eyes, and suddenly returned to her body, and to what was happening this day.

When the archbishop spoke, everyone turned to face him. He spoke eloquently in Latin, but Gwendolyn heard not a word. Her mind spun madly, and within it, she made her own vows to her husband. Then, at last, the archbishop of Exeter opened his arms wide in signal. Together, Gwendolyn and Miles knelt on the waiting cushions and gazed up at the richly dressed archbishop, as the handmaidens stood above the couple and held a sheer white cloth over their heads.

In a blurring of prayer and words, with her hand resting lightly upon his, Gwendolyn and Miles were united. The service ended suddenly, with the couple staring deeply into each other's eyes, and when the chapel doors opened, a fanfare of trumpets sounded. Standing, her hand again on top of his, Gwendolyn and her husband walked slowly from the chapel to stand within the inner ward, and listen to the cheers of the guests.

Suddenly the ranks of the people opened, and Gwendolyn saw a group of young knights moving toward them and her hand tightened over Miles's.

"It will soon be over, enjoy it." But his words were

washed away when the ten young knights reached them and separated them, hoisting Gwendolyn, with no gentle movements, high above everyone's head. Then Miles, too, was lifted into the air and, working as one, the knights carried the newlyweds toward the banquet tables amidst the raucous calls of the guests.

Gwendolyn, once aloft, forced her body to relax. Craning her neck, she saw everything spin around her until she closed her eyes against the sight and waited for it to end.

Then the hands which held her, freed her, and her bare feet were once more on the soft grass of the ward. She opened her eyes and found herself facing Miles. Lifting her arm, she placed it on his. Together they stepped up to the marriage table and, when they were standing behind their seats, waved to the guests.

Today, because of the wedding and the large number of people in attendance, the great hall had been abandoned in favor of the inner ward. And again, because of the wedding, instead of one High Table, there were two. The king, Sir Hughes, and the favored knights would sit at the first High Table. Across from them, Miles, Gwendolyn, and her three maids of honor would sit.

On a scaffold high above the inner ward, musicians played. Forceful, undulating rhythms quavered in the air, and the heat of the moment flowed through Gwendolyn's body when Miles released her hand so she could sit.

But she did not. Instead, she removed the frontal veil and handed it to Roweena, giving Miles his first unrestricted view of the face of the woman he had just wed. A moment later, she faced the crowd again, smiling fully, signaling the start of the wedding feast.

Both Miles and Gwendolyn steeled themselves for the long hours ahead. Feasting, music, entertainment, and dancing would all combine in a multeity of abandon, and through it all they would watch the festivities. But first, while the musicians played high above the gathering, came the gifts.

For two hours people came forward. Knights, dukes, earls, and finally the messengers of those who were unable to attend on such short notice. The pile of gifts grew higher before the marriage table, and with each gift, Miles and Gwendolyn thanked the bearer.

In a brief moment as one knight left and another prepared

to approach, Miles turned to Gwendolyn to toast her with a cup of wine.

"You have made me very happy, my lord," Gwendolyn whispered above the rim of her cup.

"It is only the beginning, my lady," Miles replied. His eyes swept across her face, lingering on each individual feature, until at last he turned away.

Then it began again, as the long formal procession of gift bearers continued, and the newly married couple were unable to talk to each other.

Throughout, wine and mead flowed from bottomless pitchers, the music grew louder, and the people grew wilder. Women danced exuberantly, and men laughed and yelled coarsely to each other. But still the gift procession continued. Jewels were presented to the couple and richly embroidered skins were placed before the marriage table.

By midafternoon the feast had blossomed, and the guests had abandoned themselves to their personal enjoyments. Course after course was served, and as was the habit with fetes such as this, the banquet grew almost out of control.

Lewd jokes flew everywhere, and the chivalrous knights, who rarely spoke in the presence of women, grew eloquent on their own personal bedroom habits, shouting advice across the boards to Miles.

Gwendolyn stopped blushing after the first hour's jokes and merely nodded her head. She had no appetite, and saw Miles felt the same. All she wanted was for this feast to end, and for she and Miles to be alone at last. But, glancing up at the sun, she knew there were many hours of feasting left, and many more gifts to be presented before this would happen.

From the corner of his eye, Miles glanced at Gwendolyn and saw her far-away gaze, realizing that she was as impatient to be free as he was. Soon, he thought to himself, again drinking in her beauty. Then he was lost within the music as the feast grew still louder.

When darkness fell, and the torches upon the inner walls had been lit, the madness grew in intensity. No matter where Gwendolyn turned her eyes, she found men sprawled across the boards in drunken stupor. Women, usually so shy and retiring, openly allowed themselves to be fondled.

Then Roweena came to Gwendolyn and whispered in her

ear. Gwendolyn turned to look behind her. Her three bridesmaids stood waiting, along with five of her family's women. She leaned over to Miles, who had witnessed this event, and stroked his cheek. "It is time for me," she whispered.

"Go, prepare yourself," he said in a low voice.

She stood, and a sudden hush descended on the inner ward as all those who remained conscious stared at her. Standing proudly, her breasts rising and falling evenly, she met her grandfather's eyes, awaiting his leave.

Hughes stood and bowed gracefully to Gwendolyn.

Only then did she turn and enter the center of the women who awaited her. Following their lead and holding her head high, Gwendolyn walked through the middle of the ward, listening again to the freely called advice of all those present.

When at last the procession reached the archway, Gwendolyn breathed a sigh of relief.

Tonight would be special. Their wedding night was to be spent in the marital bed of Kildrake. Her grandfather had had the servants prepare the nuptial rooms, and they appeared as they had, thirty-five years ago, when he had bedded Gwendolyn's grandmother.

Entering the room, Gwendolyn saw tapers burning brightly upon every wall. The guarderoom's tapestry was new, but the tapestries covering the other openings were as old as Kildrake.

As if the women had practiced their movements for years, each went about her duties. Roweena removed Gwendolyn's mantle, while her cousin Sanella guided her to a small table set with food.

"You must eat and build your strength for tonight," she said.

"Yes," cried Estelle Demarchier. "You must be strong, for it is rumored that Miles is like a bull." With that, all the women laughed nervously.

Gwendolyn, prepared for the lewd comments she knew must be endured, smiled wickedly at her friend. "Is it only rumored?"

"Enough!" cried yet another as she poured a cup of wine and handed it to Gwendolyn. "Drink!" she ordered.

Gwendolyn obeyed, draining the cup dutifully. Then, carefully removing the Saracen dagger, she began to eat the light repast set for her while the women continued to prepare the room for the nuptials.

She finished the meal a moment before Roweena and three other servants pulled a tub to the center of the room. When Roweena came for her, the other servants filled the tub, adding scented flowers to the water.

Roweena, conscious of everyone's stares, undressed Gwendolyn and led her to the tub, as several of the women complimented Gwendolyn on her physical shape.

Moments after Gwendolyn had gone, Miles was surrounded by his peers. They laughed and joked with him, forcing him to drink many toasts. But he held himself back, drinking only small amounts, yet doing so without offending anyone.

"A word," called Hughes as he broke through the crowd.

Miles nodded, and together they walked to a small corner that afforded privacy from the others. Above the loudness of the festivities, Hughes stared at Miles.

"You marry my granddaughter for love," he said, and cut off Miles's hesitant reply with a wave of his hand. "This is good, although rare. It is because of this that Gwendolyn's dowry is so large."

"I asked for nothing," Miles stated, wondering where this conversation was leading.

"But you shall have it anyway. When I had but one daughter, I despaired for Devonshire's future and for the future of my line. Then, when my daughter had yet another daughter, I knew my line was ended."

"My lord, this is unnecessary."

"To me it is necessary!" Hughes declared fiercely, fixing Miles with a hard, determined gaze. "Listen to what I have to say, for it concerns you deeply.

"I had given my consent, and contracted with Guildswood for a marriage that would keep Devonshire strong. At the same time, I had found a mate for Gwendolyn who could tame her wild spirit. I was wrong in not waiting as I had promised my daughter."

Hughes paused then, shaking his head slowly. "My daughter told me that Gwendolyn would marry for love. I did not believe her. Who would have a woman who dwarfed her husband? But Morgan had seemed to care not. Yet I know he had only desired her for her inheritance. You have taken that from him, and I must warn you that he will do what he can to kill you and claim both Radstock, and Gwendolyn for his own."

"I fear him not," Miles stated.

"I know that, but you must be on your guard just the same."

"I thank you, my lord."

"Do not thank me. Just produce strong sons. Our land needs it. Richard is a mighty fighter, perhaps the best that has ever ruled England, but he will not be a good king, and God help us with whomever follows. It will be your children who will make our land strong. Remember that!"

"Sir Hughes—" Miles began, but the duke silenced him with a gesture.

"Gwendolyn is a wild-spirited woman, as I've already said. But there is more. I must tell you of her birth."

"It is not necessary. I know of it."

Hughes stared at him for a moment, then shook his head sadly. "Not all of it. However, I shall not belabor the point, you will learn of it one day. Now, let me tell you of the dowry you so foolishly keep ignoring."

Hughes spoke, and Miles listened. When the duke was done, Miles gazed warmly into the older man's eyes. "You are too generous," he whispered.

"Nay . . . generosity has nothing to do with it. When I die, if there are no deeds already signed, the barons will try to take Devonshire. I will not have it. Upon my death, you will inherit my title. It has already been decreed, and Richard, because he likes you so, has agreed."

Miles nodded his head slowly, before a slow smile spread across his features. "And what did Richard demand in return?" he asked.

Hughes's barking laugh echoed powerfully from their little corner, forcing several people to gaze at the two. "I did not buy London, that is for certain." Hughes's words were a standing joke among the nobility. Because of Richard's desire and obligation to fight a holy crusade, he had sold titles, lands, and anything he could to build up his coffers. Richard had once stated, rashly, that to anyone who had the price, he would sell London itself.

"I am in your debt," Miles responded in a low voice.

"No, Son, I am in yours. Now, I believe your friends await you." Hughes cocked his head in emphasis to point to the dozen knights who were standing impatiently near them.

Miles tensed, then forced himself to relax. He turned back to Hughes and nodded his head slowly. "Devonshire shall survive, and the name of Kildrake will not be lost," he promised.

Hughes clasped Miles to him and kissed both his cheeks. Then, still holding him in a bearlike hug, he lifted the Earl of Radstock from the ground and carried him to the waiting knights. "Make him do his duty!" he cried jovially, tossing Miles into their waiting arms as if he weighed nothing.

A loud cheer swelled in the air, as Miles was passed, above the knights' heads, from eager hands to eager hands. Then, when he rested above the group of rowdy knights, they started off, following the same path that Gwendolyn and her women had taken an hour before.

Miles flowed above their heads, feeling as if he were on an undulating wave. But when they stepped inside the tower, he was suddenly returned to the ground. Still in the midst of the knights, he was pulled forward by their very numbers, until, at last, they stopped before the marital door and rapped upon it with a half-dozen dagger handles.

The door flew open, and as they entered, the tittering of the women ceased. Miles stood in the center of the room, staring at the large bed and the golden-haired woman within it. A blue coverlet separated the sight of her body from the men, but Miles only saw her eyes, calm and waiting, the way he'd always pictured them.

Gwendolyn's heart raced when the knocking came. The women screamed quickly, and then began to laugh as they rushed to open the door. When the men entered, with Miles in their center, Gwendolyn knew her tension would soon end.

She watched the women arrange themselves against the walls, while the men undressed her husband. She was also conscious of the open stares of the men, already anticipating what they would see.

Suddenly the room became silent and Gwendolyn gazed at the naked form of Miles. His body was perfect—lean and strong—with his hard muscles outlined as if he were a statue. Then the knights lifted him again, to spin him three times. With that custom finished, they carried him to the bed and waited.

When they were at the edge of the bed, Miles supported carelessly among four of them, the women rushed forward and deftly removed the covering from Gwendolyn. A collective gasp came from the knights, who unabashedly stared at Gwendolyn's naked body. Then, together, the four who held Miles, lifted him and tossed him onto the bed.

"You have indeed won a prize," advised one.

"And if you have a problem subduing her, call me. I know well how to handle such matters," called another.

Gwendolyn met each knight's gaze with her own, feeling no shame at their eyes upon her body, accepting this custom, and letting them view her.

Miles smiled tolerantly at the open-mouthed stares, surprised by the way they restrained themselves from the usual heavy-handed comments.

Again, the chamber burst forth with motion, as the women, having drunk their fill of Miles's body, began ushering the knights from the room, until at last, Miles and Gwendolyn were alone.

Miles stared at her for a moment before he spoke. When he did, his voice was heavy with desire and need. "From this moment on, I shall have to spend all my waking hours guarding you from those who feasted on your body this night, for it is a fact, they will never forget the treasure they have seen."

"So long as *you* do not forget, my lord," Gwendolyn whispered. At that very moment, Gwendolyn realized that the time had come for their vows to be sealed. She tried to say something, but Miles had seen the look on her face, and his hand came to rest on her cheek.

"Have no fear, my lady. I shall be gentle," he told her a moment before his mouth descended on hers.

Fire burst forth when their lips met, and Gwendolyn's body arched against his. Her mouth opened to accept the heated thrust of his tongue as his lean body pressed down upon hers.

Then he moved, tearing a wrenching moan from Gwendolyn's throat when his mouth ran a hot line from her lips, along her neck, until he captured her already stiff nipple in his mouth. He lavished the tip of her breast with caresses, until he bit it gently and moved across her satiny skin, to kiss and caress the other waiting peak.

Gwendolyn's fingers wove through his dark hair, entwining themselves within its thickness until she arched her back again, and pressed him harder to her. But Miles moved away from her grasp, his mouth wandering maddeningly across the expanse of skin beneath it. His tongue rasped across her abdomen, and his hands slipped beneath her tightly muscled rear, cupping it and raising her up to him.

Then he was between her silken thighs, kissing and caressing her passionately. Gwendolyn cried out when his tongue dipped within her, her body tensing, even as her blood rushed faster.

Her mind spun wildly, and she reached out for Miles. But he refused to obey her commands as his tongue and lips continued to burn fiery trails upon her.

Finally, Gwendolyn cried out, and Miles returned to her arms. But before he could fit between her legs, she, using all her strength, twisted her body and turned them onto their sides.

"I must learn of you, too, my lord," she said in a husky voice, her desire-laden eyes skipping across his face. She kissed him passionately, for a long moment, before she drew her lips away. Then Gwendolyn followed the same path that Miles had trod upon her skin, and her lips tasted the sweet saltiness of his skin. She captured each of his taut nipples between her teeth, teasing, biting, and sucking on them until his moans bounced from the stone walls of the nuptial chamber.

Her hands took on a will of their own, as they slowly explored Miles's body. She was filled with wonder while her fingers skimmed over the tight skin and powerful muscles of her husband. His stomach was flat, and every muscle was outlined perfectly. Suddenly her lips replaced her hands, and she kissed every inch of his skin until her hands went lower, and she grazed along his hardened length.

She gasped at the unfamiliar power, and slowly drew her eyes from it to look into his. "I . . ." she tried to speak, but her mouth became dry. Then it no longer mattered as she stroked his inner thighs. The strong muscles quivered under her ministrations, and he grew large before her eyes. Then her hands moved again, to capture him and feel the velvet skin throb within them.

Miles's hands went into the long gold of her hair, and grasped it tightly. He drew her slowly and inexorably back to him. Turning her gently, he rose above her and gazed into her eyes. Gwendolyn smiled, her breasts rising and falling quickly, and she opened herself for him. She had no fear of him, only desire and love.

Their lips met and Miles lowered himself to her. He entered her slowly and carefully, and Gwendolyn met him the same way.

Miles stopped when he felt the tight barrier within her break, then lowered his mouth to hers. "I love you, my wife," he whispered and plunged himself deeply within her.

Gwendolyn arched to meet him, holding him tightly to her as he filled her with his length. Then, Miles paused for a moment, until the heat of her passion flowed strongly again, and they became lost in themselves, moving together as if they had been lovers all their lives. Their mingled cries filled the chamber, as did the labored sound of their breathing. An endless time later, they lay locked in each other's arms, their breathing gentle and calm, gazing deeply at each other.

"Now, my husband, we are truly united," Gwendolyn whispered.

The chamber was dark and the sounds of revelry had finally quieted. Miles lay back on the bed, content for the moment to gaze at Gwendolyn, silhouetted within the first gray light of the new dawn. She stood perfectly straight, her body a curved profile for his hungry eyes, while she looked out the window.

"You are troubled?" he asked at last.

"No, Husband, I am at peace," she replied honestly, but her body was filled with a restless energy. It had been so since they had made love and sealed their vows. Twice more they had joined, explosively, passionately, uninhibitedly, and when each loving ended, her body seemed to become more and more vitalized until she had to leave the bed.

"Then what?" he asked, sitting up slowly.

"There is much I have to tell you, much I must show you."

"The day is still long away; come back," he ordered.

Gwendolyn walked slowly to the bed. Standing at its edge, she shook her head. "Come with me now. It is important."

Miles stared at her for a moment, then gazed at the swell of her breasts, remembering the feel of them on his lips and hands.

"I yield," he laughed, jumping from the bed to capture her within his arms. Her breasts rubbed against his chest and her thighs pressed tightly to his.

"Nay, Miles, you yield to no one." She kissed him deeply before spinning from his arms.

"The guests will be upset if we are not in our connubial bed when they barge in," he warned.

"They will find what they seek," she replied, pointing to the smattering of blood on the bedcovering. "And their curiosity will be piqued even higher by our absence. Come," she said impatiently, already moving to the clothing Roweena had put out the night before.

The gray of dawn was slowly transforming into the pink and blue of the coming day. On the silent moor, two riders galloped through the trees, uncaring of the early chill or lack of sunlight. They rode in silence, their only communication that of occasional glances, until, an hour after they'd begun, they reined in their mounts.

Gwendolyn dismounted and removed the hood of her riding cape, letting her lustrous hair fall free before glancing up at Miles and motioning him to join her.

He alighted from the horse and stood next to her. "Here?" he asked, and spoke the first word since riding out of Kildrake Castle.

"Here," Gwendolyn confirmed. "Sit next to me, my husband, for I must tell you the truth about myself. It is time."

"Another mad Kildrake!" Miles muttered even as he sank to the soft mossy grass next to his wife. "First your grandfather, and now you. What?"

"Be not so harsh, Miles, for what we must discuss is for your ears alone. Whatever my grandfather had to say could not be what I must tell you."

"Then tell the story," he whispered, sensing the time for playacting was past, and the mystery surrounding Gwendolyn would now be revealed.

"Last night we sealed our love, and throughout the night, we held each other closely. I know I have presumed much with all I have asked, but there has been good reason. There," she said in a louder voice, and her finger pointed toward the mouth of the cave in emphasis. "This cave is part of my heritage, just as is the pool I had bathed in the day you first saw me. Know you, Miles Delong, that I am bastard born?"

"So it is said," he replied.

"Yet it bothers you not?"

Miles shook his head slowly.

"Then you are truly the man chosen for me. Doubt it not, my husband, we have been destined for each other since the day the earth was formed. No," she commanded, holding his gaze with hers. "What I have to say must not be interrupted. Just listen, my husband, and when I am done, you will understand all."

Miles stared at her, a strange feeling swirling in his mind, but he nodded his head, realizing that no matter what form of madness held her, he would not give her up.

Then she spoke, and Miles's mind expanded madly. He was the second man to hear the tale of Gwendolyn's conception, and suddenly he knew what Hughes had tried to speak of last night. He listened to the story and heard the Druid's prophesy. The birds which had been coming to life within the moor's forest had stilled when Gwendolyn spoke. Everything had an unworldly silence which forced him to listen with his every sense to what his wife was saying.

She told him of her practicing with her father's sword whenever she could, and of the day he had found her, and what had transpired since. She told of the new prophesy, and of her strange new powers, and when she was finished, she stood suddenly, motioning Miles to stay where he was.

Miles watched her disappear into the cave, his mind numbed with her words. His body was paralyzed by her revelations, and he tried to rid himself of the shock she had given him. Was she truly mad? he wondered.

A moment later Gwendolyn appeared before him, cradling a long object wrapped in a chamois cloth. Slowly, reverently, she laid the object at his feet. Then she stood tall and gazed down at him.

"This is the sword of my father, the sword that shall

permit me to attain knighthood. Miles, my husband, wipe the doubt from your mind and replace it with belief."

Gracefully, Gwendolyn knelt on the earth. She glanced up at her husband and then over his shoulder. Blue sky was visible through the tree branches as day arrived to Devonshire. She unwrapped the sword and grasped its pommel. Lifting it slowly, her eyes locked with Miles's, and she held the longsword high.

The sun crested the horizon at that exact moment, and a lance of sunlight struck the silver shaft. Suddenly, the forest was filled with an explosion of silver light, a ball of infinite power surrounding Gwendolyn like the cocoon of a moth. He stared at her until he could not deny what he witnessed. Then, slowly, he breathed the scents of the morning even as the silver cocoon spread over him, engulfing him and all that was around them. She stood there for long minutes, her eyes never leaving his, while the power of the sword filled her entire being.

Then Miles stood, his eyes wide as he stared at his wife and the sword she held. All questions, doubts, and wonderings were wiped from his mind in that instant, because he, too, felt the unearthly power she had unleashed. He faced her and suddenly she lowered the sword. The brightness faded, and Gwendolyn dropped to her knees before her new lord.

Gracefully, with the blade now in her hands, she lifted the sword's handle to Miles. Rather than take her offering, Miles bent and lifted Gwendolyn to her feet. Then his hands covered hers upon the blade, and he kissed her lips gently.

"As I once gave my oath, I now affirm it, Gwendolyn, Lady of Radstock."

Silently Gwendolyn stepped back. "For that, and for your love, my husband, I pledge my life to you. For together, we shall become as no other mortals before. Take the sword, my love, and heft it. Feel it as I have done."

Again, light shimmered along the length of the blade. Gwendolyn extended it to Miles, and he grasped the hilt tightly. His eyes widened when he felt the weight of the sword, and when he raised it above his head, he knew that in his hand was something no mortal man had ever held before.

A moment later he handed the sword back to Gwendolyn. "Come with me, my husband, for I wish us to bathe in the

Pool of Pendragon, and seal our love beneath the open sky, for my mother and father to acknowledge."

Together, they mounted their horses and rode to the pool. There, with the birds singing, and the insects calling to them, they entered the cool waters and bathed each other before lying on the grassy carpet to once again join their bodies in a proclamation of love.

Book II

Of the Coming of Sir Eldwin, Knight Protector of Radstock

Chapter Seven

IN RADSTOCK, AS IN MANY areas of England, the castle sat high above the lands, looking down upon them with either benevolence or malevolence, as was the wont of its lord. With the ascension of Miles to the Earldom of Radstock, the countryside had prospered under his stern but well-guided reins.

All his vassals, from serfs to men-at-arms, respected his demands of them, and knew that for them he would always be available to help and protect them.

But, for the first time since Miles had become Earl of Radstock, and since his marriage to the Lady Gwendolyn, few people saw him. Jokes about his marriage, and the time he spent with his lady, were the usual conversations within the castle when Miles was not present. For Miles, except rarely, was only seen at night for a few hours. He had left the running of his lands to those men of his household he trusted implicitly, primarily his bastard brother Theodore, who, with Miles now married, would soon enter into the simplistic life of a monastery.

But the reason for Miles's absence from most eyes was far from what the people thought. And, the few pleasurable hours Miles and Gwendolyn shared together in view of the others of the household were but a fraction of their day together. Yet, though many believed the newlyweds saw each other for so little, in reality, Miles, Gwendolyn, James, and Arthur, spent many long and arduous hours together.

They would rise long before the sun, and after eating a

light repast, would venture into the privacy of a portion of the wooded land near the castle, to begin a day that, had any other eyes witnessed it, would cause a furor among both peasant and nobility.

But no one, save the four present, ever witnessed the events—and because of that, Gwendolyn's training in the knightly arts proceeded smoothly.

Shortly after the lord's arrival in Radstock with his wife, and after the week's celebration in honor of it, Miles had given orders to have a special chamber built, deep beneath the earthworks of the castle. It was more a huge pit than a room. Its only light came from burning torches, but that light was sufficient for the purposes intended.

The building of this chamber would take six months, and because of both time and Gwendolyn's impatience, Miles had taken his wife from Radstock a bare month after they'd arrived. They went to his lands in Wales, to a place far from the regular roads, and almost inaccessible to any who knew not where they were.

It was the castle of his great-great-grandfather, Bornmorwyn of Abergavenny, who, because of his strangely perverse nature, and his hatred of all things Norman, had hidden his castle-keep high in the hills overlooking the river Wye. The old stone-and-bailey castle was far from any life, and because of its seclusion, offered the best opportunity to train Gwendolyn.

So the newly married couple, along with their twin squires, Gwendolyn's personal servant, and ten members of Miles's household staff made the five-day journey into Wales, just as the summer grew to its most fiercesome intensity.

The procession moved on solemnly, cresting yet another hill before stopping. Gwendolyn, breathing the sweetly scented air of the valley, gazed with wonder at its emerald expanses.

"It is so different from Devonshire and Radstock," she said. "So mountainous, so filled with life."

"You will learn to hate it," Miles warned her with a stern look.

"Because of what you have in store for me?"

"Exactly."

"You do not frighten me, Husband. I have waited all my life for this," she whispered fiercely.

Miles raised his arm, his index finger pointing high and to the south. "Do you see that peak?"

Gwendolyn followed the direction of his pointing finger, letting her eyes race along the mountains, going higher and higher, until at last she was staring at the highest peak in the valley. Far above her, she saw a small dark speck on its crest.

"And the keep upon it," she answered.

"That is our destination."

It was an awesome sight, one that might leave another breathless and not a little in fear. But Gwendolyn, gazing at Miles, smiled her secret smile.

They had traversed half the distance to the keep when night fell. A tent was quickly erected for Miles and Gwendolyn, and food prepared. Later, Miles and Gwendolyn walked in the night beneath a myriad of stars and were silent, content with themselves and the peace they had found.

But when Miles turned back to their tent, Gwendolyn stopped him. "I know this is difficult for you to accept, and I will never be truly able to offer thanks for this gift you have given me."

Miles had never spoken of that day by the cave, but he had thought about it a great deal. His family had been a part of this land from time immemorial, and although Christianity had grown strong in England, the old beliefs had not fled the way the Christians had wanted and demanded. Because of that, and because of his heritage, Miles could not deny what had happened at Gwendolyn's cave. Yet, it had taken him a long time to adjust to the idea that his wife was not just a woman, that she was far more than that. His love, and the powerful desires that had filled him from the moment he'd met her, had not diminished, and by the time they'd left Radstock and started on this very journey, he'd accepted what his wife was, and knew he must help her.

"And what of our children?" he asked in a low voice.

"We will have strong, powerful children to carry on in the future," Gwendolyn assured him.

"I mean, what if you are now with child? Will you give up your training?"

"I am not with child, nor will I be until the proper time.

But fret not, for we shall leave our mark on this land for untold generations yet to come," she promised him, and Miles could not but believe her.

"Come, Husband, it is time for our sleep." She whispered, but Miles heard within her voice, not the call for sleep, but the call for a sharing of themselves, as they had almost every night since their first joining.

Silently, they entered the tent, undressed, and came together on the softness of the rush mat beneath them. Their lovemaking was strong and swift this time. Miles entered her quickly, his passion strong and urgent, made so by the unrest in his mind.

Afterward, with Miles's head resting on her breast, and her hand stroking his hair gently, Gwendolyn thought about the future, and about the hard days ahead.

It was almost dawn when she fell into a light sleep, but when she and Miles were awakened by Arthur, she rose refreshed and expectant, knowing that this day would be her last as Gwendolyn. On the morrow, when she woke again in the high keep, she would be treated by all as a man, and as a knight-in-training.

But for Miles, this night's sleep had left him unrefreshed. He had dreamed deeply and had awakened long before Gwendolyn, his mind filled with the pictures he had seen. He was reluctant to move yet, and while he lay on her soft breast, the very core of his dream seemed to help soothe his mind about what he would be doing with his wife. He had dreamed of Gwendolyn astride a black stallion, dressed in full armor, her silver sword flashing brightly above her head. Valkyrie flew in the air over her, and everything about the dream picture seemed right—even the voice he'd heard, an ancient old voice telling him his feet had been set on this path years ago, and that nothing could change what must happen. Everything he did was preordained, the voice had said, and it was important he accept this and trust in himself and in Gwendolyn.

While he lay silently during the minutes before the dawn, he thought of the dream, and by the time Arthur came to rouse them, Miles realized that his anxiety and fears were gone. It was then he knew it had been a sign for him, and rather than question further his motives in training Gwendolyn, he banished all doubts and began to look forward to the task.

That afternoon, they reached the old keep. Its very prominence took Gwendolyn's breath away, and she did not care that Miles gazed at her humorously. The old keep was surrounded by a half-filled moat, and the barbican across from them was but a high gatehouse. The bridge was fixed, but in bad repair. Yet the outer bailey, which they slowly passed through, was completely walled. Its smooth green expanse had grown wild, but within days, it would again be under control.

The procession stopped at the entrance to the old castle-keep, and Miles dismounted. He walked to his wife and brought her down to him. Together they went to the large, closed door. The wood seemed ageless, but the bolts that secured it were badly discolored.

Miles sighed loudly and tried to open one. It would not budge. He turned sideways and lunged against the heavy wood. Gwendolyn jumped when his shoulder touched the door, but stopped herself when she heard a protesting groan. Before everyone's unbelieving eyes, the giant door shifted, and, as its aged and rotted leather hinges shredded, the door collapsed inward.

"You have great strength, my husband," Gwendolyn said, trying not to let her smile break forth.

"So it appears," Miles replied dryly, shaking his head. "Come, let us see what other miracles await us within." Saying that, he took Gwendolyn's hand and led her inside.

At first, Gwendolyn stared helplessly at the stone walls. They were in terrible disrepair, on the brink of ruination, but after a few moments, she realized that Miles had indeed chosen wisely. For there would be no petty barons who would storm this keep, hoping to gain lands for themselves. This was a forgotten place to most, and few of the curious would come to pay visits.

By midafternoon, the keep hummed with life, as Miles and Gwendolyn ordered their vassals about in an effort to make the place habitable.

By nightfall their chamber had been prepared by Roweena, who had cleaned and dusted it as best she could. There was no wood-and-rush bed, but Roweena had doubled the thickness of the mat, so that the endlessly cold stone floor would not bother Miles and Gwendolyn overmuch.

That night, the small retinue feasted together upon the grass of the inner bailey. A fire roared comfortingly, and even its haunting reflections upon the old stone walls did not dampen anyone's mood.

When the meal was over, Miles stood and gazed down at the dozen faces before him. Taking a deep breath, he began to speak. "Tomorrow morning, I want everyone to begin work on the keep. Lady Gwendolyn and I will be gone for one week. When we return, I expect to find a habitable dwelling. Concentrate on the kitchen and the chambers," he said. Then, he turned to Arthur. "Go to Abergavenny, and to Lord Skinfrith's keep. I have already sent word you will be coming. Return here with all that awaits you," he said.

He extended his hand to Gwendolyn, who rose quickly and stepped to her husband's side. They walked away together, and when Roweena rose to follow, Miles turned to her. "We have no need for you tonight," he said.

Roweena stopped and looked at her mistress. Gwendolyn nodded her head in agreement with Miles, and Roweena returned to the fire and the sleeping mats that were being laid out by the other servants.

A few minutes later, Miles and Gwendolyn entered the chamber they would be sharing for many months. Within its torchlit confines, Gwendolyn saw two new bundles. She walked over to them while Miles removed his surcoat.

"Miles?" she asked as she knelt to inspect the covered piles.

Miles did not reply, but merely nodded his head. Gwendolyn lifted the light coverings and gasped. Beneath the skins were two identical piles. On top of each was a shortsword, a bow, and a dagger. Beneath the weapons were gamboise, chausses, and cuirbouilli scale armor. When Gwendolyn was finished inspecting these, she looked back at Miles.

"Are you ready now, my lady?" he asked.

"Now?"

"We start tonight. When everyone is asleep we shall leave. We will return in a week, and when we do, we shall send everyone, save James and Arthur, back to Radstock. No one must know what is happening."

"Roweena must stay. She will never speak of this."

"Can we chance it? She is still a servant. You trust her that much?" Miles asked.

"I trust her with my life. Roweena will never tell of what she witnesses."

"It could cost you your life if she does."

"She will not!"

"So be it," Miles declared. Then, with a sigh, he crossed the distance separating them, and took Gwendolyn into his arms. Her breasts were crushed against his chest, and the sudden spark of desire that rose within him was hard to push aside.

Gwendolyn sensed his reaction and kissed him deeply. Within her, too, desire coursed wildly, but even as she accepted this and opened her mouth to him, Miles drew back.

"What?" she asked, troubled by his withdrawal.

"It is not the time. We must dress."

Gwendolyn stared at him. "So be it," she replied.

First Miles dressed Gwendolyn. He had Gwendolyn stand naked before him and he put on her loincloth, and as he did so, he explained everything in the minutest detail. Then, with the loincloth in place, he lifted another strip of material.

"Your breasts must be bound, for I would see no harm come to them," he whispered, as he gazed at her dark-tipped breasts for a moment. He draped the cloth across her back, and then crisscrossed it over her breasts, catching each full mound of flesh within the material, and then binding them tightly, pressing them as flat as possible against her chest.

He lifted a short tunic and handed it to Gwendolyn. She put it on quickly, adjusting it, and smoothing it until it hung properly. When she looked down, she saw its hem reached barely to midthigh.

When Miles lifted the cuirbouilli, he smiled at her. "This was my first scale armor. My father had it made for me when I was fourteen." He unbuckled one side and put it over Gwendolyn's chest. When it was buckled, Gwendolyn was protected from her neck to the top of her thighs. The scale armor was made of wax-dipped leather, and its burnished color and deep-gouged scars told Gwendolyn much of Miles's early training.

Next Miles put on the cuirbouilli cuisses, the waxed leather pads that would protect her thighs. When that was done, he knelt before her and laced on the first of the maille she would be wearing. The chausses were in good condition, and their dark metallic color shone under the torchlight. Miles laced them until they reached her knees, where they stopped. When both legs were done, Miles stood. The only thing left was the heavy coif-de-maille, and that would wait until he was dressed.

Stepping back, Miles inspected Gwendolyn and took a deep breath as he did. She stood proudly, her shoulders straight, her head high as she met his gaze with her own. Already, she looked like a fighter. Her height was emphasized by the armor, and for the first time since he'd met her, Miles suddenly believed she would indeed become a knight.

"Do I look so strange?" Gwendolyn asked after a few more moments under his silent scrutiny.

"Not strange—powerful," he whispered. "Come," he said in a louder voice. "Now you must do the duties of the squire."

Gwendolyn nodded once, and went to Miles's armor. His pile was similar to hers, except that he had no scale armor. Instead, he had chosen a short hauberk of maille. A half hour later, Miles was dressed. Then, he put on Gwendolyn's coif-de-maille and attached it to the leather armor. Next, he put on her shortsword, then her dagger, and finally attached the bow to her back.

"Why a bow?" she wondered aloud, knowing that a knight never fought with such a weapon.

"To learn its use and to eat. What would you catch our food with? Or do you think a fast of a week will aid your strength?"

"We take no supplies?" she asked, surprised at his words.

"None," he declared, slipping his shortsword into its scabbard.

Gwendolyn went over to Valkyrie's perch. She slipped on the leather wristband and extended her arm. Valkyrie gazed at her unblinking. She held her arm before him for a moment, until the large eagle finally lifted one clawed foot from its wooden perch and ascended onto her wrist.

Ready at last, Gwendolyn turned to Miles. Silently, he pushed aside the tapestry that was their door. They stepped into the old passageway and descended to the inner keep, where they walked silently past the sleeping servants, until they reached the barbican.

The night was clear, and the multitude of stars looked like a jeweled heaven. The moon was absent this night, but the stars themselves lighted the land and illuminated a path for Miles and Gwendolyn.

They descended the incline and walked along the sparsely treed path leading down into the Valley of Wye. An hour later, Miles changed direction, leading Gwendolyn through another, more narrow path. Then they were in a forest, and the further they walked, the darker it became. Gwendolyn felt only excitement run through her veins as she luxuriated within the feel of the armor. For the first time, Valkyrie rode on her now-protected shoulder, freeing her arm. One hand rested on the hilt of her sword, while the other swung free, enabling her to move swiftly along the rocky terrain.

The maille covering her head did not bother her, nor did the unfamiliar binding that held her breasts so securely. Her eyes never strayed from Miles's broad back, and her feet maintained their balance perfectly.

"Miles," she whispered, speaking for the first time since they started out three hours before. Miles stopped and turned to face her.

"Are you tired?" he asked quickly.

"No, I am happy," she replied. "I am content," she added.

"That is good, for you will need all your contentment in the coming days." Then he turned from her and began to walk faster.

Gwendolyn smiled at his back. She had known, from the moment Miles had acceded to her wishes, that he would be a hard taskmaster. She had accepted that. She would not let him down, and wanted only the best of training. And Miles, because of his love for her, would be a relentless trainer and mentor. When they were done with the training, Gwendolyn knew Miles would have made her strong.

With those thoughts firmly fixed in her mind, Gwendolyn continued to follow Miles. She did not complain, did not speak again, and even when she fell across the thick roots of an old tree, she did not call out, but merely stood again and quickly caught up with her husband.

* * *

The sun rose, turning the sky blue with its brilliance and chasing away the gray clouds that had been with them for the last two days.

Miles stretched on the ground, and then turned to gaze at his wife. He smiled at the sight that met his eyes. Gwendolyn waited, perched above the river, as still as a statue, the long bow drawn fully, a shaft notched and waiting between her two fingers.

He did not know how long she had been like that, but when he spied the quivering of the muscles in her arm, he knew it had not been a short period.

The last six days had been more than just the beginning of Gwendolyn's training; they had been a series of revelations to him as well. He had watched his wife, dressed in her armor, walk uncomplaining through twenty miles of forest, climb a steep hill, and then spend an hour trading sword blows with him.

He had seen her watch him, as he taught her the use of the bow, and had observed Gwendolyn practicing when she thought him to be asleep. He had never seen anyone learn to use a bow as quickly as she, nor had he ever seen anyone apply such total concentration to a task in the way she did. There was nothing that he showed her that she had not learned quickly, and mastered in less time than even he had taken.

Each day since they'd left the old keep, Miles had maintained a schedule. In the morning, they would rise—he dressed in only a loincloth, she in loincloth and breast bindings, with their swords strapped to their backs. They would run along the edge of the river for half an hour before turning, to run back along the same path to their camp. High above them, Valkyrie would fly.

After returning to the camp, both he and Gwendolyn would take their bows to the river's edge to kneel motionless with their arrows notched until a trout swam beneath them.

Only when they had caught at least four fish would they undress completely and enter the cool water to bathe. Cleansed and refreshed, they would eat their breakfast, dress, and begin the heavy training.

For the morning hours, Miles would work with her on the sword, building up her muscles, and teaching her how to utilize her wrists, rather than fight with her shoulders. They would trade blows for hours, until, at last, they would fall to the ground breathless, to sleep for an hour before rising to again run through the woods.

The afternoon run was filled with excruciating pain, for Miles forced them both to run within the heavily wooded forest, where he would unexpectedly stop to spin and face her with a drawn sword. In the tight confines of the trees, he fought her mercilessly, until there was no moment she was unguarded.

Yet, throughout it all, she had not once uttered any word of complaint. Each night when they fell asleep, they did so in each other's arms, but, by the time the sun had set, neither husband nor wife could do more than hold each other before succumbing to the drugged sleep that the day's exercises had brought on.

The sudden twang of the bowstring brought Miles back to the bank of the Wye. He saw Gwendolyn quickly rise and enter the water to retrieve her arrow and the large trout that was now struggling on the shaft.

When she straightened and turned, his breath caught. She wore only the loincloth, and her breasts shimmered from the sun. She saw him gazing at her, and a soft smile curved her lips.

Miles rose and walked to her, uncaring that he was naked. Today was the last day they would be alone together, and when the night arrived, it would find them at the keep. Today, there would be no training; today was a day for them.

Gwendolyn watched Miles walk toward her, and as he did, she released the arrow and let the fish fall to where the other three were lying. She loosened her loincloth, and when it fell to the ground, walked to meet her husband.

Silently, as had been their way for this entire week, they embraced and kissed. Then Miles led her to the stream, where they bathed leisurely. When they returned to the shore, they lay on the soft grass and held each other close.

The warmth from the sun dried them even as their lips met and their passions rose. Beneath the warm summer sun, with the sounds of birds and animals floating in the air, they again joined together.

As their hands roamed across each other's bodies, Miles was conscious of the new muscles he felt beneath his fingertips. The harder, firmer flesh that he knew so intimately did not bother him; rather, he reveled within the silken touch, knowing that no other woman could ever hold him the way Gwendolyn did.

Suddenly, Gwendolyn moved, spinning them until Miles was on his back and she was poised above him. Her mouth descended onto his, kissing him fully for a moment before she tore her lips away and traced a path of maddening kisses across his chest. Her hands, so much stronger than before, gently caressed him, stroking him, and bringing him harder within her fingers' embrace.

Her mouth burned with intensity as she captured him within it, to kiss and caress him wildly, until he thought he would be able to hold back no longer.

But she stopped and drew her mouth away, only to rise above him again. Then she lowered herself onto him, taking his hard length within her. Her cry echoed loudly within the forest as she began to move upon him.

Her eyes were open and staring at her husband as he filled her. Then she cried out again as she reached a swift climax before she realized what was happening. She stopped, her head falling to his chest, but his hardness still throbbed powerfully within.

Then Miles shifted, sitting up, but holding her close. Gwendolyn's legs wrapped around him, her ankles locking behind him as her hands wound through his hair and brought his mouth to her nipple. His teeth gripped the tender tip, but did not hurt her. Then he began to move, thrusting against her forcefully, until all she could do was hold on to him. At last, he released his heated seed within her, and they fell to the ground, stroking and caressing each other until their breathing returned to normal.

A half hour later they sat across from each other, the fire between them, their fingers greasy from the trout, their silence saying more than any words would be able to.

But when the meal was done, Gwendolyn sensed some impatience within Miles. "What?" she asked, and heard Miles short laugh when she spoke.

"You know me so well, for knowing me so short a time."

"I have known you all my life. I have waited for you all my life. I cannot help knowing your moods, or sensing when you want something," Gwendolyn explained in a low voice.

"I do not pretend to understand all that has happened,"

Miles began, his voice deep and serious as he searched for the right words. "But I have accepted you, and everything that seems to happen around you."

"Miles, I wish that you could have been with me, that first time in the cave, when I discovered . . ." Before she could continue, Miles stood and came over to her. He stopped her words with a look and drew her to her feet.

"You are two people, Gwendolyn. You are my wife, and someone I do not know. I have accepted both. Leave it rest at that."

Gwendolyn gazed at him for a moment before nodding in understanding. She saw within his eyes the truth of his words. She also saw he was not afraid of the ethereal things Gwendolyn had seen and learned, but rather, would not have his mind fogged by those things which he did not understand.

"Yes, Husband, it shall be as you wish."

"Good. It is time to return to the keep, and the next step in your training."

They dressed, put out the fire, and began the fifteen-mile walk that would bring them back to the keep, where Miles would begin her formal training in arms.

Chapter Eight

THE SUMMER PASSED quickly for the five people inhabiting the old keep. Their days started early, and ended only when the sun had dropped from the heavens, and darkness blanketed all.

Both Arthur and James grew to know and respect Gwendolyn's abilities as a fighter. They watched in awe when she battled Miles, the sounds of their swords echoing loudly within the stone walls. Even Roweena, who had sworn an oath that she would not reveal what she witnessed, had grown to accept her mistress's role as a knight-in-training.

She learned, with Miles's aid, to massage her mistress and to ease the pain and soreness which had become a daily part of Gwendolyn's life. She also had seen the way Miles had wrapped her mistress's breasts, and had despaired at the bulkiness of the man's loincloth draped across Gwendolyn's hips. Roweena had taken new material and had made several garments for Gwendolyn that would be more comfortable, and offer more protection.

She had sewn leather pads into material, turning it into a halter for Gwendolyn's breasts, so that there would be no strain upon her neck or shoulders from the bindings, the thickness of leather adding extra protection to the delicate tissues of her breasts. For a loincloth, Roweena had again sewn material, folded carefully and thickened so it would protect her mistress's private area. This loincloth, rather than being knotted, used two small clasps to hold it in place.

With these aids, Gwendolyn's scale armor fit more comfortably.

As summer gave way to fall, and the weather turned crisper with each morning, Gwendolyn rose to perform her duties. They always dressed together, helping each other into the armor which Miles ordered worn, before going into the stone-walled interior of the outer keep, to learn, practice, and bring to perfection the art of knightly fighting. Each evening, when the sun had gone, and the five had eaten their fill, they would retire to their chambers, to sleep and rest in order to be fresh for the long hours of the next day.

And, as he did every night when they entered their chamber, Miles looked at his wife while she undressed. Gwendolyn had changed in the four months they'd already spent in Wales. Although she had been well-muscled when they'd married, Miles saw how much more she had developed. The hours, weeks, and months of training had refined Gwendolyn's body, bringing out the perfect definition of rippling muscles on her abdomen, thighs, and buttocks. But Miles did not desire her less for this. Even with her magnificently muscled body, she did not have the build of a man. Rather, her body was smooth and lean, and hid well the fact that beneath the satiny skin that covered her, Gwendolyn's muscles were as firm and strong as iron.

Above it all, she was the very essence of femininity. Every movement she made, every gesture she used, was that of a woman. Only when she put on her armor or hefted a sword, did the woman disappear. But in her place a man did not appear. When Gwendolyn wore her armor, only a warrior loomed.

"Turn to me," Miles commanded in a low voice, as he watched her remove her undergarment in the torchlit chamber.

Gwendolyn turned to stare at him.

"Come closer," he asked. When she stepped toward him, he saw what he was looking for. Beneath her right breast, across three ribs, was a spreading purple stain. He inspected it closely, running his fingers across the bruise. He heard her wince, but continued to probe the area carefully.

"Nothing is broken," he told her as he threw his cover away and stood. "Perhaps tomorrow we shall rest."

"No!" Gwendolyn said in a tight voice. "Time is running out."

"You cannot train tomorrow if you are in pain," he told her, "it will only make it worse."

"Miles," Gwendolyn whispered as she looked into his eyes. "I will not hold back. I cannot."

Miles, reacting to the sound of her voice, nodded his head. "Then come to bed, Wife, so that I may hold you and comfort you until the morning."

Gwendolyn fingered the bruise lightly before she followed his command. A moment later she was lying next to him, drinking in the comfort of his body while his arms held her close.

But when she awoke in the morning, and the dull gray light filtered in through the narrow openings in the stone walls, her side hurt even more than the night before. With each movement she made, lances of pain shot along her length. Cautiously, not wanting to wake Miles, Gwendolyn left the bed and walked across the chamber to a long chest set against the far wall. She opened it to reveal its contents to her eyes. On top of everything was her sword, wrapped within its timeless chamois cover.

Lifting it carefully from the chest, she sat cross-legged on the stone floor. She had made up her mind to try to learn if, among the other secrets of the sword, she could find some ability to heal herself. Gwendolyn grasped the sword tightly and felt its power within her hands. Closing her eyes, she lifted the sword high above her head. Then she cleared her mind of everything and accepted the power vibrating through her very being. A gentle heat, and the soft, familiar light of the sword filled and surrounded her. Within her mind, she directed the energy of the sword to her side, and to the bruise that ached so badly.

At first she was aware of nothing, but a moment later she felt warm tentacles of power run along her skin and pass over her breast. The gentle heat burrowed inward, to spread across her entire side. She sat still, the sword held aloft, while the power and warmth worked upon her.

A few moments later, with her mind floating peacefully, she lowered the sword and breathed deeply. Then she rose and replaced the sword within the chest, closed it, and stood straight. Looking down at her ribs, Gwendolyn saw the bruise was gone. Touching the area lightly, she found there was no pain. Gwendolyn closed her eyes and whispered her thanks.

"Take the sword out again," said Miles. Gwendolyn whirled at the sound of his voice to stare into the open eyes of her husband.

"I did not know you were awake."

"Now you do. It is time to test your blade," he informed her. "We will practice with it today."

"But the jousting?" Gwendolyn protested, not sure why she did so.

"We never joust two days in a row. The body needs to recuperate . . . at least some bodies do," he added pointedly.

"I did not think you awake."

"It does not matter. Your powers are good; they will help you in the future. But Gwendolyn, if for no other reason than my love for you, you must learn to rely on yourself. You have trained your body; do not foresake it for otherworldly help. Use the sword if you must, but do not waste its energy foolishly. A bruise will heal quickly by itself, remember that."

Gwendolyn's eyes filled with moisture as she listened to her husband's words. Slowly, she nodded her head and went to their pallet. "I will remember the words of both my husband and my teacher. I will not squander the powers of the sword," she promised as she went into his arms.

"Strike! Strike! Strike!" Miles shouted from the parapet. Ten feet below, Gwendolyn, wearing full-scale armor, fought both James and Arthur. The longsword she hefted flashed in the sun, deflecting both squires' blades neatly. She handled herself well, Miles noted, seeing just how far Gwendolyn had come since he'd first seen her fighting off the men-at-arms in Devonshire. But he was watching her carefully, knowing that the heavy weight of the longsword would soon take its toll upon her strength.

Yet he could not stop his pride from swelling as she battled the two squires valiantly. Her maille head was held high, and her leather-covered feet moved quickly. No one, unless they stood directly in front of her, would ever guess she was a woman.

"Back! Backstep!" he shouted when Arthur attacked low, and James came head on.

Gwendolyn parried Arthur's swing, and ducked low when James's sword flashed near her shoulder. She spun and used her wrists effectively to catch James's blade against hers. When she heard Miles's hurried shout, she flicked her wrists, flinging James's sword away, and stepped back quickly.

"Hold!" Miles called. Then he left the wall and came to the three fighters. "Good! James, Arthur, that was an effective attack. But remember, you must not look at each other. Rely on your training to keep you moving in accord. James, when Arthur attacked her legs, you waited to see if his stroke would reach. You should have swung at the same instant."

Miles sighed and looked at Gwendolyn. "And you should have stepped back immediately upon the attack. Instead of giving them the advantage, if you had stepped back, Arthur would have been off-stride, and you could have defeated them both before they had a chance to strike."

Gwendolyn stared at him, his words running shocklike through her mind. She had thought she'd done the right thing, but today, like most other days, she'd learned she had not.

"But you always say to press the attack when outnumbered," she defended.

"Yes, but backstepping is not running away. If you had backstepped, one man would have fallen. Your sword deflects the second man's blow, you stab the first, and then press the attack on the second!"

Gwendolyn closed her eyes and pictured his words. A moment later she realized his meaning and nodded her head. "I understand."

"Good. Arthur, bring my longsword. James, there is a sword in its sheath near the keep's entrance. Bring it to Lady Gwendolyn."

Both squires ran off to do Miles's bidding. As they went, Gwendolyn gazed at her husband. "I have never used the sword."

"I know, but the time has come. We have only a little

while left before we return to Radstock. You must learn this sword of yours now."

Before anything else could be said, the squires had returned and attached the swords to their owners. James finished linking Gwendolyn's sword and then stood behind her. Arthur did the same for Miles.

Then they were ready. Carefully, Miles drew his longsword and hefted it over his head. He whirled it several times, testing its weight before lowering it to his side. He bowed formally to Gwendolyn, a sardonic smile on his face. "Madame," he whispered.

"Sire," she replied as she drew her father's blade and lifted it high. She felt it hum in her hands, but no bolt of light flew from it. She whirled it above her head, as Miles had done, and felt its featherlike weight adjust within her hands even as she heard the whistle of the blade cut through the air.

Suddenly the air within the keep grew heavy. The squires looked at each other, their eyes wide with understanding. Today was a test. What kind they weren't sure, but it was a day of testing nonetheless.

Miles and Gwendolyn circled each other warily, their blades hovering above the ground, their eyes never wavering from each other's. In a movement that seemed faster than light, both swords rose in the air and met. A loud clash echoed, and the blades hung timelessly above. Then the slithering sound of metal grated upon everyone's ears when the blades drew apart.

"Very good," Miles said with a quick bow of his head. It took all his will power not to show the pain that had raced along his arm from the first contact. He watched Gwendolyn's face, but saw no reaction from it.

Moving quickly, Miles spun in a circle, his sword flashing out at Gwendolyn's shoulder. As the blade reached her, she, too, spun, the silver sword flying upward to deflect the blow. Before Miles recovered from his attack, Gwendolyn had completed her turn and reversed her arms.

The sword weighed nothing in her hands, and its vibrations filled her every movement. Her blood rushed through her body, and her mind rejoiced within the fight. When Miles had turned, reversing his ground to attack her from the side, she had moved as he'd taught her and caught his sword well away from her. Following both her instincts and her new training, she completed the short circle, her wrists flicking backwards to attack Miles before he had recovered.

She swung at a spot in front of him, but found her blade deflected. Angered that he had read her movements so accurately, Gwendolyn summoned up her energy from deep within and began to attack Miles relentlessly. They were both rooted to the spot, staring into each other's eyes as they fought. And fight they did. Neither gave an inch. Their blades met time and time again, sweat pouring from their faces, burning their eyes, half blinding them, but still neither gave in.

Then, in a blurring of motion which Gwendolyn could barely follow, Miles ducked beneath her blade, rolled on the ground, and regained his feet behind her, just as she turned to face him. But she was too late. The tip of his sword rested at her neck.

She lowered her blade and gazed at him. "I yield, Sir Knight," she whispered.

"Accepted," he replied as he lowered his blade. "Gwendolyn, you are my equal," he declared.

"No!" she spat suddenly, unwanted tears welling in her eyes. "No! If I were, you would not have beaten me so easily."

"I did not beat you easily, far from it. It was only my experience which aided me," he told her.

"Again," she said suddenly.

"Are you still so eager?"

"I would have another chance," she replied.

Miles nodded, and she saw his lopsided grin come fully into being. "Madame," he said formally.

"My lord," she responded, dipping her head in a slight bow. When Miles raised his sword over his head, Gwendolyn did the same, but this time, unlike the time before, she freed her mind, clearing it of everything save the sword in Miles's hand. With her fingers vibrating, she whirled the silver sword before stepping forward.

Their swords met in the air, and once again the sound of metal reverberated above them, and they began to fight in earnest. Slashing, parrying, attacking, and defending became the only things in Gwendolyn's mind. She followed every flicker of Miles's green eyes, expertly anticipating his every move. Until again, Miles turned from her in an unexpected move and was almost upon her.

"No!" she screamed in denial as she spun quickly away. Anger filled her that he'd almost tricked her again, and that very anger lent power to her arms as she faced him across the space of ten feet.

Miles lifted his sword, whirling it quickly over his head. Gwendolyn saw the flashing of sunlight from its length, but did not let that scare her. Suddenly she knew what she must do, and even as she thought it, it happened. She sensed the power flowing through her and felt herself become one with the silver blade she held. She lifted it, letting it circle over her head, controlling it with the barest of movements of her wrist. Her eyes locked on Miles's, and then they were together.

"No!" she screamed again when she swung her sword at his. The blades met in the air above, just as they had twice before. But this time, instead of the clash of metal, a loud screeching resounded, and Gwendolyn knew the power of the sword had risen. The instant her blade touched his, she felt it tear through its tempered length. Miles's sword screamed in protest as it was severed.

Then neither fighter moved, as both their eyes followed the arc of his blade until it hit the stone wall twenty feet behind. Slowly, her face filled with shock, she lowered the silver sword and stared at her husband.

In the very moment their swords had met, Gwendolyn had become aware of her anger. She realized, also, that if she had lowered the blade, she would have killed Miles instantly. She saw, too, that the anger which had gripped her could have directed the blade. Suddenly she was afraid, and because of that, opened her hands to let the silver sword fall to the ground.

She turned without a word and ran from the inner keep. When she reached the outer bailey, she did not pause, but instead continued running. She did not see the barbican when she passed through it, nor did she feel the wooden planks beneath her feet as she ran across the bridge. Her mind was filled with a horror she could barely contain, and all she wanted to do was run until she could not see, or think, or be.

With self-loathing filling all her thoughts, Gwendolyn ran

on, unmindful of the weight of the scale armor, caring not that the sun poured down upon her mailled head. All she craved was to escape, and she forced her legs to carry her until she disappeared into the thickness of the forest, leaving the castle far behind in her panic.

Miles stood rooted to the spot, watching Gwendolyn run from him. He wanted to race after her, but forced himself to stay still. He had seen the recognition of her act spring onto her face. He had felt the full impact of her thoughts and knew she must be alone to come to her senses. Nothing he could tell her, nothing he might say, would ease the torment. It was a lesson she had to learn for herself, just as he had learned it.

She was his equal; he had not lied to her. He was more experienced than she, but that would soon be a thing of the past. A moment before, she had grown angry at nearing another defeat and had summoned her reserve to fend him off. What he had seen was that she had also summoned the help of the silver sword.

When their blades met, and his had been severed, he'd seen the barest of flashes, like a lightning bolt, spew from the blades. It was then that his steel had been cut. But Gwendolyn had not seen that. She'd seen only that she had defeated him, and the knowledge that she could have killed him had struck her deeply.

Miles sighed, remembering when he had faced his father just before he had been knighted. They had fought for almost an hour, until, at last, Miles could not hold his anger in check, and had attacked and attacked and attacked his father until his blade had hit home, and he'd won the fight.

At the instant his blade had touched his father's neck, Miles had realized he'd won, and his fingers had released the handle. The blade had hit the maille, but without his strength behind it was deflected harmlessly. Yet his father carried a bruise on the side of his neck for a fortnight.

It had been then that Miles had realized he might have killed his father. He'd seen that he'd had the power to do so, and had in fact almost done that very thing.

It had taken him the entire night to understand that he, not fate or anything else, had stopped his hand from the killing stroke. And he knew that Gwendolyn, too, must come to that very realization.

"My lord?" called Arthur as he stepped before Miles.

Miles shook his head and looked down at the young squire. "Yes?"

"Your sword," he said, holding up the severed tip. "I have never seen anything like it."

Miles took the two-foot section and held it up. The metal end was smoothly torn, there were none of the ragged edges that come from a normal sword break. The only mark was a darkened line, as if it had been held over fire.

"A fault in the metal," Miles whispered before he handed the squire the sword. Then he bent and picked up Gwendolyn's sword. He turned and gazed at James. "Take your knight's sword, Squire. Clean it and sheath it properly." When James took the blade, Miles removed his coif-de-maille. When that was done, he left the bailey and went to his chamber.

There, he extended his mailled forearm to Valkyrie, who gazed at him for a moment. When the eagle was safely perched on his arm, Miles returned to the courtyard and ascended to the high walkway.

He stared out at the forests that surrounded the castle, wondering where Gwendolyn was. When he lifted his arm, he spoke to the eagle. "Find her," he ordered. "Go to her." He swung his arm upward, and when it reached the apex of the swing, Valkyrie released his talons, spread his wings, and rose from the maille perch.

Miles watched the golden eagle circle the keep once and then fly outward. He watched until the bird was nothing more than a speck against the crystal sky, and even when he saw Valkyrie dive into the dense forest, he stayed on the walkway, willing the eagle to find his mistress, and to tell her that he understood.

Chapter Nine

GWENDOLYN RAN AS SHE'd never run before. Nothing mattered save that she get away. For an hour, her strong and muscular legs pumped heavily, forcing her leather-bound feet to fly over the ground. She tried to close her mind to the images that haunted her, but that was impossible. Over and over she saw the silver sword flash, hitting Miles's blade and shearing it in half. Then she would see it again, but instead of hitting the sword, her shining blade dropped lower and severed her husband's head. She willed her legs to move faster, wanting the physical movement to banish her mental agony, but it did not.

Gwendolyn was not conscious of the path she took, nor did she realize how deep she was running into the forest. Before her eyes were only the images of the old keep, and of her husband, whom, with a bare flick of her wrists, she could have killed moments ago.

Finally, with her breath coming in harsh, tearing gasps, she could move no further and collapsed on the ground, her eyes closed, her hands balled into tight fists. Her bound breasts heaved against their restraints, and the weight of the scale armor grew heavy on her shoulders. She shook her head, but still the images would not depart.

A long while later, with her breathing under control, she blinked away her tears and sat up. She gazed around and saw tall stately trees surrounding her, and she wondered how she'd gotten so far. Standing, her muscles protesting painfully, she began to walk, but froze when she heard a loud call.

Looking up, she spied Valkyrie sitting on a large branch. She held out her arm and the golden eagle dropped from the tree, gliding in the narrow confines of the forest to alight on her mailled wrist.

Gwendolyn held the eagle's eyes level with hers and stared into them. "Hello, my friend," she whispered in a husky voice.

She put the eagle on her shoulder and together, the tall blonde woman and the golden eagle, they walked eastward to where she knew the River Wye flowed.

A half hour later she stopped. Gwendolyn's breath escaped in a loud hiss as she stared at the sight before her. The sun had just dropped behind the hills, and a soft, gentle glow radiated across their ragged tops. But she did not see nature's beauty; she saw nothing before her eyes except the perfect circle of stones.

Each stone was taller than twice her height. In the four directions of the earth, a stone rested crossways to connect the tops, forming four distinct passageways within the circle. All around her, Gwendolyn sensed a strong power emanating.

These stones were similar to some she had seen in Devon, and similar, too, to other stone circles she had heard mentioned by travelers. Yet all the stone circles she had seen and heard about had been ruins. These were not. They had always been called Druid stones. The Romans, Gwendolyn had been told, had tried to change them and make them into their own temples, but had failed. The Christian church had banned people from going to them and had tried to destroy them; but, although they decreed them banned, they had not found all the hidden places, and many people of the land still went to them with their prayers.

Yet Gwendolyn sensed this place was far different from the others. This place would only be found by luck, or by need. Although the coolness of the early night air was falling, Gwendolyn felt it not. She gazed at the Druid stones, drawn to them by some invisible lure, and could not stop her feet from taking her within.

Passing through the western gate, Gwendolyn was cognizant of only one thing—Valkyrie's loud cry and the stab of his talons as they dug through the leather armor and reached her flesh.

Then she stepped to the center of the perfect circle, stopping before the waist-high altar stone, and waited. Silence descended on the night. The calls of the night birds and insects stilled, and the last of day faded. But through the veil of darkness blanketing the countryside, Gwendolyn saw clearly where she was.

Gwendolyn waited patiently. She knew something important was about to happen. She was unafraid for herself and was still in thrall to the terrible visages that had filled her mind after her sword practice with Miles. But she forced those images away as she waited, concentrating on the smooth stone before her.

Even as she watched, she felt the power build. Closing her eyes, Gwendolyn instinctively cleared her mind. Her right hand clasped the hilt of the sword she'd left behind, but in her mind was with her now. The crackling of energy sounded loudly, and images of lightning flashed across her closed lids. Carefully, she opened her eyes to gaze at the stone.

It glowed with unearthly colors, rippling in uneven waves of white, red, and black, until it solidified to a dull orange cast. Then another streak of lightning shot from it, racing upward to the sky and disappearing within the dark blotter of newly formed clouds.

Still, Gwendolyn waited patiently.

"Have you so little faith in yourself?" came a soft, yet old voice.

Gwendolyn turned from the altar stone to stare at the robed figure standing ten feet away. The Druid priestess had returned, and within Gwendolyn's mind a new channel opened. She stepped toward the old woman, but the priestess held up one knotted hand.

"Have you so little faith in yourself that you run from who you are?"

"I might have killed him," she whispered.

"But you did not! You would not! You could not!" the old one intoned.

"Yes I could!" Gwendolyn stated defiantly. "It was my hand wielding the sword. I was angered, mad. I did not know what I was doing!"

"Today was but another lesson for you, child. It was a lesson you taught yourself. Think about it!" she commanded and, at the same time, waved her hand in the air.

Gwendolyn's mind came alive with brilliant colors. Again she heard the priestess speak within her own head.

"Watch, Gwendolyn the Chosen, watch carefully," the voice whispered. Gwendolyn felt herself floating, rising above the ground as Valkyrie was wont to do, and the night was gone, replaced by the brilliance of the afternoon sun. Beneath her she saw the old keep, and within the walled outer bailey, she saw a strange tableau.

She saw herself, the silver sword glinting with sunlight as she battled Miles. She saw Miles deflect her blows and tumble across the ground to rise behind her. Floating high above the strange scene, she experienced again the anger which had gripped her at this defeat and watched as she began to fight him again.

Her breath shot from her lips at the final moment, and she saw the spark of power leap from her sword to sever Miles's blade. But she saw also that her aim had been true, and she had been under full control of her every movement.

"Yes!" cried the priestess as she confirmed Gwendolyn's thoughts. They hovered above the old keep and watched the action below. Gwendolyn saw James take the silver sword, cleanse it and sheath it, just as Miles returned to the high wall with Valkyrie on his wrist. When he released the eagle, the images beneath them wavered.

A moment later Gwendolyn was again standing at the altar stone. She realized she had not left, but had been granted a vision by the priestess.

"Now you understand more. Gwendolyn, this lesson today was important. Important for two reasons. First, you must know that you, and only you, can control your mind. The second is that before you run from something, wait and look upon it again with a clear head. Do not run from fear, do not hide from anger. Face them both, and conquer them you shall. You are strong, Daughter of Thunder, and your mind makes you so!" she declared. Then, the old priestess stepped forward, and Gwendolyn saw her ancient, lined face. But this sight did not stop her heart from welling with the love she felt for her mentor.

"Again, I thank you," Gwendolyn said.

"Thank me not, for it is a greater power which controls us all," the old one cried. "And hate me not for setting you on the path you must follow."

"Never," Gwendolyn cried quickly.

"There will be a time you will come to doubt all those things around you. You will doubt yourself and that which you believe in. Remember my words, for when that time comes, you must face it bravely," she said. As she uttered the words, her form began to shimmer.

"I will remember," Gwendolyn promised.

"Rest, my child," whispered the priestess as her form departed, leaving Gwendolyn alone within the darkness.

She turned to look at the altar, and saw it was but plain stone again. Silently, Gwendolyn sank to the ground and laid her head against the cool stone.

She fell into a deep, resting sleep, and was not aware of Valkyrie leaving her shoulder to ascend to the top of the altar, where he perched, wide-eyed and awake, watching over his mistress with a sharp, piercing gaze.

Miles watched the sun's ascent from darkness, and when its warming rays washed over him, he breathed deeply. He stood high upon the battlement of the old keep, his eyes moving rapidly while he searched the land around them. From his vantage point, he could see for miles in every direction.

He had come up here an hour before dawn to wait patiently for the light of day; as patiently as he had sat throughout the night, waiting for Gwendolyn's return.

The long night had fled quickly while his thoughts had tunneled deeply within. He had reviewed his life, from the moment he'd met Gwendolyn, until yesterday's practice and its harsh conclusion. The only thing he'd been able to understand was that his life and Gwendolyn's were entwined in such a way that made anything or anyone else immaterial.

He had known from the instant their swords had met the previous day that Gwendolyn was his equal. The only thing she lacked was experience, and that would come with patience.

She still had much training before her, and because of the shortness of time, Miles knew he must work even harder when she returned. Whether she came back to him that day, the next, or a week hence, he did not doubt for a moment that she would return.

Valkyrie's cry drew his eyes toward the northeast, and he

saw the golden eagle soaring upward toward the keep. Miles looked to the ground beneath the majestic bird and saw the distant figure of his wife walking toward him.

Taking a deep breath, Miles nodded his head. Ten minutes later, he was astride his mount, leading Gwendolyn's horse, and riding toward her oncoming form.

When he approached her, he saw that her face, confined by the coif-de-maille, was calm and relaxed, and when he gazed into her eyes, he spied the same calmness reflected within them. He saw, too, that she had understood what had happened yesterday and had accepted it for what it was.

"I ask your forgiveness, my husband," Gwendolyn said formally in a low voice, when Miles had dismounted from his horse.

"There is nothing to forgive, my wife," he replied, with equal formality.

"There is. I ask your forgiveness for my not trusting myself in spite of the trust you have given me."

"There is nothing to forgive. Gwendolyn, what happened yesterday was a part of the training. It was something that had to happen, be it now, or at another time. It is called becoming."

Gwendolyn stared at her husband and slowly nodded. "Miles, hold me," she whispered.

Miles took her in his arms and held her tightly, his hands pressing her leather-clad form close.

When Miles released her at last, he brought her to her horse. When they were both mounted, they returned to the keep, and together, ate the first meal of the day.

That day there was no training. Rather, Miles and Gwendolyn went to their chamber and joined as man and wife, reconfirming everything they had always told each other. They spent the day talking of little things, and never once spoke of war or fighting.

But the next day, and the next weeks, the training continued, and Miles became again the relentless taskmaster whom Gwendolyn loved and needed. One morning, a month after her return from the Druid stones, she awoke to find Miles gone. She dressed quickly, choosing a long Saxon tunic, and went to look for him.

When she stepped into the inner bailey, she stopped, her hands on her arms, hugging herself against the chill of the air. She saw a strange horse, blanketed with the colors of Radstock, and saw the rider who wore the surcoat of the earl standing behind him. Miles was speaking with the squires and Roweena. It took her only a moment to realize that their time in Wales was at an end.

When Miles was finished, he saw Gwendolyn and went to her. "We leave on the morrow; the training pit at Radstock is completed," he told her.

"You have been away from your lands overlong," she replied.

"You are my lands," he whispered solemnly, "but I have responsibilities, and those, too, must be part of your training."

"I understand," she replied.

"This day will be ours," Miles declared. "We shall ride the countryside and enjoy its offerings."

"Yes!" Gwendolyn cried.

And so, Gwendolyn and Miles returned to Radstock just before the first snow of the season. For the most part, Gwendolyn's training proceeded smoothly, deep within the bowels of Radstock Castle, far away from the inquisitive eyes of the people; but now Miles was only able to spend a fraction of his time training her. He was forced to let Gwendolyn train with James and Arthur, without his supervision, when other duties called.

Life within the castle was serene. Gwendolyn led her double life without complaint, winning over the household servants by her calm manner and her common sense. She reorganized many things within the castle and also found time to accompany Miles on his excursions into the small village, and through his lands.

Radstock was a fertile area, and Gwendolyn saw that Miles was, indeed, a good lord. He was fair in his dealings with his serfs and vassals, and was considered a wise decision-maker for their problems.

But finally the harsh winter came, and in the seventh month of their marriage, Miles knew that Gwendolyn was near the end of her training.

He saw it one cold February morning when he stood on the walkway overlooking the training pit and watched Gwendolyn fend off both James and Arthur, who, although still four years away from maturity, were almost the equal of any knight Miles knew.

Miles left his vantage point and descended the wooden steps to the floor of the pit. In his hand was the last weapon that Gwendolyn would train with. He had ordered it made before they'd left for Wales, and it had been delivered this day.

Gwendolyn paused for a breath, and as she did, saw Miles approach. She smiled at him and stepped toward him, but froze when she saw the object in his hand.

"James, Arthur," Miles called in a low voice, "get the shields, the maces, and my axe."

The squires ran to the other side of the pit to do their knight's bidding as Miles reached Gwendolyn's side.

"You are almost ready, my lady," he said. Then he lifted the weapon in his hand.

Gwendolyn stared at the dark, hammered head of the battle-axe and then gazed at the polished wood of its handle.

"Why the axe?" she asked even as she reached out to touch it.

"Because it is your heritage. The Normans do not appreciate the subtle art or the beauty of the axe—they prefer the mace. But nothing is the equal of this," Miles declared, thrusting the newly made weapon into Gwendolyn's hands. "For hundreds of years the fighters of England have used this. It is a part of us."

"As it shall be a part of me," Gwendolyn replied solemnly. "It is so light," she said.

"It was made differently. Look at the handle. It is not carved from one piece of wood. It is two hollowed halves, with an iron rod in its center. The head is wider, but the shaft narrower. It will sing in the air when used. Try it, my lady knight, test its feel," he ordered.

Gwendolyn stepped back and lifted the axe. Her hands gripped it tightly, finding purchase and balance while she swung it. "It feels good," she said when she stopped her movement and looked at Miles.

"You will practice what I show you now for the next week. But, you will use the axe in a different manner than the accepted one."

"How?" Gwendolyn asked, wondering exactly what Miles had in mind.

"No shield. You will fight two-handed. The shield will hamper you; your speed will be your defense."

Gwendolyn gasped when she heard him speak and shook her head. "Against the mace?"

"Remember my fight with Morgan? Remember how useless the shield was for me?"

"But you used it at the beginning," she reminded him.

"My strength is different than yours. Gwendolyn, think about the past seven months. Has there ever been a time I have not stressed speed? I have told you to strike and move. Strike and move. You are strong, but no match for a man such as Morgan. You cannot fight his type of man with only one arm. You need all your power, and that power is in your shoulders."

Gwendolyn listened to his words and thought about them. Finally she nodded, accepting Miles's judgement. "As you say," she added in a low voice just as the squires returned.

Miles chose a shield and axe, and then faced his wife. For the next two hours he instructed her and the squires in the handling of the weapon. He made them attack him, strike against his shield, attack again, and strike again. By the end of the afternoon, everyone was exhausted from the unfamiliar fighting and gladly ended the session.

For the next week, Gwendolyn and the twins practiced their axework alone, save for the twice-daily visits of Miles, who would watch silently, offering advice only when it was necessary. By the end of the week, Gwendolyn's axe was like an extension of her hands, and her swings were accurate and hard.

But then Christmas came, and all training halted in deference to the occasion. After the holy mass, led by the Bishop Montgommery ended, a hurried announcement reached Miles and Gwendolyn as they talked with the bishop about the upcoming crusade. A visitor was approaching, and when Miles learned who it was, he welcomed him warmly within Radstock Castle.

William Marshall, Earl of Pembroke, arrived with a large retinue. After seeing to his men, Gwendolyn hastily ordered the servants to prepare a small feast while Miles escorted Richard's chief advisor to the guest chamber.

By the time everything had settled down, and the boards in the great hall had been prepared, Gwendolyn, with Roweena's assistance, was dressed for the evening.

The great hall of Radstock was large, and tapers burned in their niches, illuminating the room brilliantly. Miles's knights lined one side of the hall, Marshall's men lined the other. At the High Table sat Miles and William Marshall, with Gwendolyn between them. Standing behind the table were James, Arthur, and Roweena, ready to fill any request.

The three musicians whom Gwendolyn had sent for sat in one corner, playing their lilting music as the food was served, and the wine and mead poured.

"You are looking well, Lady Gwendolyn. Marriage agrees with you," Marshall said in compliment.

"Nay, my lord," Gwendolyn replied. "It is not marriage that agrees with me, but my husband."

Marshall laughed loudly, slapping his open palm on the table and causing his cup to turn over. He shook his head and turned to Miles. "You have won more than a wife!" he declared.

"Much more," Miles replied in a low voice before he forced a smile to cover his face.

"Would that Richard find one," Marshall said as he lifted a piece of meat and stared at it.

"He shall," Gwendolyn stated. "When the time is right."

"No, my lady. I think not," Marshall replied before he took a bite of his food.

"But he must," Miles stated. "England must have an heir."

"Miles, you know him as well as I. Do you think he will beget a son?"

Miles stared into William Marshall's eyes and slowly shook his head. "I do not know," he whispered.

"Enough!" Marshall shouted, forcing his burly features into a grimace that passed for a smile. "I bring you news," he said.

"Richard has reached the Holy Land?" Gwendolyn asked.

"Nay. Philip is playing his political games. He's had Richard waiting in Normandy for three months while he sits on his French throne and laughs at us. Now, Richard is realizing that he may have to fight without Philip and his men."

"You told him that last year," Miles reminded the earl.

"Yes, but that was last year. Richard has a short memory when he wants to fight. But that matters not. What is important is that Richard is stalled, and in need of more men and money."

"I will be joining him with fifty of my own knights. I cannot afford to give him any more money!"

"Nor would he ask it of you," Marshall said quickly, knowing well how much wealth Miles had already given over to Richard. "I have been sent to squeeze more from everyone, but Miles, it saddens me deeply. Richard will bankrupt our land in an effort to meet Saladin."

"Saladin?" asked Gwendolyn at the mention of the unfamiliar name.

"Saladin, the sultan of the Moors. He has united the Saracens, and defeated every Christian army that has gone before him. I swear, it is Richard's dream to defeat him. Not for England, or Normandy, but for his own glory!"

"And he will not be put aside?" Gwendolyn asked.

"No. It is more the shame that Geoffrey had lost good Henry's ear. For if he had not, he would be king of England and alive this day. We would not be facing the loss of our country through the sales of its lands."

"My lord, speak not so loudly, for your words are treason itself," Miles cautioned.

"No, my loyalty is unquestioned; I but wish our land ruled by a king who would stay here, rather than cross half the world to fight and possibly die. Can you imagine John Lackland as our king?"

"I pray it never happens."

"But it may. However, again I have gone off track. I have come to bring you news. Richard has declared a spring tournament to celebrate the new departure date for the Crusade. All the knights of the land are urged to participate. The only requirement is that a fee be paid to aid in the freeing of the Holy Land. The prize Richard offers is a new earldom."

Gwendolyn listened intently to Marshall's words, and when he'd spoken the proclamation, her heart beat faster and she stared pointedly at Miles. "Any knight may enter?" she asked.

"Any knight," Marshall repeated, "who but has the entrance fee."

"Richard is becoming desperate to begin this folly," Miles ventured.

"He has an army to feed, Miles, and he must raise the funds somehow. A tournament is as good a way as any."

"True," Miles replied, but his eyes were fixed on Gwendolyn's and he knew exactly what was going through her mind.

"The fee?" Miles asked.

"Whatever the knight will pay."

Unnoticed by the king's old tutor, Gwendolyn and Miles held a silent exchange as their eyes stayed locked upon each other. The look Gwendolyn favored him with spoke more than any words could, and Miles knew that there was no protest he could utter to hold back his wife from her desire. Because he had trained her himself, he knew her will and strength, and imperceptibly nodded his acceptance of her desire.

"My lord," Gwendolyn said in a voice that brought the Earl of Pembroke's eyes to hers. Before she continued, she reached to the back of her neck and unclasped the heavy gold rope necklace she wore and placed it on the table between herself and Marshall. "Will this suffice as the fee for a knight to enter the tournament?"

Marshall, eyeing the thick gold rope, nodded his head slowly. "My lady, the king thanks you. Who will be your champion?" he asked with upraised eyebrows, already sure of her answer, and enjoying this game of the newlyweds.

"You shall know at the proper time," she declared mysteriously, enjoying the sudden puzzled reaction that shadowed Marshall's face.

With that, and another quick exchange of glances, the three at the High Table returned to their food. Marshall's message had been delivered, and with his job done, they could all enjoy themselves without further concern.

But Gwendolyn's mind would not leave the subject. A restless energy filled her, and the anticipation of her first tourney began to grow within her mind.

Chapter Ten

SPRING HAD COME EARLY TO Radstock. The hills surrounding the castle turned green and lush. The air seemed to come alive with the scents of trees and flowers opening to the warmth.

But within Radstock Castle itself, and the deep pit in its bowels, nothing had changed. Every day, Gwendolyn worked, practicing with sword, axe, dagger, and lance, until she was so perfectly attuned to each weapon that they were all of second nature to her.

But this day was different, and Miles knew it as he walked across the dirt floor toward his wife. She was alone this morning, practicing with her sword the maneuvers Miles had disciplined into her mind.

When she saw Miles's face her arms grew heavy. Lowering the sword of her father, she waited for him to reach her. "What is wrong?" she asked quickly.

"Nothing and everything. Have you lost track of time?" he asked with a soft smile.

"Time?"

"In two weeks is Richard's spring tournament," he told her.

Gwendolyn stared at him for a moment before she shook her head. "It is truth, Husband, I have lost all track of time."

"We will be leaving in three days. Are you ready?"

"Am I?" she asked, returning his question with one of her own.

"You are," he declared formally.

"I thank you, my lord," she whispered.

Miles flashed a brief smile at her and then clapped his hands. Roweena appeared suddenly, and Gwendolyn stared openly at her servant. "Go with Roweena. She will prepare for this day," he commanded.

It was then that Gwendolyn understood Miles's strange formality. Her heart skipped a beat and her lips trembled slightly. She knelt quickly before Miles and bowed her head low. "Yes, my lord," she said in a trembling voice. Standing, she unsheathed her silver sword and handed it, hilt first, to Miles.

When she was gone, Miles stared at the spot she had disappeared from. He was committed now, and it could not be stopped.

"Arthur! James!" he called. The fourteen-year-old twins appeared and stood before their lord. "James, Arthur, you have both been chosen, by myself, by the Lady Gwendolyn, and by the powers that rule this land, to play a special part in our lives. I must ask you formally, for the last time, do you wish to continue in our services? If you decide not, I will find you a suitable knight to continue your training. I know that neither of you shall ever divulge what you have seen."

"We choose to stay, my lord," they said in unison, their large blue eyes staring openly at Miles as they both knelt before him.

"And I accept your service, and both I and the Lady Gwendolyn are in your debt. Rise, Squires."

The twins rose slowly, their eyes never once leaving Miles's. "I have made my decision. James, you are to be Gwendolyn's squire. Will you carry out your duties unswervingly?"

"Yes, my lord," James replied.

"Then go and put on the garments of your station." When the squire was gone, Miles turned to Arthur. "Prepare yourself and bring my full dress to my antechamber."

"Yes, my lord," Arthur said. Turning, he ran swiftly from the dark chamber to do his bidding, and to prepare himself for what lay ahead, on both this day, and the months to come.

* * *

Gwendolyn sat in the tub, willing her tense muscles to calm while Roweena combed her hair and pleated it in even rows. For nine long months she had followed the dictates of her fate and had worked ceaselessly to attain her goals. Today she had realized when she stared into her husband's eyes, would be the day she'd see the goals reached.

Although she knew that this would merely be another step on the path that led to her destiny, she believed it to be the most important step.

She and Miles had spent much time discussing how she would be able to remain undiscovered as a woman, yet fight and tourney as a knight. It had been only the week before that they had come across the perfect method.

"There is only one way," Miles had declared.

"Tell me, Husband, for I can not think of any."

"Your voice is not deep enough, you can not speak. Your face is too beautiful, it can not show. That is the answer."

"Unravel this riddle for me," Gwendolyn had begged when she had heard his words and seen his smile.

"It is no riddle; rather, it is the true way of things. You must swear a double oath to me, and because it will be to me alone, I am the only person who can release you from it," he'd stated smugly.

"And that oath?"

"The first part is an oath of silence: that until the Holy Land is freed from the hold of the Saracens, you shall not speak. The second part is similar. You take oath that until the Holy Land is free, no man may look upon your face."

"But," Gwendolyn had cried when his words echoed through her mind, "it will not be possible."

"Yes, it will. Your squire will be your spokesman. When you are not about your knightly duties, you are the Lady Gwendolyn of Radstock and unbound by the oath of your knightly self. As for your face, a leather mask will be made revealing only your eyes, and with small holes to breathe through."

"Are you sure it will suffice?" she'd asked.

"It is your only chance. Do you agree?"

"I agree, my lord," she'd replied.

When Gwendolyn had more time to think about Miles's idea, she saw it was not only the perfect solution, but the only one feasible.

"My lady?" Roweena called for the third time.

"Yes?" Gwendolyn asked, drawn from her thoughts. She looked up to see Roweena standing with her bath sheet. She stood, letting her servant wrap her tightly. "Where are my clothes?" she asked.

"My lady, Lord Miles ordered me to bring you to his chamber without clothing," she stated.

"So be it," Gwendolyn replied. She followed Roweena across her own antechamber and waited until the young woman opened the heavy door leading into Miles's formal dress chamber.

When she entered the room, she paused. Lined on the floor were all the garments of her rank. Standing to one side was James, fully dressed, and with a new surcoat. Gwendolyn stared at its coat of arms, until her throat constricted tightly.

The coat of arms was completely new. It was the full coat of Radstock, surrounded by a golden border, and sitting upon the border was a golden eagle with its wings spread wide.

When Gwendolyn finished looking at it, she gazed into James's eyes. "Leave us," James commanded Roweena in a voice that brooked no argument.

Roweena stiffened momentarily, then turned and left the small chamber.

"My lord," James said as he stepped toward Gwendolyn. "I am James, son of Harold, who died in the service of good King Henry. Will thou accept me as your squire?" he asked, going to one knee before her.

"Rise, James, son of Harold. I accept thee as my squire and accept my responsibility to you as your lord."

"I thank you, my lord," James replied when he stood. "It is time to dress," he said. Gwendolyn lifted her arms, and James unwound the bath sheet. She stood naked before him, not bothered by him seeing her so, knowing that he did not look upon her as a woman. When he had offered his service as squire, he had looked upon her as he would any other knight.

James moved swiftly and surely as he dressed Gwendolyn. He dressed her the same way that Miles had every day of the past nine months. First her loincloth, which James clasped over her hips. Then he held her breast support, and when it was slipped over her arms, James stepped behind her to buckle it closed.

He returned to the garments on the floor and carefully lifted the first. He held it up for Gwendolyn to inspect, and her breath caught in her throat. It was a new gamboise, the stitching of the quilt showed that fact plainly. He held it toward her, and she put her arms through the proper openings. Stepping behind her again, James laced the protective undergarment closed. Gwendolyn stood proudly, gazing down at the gamboise. It reached to midthigh and was split in the center as would be the hauberk.

"Sewn into the middle of the gamboise," James said in a low voice, "is a metal breastplate. Sir Miles thought it would be best."

Gwendolyn didn't reply as James continued to dress her. Next came the cuisses, the protection for her thighs, knees, and shins, and over that, James laced on the full maille chausses. When he was done, he stepped back to inspect his work. Nodding, he returned to the waiting objects and picked up the next.

Twenty minutes later, Gwendolyn's arms were protected by rarebraces, and vambraces of leather, and maille, and James was holding up the shining new hauberk for Gwendolyn's inspection. The coat of maille glowed from the light of the tapers, and, again, Gwendolyn's breath caught. She held up her arms, and James draped the hauberk upon her. The weight of the maille was not light, but Gwendolyn felt it not at all as chills of anticipation and excitement coursed along her skin. When the maille was in place, she breathed deeply, adjusting her body to its weight.

Carefully, James placed the arming coif over Gwendolyn's head and laced it at her throat. Then he lifted Gwendolyn's coif-de-maille, with its full-shoulder coverings, and settled it on her.

After he attached the coif to its hooks, James turned from her and went to the table. There he lifted some folded material and returned to Gwendolyn. "My lord," he said as he unfurled the surcoat. Emblazoned on its front was another coat of arms. This time no shield of Radstock showed. The coat of arms was simple in the extreme, yet it sent Gwendolyn's blood running molten within her veins.

Embroidered upon the surcoat was a perfect circle of

black. Within the circle was a golden eagle, its wings outspread. In the eagle's talons was a silver longsword, and beneath the horizontal longsword was the winged dragon of Wales. Gwendolyn closed her eyes for a moment as her mind whirled happily. She opened them to find James holding the surcoat up, ready to slip it over her head.

It took only five minutes more for James to finish. He attached the weapon hooks and placed her long dagger on one, her battle-axe upon the other, and then reverently, for he had witnessed the power of the silver sword, attached the sword in its scabbard to the proper place.

When that was done, James bowed to Gwendolyn and left the chamber. While she was alone, she tried to calm her mind. The unfamiliar feel of her new armor did not bother her, and her only thought was a prayer that she would be able to handle herself without giving away her true identity.

Then all thought was wiped from her mind when she heard movement from the other chamber. She gazed at the doorway and then held her breath. James and Arthur stepped inside. They were now dressed differently. James wore the same surcoat he'd had on when he'd dressed Gwendolyn, and Arthur wore the coat of arms of Radstock. They stepped forward, separated, and stopped in unison. When they did, Miles entered.

He was dressed exactly as she, in full knightly armor, and upon his surcoat was the emblem of Radstock. His longsword hung almost to the floor, and his mailled hand rested on its hilt.

He stopped three feet from Gwendolyn, and his deep green eyes stared into her lighter ones. Then a shadowy smile etched the corners of his mouth.

"Kneel," he commanded in a low voice.

Gwendolyn shook herself free of his haunting gaze and lowered herself to both knees. There, below her husband, she raised her eyes to his.

"On this day, we do perform a service for our country," he proclaimed in a smooth, rolling voice. He withdrew his longsword and raised it above her head with both mailled hands. "By the right given to me as a knight of England, I do proclaim in the very name of England," he intoned and touched her left shoulder with the blade before lifting it and speaking again. "And, with the grace of our king, Richard

I," he said, lowering the sword to rest upon her right shoulder for a moment, before lifting it above her head again. "And, by the powers that oversee all that happens upon this earth," he intoned as the sword dropped for the third time to rest upon Gwendolyn's mailled head, "I declare you a knight of England, and charge you with all the responsibilities and obligations of your new rank. Rise, Sir Eldwin, Knight Protector of Radstock," he finished.

With her eyes filling with teardrops, Gwendolyn rose to face her husband on equal footing.

"Your sword, Sir Eldwin." Gwendolyn withdrew her sword, and handed it to him. "Upon this sword, you must now swear your oath."

Gwendolyn looked at the silver sword and cleared her mind of everything. She sensed the power of the blade and willed all other thoughts, save the thought of it, away. Kneeling upon one knee, she took the sword in her mailled hands, and, holding it in front of her, with her eyes locked upon Miles's, she spoke.

"I, as Sir Eldwin, hereby swear that until the Holy Land is freed of Saracens and returned to the rightful hands I shall not speak, nor shall I let any gaze upon the face beneath the armor I wear." Then Gwendolyn brought the blade to her lips and pressed it close.

"Rise, Sir Eldwin, and receive a gift."

Gwendolyn stood again, and looked at Miles's outstretched hand. Hanging from his fingertips was a chamois mask. Instinctively, she knew it had been made from the soft leather that had always held her sword. She nodded, knowing that she could not speak as long as she wore her armor and stood in the guise of Sir Eldwin. But she had no need for words.

"James, see to your lord," Miles ordered. "I would like to spend the rest of the day with my wife," he added dryly as he turned, sheathed his sword, and left the dress chamber with Arthur in attendance.

Twenty minutes later, naked as the day she had entered the world, Gwendolyn went to the marital chamber she shared with Miles to find him awaiting her in their bed.

"My lord," she whispered, her voice thick with emotion.

"My lady," he responded as he held out his arms to her.

She went to him and they joined together as man and wife.

Sir Eldwin set aside for the moment, the only inhabitants in their world were Miles and she, locked together in a passionate embrace that excluded all else.

During the next three days, while the preparations for the spring tournament progressed, both Miles and Gwendolyn rode the lands, checking on the planting and the birthings of the flocks. Because of the long months of her training, it was as if Gwendolyn were again seeing the land for the first time.

The sloping lands and rolling hills were unlike Devonshire, but they held their own beauty and lure. It was an open land, filled with crops and sheep, and not a few head of beef.

It was the custom of the lord of the land to inspect everything. It was also his right and due. But Gwendolyn marveled at the respect shown to him by his vassals and noted how even the lowliest of the serfs and slaves showed him their regard.

Yet, even though she witnessed this display of affection for her husband, she also saw the poor state of most of the homes. When she asked Miles about it, he explained.

"Richard is bankrupting the country. He takes every free shilling for his wars. But we must pay, not because we are vassal to him, but because he is the figurehead England needs to pull her together," he said as he drew his horse to a halt near the summit of a low hill.

"Who says Richard will bring the land together?" Gwendolyn asked, unsatisfied with her husband's answer.

"Gwendolyn, for two hundred years England has been at war with herself. The barons, and the rest of the nobility, have spent their lives feuding with each other, enlarging their lands, and fighting endlessly. When Henry became king, he was able to stop it to some small degree, but even he had a greed for wealth which could not be stopped. Richard is the first king to sit on the throne that cares not for property."

"No," Gwendolyn said quickly, stalling any further explanation from Miles. "No, his greed is for glory and to raise his soul and image above all others. His greed is for war. It is his sickness!" she declared.

"Yes," Miles agreed, surprising Gwendolyn. "But for our country it is a better sickness than the other. We are at peace with ourselves. At Richard's coronation, we gathered not as knights of the realm, nor as Richard's vassals. We met, all the barons, dukes, and earls of England and agreed to support Richard in his fierce quests, so long as England remained untouched and could heal from its age of sickness."

"But so much money, so much of our property lays in ruin because of this."

"And while I am gone, it shall be on your shoulders to make do as best you can," he told her.

"I shall, my lord," Gwendolyn promised.

When they returned to Radstock Castle, the conversation weighed heavily on her mind, and she made herself another promise. Somehow, she would improve the lot of the people of Radstock. How, she did not know, but she would find a way.

The days had passed quickly, but not quickly enough for Gwendolyn. With the sunrise of the fourth day, Gwendolyn woke anxiously. She put on a tunic and, without waking Miles, left their chamber and ascended the stairs, stepping onto the high battlement of Radstock.

The sun was just rising, and the sky was clear and cloudless in all directions. Below her, in the outer ward, the horses and equipment waited. Twenty horses, along with her own palfrey, and Miles's heavy charger, were lined up and being attended.

They would be gone for two weeks, and in that time, Sir Eldwin would ride for the first time, and the deception of Radstock would begin. She and Miles had discussed this, but it had been she who had devised the plan for Radstock. Whenever she rode as Sir Eldwin, Roweena would tell all that the Lady Gwendolyn was ill and in her chamber.

Anything that had to be dealt with, Roweena would handle, deferring all important decisions until Gwendolyn returned.

"My lady," called James from behind her.

Gwendolyn turned and saw the boy standing near the staircase. "Good morrow, Squire," she greeted him.

"It is time," he informed her.

"I shall be down in a moment," she said. James bowed and left her, sensing her need to be alone for a minute longer.

Gwendolyn sighed and looked across the lands once more.

Then she willed her nerves to steady and closed her eyes. She built a picture of her silver sword within her mind and saw the purity of the light surround it. She felt the perfection of the light fill her and let it soothe her anxieties. When the mind-picture faded, she opened her eyes and went to the stairs.

In their chamber, Roweena had laid out a meal for both her and Miles, and while the squires set out their knightly apparel, Miles and Gwendolyn broke fast together, both issuing instructions to Roweena for the time they would be gone.

An hour after the meal was finished, Miles left the chamber dressed as befitted his station as Earl of Radstock. Although he was not in full armor, Gwendolyn could not but help the desire surging within her breasts at the sight he presented. He stood tall and proud, his legs encased in leather, his short hauberk of maille covered by his white surcoat, and his hands encased in leather gauntlets.

Because none must know her true identity, Gwendolyn was forced to wear full armor for the trip. But, since she would be riding and not fighting, she chose not to wear her maille chausses, and instead let James wrap her legs in leather bindings. She did wear the gamboise beneath her maille hauberk so that none could tell the shape of her torso. Instead of her coif-de-maille, Gwendolyn put on the chamois mask, and the arming coif of leather.

With James guiding her, they took a back passage through the castle and then followed a secret tunnel that Miles's father had constructed. In the emptiness outside the high wall of Radstock, James led Gwendolyn, as Sir Eldwin, to her horse. After they mounted, they rode slowly toward the spot Miles had told them to wait.

Within the outer ward, Miles signaled his men out of the castle. His every nerve was tautly stretched with the knowledge that the next few minutes would decide the fate of Sir Eldwin, and the Lady Gwendolyn.

When the last knight passed through the gate, Miles ordered a halt. Just then the armored figure of another knight rode toward them.

Although his men were always prepared for a fight, Miles sensed that this new knight with the face covering disconcerted them. Not knowing what to expect, they waited for some signal from their lord.

Gwendolyn rode slowly until she was within touching distance of Miles. Then she dismounted and approached him. Stepping before Miles, she drew her sword and kneeled in one smooth movement. She extended the sword upward to him and waited.

Miles dismounted and stood above her. He took the sword from her mailled hand and spoke. "Rise, Sir Knight, and speak your mind," he commanded formally.

Instead of speaking, the knight withdrew a rolled parchment and handed it to Miles. Miles opened it and read it quickly. Then he signaled to James, who was standing by his horse's side. James strode purposely forward, and when he reached Miles, dropped to one knee quickly before rising.

Then James spoke in a voice loud enough for all to hear. "My lord, this is the knight you sent me to find. Sir Eldwin of Maidstone, sworn to the service of Lady Gwendolyn of Radstock. Sir Eldwin is under the vow of silence and may not speak."

"Sir Eldwin," Miles said in a loud voice, "we welcome you to Radstock and gladly accept your services," he intoned as he handed Gwendolyn back the silver sword. "Because we value the Lady Gwendolyn, and because we know she values you so highly, I accept your services and appoint you to the station of Knight Protector of Radstock. Join us, Sir Eldwin," Miles commanded.

Gwendolyn, through the eyeslits of her mask, watched not only her husband, but the knights mounted behind him. She knew he had already spoken to his men about the knight who would be joining them. He had told them he'd hired the services of this knight when he had wed Gwendolyn, and that this religious, yet fearsome knight would stand his place while he went with Richard to the Holy Land.

This tourney of Richard's, should Gwendolyn be victorious, would solidify Sir Eldwin's position and earn her the respect of the knights of Radstock, for there was no knight who would begrudge the king's champion his due.

With the formalities completed, Miles, with Sir Eldwin riding beside him, ordered his men forward, and thus they began the three-day journey to Windsor, where Richard had ordered the spring tournament to be held.

Chapter Eleven

WINDSOR WAS EVERYTHING Gwendolyn had heard it was. King Henry's massive, round keep dominated all and was visible for miles. Yet not even that imposing tower could hold anyone's eyes for more than a moment. Surrounding the castle, spreading out in all directions, were thousands of tents. Nearly all the nobility of England, and almost every knight and mercenary who had dreams of gaining an earldom, was camped around the high walls of Windsor.

The streets, actually pathways of the tent city, were filled with a multitude of people. Some were going about their business, while others hawked wares and food, and yet others did nothing except watch and join whatever merriment happened along.

Women, be they camp followers, slaves, or peasants trying to find a master to serve who would ease their lot, scurried to-and-fro. Watching it all was the mysterious hooded knight who spoke not a word, nor ventured from his tent, save to exercise with his squire.

It was the day before the tournament would commence, and a festive mood filled the air. For most, the putrid scents of rotting food and unwashed bodies differed little from normal day-to-day life, but for Gwendolyn, in the guise of Eldwin, each passing hour taught her more and more about the people of her homeland, and the perilousness of their lot.

Inside the walls of Windsor, Richard sat on his high chair, addressing the gathered nobility before him. For this occasion, the great hall of Windsor had been turned into a meeting room, and everywhere within the hall, Richard's knights, barons, dukes, and earls stood in attendance.

They had listened to Richard talk of the coming war, and had heard him read aloud the communication he had received from the French King Philip, that Philip and his army were finally ready to join Richard.

Richard boasted that it was he who had forced the deceiving king to hasten his preparations by sending a missive to the pope.

He laughed when he related the story, and laughed even louder when he told his men that Philip had been warned by the pope to either make ready, or face excommunication.

"It was a wise move," called Alfred of Wight.

"It was the only move left," replied Richard candidly. "We leave a fortnight after this tournament." Spontaneous cheering reached the heavy rafters of the hall, as all the knights gave vent to their yearning for combat and blood.

"But now," Richard went on, "prepare for our feast, and for the games on the morrow." Everyone bowed when Richard stood, and they stayed that way until the king had left.

The milling nobility broke into small groups to discuss what they had heard, and Miles, seeing his chance to escape, began to make his way toward the door. But before he reached it, a large hand fell on his shoulder.

"Hold," William Marshall said in a low voice. "Richard would see you."

Miles nodded and followed the earl to a door which led into the large walled keep. A few minutes later, Miles stepped into Richard's chamber and bowed low before the king.

"Rise, Miles, we have no need of formalities in private. We have missed your presence over the winter months."

"My apologies, my lord," Miles said in a low voice.

"But we understand the reasons. Does the Lady Gwendolyn still please you?" he asked.

"Daily."

"And you have planted the seed for an heir?"

"At this time I know not."

"But you have worked hard to try, have you not?" Richard said with a wide smile. "I have heard the stories of your disappearance from Radstock for many months. I envy you."

"Thank you, Sire,"

"But we miss the Lady Gwendolyn. Why is she not in attendance?"

"She has taken sick, my lord, and I would not have her travel in that condition."

"Is it serious?" Richard inquired quickly, and Miles saw a true concern cover his features.

"I think not; the change of season has affected her," he explained, strangely pleased with this new revelation of his king.

"I understand. I have seen many strong men felled by the same. Yet I had hoped to feast with her this night. She is a woman worthy of the company of men."

"I will convey your words to her; she will be pleased."

"And what of you? Are you less anxious to be off to war now that you have such a woman warming your bed?"

"I am only anxious to have done with it, and to defeat the Saracens so that I may return quickly to her," Miles said truthfully, realizing for the first time that he did want a fast end to this crusade.

"Then we shall have to be swift. This tournament has helped to fill our coffers, and with it I have added hundreds of knights to my banner. When we reach the Holy Land we will be strong!" he declared in a loud voice.

"So I pray, Sire," Miles said as he stole a glance at William Marshall, whose face had flickered sourly.

"But I am troubled," Richard continued. "We have fought many times together, and yet you do not enter the tournament. Why?"

"I have no need of more lands. I am content with what I have."

"Yet, I had hoped to watch you defeat all others. Miles, it saddens me that these knights will not see a true warrior battle."

Miles gazed at Richard, wondering how far he dare go, yet sensing that Richard's disapproval was only due to his thirst for the fight.

"Fear not, for there will be a knight fighting under my banner. His fee was paid months ago by the Lady Gwendolyn."

"Is that so?" Surprised, Richard glanced at Marshall who nodded in confirmation. "And who be this knight you have such trust in?"

"His name is Eldwin, and he was knighted by my own hand. I have appointed him Protector of Radstock in my absence."

"To have such trust in a mercenary is foolish, Miles. You of all people should know better."

"I have full trust in this knight, Sire. He is like no other in all England."

"Your judgement has always been good; I pray it is in this case."

"It is," Miles declared.

"Yet, if he is victorious, as you seem to think he will be, you would lose this knight to the earldom he wins," Richard stated smugly as he ran his fingers across his lips in a characteristic gesture of thought. "Yes, I would see the mettle of this knight. You will point him out to me tonight," Richard ordered.

A warning chill raced along Miles's spine as he held the king's gaze tightly. "I am sorry, Sire, but Sir Eldwin can not join the feast."

"Why?" Richard demanded harshly.

"He has taken a vow of silence until you have succeeded with your mission in the Holy Land."

"Silence does not stop one from feasting or enjoying life!"

"True, but he is sworn never to show his face to another until the Saracens are defeated, and because of that, he wears a hood to shield his face from other eyes."

"Then how does he eat?"

"Privately, and I would beg you to not force him to break his vow. He is not like most," Miles added in a low voice.

"I dislike not knowing the faces of my vassals," Richard growled in defeat.

"Sir Eldwin is loyal to England, Sire. I stake my life upon it."

"It will be your life if you are wrong. And if he wins the tourney, how can I make an earl of a faceless man?"

"You cannot. Sir Eldwin seeks no title. If he wins, he has but one simple request," Miles informed Richard.

"Simple?"

"Yes, Sire. He wants to be knighted, again, by your hand. That is the only reward he seeks."

"If he wins, he shall have it," Richard declared, flinging his hand before him in dismissal. Miles bowed low and began backing toward the door, but Richard's voice stopped him. "I thought you should know that Morgan of Guildswood has petitioned to fight by my side in Jerusalem and offers two hundred knights."

"He is a strong fighter," Miles replied carefully, forcing away the warning produced by Richard's words.

"He is," Richard said and waved his hand once again in a final dismissal.

Miles left the audience and walked through the large keep, his mind whirling with the last words Richard had uttered. Why did Morgan choose to make his petition now? But Miles knew that the enemy he had made in Devonshire had returned to haunt him and understood that once the crusade was under way, he must watch Guildswood carefully.

Shrugging the thought away, he entered the crowded tent city and strode purposefully toward the banner of Radstock which flew high above his tent.

Within her large tent, her mask always in place, Gwendolyn sat upon a rush mat awaiting Miles's return from his attendance at Richard's court.

She had used her time wisely, forcing herself to remain calm and relaxed, repeating silently to herself all the lessons she had been taught by her husband. When the flap of the tent parted, her concentration dissolved and she looked into the worried face of Miles.

She watched him secure the flap so that no one could enter, and when that was done, Gwendolyn removed the mask, and took a deep breath.

"What is bothering you?" she asked.

"Morgan."

Gwendolyn waited patiently until he explained what had happened with Richard. "But that should make no difference to you. You care not for the glory Richard and the others seek. You go only out of your obligation as the king's vassal."

"It is not the crusade I worry about. I do not fear Morgan,

but I fear for you tomorrow, and for the entire tournament. When I left Richard I went inquiring among the knights I know. Morgan has been boasting that he will defeat me in this tournament and recoup his losses from our last meeting."

"But you are not entered in the tourney."

"Morgan has not yet learned of that. When he does, he will go after you with a vengeance. I had not thought of that when I agreed to this tournament and am at fault."

"Fear not, Miles, for Morgan does not frighten me."

"He frightens me!" Miles spat. "I've fought him. I know his power. He is strong and ruthless and will stop at nothing to defeat anyone under the colors of Radstock."

"Calm yourself, my husband. I shall not give Morgan the opportunity to harm us."

"You may not have the choice."

"I will stay across the field from him until there is no other opponent. Perhaps someone will defeat him first," she said hopefully.

"I will pray for that, but his hatred is a strong force within him."

"And one that may help to defeat him. But," she said as a smile brightened her face, "did you speak with Richard about my request?"

"Yes. If you win, you shall be knighted again by Richard himself."

"Thank you, my lord."

"Do not thank me until the deed is done," Miles cautioned.

They sat silently until darkness fell, and Arthur came to dress Miles for the banquet. When he was gone, Gwendolyn again put on the mask of Sir Eldwin and sat cross-legged on the rush mat with the silver sword resting upon her thighs. She cleared her mind and fell into a trancelike state, willing the channel that linked her to the sword to open, and when it did, she drew from it the strength and calmness she would need on the morrow.

The tournament began as none other save the king's would. The long procession of knights was led into the wide green swarth by the king's bodyguards and was proceeded by five ranks of trumpeters blowing the call to arms.

The knights, dressed in full armor and colors, presented a picture that would not be forgotten quickly. Three hundred proud warriors rode into the arena. Of the large group, a full three-quarters were landless knights, each of whom was hopeful that at the end of three days, he would be proclaimed an earl and elevated to the ranks of nobility. Of the others, who already ranked in the nobility of England, each of them wanted two things: the prestige and glory of winning the king's tournament, and the added riches of more land and yet another title.

For the crowd who gathered to witness this day, excitement swirled thickly in the air. Women called out to their husbands, mothers cried to their sons, and all felt the thrill of the battle that would soon commence, for a battle it would truly be.

Gwendolyn, wearing her full armor and sitting astride her mount in the second rank of knights, gazed steadily at where Richard stood on his platform. Waiting for him to speak and order the tournament to begin, she thought back to the morning, and the words of caution her husband had given her.

The early cock's first cries drew Gwendolyn from her sleep. She had awakened instantly and opened her eyes. Blinking, she had seen Miles's shadowy form sitting next to her.

"Your day begins," he had whispered.

"Our day," she had replied as she raised her hand to caress his large shoulder. His hand covered hers and squeezed it gently.

"This is your first tournament. I must speak to you of it," he had said in a low voice. He had waited until Gwendolyn nodded her head before he went on. "Although you have witnessed many tournaments, there is nothing to prepare you for it. Gwendolyn, you must remember that the difference between a tournament and a true battle is almost indistinguishable. Those knights whom you will face today, and in the coming days, are fighting for something they want. They will fight their opponents as if it were to the death, and indeed, there will be many who will lose their lives."

"I understand," Gwendolyn had told him, and she did. She knew well the history of the tournament. It was a

Norman tradition, used to train their knights for battle. Only rarely was there a tournament such as Miles and Morgan had fought, when only one knight faced another. Most were like the one today, a melee. There would be two sides—two armies—who would fight each other. And, as the losers fell, the victors would ride again, and again, until there were but two knights left to face each other. At the end of the day, only one out of three hundred would be the winner.

And then it would begin again the next day, and the day after, until all methods of fighting had been used, and there was but one knight who stood above the rest.

"You must concentrate. You must pick your first opponent, and your concentration must not be broken by anything. Look not right nor left when you charge. Pick your knight and picture him unseated. That is the way of victory," Miles had declared heatedly.

"I shall, my teacher, I shall," Gwendolyn had whispered. Then she had gone into his arms and drawn from his strength all the security and confidence she needed.

The trumpets signaled a fanfare, pulling Gwendolyn from her thoughts. The crowd stilled, and King Richard, resplendent in a long red mantle, moved forward on the specially erected platform. A narrow gold crown rested on his head, and his shoulder-length hair sparkled in the sunlight. He raised both hands high, and when he did, the Archbishop of Canterbury stepped forward.

The archbishop lifted his gold-encrusted staff, and the blessings of the tournament rolled smoothly from his tongue. When he finished his benediction, he stepped back to the carved wooden chair next to the king's and waited.

Richard stepped forward, and the crowd began to cheer again. "For the glory of England, for the love of God, and under the code of chivalry, I hereby order this tournament begun."

From a thousand throats came a loud, animal-like cry. The knights lined up before Richard and lifted their swords high before wheeling their mounts around and racing to their squires.

Gwendolyn felt a surge of energy race through her when she spurred the stallion toward James. Excitement made her nerves hum tightly.

Reaching James, she dismounted and let her squire help her to mount Miles's heavy charger. When she sat in the special saddle Miles had designed, which would hold her securely against the hard thrusts of a lance, she gazed across the field to survey her opponents and felt the full impact of Miles's earlier words. Across from her, the opposing knights were gathering and the wall they created sent a chill racing along her spine.

No specific knight would face off against another until the field was narrowed down. Because of the great amount of entrants, the full numbers of knights could not participate at the same time. So, the marshal of the tournament had declared there be two opening jousts. One hundred and fifty knights, seventy-five to each side, would battle. When this first wave of jousting ended—and it would end only when there were but seventy-five survivors—the next hundred-and-fifty knights would take the field. Again, only when there were seventy-five victors, would the knights of the first wave face those of the second.

Gwendolyn was in the first wave, which she was pleased about, and as she looked across the field, she saw that Morgan was not mounted and would be in the second wave.

Glad to postpone what she knew would be the inevitable, Gwendolyn accepted the lance James handed her. "Be aware of the riders on both sides," James cautioned. "They may put you off-stride."

Gwendolyn adjusted the shield on her left arm and used her spurs to move the heavy charger forward. Concentrating on the line of knights thirty yards across from her, Gwendolyn prepared her body for the first assault.

The trumpets signaled, and the sounds of hooves rose in the air. She braced herself in the saddle and charged forward. Her body moved as one with the horse, and the weight of her armor added to her comfort and confidence. As the two lines closed, she picked her opponent and dipped her lance once. Then only ten yards separated them, and the tip of the other knight's lance grew large.

Her body tensed, but she forced the tightness away as she heard Miles's voice in her mind. "Do not tense. Do not wait. Attack and believe your opponent unseated." And she did. Sir Eldwin, with her lower back braced and her shield held firm along her left side, met her first opponent. A bare second before their lances reached the shields, she saw his eyes go wide in warning and braced her arm. The sound of her own lance hitting his shield came at the same time as she felt the jarring impact upon her leather-covered shield, and a wave of unexpected pain raced through her shoulder.

She was lifted in the saddle, but did not loosen the grip on her lance. Suddenly, there was no more resistance, and she rode past the now riderless horse of her opponent.

It had ended faster than she'd thought possible. She had won her first joust, and the thrill of her victory raced headily through her mind. Wheeling her mount around, she gazed at the fallen knight. She did not know him, but he stood proudly before her and bobbed his head in salute. Gwendolyn rode close to him and returned his chivalrous compliment by dipping her lance in his honor.

Then, with the cheers of the crowd dwindling, Gwendolyn rode back to James and, with his help, dismounted from the ungainly charger.

"You did well, my lord," James stated proudly. "You defeated Simon of Northumber, a worthy knight."

Gwendolyn nodded, the only form of communication she could use while attired as Sir Eldwin, and watched the continuation of the first wave of jousts. A third of the knights of the first joust had been unseated, but until there were no more opponents, the second wave would not begin.

The horses charged, and the joust continued. Gwendolyn surveyed the crowd for a moment before glancing toward Richard. Seated around Richard and the archbishop was his military council, and among them, she saw Miles.

She wanted to go to him, but knew she could not, and only hoped he was as proud of her as she was of him. Knowing she must keep her attention focused on the fighting, Gwendolyn drew her eyes from Miles's form and concentrated on the men in the field.

Another hour passed and the first wave was ended. The survivors of the joust rested now, preparing for their next fight while the second wave mounted and rode onto the field of combat.

Gwendolyn glanced quickly to where Miles sat and saw his eyes fixed on Morgan. She, too, looked at the wide-set knight and felt the old familiar shiver of disgust when she saw his smiling lips.

Then the trumpet sounded and the horses charged. She watched Morgan's lance go level and saw him spur his horse harshly. The two lines met in a loud crashing noise. The sound of shattering lances echoed, and the screams of one knight ripped through the air.

The dust settled, and Gwendolyn gazed at the seated victors. Morgan sat on his horse proudly, but his lance was gone. Then Gwendolyn looked at the ground and saw Morgan's opponent writhing in pain, a piece of the lance's shaft protruding from his chest.

Revulsion filled her, and she tasted the bitterness of bile in the back of her throat. Death was no stranger to tournaments, but she still despised this senseless need to kill. When she looked at Morgan's face, she realized that death was the only thing he sought when facing an opponent, whether on the game field, or on the battlefield.

"You shall not win," she promised, but the words did not pass her lips; they only echoed in her mind.

By the time the sun passed its zenith, the first rounds of the joust were over, and the second had begun. This jousting would differ from the morning's in only one way. Half the knights had been eliminated, and there would be but one initial wave. This joust would continue, no matter how long it took, until the final two surviving knights faced each other. And, Gwendolyn was determined to be one of them.

Gwendolyn sat astride Miles's charger and gazed across the field. She had purposely chosen a spot diagonally across from Morgan, not because she feared him, but because she wanted to face him later.

The trumpet sounded, and again Gwendolyn's skin rippled with excitement. One hundred and fifty lances fell to the horizontal and the horses rushed forward.

Forcing her body to relax, Gwendolyn braced herself in the saddle. She met her opponent, and the loud cracking of lance on shield sounded in her ears. But this time she was not lifted from her saddle as her opponent's lance shattered at first impact. Her own lance shattered as well, and when she halted the charger, she turned to face the other knight. They bowed their heads and raced off to their squires to retrieve new lances, and Gwendolyn renewed her concentration and determination to be victorious.

By midafternoon there was not a part of Gwendolyn's

body that did not hurt. It had taken four runs to finally unseat her first opponent, and only her own self-confidence had helped her to win. Five more times she had ridden against other opponents, but none, save the first knight she'd faced, had survived her first charge. Gwendolyn, her mind blank except for her purpose, had become not only an extension of her charger, but had become as one with the lance. She had fought unmercifully, charging across the green swarth to hit her opponent's shield, and to be rewarded by the sound of a clean hit against the onrushing knight.

She had thought not about anything, but had concentrated solely on her immediate opponent. And, when the seventh knight who faced her had been dismounted, and she had returned to James's smiling face, she breathed a sigh of relief. She saw in his face that she had done what most would consider impossible. She had survived to the very end. But her taste of victory and relief was short-lived when the cheers of the spectators grew louder.

Turning, she froze. There was but one knight left to face, and recognition burned tightly in her chest. Morgan of Guildswood sat astride his charger, his shield lowered to his side, awaiting a new lance.

Gwendolyn thought of her sword, and of the powers it contained to help heal her, but even before the thought fully formed, she chased it away, as Miles's face floated before her eyes. "Do not waste the power. Your body is strong; rely on it."

I will, she thought, taking the new lance from James and riding to the center of the arena. The crowd quieted, and their silence made Gwendolyn's nerves grow tighter. Then Morgan rode up to her and stared at her masked face. A ripple of fear tugged in her mind that he might see through her mysterious facade and know whom he faced, but with his first words, that fear dissolved.

"Are you so ugly you cannot show yourself?" he asked.

Gwendolyn stared at him through the eyeholes for a long second before she turned her head toward the king.

Richard was standing, his arms again upraised. In one hand he held the scarlet sash of victory. "Let the joust be joined," he intoned. Both Gwendolyn and Morgan bowed their heads to him and turned their horses to face each other's. Gwendolyn dipped her lance in salute, and Morgan replied in kind.

But before she could spur the charger away, Morgan spoke again. "I will be the victor today, faceless one, and you shall lie broken at my feet in the place of your master, the coward who is too afraid to meet me on this field of honor." With that, Morgan spurred his charger across the field, accompanied by the cheers of his men-at-arms.

Yet Gwendolyn, upon hearing his words, felt no fear. Instead, a searing anger filled her, making her want nothing else but to defeat Morgan quickly and decisively, to pay him back for his cruelty, deceit, and hatred. She urged her mount across the field, but refused to force the now-tired horse into a run. She rode regally, and in response to this show, the crowd called loudly to her.

Gwendolyn stopped the charger at the gate and turned to face the crowd. She stood tall in the stirrups and dipped her lance once again to Richard. Then she sat deep in the saddle, hefted her shield, and lowered the lance.

As she did all this, she opened that special channel in her mind to draw upon its warmth and comfort, but did not call for its ethereal aid, nor ask for its help in defeating Morgan. Today was her first test, and Gwendolyn knew that she must win this joust by herself, for both herself and Miles. She let the light fill her, soothe her nerves, and shore up her determination. Her eyes focused on Morgan across the field, and she was suddenly aware of a dark aura surrounding him. She realized then that he was evil, that all about him radiated a black visage which could not be denied.

The trumpet sounded, and her highly trained instincts took over. Closing her mind to the light, she charged forward, the blackness surrounding Morgan also dissolving. All that remained was his bulky countenance. Then there was nothing left in creation, save the muscular horse beneath her, and the oncoming knight.

Adjusting her shield as she rode, she moved it a fraction to her left so that when their lances met, his would follow the curvature of the shield and be deflected properly. Suddenly time slowed, and it seemed they would never meet, as everything around Gwendolyn took on an otherworldliness.

Morgan grew larger, wider than before. The helmet he wore was stained dark, and the crossed nasal bar looked like a scar rather than metal protection.

Gwendolyn was aware of everything about him, including the point of the lance that suddenly dropped lower. *No!* she screamed in her mind when she saw his intent. He was going after her horse. It was a legal move, but one that was frowned on.

Reacting quickly, Gwendolyn pressed her knee into the charger's side and the horse moved over a foot. This move took Morgan by surprise and he lifted the lance higher while he maneuvered his mount anew.

Then there was no time for him to readjust as their lances met. Gwendolyn, her teeth clenched and her body ready, accepted the full force of his lance on her shield, and even as the wood met the leather, her arm moved instinctively, deflecting the blow as her lance hit the center of his shield. This time, unlike the previous jousts, Gwendolyn did not let her lance waver mercifully, but instead tightened her arm against her side and kept the long wooden pole firm.

She heard a loud cry of denial and saw Morgan's arms fly in the air as her lance ripped his shield from its binding. Then Morgan was flying backward, even as she passed him and slowed her mount. Everything returned to normal, and time resumed its usual fast pace.

Turning, Gwendolyn watched Morgan rise to his feet and glare at her. Although she did not hear his words, she read his lips plainly.

"I will have your life," he mouthed.

Then she could not watch any longer as James took the reins of the charger and led the hooded knight before King Richard.

She dismounted quickly and knelt before the king.

"Rise, Sir Eldwin, champion of the jousts, victor of the first day of our tournament," he said in a loud voice.

Gwendolyn did as she was told and faced her king. But when she looked at him, she also saw Miles behind him, a smile on his face, his green eyes sparkling proudly.

Richard placed the scarlet sash over her head and stepped back. "I have heard of your vows and accept them as they are meant."

Gwendolyn bowed low before Richard and then turned to the crowd. The spectators rose to their feet and cheered. Many women, seeing a mystery beneath the masked face, threw wildflowers at Sir Eldwin's feet when she walked toward the edge of the tournament field. They would return tomorrow to urge on this unknown knight in his quest for victory. The crowd now had a champion, and such a one as only the legends of their forefathers had spoken of.

Chapter Twelve

THE NIGHT OF THE FIRST day's tourney was one of celebration. The great hall was filled with people, as was the entire keep and the streets of the tent city. Within the great hall, knights talked of the day's joust, pointing out to each other just where they had made their mistakes. Boasting would then begin anew of how each of them would regain their prominence the next day, with either the bow, the axe, or the mace.

Richard, sitting at the High Table, joined in with his own comments, telling each of the bested knights what he had done wrong. But, as Miles watched, he wondered if Richard was but goading each of them so that his own blood-thirst could be sated.

Miles understood that for Richard, who had spent his life fighting, to sit and watch a tournament was a form of torture to the young monarch. Yet Richard, as king, could not be a part of this tournament.

Lifting his pewter cup, Miles sipped the wine and continued to watch the knights in the room. He wanted to be with Gwendolyn, for their time together was coming to an end. He would soon have to honor his obligation to Richard and leave with the king for the Holy Land. But the hour was still early, and the revelry in the hall not fully under way, and, therefore, he could not leave yet.

"Morgan is coming," whispered Arthur, covering his words by pouring Miles more wine. Following the direction of the squire's gaze, Miles saw Morgan of Guildswood enter the great hall.

Morgan wore a short tunic with the crest of Guildswood on his breast. Full leggings covered powerful thighs and calves, and a long dagger rested against one hip. Halfway across the hall his eyes met Miles's and he stopped. Hatred sparked from Morgan's dark orbs, but rather than react to it, Miles lifted his cup in salute.

The gesture caught Morgan off guard, and he turned from Miles to speak with another knight standing near him. Just then, Richard leaned over and called to Miles.

"Your Sir Eldwin has caught the people's fancy," remarked Richard.

"Their fancy?" Miles questioned, his eyes still on Morgan.

"All I have heard about since the end of this day's fighting has been about your knight. The people love this mysterious man. But Miles," Richard said, and the tone of his voice forced Miles's eyes from Morgan's, "will he win tomorrow, and the next day?"

"I believe Eldwin will be the victor when the tourney ends, Sire," Miles replied in a low voice.

"Morgan is not one to let it happen easily," came the deep voice of William Marshall as he took the seat between Miles and Richard.

"I have faith in Eldwin," Miles declared.

"You must. Wasn't that one of your squires attending him?" Richard asked.

"Yes, Sire. I have given James over to Sir Eldwin's service."

"Why have I never seen or heard of this knight before?" Marshall asked suddenly. His dark blue eyes probed Miles's face intensely.

Miles knew he was being tested by both men. "His father and mine were friends. My father made a deathbed promise that he would see to the young boy's training. But before he could, his uncle claimed him and there was nothing my father could do."

"A petition to the king?" Marshall queried.

"No, sir; the uncle took the boy to northern Wales. We could not go after him at the time; King Henry forbade it. It seemed your father," Miles said pointedly to Richard, "had plans for that area of Wales and did not want my father to do anything that would hold him back."

"That sounds familiar," Richard muttered.

"Then how did he come to your service?" Marshall asked, again proving that he never let anything deter him from his goal.

"Five years ago, his uncle died. Eldwin escaped and made his way to Radstock. There, he came to me and told me who he was. From that day on, he trained as a knight as my father had promised," Miles finished.

"But why the oath?" Richard asked, drawn into the story as only one who had felt the restraining hand of battling guardians could.

"Sire, it seems Eldwin had a very powerful vision, and because of that he took his oath."

"He must be strong-willed," Marshall muttered.

"Sir Eldwin is more than that," Miles shot back, holding Marshall's challenging stare with his own.

"No matter what he is, and no matter if he wins the tournament or not, I shall knight him for this day's victory alone, if need be," Richard said.

Miles held his face expressionless, but felt relief. Richard believed the story, and that was what mattered. Yet Marshall's face still held some doubt.

"No, Sire. Eldwin will not accept that. He wants to prove himself and earn his reward."

"He is prideful," Richard said after a moment.

"Sir Eldwin is as idealistic as he is good. He will win," Miles declared.

"He will not!" came the coarse voice of Morgan who had come to the High Table unobserved by those in conversation.

Miles gazed into Morgan's sneering features and felt a cold chill. He shook his head slowly and insultingly turned back to Richard. "As I have said, my lord," Miles repeated, "Sir Eldwin will be victorious."

"Or dead!" Morgan stated as his hand went to the hilt of his dagger. Miles refused to look at the knight, and kept his eyes level with the king's.

"You fought well today, Morgan of Guildswood. There is no shame in losing to Eldwin," Richard told the angered knight.

"It was but a trick. He swerved his horse at the last moment," Morgan defended.

"Do you think a Saracen would do elseways?" William Marshall cut in. Morgan, again caught off guard, glared at Marshall.

"I would expect such from them, but not from a Frankish knight, as they call us."

"Was not your lance held low?" Miles asked in a mild voice.

"Do not anger me, Delong, or there will be yet more blood spilled!"

Miles had trained himself to hold his anger in check, but Morgan's brash threat broke his will power and a sudden rage took hold of him. Standing quickly, he grasped the handle of his dagger and faced Morgan across the wide table.

"If it's blood you hunger for, perhaps you should drink of your own," Miles spat, drawing his dagger. Morgan's blade was out in a flash. A sudden silence fell in the hall, as all eyes focused on the two knights. Before anything could happen, Marshall grabbed Miles, pinning his arms to his sides.

"There will be no fighting among my men!" decreed Richard, who stood, glaring at both Miles and Morgan. "May I suggest, Sir Morgan, that you save your energy for the field tomorrow. You have points to regain."

Shaking with anger, Morgan bowed to Richard. "As you say, Sire." Morgan sheathed his blade and walked from the great hall with every eye following his exit.

"That was stupid," Marshall chided.

"The man angers me," Miles replied after he, too, had sheathed his dagger.

"You took something from him; he seeks revenge. I hope your Sir Eldwin does not fall victim to it," Richard said.

"Or to the women who have besieged his tent," Marshall added with a laugh.

"Besieged?" asked Miles, taken aback by the old knight's words.

"Aye, it seems the bards are already telling the tale of the masked knight. He is a romantic figure to all the maidens, and to quite a few who are far from that age."

Smiling, Miles shook his head slowly.

"Do you know something we should?" Marshall asked when he saw Miles's strange reaction.

"No, I find it amusing that with all the men who seek the maidens' charms, they should chase the only one whom they cannot have."

"He has taken a vow of chastity, also?" Richard asked, incredulously.

"Hardly, Sire, but when in tournament, he reserves his strength for his opponents."

"Perhaps a few of these men should learn from that example," Marshall said with a barking laugh as he swept his hand around the room. Miles and Richard both joined in his laughter as they saw various knights fondling whatever women came within reach.

A moment later, Miles called Arthur to him and whispered orders. Arthur quickly departed, and within half an hour, Miles bid his king and Marshall good-night.

"We look forward to seeing your knight upon the field tomorrow," Richard called in parting.

Miles left the great hall and walked directly to the tents of Radstock. Twenty feet from the tent he froze. The path was five deep in people, and most were the peasant women of whom Marshall had spoken. They stood patiently, awaiting just a glimpse of their new champion, and more than one lewd comment reached Miles's ears.

Taking a deep breath, Miles headed into the crowd. The insignia of his rank opened a path and, without looking at the people, he went straight to the tent's opening where Arthur and James stood guard at the entrance. When Miles reached it, they opened the flap and let him in, following quickly behind.

When he stood in the center, Gwendolyn rose and embraced him. "What do they want of me?" she asked when they parted.

"You are their hero today. They just want to see you again. Put on your surcoat and mask."

With her mask in place, Gwendolyn paused by her equipment. She didn't know why, but some inner sense warned her to take the sword. Carrying it unsheathed, she stood next to Miles.

James and Arthur went first, and then Miles. Finally, Gwendolyn stepped into the night, and as she did, a loud cry rang out. Her throat tightened when she surveyed the crowd. Slowly, she bowed her head. The name of Sir Eldwin rose from fifty throats, and Gwendolyn lifted the silver sword high.

Satisfied that their hero had come out to greet them, many in the crowd began to leave. Miles turned to Gwendolyn, smiling as he motioned the squires to open the tent's entrance.

When she turned, Gwendolyn's senses flared in warning and, lifting the sword, she spun around at the ready. The whistling of an arrow sounded loud in her ears, and her hand, guided without her realizing it, moved in a blur.

The sound of an arrowhead hitting metal echoed distinctly. Everyone froze as a feathered shaft fell to the ground. Then a new cheer rang out, for those who had witnessed Sir Eldwin's deflection of the arrow by the sword cried out a new belief of their champion. Miles, reacting quickly, ushered Gwendolyn and the squires inside.

"Why?" Gwendolyn asked after she took off her mask.

"Morgan." Miles spat and related the tale of what had happened in the great hall between himself and Morgan.

"He will pay for this," Gwendolyn swore.

"No!" Miles stated fiercely.

"He tried to kill one of us," Gwendolyn whispered.

"Not one of us—you. But he failed. Gwendolyn, how did you know?"

"I didn't. I sensed something, and it happened. Miles, I can't explain it. My arm seemed to move of itself."

"Arthur, I want three of my knights posted outside . . . Guy, Poole, and Talen. Tell them what has happened, and to be on the watch for any of Guildswood's men. James, stand the first watch until the men arrive. Then I want you and Arthur to sleep in my tent. Answer no summons except for mine," he ordered.

When the squires were gone, Miles held Gwendolyn's hand tightly. "Do not let this disturb you; you need your concentration for tomorrow."

"You were wrong," she told him when the squires had gone.

"Wrong?"

"The arrow—it was not meant for me, it was meant for you."

"No."

"Yes. Miles, if you were killed, Morgan would be free to

take me from Radstock. He would petition Richard and show prior claim. He would also take the lands."

"I think not."

"It is so. Miles, I did not stop that shaft. I heard it and my arm moved. But I did not do anything!"

"Your instincts are good," Miles argued, choosing to ignore the meaning of her words.

Gwendolyn sighed and shrugged her shoulders. "Miles, I . . ." But she could not go on.

"Come, let us sleep together. You must rest and be fresh for the morrow."

"Yes, my lord," Gwendolyn replied. And in that moment she realized Miles had known the destination of the shaft all along.

The morning of the second day of the tournament was as cloudless as the first. The air was crisp, and the scents of the cooking fires chased away the smells of the overcrowded streets.

Within the tent of Sir Eldwin, James was dressing the knight for the tournament while Arthur checked each shaft that Gwendolyn would shoot.

"It will be a long day," Miles warned as he began to explain to Gwendolyn what she would be facing today. "They say the archery will be the fiercest in years. Richard has once again shown his greed and opened the competition to all, even peasants. If a peasant wins, he will gain a gold purse, but they have also paid dearly."

"You have taught me the longbow's use quite well," Gwendolyn replied confidently.

"I speak of this only because I want you to know that if you do not win, it has no effect on the tournament as a whole."

"I shall do my best."

"It is this afternoon that worries me," Miles admitted.

"Hold your worry until the proper time. I will avoid Morgan for as long as possible, I promise you that."

"You must be quick. You must not let anyone's blow land on you."

Gwendolyn stared at Miles for a moment while James cinched her gambeson. Then, with a half smile, she lifted her mask and put it on, effectively ending any further conversation.

Miles shook his head, but knew there could be no more talk. "I will cheer for you," he told her as he left the tent.

"He worries greatly for you," James said while anchoring her coif-de-maille into place.

Putting her hand on his shoulder, Gwendolyn squeezed it gently. She saw within his young, intelligent eyes the understanding of what she tried to convey.

With James walking behind her, she left the tent. Outside, people lined the pathway, cheering for their mysterious champion.

Then she was on the field. Together with all the contestants, she walked in rank before the king's stand. The sun was strong today, and Gwendolyn sweated beneath the maille. But she ignored the unpleasantness while she surveyed her competition. All the knights who remained uninjured from yesterday's joust were on the field and, in addition, there were perhaps thirty peasants.

Again, as he had yesterday, the Archbishop of Canterbury stood next to the king and offered the day's benediction. When he finished, Richard spoke.

"The archers of England have always been the finest in the world. Their aim has always been true, and because of them, we have been victorious time and again. Today we shall learn who is the best longbowman in our country."

The spectators were silent as they watched the most colorful king England had known for generations. But, when his hands rose, and the fur-collared mantle fell back from his arms, a low roar grew from their combined throats.

"Let the tournament begin," he proclaimed.

Bedlam broke loose when the contestants returned to their squires and the first of the archers lined up on the mark. Even while Gwendolyn walked toward James, she became aware of a sound breaking above the noise of the crowd. She stopped when she realized what it was. From hundreds of throats, the name of Sir Eldwin was being called. Turning, Sir Eldwin looked toward the spectators and raised a mailled hand in salute. The shouts grew louder, following Gwendolyn as she walked towards James.

There, she watched the first fifty archers notch their

shafts. Her eyes were drawn to a tall, thin man who stood half a head higher than the rest. No matter how hard Gwendolyn tried to draw her eyes from the tall man, she could not. His face was gaunt, its lines severe, but she saw that among them all, he was the most relaxed.

Then the king's chamberlain lifted his staff and banged its tip three times. The archers, who were made up of the thirty peasants, as well as twenty squires who wanted to test their aim, drew their longbows and let fly the shafts.

Two minutes later, the three judges, William Marshall among them, returned from the targets. They went to the chamberlain and gave the results.

"Ten archers have hit the center mark," declared the chamberlain. He called out the names, and the crowd responded with applause. But Gwendolyn still watched the tall archer who she knew had hit dead center. "Robin Locksley," called the chamberlain at last. The tall man bowed once and walked from the field.

The next group of fifty went to the mark, and when their arrows were scored, only two had reached center. The third wave of archers stepped forward, and Gwendolyn's eyes locked with Morgan's. He stood at the mark, but he looked at Sir Eldwin, and all could see the challenge written across his features.

The arrows were notched, yet Morgan still stared at Gwendolyn. Only when the signal to shoot came did Morgan take his eyes away. He seemed careless to those who watched. Drawing back his bow, he fired almost without taking aim. As soon as his shaft was loosened, his eyes went back to Gwendolyn, seemingly uninterested in the results.

When the winners' names were called, only one rang out. "Morgan of Guildswood, dead center." Even with his name ringing in the air, Morgan acknowledged nothing. His eyes remained fixed on Gwendolyn's in challenge.

Then Gwendolyn was walking toward the line, and the air was filled with the name of Sir Eldwin. Forcing herself to concentrate on her task, Gwendolyn shut all else out. She stared at the target two hundred feet away and made herself breathe easily. She strung the longbow and lifted three shafts. Gazing at each carefully, she chose the one that looked the most perfect.

When the call to mark came, she once again heard Miles's patient voice within her mind. *"Do not rush. Breathe deeply and hold. When you are ready, exhale while you release the shaft. Concentrate on your target, concentrate. . . ."*

Gwendolyn drew her breath in slowly while she pulled back the gut. Concentrating on the target, she let herself become one with the powerful hardwood bow. Suddenly she felt the bow vibrate and forced her muscles to steady it. When the tip of the shaft pointed properly, she let loose the string.

The shaft arced smoothly, and as the rest of her breath left her, she watched it fly true to its mark. Lowering the bow, she waited until the judges withdrew the shafts.

Three names were called this round, Sir Eldwin's the first. When her name was announced, Gwendolyn turned to face Morgan. The sneer on his mouth sent a lance of rage shooting through her, and it took all her will power not to challenge him directly. Instead, still staring at him, she bowed her head, and was rewarded by Morgan turning his back to her.

Gwendolyn stayed where she was, and the rest of the survivors of the first round came to their marks. There were twenty-two of them. Morgan stood three men away from Gwendolyn, but to her surprise, the tall peasant came to the spot next to her.

"My compliments, Sir Eldwin. That was a fine shot."

Sir Eldwin nodded to him, in reply.

"I have heard of your vows, and respect them. I am Robin Locksley, of Nottingham," he said in introduction.

When the call to mark came, Gwendolyn chose a new shaft. She glanced at Morgan, who was again glaring at her.

"Concentrate," whispered Locksley, "do not let his anger reach you."

With that, Gwendolyn drew back the longbow and willed herself to think only of the target. She let fly her shaft and heard the echoes of the other bows. Again, when she looked at her target, she saw her aim had been true.

"Well done," Locksley said. Gwendolyn nodded to the man, wondering just who he was. He wore the poorly dyed clothing of a peasant, but spoke with the accent of a nobleman.

Of the twenty-two, only ten survived—Sir Eldwin, Morgan, and Locksley among them. The remaining archers toed their mark, and once more Gwendolyn drew back the powerful bow. Letting loose another shaft, she saw her arrow strike dead on center.

This time Morgan did not look at her. His arrow, too, had reached the proper mark, but just barely. Now there were six. The crowd was on its feet, every voice exhorting its chosen champion. Yet, as Gwendolyn listened to the names called out by the populace, she heard not the name of Locksley.

But Gwendolyn had recognized in the way the man stood, and the way he held his bow, that there was not a better bowman in the tournament. She could not cheer him, so instead, as the archers chose their next shafts, Sir Eldwin's mailled hand fell across Locksley's. In it, was one of her arrows.

Locksley gazed at the knight's masked face for a moment. "My thanks, my lord," Locksley said in a low voice. Gwendolyn watched him notch the arrow and face the targets. Behind him she saw Morgan, his face dark with silent rage at this new affront.

Gwendolyn drew back her bow, and at the call, loosened the shaft. But even as it flew, she knew she had lost her concentration. When her shaft sank into the target, she saw it had barely missed the center mark. Quickly, she glanced at the other targets. Morgan's shaft was again dead center, as was Locksley's. She and the other three knights had lost. Only Locksley and Morgan were left.

Gwendolyn turned and looked toward the king's stand. She saw Richard, and behind him, Miles. Miles nodded, no disappointment showing on his face. But, by the time Gwendolyn reached James, Miles had appeared.

"You let Morgan break your concentration," he whispered.

Gwendolyn stared at him for a long moment, forcing herself to think back to the final shot. Then she remembered when she had drawn the shaft back, letting her eyes flicker toward Morgan.

"He will not win in any event," Miles remarked.

Gwendolyn studied Miles's features for a moment, before

looking back at the two remaining archers. The chamberlain stood behind them, waiting until their arrows were notched. Then he called them to their marks.

She watched as Morgan drew back his bow, and Locksley did the same. They released the arrows at the same time, and the sound of gut reverberated in the air. The arrows flew true, and both landed dead center.

Then Richard stood, and in a loud voice called for the final shoot. "One target. One shot," he decreed.

Both Morgan and Locksley bowed to signify their acceptance. This time, with the crowd shouting only Morgan's name, the two archers stood side by side and drew their bows. Gwendolyn's breath caught when she saw it was her arrow Locksley had notched once again.

Morgan let loose first, and even as his arrow was sailing toward the target, Locksley's bow twanged and his shaft followed.

A great cry wafted from the crowd when first one arrow struck the target and then the second. This time no one could see the results as Marshall and the two other judges stepped directly in front of the target. They lifted the leather-covered board and carried it to Richard.

The crowd gasped as one when they saw the two shafts almost touching. Carefully, Marshall pointed to the one closest the center.

"Robin Locksley of Nottingham!" he yelled for all to hear.

Both Gwendolyn and Miles stared at Morgan, whose face grew darker with Richard's words. He turned and walked to his men, and Gwendolyn felt a twinge of fear as she suddenly remembered the dark aura she had seen surround him yesterday. She knew that this afternoon Morgan would be more dangerous than ever.

But not even her worry of Morgan interfered when she listened to Richard commending Locksley.

"You have stood well today, Robin Locksley, and all the men of England are proud of you. Your victory has earned you a purse of gold," Richard declared, holding up a heavy leather purse. "To the victor goes the spoils," he added, throwing the purse to Locksley.

But when the tall peasant rose from his knees, the purse

clutched tightly in his hand, he did not turn to leave; rather, he faced Richard bravely and spoke. "Sire, may I request a boon?" he asked.

The crowd hushed at his words, some plainly frightened, others aghast at his audaciousness. Yet, Gwendolyn sensed there was more to this peasant than met the eye, and silently cheered him on.

Richard, for his part, always the champion of the brave and foolhardy, merely nodded. "I seem to be plagued with requests and boons for this tournament," he stated acerbically. "Speak your mind."

"Sire, I wish you to know that the men of the north country are behind you and look forward to many years of a good reign. Because of this, and in the name of the common people of England, I wish to donate this purse to aid you in your fight against the Saracen."

Richard seemed taken back by the peasant's words, but his majestic bearing overcame the surprise and he nodded slowly. "With my thanks, and England's, I accept your offer," Richard replied.

Locksley smiled and insolently tossed the heavy purse back to Richard. Then, instead of leaving, he spoke once again. "Sire, do not leave your country unattended for too long; there are those who would take it from you."

"And you?" Richard asked quickly, staring intensely at the peasant dressed in green.

"I will but try to hold it for you, your Majesty," he said in a tight voice.

The tension was thick in the air, and the grumblings of the nobility sounded dangerous. Richard merely laughed, then became serious. "I shall count on you."

"Thank you, Sire," Locksley said, bowing once again. The cheers of the common people grew louder, for before them was a champion who had stolen the day from their lords and masters, and for one very rare moment, they felt themselves transformed from their poor existence.

"There is something about him that is strong," Miles commented, studying the man who walked toward them. Locksley stopped three feet away, bowed his head, and then extended Gwendolyn's shaft to her.

"I thank you for not looking down upon me, and am in

your debt," he said formally. "Guard yourselves well this day, for word is that Morgan means to destroy you both." With that, the tall archer left.

"We must discuss this this afternoon," Miles said suddenly, but he was not looking at Gwendolyn; rather, his eyes stayed on Locksley's back until he was swallowed by the crowd of celebrants.

Chapter Thirteen

"DAMN IT, WOMAN—LISTEN to me!" Miles yelled through clenched teeth, his tall, muscular body blocking Gwendolyn's.

"Don't yell at me, my lord. My mind is made up."

"I forbid it!"

Gwendolyn stared at Miles for a moment and then reached for her leather mask. His fingers grasped her wrist and held it steady.

"Don't hide behind the mask. Face me. You cannot do what you are planning," he told her in a quieter voice.

Gwendolyn tried to raise her arm, but Miles's strength was too much for her. Yet she refused to yield, and he refused to relinquish his hold. A moment later she nodded, and Miles released her wrist.

"I am not fighting you, Husband, I am doing what I must."

"You are going to be hurt."

"Do you think your training bad? Or do you have so little faith in my ability?"

"You cannot face Morgan with a mace," he said.

"I have no intention of doing so."

"He will come after you," Miles warned.

"Miles, please, I know what I'm doing. Morgan is a good strategist. He has baited us, and he has made you afraid for our confrontation—no," Gwendolyn said, cutting off Miles's protest. "I do not mean you fear him, but he has made you afraid for me. I must face him eventually, because we both know that by the end of this tournament only Morgan or I shall be victorious."

"He has a bloodlust for anything of Radstock."

"And that will be his defeat. Trust me, Husband, I know what I must do. I know as surely as I know Morgan."

"Then do it," Miles said, relenting against what he knew would be an argument without end.

"My lord," Gwendolyn whispered. "Your blessings?"

"They are always with you. James! Arthur! Attend to Sir Eldwin," he shouted.

The squires returned to finish the job Miles had interrupted, and soon Gwendolyn was ready. Hanging on a double-hooked sash was the battle-axe Miles had had fashioned for her, but in her hand she held the heavy wooden handle of a tournament mace, with its leaded morningstar hanging menacingly. That was what she and Miles had argued about. He wanted her to fight only with the axe, but Gwendolyn wanted to begin with the mace.

What she had in mind was a risky plan, but if it succeeded, it would enable her to face Morgan late in the fighting and be better prepared.

Although she held the same fears that Miles did, she knew Morgan would not go after her in the beginning. He wanted the crowd to see them battle, and see him defeat her. His two biggest flaws were his anger and his ego. She was confident she could use them against him.

Finally, within the heavy protection of her chain maille armor, she heard the trumpets call the combatants to the field. With Arthur and James behind her, carrying extra maces and shields, Sir Eldwin walked to the field and joined ranks with the other knights to face King Richard and begin the third phase of the tourney.

Of the three hundred knights who had begun the tournament, hoping to be named an earl at its conclusion, barely a hundred stood on the field. There was no naming of opponents, just a challenge from one to another. Like the jousting, the mace wielding would involve all knights. After the first combat, those who were victorious would face another, and the battle would continue until there were but two knights fighting in the final confrontation.

Gwendolyn was troubled by Miles's outburst, and his anger at her desire to fight with the mace. She knew she could handle it well, as Miles himself had often told her. But she recognized, too, the need within herself to prove she could battle as a knight, with any type of weapon.

Gwendolyn also knew that her speed and mobility, even with the extra weight of her armor, would be an asset in this fight. Miles had spent many long hours teaching her how to move; how to fall and roll and regain her feet without conscious effort.

The sun was burning brilliantly in the sky when the call to arms came. From the moment she stepped upon the grassy sward, she fixed her eyes on Morgan's bulky figure, watching him maneuver himself until he had chosen his spot. When he was set, Gwendolyn moved across the grass to stand on the same side as he.

Glancing at Miles, she saw his approving smile. Sir Eldwin would not face Morgan in the first round.

Standing beneath the blistering sun and ignoring the heat, Gwendolyn gazed through the eyeslits of her mask and chose her opponent. With a nod, and a flick of the mace's ball, she challenged the knight. The man accepted and bowed his head to her. That very gesture was being repeated along the two lines of knights, as they followed the code of chivalry that governed this tournament.

When the trumpets sounded again, the knights came forward. Gwendolyn lifted her shield and let her opponent's ball ricochet harmlessly from it. It was a testing shot, and she felt barely a twinge on her arm; yet, she held her mace back, still waiting. She knew not to waste her strength or energy in testing an opponent with this weapon. When she was ready to strike, it would be swift and sure.

Suddenly the knight lifted his mace and whirled it over his head. Gwendolyn did not let the movement distract her, and held her eyes on his dark brown ones. With his mace spinning in a blur, Gwendolyn dropped low, raised her shield, and flung the head of the mace in a sideways arc. The rounded ball hit the knight in his side, and, once again, Gwendolyn avoided her opponent's deadly sphere with her shield. But this time the ball landed solidly, and the shock of the contact raced along her arm.

Ignoring it, Gwendolyn recovered. She whirled the mace's ball and charged the knight. His shield came up, but too late, as the heavy ball hit his shoulder squarely.

She saw pain flash across the man's face, even as she backstepped and began to whirl the mace anew. But she did not attack. She waited until the knight had regained his balance, and only then did she come ahead. Respect shone in her opponent's eyes as he met her new charge.

Time flew quickly while they traded blows. Her shoulder was becoming numb from the repeated assault on her shield, and she realized she must not let this go on much longer. Ducking a swift blow, Gwendolyn turned, holding the wooden handle behind her back. Lunging suddenly, she cast her arm forward, and the ball whistled in the air. The knight misjudged Gwendolyn's reach, and the ball skimmed over the top of his shield, crashing into his helmet.

Gwendolyn held herself ready while she stared at the man. Then, slowly, his eyes closed, and he fell to the ground unconscious.

Her breath came in harsh gasps as she fought to control the surging of her blood. She had won, and won with the mace. Glancing around, she saw many knights still fighting, and knew she would have a few minutes to recover.

James ran out to her, taking her shield and mace as her opponent's squire raced to his master's prostrate form. Gwendolyn stood there waiting, watching the thin streak of blood seeping from beneath the other knight's helmet. But, by the time the squire had helped the knight to his feet, he had regained his senses.

"Well done, Sir Eldwin," the knight called as he leaned on his squire.

Gwendolyn bowed low to her opponent in reply. Turning, she walked back to James. "You fought well, my lord," James said.

"But you were slow on the second assault," came Miles's voice from behind her.

Gwendolyn spun to face him. He smiled warmly, and the tension eased from her muscles.

"Don't be so gallant. You were lucky. Sir Jason believes in fighting honorably. Very few do. Damn it! Realize that you're facing mercenaries. They are fighting out there to win more than praise. They want an earldom, and they'll do anything they can to gain it. Don't hold back again; I want you alive," he added in a quieter voice.

Gwendolyn stared at the hand he had balled in emphasis of

his words. Silently, she covered it with her gauntleted one and pressed it tightly.

Then, James was at her side, slipping on a new shield and handing her the mace. She glanced quickly at Miles before walking out on the field again.

Although there had been fifty victors, only twenty knights remained. Many of the victors had been too badly hurt to continue. As Gwendolyn stepped into the ranks, she saw Morgan eye her and then join the same line as she.

Smiling to herself, she knew she had baited him properly. He would face defeat rather than miss the opportunity to face her alone.

The trumpets sounded, and Gwendolyn dipped her head formally to her new opponent, who unlike Sir Jason, ignored this formality and charged her straight on.

Gwendolyn spun and raised her shield simultaneously, ducking under the hiss of the mace and, as the knight slipped past her, using her shield, rather than the lead ball, to hit his unprotected side in warning.

Then, when the knight faced her, she heeded Miles's words and attacked him relentlessly. The mace was like lightning in her hands, as she used it in the double-circle method of striking that Miles had taught her. The other knight tried to ward off her attack, but Gwendolyn was lost to the music of the fight and the whistle of the morningstar. Nothing could prevent her charge. She heard not the cheers of the crowd, nor the sounds of the other knights in combat. All she saw was her foe before her, his shield torn to ribbons, his mace never landing upon her.

Her attack was so furious that the knight could not stand in place and was forced to retreat. He backstepped, continually deflecting the lead ball with his shield, until there was nothing but tattered remains of the once-leather-covered wood.

Gwendolyn, heedless of the spectators' cries for blood, continued on. Then it happened—the knight tripped over another fallen victim and lay on the ground defenseless.

Gwendolyn, with the sweet taste of her victory filling her, jumped over the body of the first knight to stand above her opponent.

Her mailled foot moved like lightning, pinning his wrist to

the ground, his mace useless. Whirling her mace above her head, Gwendolyn saw the knight's eyes widen. She swiftly swung it down, and the dull thud of lead upon the earth, inches from the knight's head, sounded loud in her ears. Then wordlessly, she waited.

"I yield," the knight whispered. Instantly, Gwendolyn's foot left his wrist and she stepped back. She waited for the knight to rise, and when he did, she once again bowed to her conquered opponent.

Grudgingly he returned the courtesy before turning his back and walking from the field in defeat. Again, a loud cheering rose when Sir Eldwin looked at the crowd. Turning, Sir Eldwin looked to see who remained.

As Gwendolyn glanced across the field, she saw Morgan standing over his opponent, his mace hanging limply in his hand. A wide, animalistic sneer was on his face as he looked at her in renewed challenge. Looking down, Gwendolyn saw his opponent unmoving upon the ground, and saw, too, a steady stream of blood flowing from beneath the cracked helmet.

Instantly, she knew he had killed yet another of England's knights in his attempt to win everything set before him. She shook her head sadly at the sight before walking back to her position by James.

Upon reaching James, Gwendolyn sighed loudly.

"Have you been hurt?" he asked quietly.

Gwendolyn shook her head and dropped the mace. She began to wind her arm in circles, loosening the cramps the last contest had brought out. She realized she was tiring, but fought against it with every ounce of strength she possessed.

"Hold this," Miles said, handing her a rope-encased stone. She looked at it and then at Miles. "It's much heavier than the mace. Hold it for a while, then the mace will feel lighter."

Gwendolyn took the heavy rock, and while she held it, Miles spoke again. "You handled the last man well. Try to end the next fight quickly. You were right; Morgan is counting on you to win. He wants you badly."

When the trumpet sounded, Gwendolyn released the rope and took the mace from James. It was just as Miles had said. The mace felt light once again. Taking several deep, preparatory breaths, she crossed the field and stood next to Morgan. She faced her next opponent, the one she must defeat in order to meet Morgan.

This time, instead of waiting for the call, she bowed formally. Her opponent returned the courtesy, squared his shoulders, and hefted the mace. She watched the man's eyes, tensing her body for the first attack. The trumpet sounded and, moving swiftly, Gwendolyn backstepped before the knight could strike.

He shook his head and came on. She saw his lips moving, but did not hear his words. Then she realized he was not speaking aloud, but urging himself on. He had seen Sir Eldwin's prowess and was nerving himself to best her.

Intuitively, Gwendolyn stopped and, even as she lifted her mace, charged the knight. She accepted the full strike of his rounded morningstar on her shield while she whipped her own mace over the leather rim. She caught the chain of his mace with her own and, still having the advantage of surprise, moved her wrist whiplike and yanked sharply.

Before the knight realized her strategy, his mace was entangled in hers, and was ripped from his hand. The duel had taken no more than twenty seconds, but with the knight weaponless, there was no choice but to yield. Gallantly, Sir Eldwin lowered her mace, and shield and waited.

Her opponent threw down his shield and bowed. "I yield," he said in a bitter voice.

Again, from a multitude of voices, the name of Sir Eldwin carried across the field. But Gwendolyn did not look at the people calling her name. Instead, she watched the final battle between Morgan and his opponent. The man Morgan fought, fought well, and it seemed an even fight.

The blows of their maces upon each other's shields were like a musician's beat. For several minutes they fought, maneuvering around each other carefully. Then Morgan turned, and Gwendolyn knew he saw her from the corner of his eye. A loud bellow spewed from his mouth and he attacked his opponent. The mace flew so fast it was barely a blur, and under his bull-like assault, the other knight gave way. Slowly, unmercifully, Morgan weakened his opponent's defenses.

With a sudden change in direction, Morgan lashed out, and the leaded morningstar crashed through the knight's shield, splintering it to pieces. The knight fought vainly, but without his shield his body became the target of Morgan's ball.

The fight was over, everyone saw that, but Morgan of Guildswood gave him no chance to yield. A sudden rage filled Gwendolyn, forcing her toward the fighting knights. Just as Morgan was about to raise his mace again, Sir Eldwin jumped between them, holding her shield high to protect the other knight.

"I yield!" he shouted loud enough for all to hear.

When Gwendolyn lowered her shield, she stared into Morgan's hate-widened eyes. Knowing he could not strike with impunity, he spat at her feet and threw down his mace. When he turned his back, Gwendolyn slipped her shield from her arm and flung it at him. It struck his shoulder and Morgan spun.

What he saw froze him to the spot. Sir Eldwin's gaunt-leted hand was outstretched, a mailled index finger pointing directly at him in challenge.

"You will not walk from this field!" he swore. Then he turned and went to his squire. While he did, James ran to Sir Eldwin, a new mace hanging from his hand. The squire picked up the discarded shield and handed it to Gwendolyn.

The crowd had become silent. Tension filled the air, and the smell of excitement wafted from the people. While she waited for Morgan to arm himself, she glanced at Richard and saw him staring intently at her while William Marshall spoke in his ear.

Then she sought Miles and found him standing with Ar-thur near her equipment. Their eyes met and locked, and Gwendolyn saw both his faith and his trust in her reach out.

Then Morgan was crossing the field again. On his arm was a fresh shield, the dark crest of Guildswood covering its surface. Her eyes moved even as she heard the gasp from the crowd. He carried not a mace, but a Saxon axe.

Gwendolyn's eyes narrowed as she gave James back the shield. She had hoped to lure him to her own fight and had done so. The crowd gasped when they saw James walk from the field with the kite-shaped shield and cheered when Sir Eldwin unhooked the curved-handled axe that had been affixed to the armor throughout the afternoon's fight.

Gwendolyn stared at Morgan and, for the first time, she

saw a flicker of doubt cross his face. Hefting the specially made axe, she swung it several times in the pattern she'd always used in practice.

She stared at Morgan and bowed her head. Then she turned her back to him and bowed toward Richard. The crowd cried out, but she was prepared for Morgan's surprise attack and rolled forward in a neat somersault, letting Morgan's axe whistle harmlessly in the empty space she had occupied just a bare second before.

Then she was on her feet, stepping toward Morgan before he could recover from the swing. Her axe whipped between them to bite into the center of his shield. With a quick two-handed jerk, she freed the head and stepped back just as Morgan swung at her again.

Then he stopped and began to gauge her. His first attempts had failed, and Morgan knew he was in for his toughest fight. He lunged forward, using the pointed backend of the axe as a lance, but Eldwin sidestepped and used her axe shaft to knock his blow aside.

They circled each other, and suddenly Gwendolyn saw the dark aura that encased him. She tried to force it away, but could not, and thus misjudged his next attack. She was unable to move aside, and the edge of his axe hit her shoulder, biting through the chain maille and leather. She fell with the blow, letting her body be directed by its force, thus lessening the axe's strike and avoiding the sharp edge's full penetration. When she hit the ground she rolled quickly, bringing the handle of her axe across her face, knowing that Morgan would be trying for the kill.

She ignored the pain that lanced through her shoulder and saw that she had been right. Morgan's axe was descending in a killing blur. Gwendolyn bit her lip to stop from screaming out her rage and straightened her arms.

Morgan's axe head missed her handle, and when his own handle struck hers, it was like the sound of a thunderclap. Pain raced along Gwendolyn's arms, and again she thought she would cry out.

Morgan did not pull the axe back; rather, he leaned his weight full upon it, trying to break the lock Gwendolyn held her elbows in. Suddenly, Gwendolyn drew her knees in and lashed upward, drawing on her will power to make her muscles obey. Morgan's scream of denial rang loudly as she lifted him from the ground and, using a combination of legs, arms, and his own bulkiness, flipped him over her head.

She rolled again and quickly stood, her breathing ragged, her muscles screaming out their protest. Still she held her ground and waited while Morgan regained his feet.

She forced herself not to see the blackness that surrounded Morgan. She saw only his eyes, and the hatred pouring from them. Before he could move, Gwendolyn, using both hands, swung at him. Morgan stepped back, and the blade passed within an inch of his face. Relief swept across his features, but he had never seen Sir Eldwin work the battle-axe.

Even as she swung, her arms were reversing, and when the axe passed near Morgan's face it seemed to waver in the air. Then, it was returning from the opposite direction, and Morgan barely raised his shield in time. He deflected the blow, but again, Eldwin's axe wavered hauntingly before coming at him again.

Morgan backstepped quickly, trying to adjust to this new attack. But the faster he moved his shield, the faster Eldwin changed the axe's direction.

Gwendolyn followed his retreat, knowing she must not let up. She swung ceaselessly, and with each pass, pieces of Morgan's shield flew away. Her left shoulder was beginning to ache badly, and she realized that his axe had penetrated the three layers of armor, striking her flesh.

Forcing away the pain, Gwendolyn continued her attack until suddenly, Morgan ducked beneath one harsh blow and spun away. He screamed and charged. Gwendolyn sidestepped, and Morgan's wild slash grazed her left arm, another blaze of pain erupting even as she withdrew to await his next attack.

Then she saw his face, and the savage smile that spread across it. He had seen the blood seeping through the maille, and now stalked her mercilessly. Taking a deep breath, Gwendolyn prepared to face him. Morgan came on, but he stopped suddenly. Gwendolyn held herself at bay, waiting to see what his next move would be.

Morgan began to circle her slowly, and she had no choice but to follow. Halfway around, he lunged toward her. Gwendolyn raised her axe and warded off the blow, spinning to her left, and at the same time lashing out at him.

Her axe met Morgan's and the two shafts of wood came together. Then Morgan, using all his great weight, lunged forward, forcing Gwendolyn back. He stepped back suddenly, freeing her, only to begin his circling movements again.

"You are good," he yelled, "but I am better!" Morgan stopped and waved his axe in the air. Watching him carefully, she saw both the lifting of the axe, and the slight movement from his shield.

She set herself for the attack even as he lunged at her. She swung quickly, and the axheads met in the air. Sparks flew, and a loud metallic sound rose above them.

But when she tried to bring her axe down, Morgan's shield rammed into her chest. She was lifted from her feet and thrown onto her back. The sudden meeting of earth and armor stunned her, knocking the breath from her as the axe flew from her hand.

It was over, she realized bitterly. Fighting to regain her breath and trying, also, to raise her hand in the gesture of yielding, she saw Morgan's distorted features glaring down at her. Then she saw his axe raised high, even as the crowd screamed its denial.

Morgan stood above her, his eyes growing wider while he savored his moment of victory. Then his arm reached back further, and Gwendolyn realized he meant to kill her. Before she could move, a dull thud sounded, and an inch below the head of Morgan's axe an arrow shaft appeared.

A loud cheer erupted, and with it, Gwendolyn rolled from beneath the axe's blade. Regaining her feet, she glanced quickly around. She saw Miles, halfway to her, his longsword drawn. Then she saw the green-clad peasant standing twenty feet from Morgan, his bow notched with a second arrow, his eyes fixed on the wide-set knight.

"Your opponent has yielded, Sir Knight. Know you not the chivalry you represent? Does a mere peasant have to teach you?" he called derisively.

Before anything could happen, Richard was striding across the field, his face held in stern lines. He stopped next to the archer, and his hand covered Locksley's, forcing him to lower the longbow.

"We thank you for your swift action and are indebted to you. Morgan, I hold that you were but caught up in the fever of battle. And, we pray it will not happen again in tournament," he said pointedly.

Morgan shook himself, and then bowed before the king. "My apologies, Sire. I was unaware of my actions."

"So we have noted. Try, good Knight, to keep some restraint on yourself, at least until we face the Saracen. We need every noble man to hold our country strong."

"Yes, Your Majesty," Morgan said, but no one present missed the glare of hatred he shot at Locksley.

"I declare Morgan of Guildswood victor of the second day of tournament," Richard proclaimed to the crowd.

Although the cheering was loud, Gwendolyn heard the name of Sir Eldwin again being hailed as Richard draped the scarlet sash of victory over Morgan's head.

Turning, she walked toward Locksley, and although she could not speak, reached out her hand and grasped his.

"If ever you are in the north country and seek aid, call out my name to any, and I will hear," he said. "For you are not like the others; of that I am certain."

"And you, Robin Locksley, if you should require aid of any sort, send to Radstock, for I and all my people are indebted to you," Miles Delong stated, covering both their hands with his own.

Chapter Fourteen

GWENDOLYN WAS IMMOBILE, staring vacantly as she sat inside the large tent. Her defeat at Morgan's hands was a blow she had been unprepared for, and one which gave her more pain than the axe blade's bite.

She had been silent from the moment she'd entered the tent, and even after James had removed her armor, and Miles had cleansed and dressed her shoulder, she had not said a single word. Hours later, with tapers illuminating the interior, she could not take her thoughts from the afternoon's fight.

She relived, over and over, all her mistakes, trying to ascertain the cause of her defeat. She knew in part that overconfidence had reared its ugly head. But at the same time she wondered if Morgan's superior strength had also been a determining factor. Yet, no matter what reason she sought, what excuse she used, only one fact remained. She had failed!

Miles had been sitting near throughout Gwendolyn's silent ordeal and had wisely let her be. But as the hours passed, he sensed that if this continued, she might never recover the confidence to fight again, and he knew he could not let that happen. Others might want a simple wife, but during the last year, Miles had learned that anything less than the strength Gwendolyn possessed would not be enough for him.

She was unique, and he knew that in marrying her he had been granted a rare privilege. But, for that privilege he must prove himself, and Miles Delong, of the original seeds of England, would do what was necessary.

"You must eat."

"No."

"Gwendolyn, there is no shame in losing."

"For me there is."

"No. Your shame is in your pride!"

"It is shame nonetheless."

"And because of today you will let Morgan take what he wants?"

His words struck at her, but no anger welled to stop their passage; instead, there was only a dark void. No tears of release came to her aid, and she felt as if a part of her had died.

Miles stood suddenly, the movement in the quiet tent forcing Gwendolyn to look into his face. His green eyes, usually so gentle and compassionate, were hard. His lips were drawn in a tight line, and a muscle spasmed angrily in his cheek. But not even this sight affected her.

Miles strode purposefully across the tent and went to her equipment. A moment later he stood with her silver sword.

"It has been almost a year since you swore me to my oath and took me to your cave to show me this sword. You told me of your destiny—and of mine. I believed in you. I trained you. I gave in to your desires. No woman has ever become a knight before. Perhaps, it is for the very reasons you show now," he finished, his voice dropping derisively at the last.

But still no spark of will reflected in her sky-blue eyes. Miles shook his head sadly and looked at the sword in his hands, his anger growing in proportion to her apathy. "Shall I give this blade to Richard? He could melt it down and fill his war chest even fuller."

Gwendolyn listened to everything Miles said, but though she knew him to be right, she could not find the strength to bring herself to action. His words struck cruelly when what she wanted from him was comfort.

"Hold me, Husband," she pleaded.

"I hold only my wife who is my equal. I take no weak-willed female into my arms."

The harshness of his words, coupled with his unyielding glare, brought home to her the truth of everything he'd said. Her gaze shifted to the sword he gripped with white-knuckled hands. She stared at it and, rising, took the blade from him.

She searched for the comfort of its power, but felt only the coolness of the metal. "There is nothing," she whispered.

"You feel nothing? How could you? It takes more than a witch's words and a sorcerer's sword to make one a knight. It takes something far greater!"

"What has happened to me?" she asked as she stared at the blade in her hands.

"You must find that answer yourself."

"Damn you!" she screamed, rage sweeping through her in unreasonable waves. Spinning from him, she angrily flung the sword into the ground. The blade bit into the earth and held. The sword swayed back and forth, a metronome to her haunted thoughts.

Miles watched carefully, relief flooding through him when she cast the sword from herself. It was not what she did, but the fact that she did something. At last some spark of life had returned. He called her name, but she did not turn. Stepping next to her, he saw her eyes fixed on the sword and realized that she was fighting a battle within herself. Anything and anyone else would be nonexistent until the fight was done with and the results determined.

Walking quietly, Miles left the tent, and when he stepped outside, he ordered the squires to stand guard and let no one enter. All around him were the sounds of revelry, but he had no desire to join in. He walked away from the tent city to find some peaceful spot where he could sit in solitude and ponder his thoughts.

Inside the tent, the sword continued to sway, and Gwendolyn was unable to take her eyes from it. She did not hear Miles call her name or leave, but sensed she was alone. She sank to the ground a bare inch from the upright blade and reached out to touch the silver hilt.

"I believed in you," she whispered hoarsely, her fingertips caressing the cool metal. "Were you only in my imagination?" Wrapping her hand around the hilt, she drew the sword from the ground. With the sword in her hand, she closed her eyes and thought back through the years. Her memory responded with a rare crystal clarity, and she saw her mother again, taking her to the Pool of Pendragon, as well as to the cave for the first time. The excitement and thrill of holding her father's sword was rekindled in her mind as she once again felt its pulsating power.

But when she opened her eyes the power vanished. Concentrating, she willed the channel in her mind to open, but found only a dark void. "What has happened to me?" And the words Miles had spoken earlier returned to echo hollowly in her ears. *You must find the answer yourself.*

"Help me. . . ." she pleaded, and her body obeyed her as her eyes filled with tears. And suddenly she knew some of the answer. It had been she, rather than Morgan, who was responsible for the defeat. Because he, of all the men she had faced since the start of the tournament, had been the only one who had ever brought out fear within her. In the joust she had been lucky, she realized, because Morgan had not been prepared for a decisive thrust at the first charge. But this afternoon, when she'd faced him, she'd been deceived by the blackness of his aura and had lost her concentration and will power.

She had defeated herself. It had not been Morgan, it had been she. At last in accord with her thoughts, she held the sword high. It began as a gentle hum in her mind, until it increased, and she felt the sword vibrate in her hands at last.

It had returned to her, and relief flooded her mind, awakening the senses she herself had turned off.

With this new singing in her blood, she understood what Miles had tried to tell her earlier. It took more than a sword to make a knight—it took more than training, and more than knightly trappings. Gwendolyn had just learned exactly what it was: It was a state of mind.

Concentrating, Gwendolyn opened the channel, and as she did, the interior of the tent filled with light. Her blood rushed through her veins, and the sword came fully alive.

Remembering the lessons of the priestess, Gwendolyn released the hold within her mind, and the sensation of separation from her body returned. She rose, bodiless, within the tent and willed herself to see the afternoon again. Suddenly, the afternoon's bright sun washed across the tournament field, and she saw two figures beneath her. She watched again those final minutes of the duel between herself and Morgan and saw her fatal mistake when she left herself open to Morgan's timely shield thrust. She saw, too, the dark ugly aura surrounding him and watched it expand while she lay defenseless beneath him.

"You are learning, child." The words filled her mind, returning it to her body, but she did not look for the priestess. Gwendolyn knew she was alone. The heaviness and despair that had held her for so many hours now vanished, and once again, Gwendolyn's body swelled with life as she gave herself over to the powers that roamed the heavens and drew sustenance from within her own soul.

"I want to know who he is!" roared Morgan, his face red with anger as he glared across the table.

"My lord, he is but a peasant."

"I want him! I want him dead!" Morgan declared.

The two mercenary knights glanced at each other in warning. Then, the one who had spoken, stood. "I will put out the word."

"No, not yet. He is a hero to the rabble. Just find out who this Robin Locksley is. I will deal with him another time." Morgan turned to the other knight and fixed him with a hard stare. "And Eldwin? How badly is he hurt?"

"We learned nothing. Delong's tents are well-guarded, and no one will speak of it."

"Something is not right about this masked fighter; what?" he asked, more to himself than the others. The tournament had changed greatly in the last two days. When the longsword duels commenced the next day, there would be but a handful to compete. And Morgan knew that at the end it would be he and Eldwin.

"You must work on his shoulder," advised the first man.

"Of that you can be sure," Morgan stated. "And both of you must find out about Eldwin. Spend whatever is necessary. I want to know who this man is!" Then he stood and called his squire. "Bring her in now. I have need of her."

A few moments later the squire returned, bringing with him a young girl dressed in an old, stained tunic, whose face reflected a combination of loathing and fright. When they entered, the other two men left. Just as quickly, the squire released the girl and withdrew.

Morgan fingered his chin while he studied the peasant girl. She was young, no more than thirteen, with wide, tear-filled

It was after midnight when Gwendolyn arose from the floor. Her mind was no longer heavy with tortured thoughts of self-loathing; rather, a new resolve had come to ease her loss. She stretched her cramped muscles and went to the front of the tent where she called Arthur and asked after Miles.

"I do not know where he is."

"At the hall?"

"No. He walked in the opposite direction. I think he wanted to be away from the crowds, my lady."

"Thank you." Gwendolyn went to the chest and drew on the single woman's tunic she had brought. After that, she took out her long hooded mantlelike cape. She hung the Saracen dagger around her neck and put on the mantle, wrapping herself completely within its folds, before drawing the hood low across her brow.

"You can't go outside, my lady."

"Put out the tapers. Stand guard with your brother and let no one enter," she ordered, disregarding his protest as she strode across the tent floor.

She ignored James's startled glance and turned into the street to begin her search for Miles. Behind her, Arthur whispered urgently in James's ear. The squire nodded quickly, loosened his dagger, and began to follow Gwendolyn.

The streets were quieter now, but still the people carried on the spirit of the tournament. Everywhere she looked, Gwendolyn saw couples fondling each other openly. The senseless bodies of those who'd drunk too much littered the ground, and while she walked, she could feel the eyes of the men mark her trail. But something about her carriage stopped those who would, from following the dark form of her passage.

She kept up her fast pace until she reached the edge of the tent city. She stopped there, closing her eyes and willing herself to feel Miles's presence. Cautiously, she walked in the direction her senses led. Moments later she found herself near a crumbling ruin.

It was an old place, probably the keep of whomever held the land before King Henry took it for himself. But she felt no malaise about it and knew only that she had been guided here. Stepping over a low pile of stone, she entered the ruin and froze.

Across from her, silhouetted by a shaft of moonlight,

stood Miles. He was gazing into the night, and his strong features were softened by the low wash of the moon. As it had happened so many times since she'd first met him, she felt her heart flutter. Quietly, she walked before him and knelt. "My lord?"

"My lady," he replied, seemingly unsurprised by her presence. "Why are you out in the night?"

"To find you."

"You have done so."

"To tell you Sir Eldwin has come to understand the meaning of knighthood, and to thank you, my lord."

Miles lifted Gwendolyn from her knees and drew her into his arms. "How did you find me?"

"There is no place where I could not," she replied simply. He kissed her then, a deep, loving kiss. But as his hands tightened on her shoulders, she gasped.

Miles saw her wince of pain and released her. "When we return, use the sword to heal your shoulder."

Gwendolyn sucked in her breath and slowly shook her head. "I can't."

"The power did not return?"

"It returned, but that is not the reason."

"Then why?"

"You. I used the sword once in that way and was wrong. You, yourself, have taught me that. Tomorrow I will trust in my body, as I did not today."

"You will not use the sword?"

"Not to heal the wound. I will carry my father's sword if I face Morgan tomorrow, but I will not use it against the others."

Miles thought about her words, and nodded his head in agreement. Her decision was the proper one. He realized proudly in that moment, that his wife had truly become a knight.

The final day of the tournament arrived, but unlike the two previous ones, the sky was overcast, rife with dull gray clouds. This did not dampen the enthusiasm of the people who eagerly waited to cheer on their favorite knight and to see who would become the champion of the tournament.

Today the dueling was in two parts. There were but four knights who returned to the field of honor: Morgan of

Guildswood, Eldwin of Radstock, Hugo of Hereford, and Archibald of Corfe. And so, after the first round there would be a rest before the final confrontation.

Because there were but four knights remaining, it was decided that lots would be drawn for the first pairing. After the archbishop called out the blessings, and Richard spoke, the four knights, with their squires in attendance, drew their lots.

Morgan smiled when he held up the same length reed as Archibald, and Eldwin turned to face Hugo, who was slimmer, and shorter than the other three. While she studied him, she recalled what she'd heard. Hugo, one of Richard's mercenaries, was a fast and wiry man who relied on speed more than the subtleties of the blade. His swordsmanship was said to be good, but his weaknesses were in head-on conflict and a lack of self-discipline in single combat. The trumpets interrupted Gwendolyn's thoughts and brought her attention to the king's stand.

"The field is narrowed to four," Richard declared loudly. "These knights standing before you now represent everything that is great within our kingdom. Sir Archibald, Sir Hugo, Sir Morgan, Sir Eldwin, upon your shoulders rests victory. Let the tournament begin!"

The people shouted lustily, but unlike the past two days, their cries carried an undertone of fierceness. Gwendolyn forced their bloodthirsty yells from her mind as James slipped her longshield onto her left arm and handed her the sword.

Like the battle-axe which Miles had designed, this longsword differed from others in several ways. Although it was of the same length as a normal longsword, its blade was lighter and narrower than others, and its quillons were shaped differently than most handguards. Instead of being a straight bar, the quillons curved slightly inward. Because the sword was lighter, the curved guard would aid in deflecting a sliding blow, and allow her to spin from beneath it.

Throughout her training with the longsword, Miles had stressed speed and swift attacks to make up for the difference in strength between Gwendolyn and most men. Although Gwendolyn preferred fighting two-handed, as she did with her father's sword, she was the equal of most with sword and shield.

Swinging the longsword gracefully, Gwendolyn stepped toward Sir Hugo. When the four knights were prepared, they turned to Richard in salute.

Richard lifted his arm, and as he did the chamberlain's staff sounded loudly, signaling the start.

Sir Eldwin saluted Hugo and then came to the ready. A second later the clash of blades rang out, and Gwendolyn heard nothing else as she deflected Hugo's first stroke.

He was faster than she'd thought possible, and at first Gwendolyn was hard pressed to do anything but defend herself. Yet she did that perfectly. Using her shield effectively to deflect Hugo's strikes, she gauged the knight's strengths and weaknesses. A few moments later, Gwendolyn retreated from his assault, only to release her own attack. Their swords met time after time, and the screeching of metal tore through the air. But no matter what feints she tried, Hugo met them, his speed enabling him to catch even her swiftest strokes.

Gwendolyn, remembering the advice about his weaknesses, did not ease up. When Hugo took the offensive again, his blade whistling through the air, she held under the assault and slowly advanced on him, pressing the fight forcefully.

Hugo seemed to sense what she was doing and, feinting toward her shield, he spun from her attack to step just out of reach. Gwendolyn's breath was labored. Her breasts pushed against their binding, and even in the coolness of the day, she sweated profusely within the confines of her leather mask. She paused when Hugo did not attack and waited for his next move. Staring into his eyes, she willed her body to separate from her mind, and react on its own accord.

Hugo moved and Gwendolyn's sword flashed at the same instant. She leaned under his swing, lifting her shield to take the brunt of the heavy blow while her own blade reached under his shield toward his unprotected side.

The instant her sword passed beneath the rim of his shield, pain exploded in her shoulder, making her own strike ineffective.

His sword had struck her shield so savagely that it tore the leather straps from her arm, knocking her to the ground and causing a sickening rush of pain to claim her.

As she fell, she instinctively rolled, ignoring another lance of pain in her efforts, and before Hugo recovered to strike the fatal blow, Sir Eldwin was on her feet. Shieldless, and banishing the pain from her shoulder with all her will power, she gripped the longsword in a two-handed hold and circled Hugo warily. Gwendolyn's mind whirled, and relief flooded her with the realization that she had been able to recover. Although she had lost the protection of the shield, it in no way affected her abilities. Now, she knew, would be the real test of her agility and ability as a knight, and she welcomed it freely.

Gwendolyn reacted to the new situation by charging forward, her sword flying in the air, to meet Hugo's blade with jarring impact.

With the blades joined, Gwendolyn swiveled suddenly, slipping beneath the upraised steel to pull her sword free. She spun again, before Hugo could react, her sword striking his shoulder powerfully. His maille held, but she saw pain flash across his features. Without letting up, Gwendolyn spun yet again, but this time Hugo was prepared, and he deflected the blow.

Gwendolyn stepped back when Hugo resumed attack. She waited, her nerves racing as he pressed on. Planting her mailled feet firmly and using her wrists and shoulders, she fought him, deflecting every blow with a simple twist of her wrists, making him expend his energy uselessly. Suddenly Hugo gave vent to a war cry and his sword arced in the air. As it descended, Gwendolyn moved. She twisted under the coming blow, and when his blade met hers, and slid along the length of the shaft, she flicked both wrists in a full circle at the exact instant his blade touched the quillons. The resultant shock tore the hilt from Hugo's gauntleted hand.

Without stopping her momentum, Gwendolyn swung again, striking his shield harshly. Hugo backstepped, his shield held before him, but Sir Eldwin had already stopped the attack and stood waiting.

"I yield," Hugo declared in a clear, proud voice.

Gwendolyn bowed to the knight, and then surprising everyone, turned, bent, and lifted Hugo's sword. Gallantly, as had marked all her bouts except those with Morgan, she returned the sword to its owner.

Sir Hugo, after accepting the sword, bowed. "If ever you

have need, call upon me, Sir Eldwin, for there is no shame in serving you."

Gwendolyn stared at him through the eyeslits for a long moment and then held out her gauntleted hand. Hugo's hand joined hers, their thumbs interlocking, their fingers clasping the back of each other's hands, and together their clenched gauntlets rose in the air.

Voices cried out from the crowd, and the name of Sir Eldwin flew from a thousand mouths. There was no longer any doubt as to whom the people wanted for their champion.

A moment later, Gwendolyn released her grip on Hugo and turned to see Morgan, victorious over a fallen Archibald, staring at her. But unlike yesterday, his face was calm; no anger showed in it at all.

His only expression was a predatory smile, like that of a hungry wolf sensing its victim before it.

Chapter Fifteen

"It has opened again," Miles said as he swabbed her shoulder with a clean piece of cloth and looked at the jagged tear in her porcelain skin. "Use the sword."

"Not yet," she replied, gritting her teeth against a stab of pain. "Bind it tightly."

"Perhaps it is your hands I should bind."

"Morgan would like that."

Miles's sudden laugh broke the tension, and Gwendolyn smiled, too. "I can win as I am; you have taught me that."

Holding her gaze with his, Miles placed the mixture of herbs Gwendolyn had prepared on the wound and wrapped and bound her shoulder with a strip of cloth. "Move your arm." She did as he ordered, testing the mobility of her arm and shoulder under his watchful scrutiny.

"I can do no more. James," he called, signaling Gwendolyn's squire within. James silently began his duties, and twenty minutes later Gwendolyn was again dressed in full armor.

She had not yet put on her mask, and the coif-de-maille rested loosely on her shoulders. "My sword."

James stepped back, and as he did, Miles and Arthur watched him lift the silver sword. He settled the scabbard onto its hook and adjusted the sash across Gwendolyn's surcoat. For this fight she had chosen to wear her gipon, the lightly padded armorial surcoat, to add to her protection.

"Morgan will stop at nothing; he will break every rule to defeat you."

Gwendolyn's eyes fastened on Miles's face when he spoke. Slowly, she drew the sword. A narrow beam of light filtered in through the small smoke-hole at the top of the tent, and as Gwendolyn lifted the sword above her head, the light struck it.

James and Arthur gasped. The silver sword shone softly and Miles saw a change in Gwendolyn's eyes. They glowed like the early morning sky, and within them, Miles sensed a renewal of all the power and strength Gwendolyn possessed.

For several minutes, while the sword was suspended above everyone's head, a calming silence bathed the four. Then Gwendolyn lowered the sword from the shaft of light, sheathed it, and reality returned to the tent.

James recovered quickly, but his eyes were still wide when he slipped the mask over her head and placed the coif-de-maille atop it. He adjusted her beaver, hooked and laced the coif securely, but when he reached for the helmet, Miles stopped him.

It was Miles who put Gwendolyn's helmet on, and as he did, he spoke in a low voice. "Fight well, my love, my spirit and my heart will be with you on the field."

James lifted a new shield, but it was Miles not Gwendolyn who reacted. "No shield," he said just as the trumpets blared their first call.

Gwendolyn's mind raced madly when she walked onto the field. Behind her she sensed Miles's eyes following her every step, but she forced away all thoughts other than the coming battle. She was confident, but not overly so. Her sword would aid her, but she could not use its unlimited powers. She must draw from her own reserves, yet she knew that she had some small advantage. Gwendolyn's faith, almost shaken from her yesterday, had returned stronger than before, and that faith gave her belief in herself.

When she had held her father's blade to the light of the tent, she'd felt power build within her. The pain in her shoulder had lessened even though she'd not consciously willed it. Her breathing was deep and even, and the heaviness of the armor bothered her not at all. She felt strength and power flow in her arms, and knew that this day she was ready to face the next step in her destiny.

At the same time Gwendolyn started onto the field, Morgan crossed from his position. He timed his steps to match hers so they would reach the king simultaneously.

Stopping four feet from the stands where Richard sat, Gwendolyn knelt and bowed her head, fully aware that Morgan had done the same.

"Rise, Morgan of Guildswood. Rise, Eldwin of Radstock." When both knights were standing, Richard rose and gazed at each in turn. "Of three hundred, only you remain. You have fought well, we commend you. Now, for England, for God, and for victory, we declare the final match begun!"

The trumpets sounded in response to his words, but beneath their call, Richard spoke in a low voice meant for the two knights only. "I charge you both to see that this fight is not to the death. We are aware of your feud and will not have it!"

The two knights walked to the center of the field where their squires waited. Tension swirled thickly in the air, and the thousands of people watching all held their breath at the same time, waiting expectantly for the first clash of metal.

Morgan's squire held out his shield, and Morgan slipped his arm through the twin leather straps. But his eyes widened when Eldwin motioned his squire from the field. It was only then that Morgan noticed the squire held no shield.

"You want this to end so swiftly?" he mocked in a voice that carried to the people. Without waiting for an answer, Morgan stepped back, his hand on the hilt of his sword, and bowed gallantly for the first time in the tournament.

Gwendolyn was not surprised by either his words or his gesture as she returned the bow and drew the silver blade. She saw Morgan's eyes widen at the sight of it and smiled behind the mask. No blade like hers had ever been seen in a tournament. Its width was wider than Morgan's, its length longer, and its gleaming surface unmarred.

Through her gauntlets, through the maille beneath them, and into the flesh of her hands, Gwendolyn felt the sword come to life. Yet it did not glow as it always had, it did not hum or vibrate; rather, it joined with her, the silver blade's weight seeming to become even lighter.

The chamberlain's eyes went from Morgan to Eldwin before he raised his staff of office. The instant the staff struck the ground, Morgan's sword blurred in the air.

Giving herself up to her instincts, Gwendolyn let the sword and her mind come together. Morgan's sword reached toward her, and with the barest of movement, she deflected it. He spun, his mouth curved in a leer, as he came on again. Gwendolyn settled herself to his attack and, once again, deflected his blow easily.

But then Morgan, sensing his opponent to be better than he first thought, began to draw on his expertise. Tricks that were only learned on a battlefield began to emerge, and slowly, Morgan forced Gwendolyn to lose ground.

After the first few strokes, Gwendolyn held herself back. She knew that by opening the channel in her mind, she could easily defeat Morgan. But she stayed herself, as the need to prove her abilities returned. It was not a foolish decision, but one of necessity. No power on this earth could keep her alive if she did not have the ability to do so herself. On the field of honor, fighting against the man who had once claimed her as his own property, Gwendolyn again found a new realization.

The sword, used properly, made her not greater, but the equal of any. She did not need to use its unearthly powers to win; just become part of it, and use her own strength to wield the blade.

All of these thoughts flashed through her mind in the space of a breath as Morgan stepped back and assessed his opponent once more.

"You are better than I thought, but you are still dead," he whispered. He lunged suddenly, taking Gwendolyn off guard, and the tip of his sword struck her shoulder. For the first time since stepping onto the field, pain lashed out.

Laughing, Morgan drew back before Gwendolyn could strike. She stared at him, again seeing the dark aura encompass him like a malignant cloud. But the aura did not distract her; instead, it lent power to her anger, and swiftness to her hand.

She charged Morgan, rage directing her swing, and suddenly, the tip of the silver blade ripped through his shield, passed through his maille, to taste of the flesh and blood of his shoulder. Pulling back harshly, Gwendolyn freed the blade as if it had only been in a straw sack.

Morgan's scream of enraged pain shook the air around him and, as he glanced at his shoulder, he attacked. His blade moved like lightning, but with each stroke, Gwendolyn deflected the blow, and to add insult, struck his shield with the flat of her blade.

Then she saw his eyes change. They narrowed into slits, red rims turning bloody against black pupils. Setting herself for what she knew would be a killing assault, Gwendolyn released the hold she had placed on her mind and, again, blended with the sword. Her blood rushed within her body, and she could hear its singsong rhythm in her ears. Her breathing steadied, and renewed energy flowed to every muscle in her body. A calm fell over her mind, and she cast all thoughts away, giving herself up to the sword, and uniting with its power.

Morgan's eyes flickered for a bare second as he watched Eldwin. The knight stood his ground, awaiting the attack, but Morgan sensed a strangeness about Eldwin, a calmness that should not be there. While his anger at being blooded held him fast, he heard the cries of the people for Eldwin. Still he did not move as he watched the leather-masked face, and the gauntleted hands which held the overlarge sword.

Suddenly, he flung his arm outward, casting his shield away and gripping his own sword in two hands. The spectators cheered this new move, and Morgan realized he'd won back some support.

Gwendolyn watched Morgan throw his shield away and face her with his blade in both hands. She saw the stain of red on his maille, but knew it would not affect him. He was a bull of a man, and only the severest of blows would stop him. Then he moved, and Gwendolyn's body flowed to meet him.

Their blades met in the air, and sparks of metal flew. With an easy flick of her wrists, she deflected his blow. But Morgan came on again, attacking in a mad rush. Gwendolyn stood her ground, her sword moving so fast it was almost invisible, the air whistling with its passage. Her arms seemed to grow lighter, and her body vibrated with unseen powers as she held off Morgan's charge.

Then she spun from his next swing, and its force carried Morgan past her, pulling him off-balance and sending him crashing to the ground. A loud cry filled the air, and the bloodlust that held so many people exhorted her to end the fight, but Sir Eldwin did not take advantage of Morgan's fall.

Gwendolyn glanced behind her when Morgan fell, and saw Miles standing relaxed, his face showing no sign of tension. He knew, she saw, and he approved of what she was doing. Then Morgan was on his feet, rage bellowing from his mouth as he lifted the sword high above his head. He ran at her, charging like the mad animal he resembled, and Gwendolyn saw in his attack all the hatred and greed of one who must have everything.

She stood her ground, and only when his blade swung did she move. His sword hissed through the spot she had just left, but before it completed its arc, Gwendolyn had turned completely around, and her blade and his rang out again.

Morgan recovered quicker than she expected and launched a side stroke. Reversing her wrists, she deflected the blow neatly.

"Face me, coward!" Morgan roared, his chest rising and falling with the force of anger and pride.

Gwendolyn nodded her head, accepting the challenge, and when Morgan raised his sword, Gwendolyn set herself. He swung just then, bringing the blade in a half arc over his head and putting every bit of strength he possessed behind the blow. As he did, Gwendolyn, moving swiftly, brought the silver blade in a full circle over her head, lifting herself onto the balls of her feet.

In that instant, her masked head was a foot above Morgan's. The crowd screamed as one at the blur of silver lashing forward. When their blades met, the very air seemed to explode.

The blades held, and four gauntleted hands were separated by inches. Eyes stared into eyes as Morgan and Eldwin held their blades tightly. "Die!" Morgan screamed and for the first time in the duel, he spun.

Gwendolyn was again caught off guard, but instinct, and the sword, saved her. She whirled in the opposite direction, and again the blades met. Morgan's eyes widened for an instant before they returned to their snakelike slits. "First you, then Delong, and then all of Radstock," he threatened.

Rage and denial flared through Gwendolyn's mind, and she tore her blade free. Then she attacked, swinging mercilessly, letting the power of not the sword but her anger direct her. She attacked, trying to strike through his defense, as a red rage filmed her vision. Mercilessly, she went after Morgan, her only thought to wipe his image and body from the face of the earth.

She beat at him, her blade moving faster than anyone had ever seen before, forcing him back and back, until they were at the very edge of the field, fighting before Richard himself.

Morgan's back hit the wood of Richard's stand, and he could retreat no further. No thought of yielding entered his hate-maddened mind, but he knew the end was near. He had never faced a man like the one before him. His own arms were screaming in pain, and he was barely able to deflect the unending blows that rained upon him. But he would not give up, and he summoned his anger and hate to help him.

"Yield! Yield! Yield!" cried the crowd, but their calls only added weight to his rage. The dark mask of Eldwin loomed near, and he could almost feel the heat from the other's body. Then Eldwin's blade descended again, and tensing, he met it with a side stroke that deflected the ominously shining sword. Eldwin's blade struck the wood of the stand, and splinters flew, but Morgan saw it not as he jumped away and drew the fighting dagger at his waist.

He leaped toward Eldwin, the dagger aimed at the knight's vulnerable side, but Gwendolyn had seen the surprise attack and brought her sword back in a quick move.

Gwendolyn's mind screamed its warning and she windmilled her arms, moving the silver sword in an effort to stop the dagger's path. Her sword nicked the dagger, and it passed her side harmlessly. She stepped back quickly as Morgan dropped his dagger and again gripped his longsword with two hands.

When he blinked, Gwendolyn moved. She gave herself no conscious directions; she merely let her body take over. Morgan's blade was whistling in the air, but to her eyes, it barely moved. Her own blade seemed to move by itself, pulling her arms along effortlessly. The swords met, and Gwendolyn felt no resistance. It happened suddenly, amid the screams of the people—Gwendolyn's blade passed through Morgan's, severing it in the exact center.

Without stopping, Gwendolyn followed the blade, turning under it, and bringing it around. Again the silver sword met Morgan's metal, and this time his blade was severed at the hilt.

Before Morgan could raise his arm, the tip of the silver sword was at his throat, penetrating the maille and stopping only when it reached his skin.

Gwendolyn's arm trembled, and the power of the sword vibrated through her soul. She longed to plunge the blade deep, but even with the advantage she had, she could not bring herself to murder anyone. The battle was done, the fight ended, and the bloodlust that claimed her, eased.

Carefully, she withdrew the blade and held it toward Richard so that he would see she had not drawn blood in the finish. But while she held the blade toward her king, her eyes never left Morgan's hate-filled gaze, still ready for any further treachery on his part.

"Well done, Sir Eldwin," Richard said, his voice not quite as steady as usual, but respect filling every word.

Morgan, upon hearing Richard, turned from Eldwin, and without the customary bow, walked silently from the field, his ears awash with the name of Eldwin pouring from everyone's lips. When he reached his squire, he turned. Rage shook him, and when the squire went to take the remains of Morgan's sword, Morgan lashed out, knocking the young boy off his feet.

Gwendolyn, standing before the king, saw none of that. Her eyes held Richard's and she waited. Gracefully, England's warrior king stepped down from the platform to stand before her. A moment later, Miles was on one side of Richard and William Marshall on the other.

Richard spoke, but his voice was not loud. "You are the victor, the champion of the tournament. You have gained an earldom, but I am told you want it not. Have you changed your thoughts?"

Gwendolyn shook her head once.

"You are different from any other I have known. I have never met a man who turned down rank. I have never seen a knight wield a sword as do you. Sir Eldwin, although you turn your back on the prize, I proclaim that for as long as I live, should you but ask, the earldom is yours. Kneel, Sir Eldwin of Radstock, and receive your victory boon."

Gwendolyn, her heart racing, knelt slowly, her hand still holding her father's sword. Above her, Richard turned to Marshall and waited. William Marshall lifted the long cushion on which rested the sword of state, the wide gold blade allowed to be held only by England's king. Marshall, his lined features held immobile, offered Richard the cushion.

Taking the heavy sword into his hand, Richard looked down upon Sir Eldwin's bowed head. "Remove your helmet," he instructed.

Gwendolyn took off the metal cap and placed it on the ground before her.

"I, Richard, King of England, Duke of Normandy, by the grace of God, and by the powers given to me by the people, and, in the name of God, with the spirit of knightly chivalry, and for the sake of England, do hereby proclaim Sir Eldwin of Maidstone, Knight Protector of Radstock, a knight of the Realm."

Carefully, aware of all eyes upon him, and with a respect he felt for very few, Richard *Coeur de Lion* lifted the gold sword of England and dubbed Eldwin.

Behind them an eruption of voices shattered the solemnity of the moment, but for the four principals, nothing would ever interfere with the magnificence of what had happened. When Gwendolyn rose, her eyes did not stare at Richard, but fastened upon Miles. She saw on his face a pride that made her eyes water and her heart stir.

It was not just she who had been knighted, it was also he, for Gwendolyn now knew one truth of the priestess's: Miles and she were one. They had been since the beginning of time, and would be for all eternity.

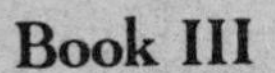

Book III

Of the Crusade of Richard Coeur de Lion, *and of the Treachery of the Dark One*

Chapter Sixteen

MILES URGED HIS HORSE TO run smoothly along the half-sand, half-rock ground. He was in the lead of a small group of knights who were scouting ahead of the main column of Richard's army.

He had not been told to do this, but chose to in order to get away from the loud voices and stench of fetid, unwashed bodies, so he could regain some small grip on his sanity.

He had never imagined in his wildest dreams the reality of the crusade he had embarked on. The hot September sun of Palestine beat down upon his armor-shielded body, as it had for many months; yet he did not feel its draining effects, or hear the voices of the knights behind him, as he lost himself to the thoughts of what had passed since arriving in Sicily. For more months than he wanted to remember, Miles had been following Richard, wondering what more could possibly happen. The crusade had begun with delays and deceit and had continued in just that way.

They had been stranded in Italy for a year, treated like dirt and vermin, until Richard was forced to capture and subjugate the Sicilian city of Messina, wasting valuable time and men. Once this had been accomplished, Richard's and Philip's army had been able to rest and replenish its supplies.

In the spring, Miles had watched Philip, ill since the start of the campaign, sail with his men to Tyre, and from there on to Acre. He, along with Richard and the English army, went on to take the financially valuable island of Cypress before joining the French monarch.

Everything about the crusade had shaken and sickened Miles: the unnecessary slaughter of innocent people, the bloodthirst that seemed to hold the knights captive. He had known this war was to better the chances of Christianity, but after seven months of watching the senseless brutality of both sides, he had come to doubt not only the benefit of religion, but found himself questioning the validity of life, itself.

All the horrors Miles had heard about in stories of past Crusades, he became a part of. The atrocities which had always been laid at the feet of the Saracens, he witnessed being done by the supposedly chivalrous Christian knights with whom he rode. He had known there would be no mercy shown from the lesser knights in their efforts to increase their own coffers with the legitimate gains of war. But he had not expected to see the same greed from the nobility he had fought with and known all his life.

These dukes and knights had changed when they'd set foot upon the soil of the Holy Land. They had become ruthless to the extreme; their greed exceeded only by their hunger for killing.

Even Richard had reached new heights of bloodlust at Acre and had brought shame to the side of the cross. When Saladin had not produced the ransom as quickly as Richard had demanded, Richard had put to death twenty-six hundred Saracen knights. Not even Saladin had been so bloodthirsty.

Miles had argued futilely that Richard should not do this thing, for never had Saladin taken the lives of his prisoners without first giving ample time for ransom. And, in fact, there were many known instances when, because of the inability of a prisoner's family to raise the ransom, Saladin had reduced the sum so that the knight was able to gain freedom.

"But look at the cost!" Richard had declared. "Part of the ransom was the knights' pledge of parole to leave the Holy Land and return home."

"Sire, I can only repeat that what you are about to do is wrong," Miles had argued.

"We cannot feed them! We cannot let so many stay among our midst. We must rid ourselves of them. Tomorrow, at midday, if Saladin does not present the ransom, they must die."

Richard's words were echoed by the half-dozen members of his staff. Miles had wanted to fight, to argue until he won his points, but when his eyes had swept across the faces of the men gathered in the king's tent, he knew he could not win. Morgan's tight-lipped smile taunted him, and Miles knew the man had gained Richard's ear in this matter. The next day, as the sun beat down upon the city of Acre, Richard cold-bloodedly slaughtered the prisoners, ending the negotiations that had begun with Saladin after Philip, who had grown progressively sicker, had returned home.

With the failure to negotiate further with the Moors, Richard had decided upon a two-fold plan of attack to free the Holy City. The first part was to ride toward Jerusalem in an effort to free the city. The second part was one of ongoing parley with Saladin, to try and negotiate a peace that would save them both.

Richard had advanced the plan of offering his sister in marriage to Saladin to secure this peace. But Miles, along with several of Richard's advisors, had thought this unlikely.

So at present, no negotiations since Acre had come about, and Richard's army was advancing deep within the hold of the Saracens. They were en route to Jaffa, to rest and replenish the army's supplies, before going on to Jerusalem, and the final confrontation between Christian and Moslem.

Miles shook himself free of his memories and reined in his horse. Spread out beneath him was the valley he had come to scout. Gazing down upon the bleak land, his eyes swept across its barren surface. Yet he saw that this valley, as most of the land of Palestine, was a strange mixture of sand and growing life. Although the valley itself was made of sand and rock, the hills rising along its flanks were filled with a multitude of trees.

A feeling of dread and wrongness held Miles in its grip, but he could find nothing to substantiate it. He looked closely at the hills, but saw no flicker of life within them. Yet the air seemed heavy with warning, a warning he could not understand.

"My lord, the valley looks peaceful," Arthur said in a low voice, reminding him of where he was.

Miles did not reply; instead, he again looked at the valley they must cross on their way to Jaffa. On the other side was the small town of Arsuf, the only place they might find resistance before reaching Jaffa and the sea. But on this warm September afternoon, Miles saw nothing out of the ordinary and, shrugging away his doubts, signaled the men back to camp.

As Miles rode, he wished Valkyrie were here, flying high and wide, looking for any hidden Saracens. But neither the golden eagle nor Gwendolyn was here, and Miles willed away the thoughts that tore through his mind to threaten his very existence.

Perhaps it was because he was fighting with himself that he did not see the lone rider, wrapped in a dark mantle, emerge from the rocks behind the small group. No man saw this other, and while Richard's knights returned to the sprawling camp, the single man rode swiftly into the valley.

While Miles reported to Richard, the other rider rode deeper into the level valley, until he reached a predetermined spot and stopped his horse. He dismounted, and when he had done so, threw the mantle over his shoulders to reveal a broad, powerful body.

Then, Morgan of Guildswood waited, his dark eyes never once staying still, his hand never straying from the hilt of his sword. A few minutes later, five riders in flowing burnooses broke from the cover of the trees and rode their wiry horses to where he waited.

Morgan watched the newcomers dismount and carefully inspected each of them. His unfaltering gaze swept each of them from boots to face, and noted well the long curved scimitars they carried. After another moment of silence, one man stepped close to Morgan and spoke.

"You have asked to speak with me. Do you wish to join with us, embrace the true faith, and accept Allah as your God, and Muhammad as his prophet on earth?" the Moor asked in perfect French.

"There is no true faith except in one's mind. I have not come to join you, only to offer you something," Morgan stated, drawing himself straighter in front of Saladin.

"You believers of Jesus are a strange breed. I could cut your throat right now and have one less infidel to bother me."

"And you would be one step closer to losing Jerusalem."

"You would help me keep it?" Saladin's voice dripped with sarcasm. He had dealt with many Frankish knights in his life and had found few of them to be honorable. Saladin was a man used to leadership, and one of his traits was an inherent ability to know the type of man with whom he spoke. He knew this knight standing before him was not honorable, yet necessity made him listen.

"No, but I want this damned war over. I do not want to wait until all eternity ends before I return home. I have lands to rule, and matters that must be accomplished."

"So?"

"So, I make you an offer. I will give you Richard's plans so that you will be able to thwart them."

"Why?"

Morgan held himself still under Saladin's increased scrutiny. He was unafraid of the Saracen, confident that he would leave this meeting alive and with what he sought.

"Because if you know Richard's plans, you can stop him long enough to force him to negotiate and join with you in a truce. The war will end, and I will be able to return to my lands."

"And to your great ambitions. What do you want in return?" asked the ruler of the Moslem world.

"I want one knight captured—not killed. And I want your word that there will be no ransom accepted for this knight. I want your solemn promise that this knight will be held, even after the war is ended, and that he will fare no better than a slave!"

"Why?"

"The reason is not your business. Your benefit by doing this should be enough of an answer," Morgan stated brashly.

"You would accept my word on this?"

"It is said that you keep your word."

"Unlike you infidels, when a Moslem makes a promise, it is his duty to keep it."

"Then you agree?"

"I agree," Saladin replied, willing to accept whatever help necessary to end this war that was draining his lands of both wealth and people.

"Then speak the words." Morgan stared at Saladin and waited.

"I swear, by Allah the merciful, and Muhammad his prophet!" Saladin clapped his hands, and without issuing further orders, a blanket was spread on the sandy ground.

Food was placed upon it, and for the next hour, Morgan talked and Saladin listened until Morgan had nothing else to say and the audience drew to a close.

"And the knight you wish taken?"

"He rides near Richard, always." Morgan took out a rolled sheet from his waist and handed it to Saladin.

The King of the Moors opened the vellum and gazed at the crest drawn upon it. He studied it for a moment before looking at Morgan. His expression was one of dark thunder, and Morgan felt the first shred of fear since the meeting had begun. "I have seen this one fight. Be gone!" he ordered fiercely.

Morgan left then, mounting his horse and riding from the valley. He did not care what Saladin said, only that he would do what was necessary. Morgan's plans would go ahead, and when he returned to England, his power would be increased immeasurably. That, and the agreement he'd made with Prince John before leaving England, would produce all he wanted.

But behind him, Saladin and his men waited. They watched the Frankish knight ride away, and after he was gone, Saladin held up the drawing.

"He is evil," whispered Borka-al-Salu, the grand vizier to the king.

"But his evil will help us."

"Oh Master, Right Hand of Muhammad upon this earth," Borka intoned solemnly, using only one of Saladin's hundreds of titles, "you have said time and again, that if all the Franks were like this one, we would not be at war." When he spoke, his finger pointed to the crest of Radstock which Saladin held in his hands.

"I know. But I would do what is necessary to end this futility."

"It is wrong. It will not go as you think. You have made a bargain with the devil." The grand vizier's eyes sparkled brightly as he gazed at Saladin.

"Enough!"

"No, Revered One, take my head if you must, but heed my words. A pact with that spawn of hell will not win you the seat of paradise you seek. Do not do this thing; the stars have spoken to me that it will tempt fate and bring hurt to our land."

"I have given the Frank my word," Saladin said in a low voice.

"As Allah is my judge, I pray you do not suffer because of it."

"As do I," Saladin replied, remembering the two brief times he had faced Miles of Radstock. Of all the knights he had fought against, and of all the reports he had received, only this knight stood out, both in his fighting, and in the gallant way he treated his enemy.

Saladin had spies everywhere, and he knew that when Richard had ordered the deaths of his people in Acre, only this knight had stood against it, and when the slaughter had taken place, he'd not lifted his sword to strike a single Moor. Saladin, despite all his fierce thoughts and hatred of infidels, respected this man, and his heart was heavy with what he must do.

The sun bore down on Richard's army as it traversed the valley. They were on the primary road leading to Jaffa and would reach the town of Arsuf by nightfall. From there it would be a short journey to Jaffa, where green and bountiful lands met the sea, and Richard's army could rest and reprovision itself for the attack upon Jerusalem.

Miles rode next to the king, his eyes constantly darting this way and that. He was uneasy, but only intuition held him so, as there was nothing concrete for him to see.

"I dislike the grumblings of the French," Richard said to Miles.

"More of them desert daily." And it was true. Every day, five or six of Philip's men left. Without their king to lead them, they did not have the heart to do battle.

"We do not need them. Miles, we are strong."

"Are we, Sire?"

"Are you, too, beginning to doubt us?"

"No, Sire, I do not doubt us. I only doubt the flesh we are made of."

"It will be over by Christmas," Richard promised foolishly.

"I hope so."

"It must be. I have received too many missives from home. John is beginning to flex his muscles and I like it not."

"I know," Miles responded. In the last message he had received from Gwendolyn, she had written that Richard's brother was gaining power and lands, and was ruling the country in a harsh way. The people were hurting, and the word of his ruthless reign was spreading widely.

"Attack!" screamed a knight. Simultaneously, Richard and Miles turned their horses. From out of the tree-lined hills, a wave of Saracens charged down upon them.

Orders were called out and ranks formed. The archers knelt and unleashed a fury of arrows upon the attackers. The knights joined together, with lance and sword, awaiting the charge of the mounted enemy.

"Hold!" cried Richard, too aware of his earlier losses to let his knights charge the rushing force. "Archers, keep up the fire!" he commanded. Quickly, Richard rode his horse to the front of the knights. "Form ranks and wait for my command!" he ordered.

The knights of the Christian army did as their king ordered and formed their battle ranks. In the center were Richard's knights, and upon the left flank stood the French. The right flank belonged to the Hospitaller knights, who lived for nothing more than to kill the Saracens.

Then Richard turned to watch the advancing Moors. The archers were accurate, and wave after wave of Saracens fell, but they kept on. Miles sat still in his saddle, his sword held tightly in his hand, waiting for the word to attack.

On the crest of a hill he saw a single rider and knew it was Saladin. But he could not watch the leader, for the Saracen knights were almost upon them.

"Wait!" Richard implored harshly. He raised his hand to signal the trumpeters, but still he held back.

Miles saw that Richard was in control. There was no finer military mind in the world when it came to warfare than his king's. But before Richard could give the command, a line of Hospitaller knights charged forward. Unable to stand and wait under the attack of Saracen arrows, they had gone forward to meet their sworn enemy.

Still Richard held his men back. The Hospitallers met the Moors, and the clash of battle sounded. Only then did Richard give the command, leading the mounted knights himself. Miles spurred his stallion on and when he met his first foe, he was at Richard's side. They battled mightily for over an hour, and time became suspended within the fury of the fight.

At one point, Miles became separated from Richard and had to fight his way back to the king's side. Richard's defense soon changed into an attack that became like a pincer of the desert scorpion. His knights closed in from two sides while the archers continued firing toward the center. Suddenly, Saladin's men were pressed tightly together, and the hell of battle grew to its fullest.

Miles lost track of everything except the enemy before him. At one point five Saracens ringed him, but Richard burst through and killed two of them while Miles defeated a third.

Before he could meet the fourth, a sudden cry went up, and the Saracens fell back, running and fighting from the field in a mad retreat.

"The day is ours!" cried Morgan, who had ridden to Richard's side, his surcoat and sword covered with scarlet blood. But for Richard and Miles, who stared at each other and then at the bodies strewn across the battlefield, it had been a hollow victory. Neither Miles nor Richard had seen the shocked look on Morgan's face when he had recognized Miles. Nor did they see the dark flash of anger in his eyes.

By nightfall the dead had been counted. Seven hundred Christians died that day; two hundred more were wounded so badly they would never fight again.

The Saracens had lost more—over a thousand dead. But this was their land; Saladin would be able to replace them.

It was long after midnight when Miles, Richard, and several others sitting in the king's tent heard the returning cries of the men sent out to spy on the Saracen army.

A tired Sir Hugo, one of the king's most trusted mercenaries, and one of the few knights fluent in the Saracen tongue, entered the tent, bowed to Richard, and drank from a quickly offered goblet. Then he spoke. "They are already packing their equipment. I got close, very close, and listened to two men talk. Saladin has ordered a return to Jerusalem."

"That is good," stated Alfred of Wight.

"Why?" asked Richard. "So that he can strengthen his army? So he can plan another campaign even as we recuperate in Jaffa? No. We must again begin to negotiate with Saladin. We have been too long away from our homes."

Miles thoughts echoed Richard's, but he saw the strange look in Morgan's eyes. Miles had been aware of Morgan's black mood since the fighting ended. Now he sensed Morgan's new unhappiness in Richard's proposal and wondered why he would want to stay and fight. But he brushed the thought aside when Richard gave his orders for the morrow, choosing his representative to make the first approach to Saladin.

"What if they refuse to parley?" Morgan asked.

It was Alfred of Wight who spoke again, and his voice was heavy with sarcasm. "It appears as if you view this day as a loss, Sir Morgan. Why are you in so foul of temper? Your sword blooded many Saracens, did it not? No," he went on before Morgan could protest, "the Saracens will parley."

"They will," seconded Richard. "The question is, will they agree to what we must have?" Then Richard shook his head slowly. "Saladin is a proud man, and I have fought no greater a general in my life. Mark my words! If we do not reach an agreement, we could spend the rest of our lives fighting." Everyone's eyes locked on Richard's, within the sudden silence of the tent, and all read within their sparkling depths the truth of his prophesy.

The scents of the late fall were carried by the November breezes to Gwendolyn's sensitive nose. She reined in the black mare and breathed deeply. Then, in a field of yellow stalks that would soon become dry and cracked, she dismounted and sat down upon the fertile ground.

Behind her, James and Roweena did the same. For more than a year and a half, Gwendolyn had ridden the lands of Radstock, administering to the people, making certain that all was well. She maintained her husband's properties with determination and good sense, and under her gentle but firm guidance, all of Radstock prospered.

But within her, a hollowness festered. Her life seemed empty and meaningless. She drove herself unmercifully in an effort to hold back her loneliness, but whenever she saw something soft and beautiful, the emptiness of her life threatened to overwhelm her.

Since Miles had left, Gwendolyn had filled her days to

their limit: Making the rounds of the lands, seeing to the health and care of Radstock's vassals, and continuing her training as a knight. In the milder weather, Gwendolyn would train out of doors, in a hidden glen. But in the winter, she would go into the bowels of Radstock Castle, to the special pit, and practice her skills with James.

More times than she could remember, Gwendolyn had ridden in the guise of Sir Eldwin to meet any who would try to take from Radstock what was not theirs to take. In the long months she ruled Radstock, Gwendolyn had lived the double life of man and woman, and so far, none had learned of the secret.

But she did not want to continue this much longer. She had realized soon after Miles left that she had become half a person and had learned that she needed Miles in order to be whole.

Whenever her emotions became too much to bear, she would ride as Eldwin, leaving Roweena to issue instructions in her place, letting those in the castle think her ill again and confined to her room.

Dressed as Eldwin, Gwendolyn would go to a lonely place, far from Radstock, and miles from any people, to sit throughout the night and day in a deep trance, protected by the silver sword. She would let her mind go and would travel the myriad paths of the otherworld, drawing comfort and solace from her feelings. But during the last few months it had become more and more difficult to find surcease from her troubled thoughts. Transcending everything was her driving need to be with Miles again.

She had traveled, with the use of the silver sword, to the far reaches of the world. But try as she might, she had been unable to find Miles as she floated on the planes above the earth. She had called to the priestess for help, but had been unable to find her.

She had taken to learning more and more of the strange powers the sword had given her. She became strong within her mind, confident that she could control it. Yet, there always seemed to be another force watching her, holding her back, and shadowing everything she did.

"My lady," called James.

Gwendolyn lifted her eyes from the stalks to gaze at the youth.

"It is getting late; we must return to the castle."

"I know," she whispered.

A few moments later she was mounted and the three were riding toward home. They were a mile from the castle when Gwendolyn suddenly reined in her mount. James and Roweena came alongside, but she didn't see them. A darkness spread through her mind, washing everything from her sight. Something was wrong. Something was wrong with Miles. A dizzying wave attacked her, and her stomach twisted painfully.

Swaying in the saddle for a long moment, Gwendolyn tried to clear her mind, but she failed, and the darkness claimed her even as she fell.

James and Roweena reached her side a moment later, and Roweena screamed when she saw her mistress's chalky white face. But it was James who acted quickly as he lifted her.

"Help me!" Roweena instinctively reacted to James's command, and together they put Gwendolyn on her horse. With James mounted behind her, holding her unconscious body to his own, they rode quickly into the castle.

At the castle, the sight of the stricken Lady Delong brought immediate response from the people. Two minutes later Gwendolyn was safely within her bed. Once James had cleared the chamber of everyone save Roweena, he tried to awaken her. But it was to no avail. Roweena was desperately worried, afraid for her mistress's life.

James, again, acted decisively. Noting Gwendolyn's pale features, and the barest movement of her breasts, James tried to comprehend what was happening within her body. He knew Gwendolyn was unlike any person—man or woman—he had ever met, and he knew how physically strong she was. This was no normal illness.

"I'll call a leech," Roweena whispered.

"No! Stay by her side. Do not leave her. Do not let anyone come in!" he ordered. Moving quickly, James went from the bedchamber to the anteroom where Eldwin's arms were hidden. There, letting his intuition guide him, he lifted the silver sword and returned to Gwendolyn.

When he stepped into the chamber, he paused. Roweena was kneeling on the floor, her hand holding Gwendolyn's.

Tears fell from the servant's eyes and low sobs rocked her body.

Gently, James lifted the girl to her feet and stared into her face. "She will live," he proclaimed. "Stand by the door. Let no one enter."

When Roweena did as he ordered, James stepped next to the bed. He drew down the coverlet and exposed Gwendolyn's unclothed body. Since the day James had become Gwendolyn's squire, he had banished all thought of her sex and had accomplished the impossible. When he gazed upon her nakedness, he saw not a woman, but the body of his lord—his knight.

Carefully, he placed the silver sword on her body. The hilt rested between her breasts, and the tip of the blade was on her knees. He took both her hands and placed them on the hilt, and only then did he step back.

He watched carefully. A minute later, he sensed a change in the room. Warmth emanated from everywhere, and his eyes were drawn to Gwendolyn's body. He saw it then and was reminded of that long ago day in Windsor when Eldwin had held the silver sword aloft and it had glowed within the tent. Once again the sword glowed. A low silvery light flickered along its length, spreading slowly until it encompassed the sword. Then the glow grew, and, before James's eyes, Gwendolyn's body took on the same illumination.

She seemed to become iridescent and shimmering, but rather than being frightened, James breathed easily. He realized that he had done the right thing. Somehow, the sword would help Gwendolyn, and he would wait until it had done its work.

An hour later Roweena returned. She gasped when she saw Gwendolyn, but James waved her to silence, and then left the chamber with her.

"What is happening?" she asked.

"I do not know, but our mistress will be better."

"When?"

"I do not know that either."

"No one must see her this way," Roweena said.

"You must see to that."

"You will stay with her?"

"Yes."

"Then guard the door so I may bring you food," Roweena ordered quickly. Before James could reply, she was gone.

When she returned, James reentered the bedchamber and sat on the rush mat near the bed to begin his vigil.

Patiently, with love and devotion, both he and Roweena watched over Gwendolyn, caring for her while she slept in her trance.

Chapter Seventeen

DARKNESS. SWIRLING, THICK darkness engulfed her every sense. In the space of a heartbeat the distant castle slipped from her sight, hidden within folds of seeping darkness.

Gwendolyn fought this attack with all her strength, but no matter how she battled, she sensed her heart slowing. Her breathing seemed to stop, held back by the thickening blackness. Then there was nothing. She sensed movement, and in the part of her mind that still functioned, she knew she was being brought to Radstock. But nothing penetrated the veil of darkness she floated within.

For a long while she could feel nothing, and sensed she was losing something of value. The emptiness she floated in called for her surrender, but she fought its alluring song, trying to focus her mind and cry out for her sword. Then a pinpoint of light broke through the blackness in her mind, and she felt the warmth of the sword spread through her body. She realized, with the coming of the small dot of light, what she was losing. Miles! Something had happened to Miles!

She waited, drawing comfort from the sword and preparing herself to battle this mysterious void that claimed her. Time was meaningless in this world of darkness that held her. All she was conscious of was her determination to battle against this new enemy, and to find out about her husband, the other half of her being.

Fighting within herself, drawing on her love for Miles, Gwendolyn curled her fingers around the pommel and willed her mind to push back the veil. She concentrated completely on her objective, using Miles's training, rather than the priestess's, in her effort. She focused on the small pinpoint of light, willing it to grow and push back the dark. A wrenching suddenly tore through her, pulling her madly asunder, until, once again, she felt herself separate from her body. She floated upward in the darkness toward the speck of light, clinging to it with the singlemindedness of purpose that would not be denied. And just as suddenly as the darkness had claimed her, she emerged within a sparkling universe of brilliant light. Rainbow hues caressed her body, and the soft sparks of stars washed along her length. But above it all, was the sensation of peace and right.

She sped through the heavens of this place, searching everywhere for some sign to follow. Then she broke through a crimson layer of mist, and before her was a plateau of shimmering green grass.

She floated to the ground and let her feet sink deeply into the living carpet. Then she looked around. To her right she saw a circle of stone. The surfaces of the stones glowed with an unearthly power and beauty that drew her to them.

Gwendolyn could feel every blade of grass under her feet. The very texture of the grass, and the soft dirt beneath it, sent vibrations of calming waves through her. Her muscles rippled in response, and the gentle heat that fell from above washed her body with love. She stopped just before she reached the stone circle to raise her arms and look into the sky of the multihued universe. Naked to whatever powers rode there, she presented herself for inspection. A moment later she lowered her arms.

Entering through a stone arch, Gwendolyn stopped only when she reached the altar stone. There, gazing into the misty orange surface, she spoke.

"What has happened to my husband?" she asked. The dark hollowness which had been growing within her since Miles had gone, was also a part of the black curtain which had shrouded her mind and carried her senses from her earthly body. Yet she knew it was only a part. Something else controlled the black void. Something terrible.

The altar stone glowed brightly, and before her eyes she

saw a scene unfold. Even before she recognized anyone, she knew she was seeing Palestine. Gwendolyn stood transfixed by the scene within the stone. Her hands curled tightly, and her knuckles turned white.

Before her eyes, she watched two armies gather. She saw the banners of the Christians flutter in the gusty wind, and watched the Saracen army charge forward. Murky clouds shrouded the battlefield, and wet ground made the horses lose their footing easily. The rainy season was full upon the land, and with it, Gwendolyn knew, came the caprices of life and death.

She saw Morgan of Guildswood, the dark aura of his evilness surrounding him, giving orders to several men before the battle was joined. She cried out when the two lines met and trembled when Richard and Miles were attacked at the head of the troops.

She watched helplessly when Miles was separated from Richard by a large group of Saracens. Then she saw even more of the scene as Miles was surrounded by a large band of Moors. He fought gallantly against them and Gwendolyn's heart throbbed in response.

She watched Richard and five of Miles's personal knights vainly try to break through the ring of Saracens to come to Miles's aid, but the greatest fighting king in history could not breach the wall of men.

She saw Morgan withdraw slightly, and with him half the men who fought. More knights rode to Richard's side to force him from the melee. He argued, fought his own men, but soon logic claimed him, and he knew he would be unable to rescue Miles. Gwendolyn saw it all, and saw, too, how Morgan held back.

Soon the battle ended, and as each side withdrew, Gwendolyn was the sole witness to what happened next. She saw her husband, his body covered with blood, carried to a horse and tied to it. Then, with a hundred men forming an unbreachable phalanx, the Saracens rode off with Miles's body in its center.

Why did they want it? she asked herself, her sadness overcoming her and shaking the very beliefs that had brought her here.

"Miles . . ." she cried sadly. "No!" She screamed her denial loudly within the stone circle and felt herself swell with power. The stones themselves seemed to call back to her, increasing the loudness and rage she cried out with.

But when she looked into the altar stone again, she saw nothing. Turning, Gwendolyn gazed at the stones surrounding her. She did not speak; rather, she formed her questions in her mind and hurled them upwards at the violet clouds hovering over this unearthly world.

"You are power. You are beauty. You are good." The reply seemed to come from everywhere, including her own body. But she stood still and waited.

"I am Gwendolyn, daughter of Gwyneth, wife of Miles. That is all I am."

"You are that and more, Daughter of Thunder," came the voice of the Druid priestess.

Whirling, Gwendolyn faced the black-robed figure. "I am only that. I am more, when I am complete. Now that will never happen."

"You have learned well, my child. It is as you say, but not as you say."

"Have you brought me here to speak more riddles? Or to verify that I have died this day with my husband?"

"I did not bring you; you came by yourself. You have not died this day, nor has your husband. He lives as do you!"

"I . . ." But Gwendolyn was taken aback by her mentor's words.

"The darkness was not of our doing. The darkness was of the other powers, the powers that would rule your world."

"Morgan?" she asked.

"Is within their power. He was born vile and he lives only for his own satisfaction. Yes, Morgan, although he is but a tool, is the earthly visage of your enemy."

"But I defeated him before."

"A testing. They were unprepared for you. It is not so now."

"But why does he plot against Miles?"

"Why does man war upon man? Ponder not in terms of your own mind, innocent Gwendolyn, but in the terms of others."

"Then what vision did I see before me?" But Gwendolyn already knew the answer.

"You saw but the truth."

"Yet you say Miles lives?"

"It is time to prepare yourself. Make ready to leave your home. You must travel across the world. It is part of your destiny."

"And you will say no more?"

The Druid priestess threw back her hood to stare at Gwendolyn with dark, berrylike eyes. "You will learn soon enough the answers you seek!"

"No!" The uncontrollable anger flaring from within Gwendolyn's mind was unlike any before. A cold rage shook her, filling her mind, her body, and her soul. Within her hands, she pictured the hilt of the sword that at this moment rested within her earthly fingers far from where she stood. "I will have the truth," she demanded, directing the sword toward the priestess.

A flash of sparks exploded within the stone circle, and where the priestess had stood was empty space. Spinning, Gwendolyn searched for her mentor but could find her nowhere.

"Do you presume to fight me?" asked the priestess.

Gwendolyn looked up and saw the robed figure standing astride the top of a stone.

"Only if you force me. I want the answers to my questions!"

"You think yourself so strong then?"

Gwendolyn didn't answer; instead she drew on the power within her mind, directing another thrust of her swordlike thought.

Again, sparks flew at the spot where the priestess had stood, but as before, she was gone. "You surprise me. You have learned more than I thought."

"I have learned only what you told me." Gwendolyn stated bitterly to the priestess who had materialized before her again.

"Yet, I did not tell you of the powers within your mind when you are in the trance of knowledge."

"You told me all, when you told me of the sword."

"I bow before you, Daughter of Thunder, for you now teach to me what I failed to see."

Confusion reigned within her mind as she tried to understand and make sense of her mentor's words.

"Worry not of what you hear, but look upon that which has not been said." Gwendolyn followed the priestess's long pointing finger and found herself gazing deeply into the altar stone.

She was looking at the walled city of Jerusalem. Then the scene changed, and she was within a large, ornate room. Bright tapestries hung on the walls, and torches burned brilliantly over the mosaic-tiled floors. She watched a single man, resplendent in finely woven robes, walk into a chamber. There he bent and lifted the head of a prone figure. Gwendolyn gasped when she saw Miles's blood-smeared face. Then the man began to issue orders and, following that, a dozen slaves swarmed over Miles, removing his armor and treating his wounds. She stared at the man for a long moment, impressing within her mind every detail of his face.

"Saladin," she whispered. "The devil!"

"No, child," came the soothing sounds of the priestess. "No devil, only man." The picture dissolved, and with its surcease Gwendolyn lifted her head.

"Come, child," called the other, and the warm caress of the priestess's mind blended within hers. "Have faith, for I warned you the road you travel is a harsh one. And today you have seen for yourself just how hard it is."

"But why?" Gwendolyn whispered.

The priestess opened her arms, and Gwendolyn, a full head taller than she, came within the robed arms, sinking to her knees and pressing her cheek to the priestess's breasts, accepting the comfort of the old one.

"We must all fulfill a destiny. Our roles in life have been chosen, and yours is the most important of all. Wonder not of why you must walk this road, but of how it is best done," she cautioned.

Gwendolyn let herself go and relinquished her anger and fight as she listened to the woman. "Prepare yourself, for soon will come your confrontation with the dark powers. Think not of other things, for when you have proven yourself to be the chosen one, you will become whole again. There is reason and need for this earthly confrontation. And when you have given of yourself, your rewards will live to bring about a new world."

"I must go to Miles," Gwendolyn stated.

"Yes, but not until the proper time. The dark powers must be lulled. They must think themselves victorious. Here, in the old land, the people suffer. Their golden warrior, their lion-hearted leader is fighting another's battles and leaves them in the care of the black prince, yet another tool of darkness.

"John . . ." whispered Gwendolyn.

"The black prince must be fought another time, in the years ahead. Think only of Miles."

"But . . ."

"There is nothing else."

"I understand. I will prepare myself." And Gwendolyn did understand. She knew why she had fallen victim to the darkness that had claimed her and she also understood how she had won free. The spectre of Miles's death was the darkness, and the pinpoint of light had been his life returning. Miles needed her and she would be ready when the time came.

"Give nothing away. Allow no one to know what you do, lest they gain the ability to stop you. When the word comes, you will go because you are ready."

The priestess pushed Gwendolyn from her and waved her hand in the air. Light encased her in a whirlwind of brilliance. It caressed her skin and filtered into her mind, easing her hurt and loss while it guided her safely back to her earthbound body, and the sword that was in her grasp.

When she felt her mind joined with its earthly covering of flesh and bone, she took a deep breath. She was suddenly aware of all that had happened, from the moment darkness had captured her, until she rejoined her body. In the instant she'd drawn her breath, she knew that James and Roweena had sat watch for three days and three nights, and the castle had become rife with rumor and frightening tales.

Slowly, Gwendolyn opened her eyes.

"Thank God," Roweena cried. But James only gazed into Gwendolyn's strangely iridescent eyes.

Gwendolyn held his gaze for a long moment before she spoke.

"We have much to do."

Rising through the foggy bonds of his mind, Miles tried to remember what had happened to him. He started to open his eyes, but could not, and a low moan was torn from his throat by the effort.

A voice spoke to him in an incomprehensible tongue.

Then he remembered what had happened and stopped his struggles. A cool cloth was pressed to his brow, and Miles forced himself to stay calm.

He remembered the battle clearly, up until the last. He and Richard had been leading their men in a surprise attack against Saladin's fortifications on the outskirts of Jerusalem. Richard, master strategist that he was, had taken it badly when Saladin had refused to negotiate any longer and had thrown the offer of Richard's sister back at the English king.

Angered, Richard had set out to teach the Moor a lesson in courtesy by following his original plan, which he'd set aside for the negotiations. It was a good plan, made even better by the early winter rains, but something had gone wrong, and Saladin had been prepared.

When they'd started their attack, Miles had seen that the Moors had more men than usual. Before he could warn Richard, another wave of Moorish knights charged from behind.

While Miles had fought, he kept the king in his sight and soon realized that the day was lost. But before he could reach Richard to fight by his side, he had been surrounded by Saracens.

Yet, though surrounded, he shouted orders to his own knights to protect Richard at all costs. And then Miles had seen his fate. He was cut off from his army, totally. Not even Arthur was near him, and for that, Miles was glad. Arthur was too young to die so far from his home. With a prayer to Gwendolyn, he turned to meet his enemies. Miles Delong knew he would die on the field, and his only regret was that he would never see his wife's face again. But the thought of Gwendolyn only served to make his arm stronger, and he fought as he had never done before.

The knights of Saladin who faced him had never known fury as they fought against. Before they had Miles ringed, a full half dozen had fallen. Then something hit his helmet and he almost lost his balance. With his ears ringing painfully, Miles readied himself for his last act upon this earth.

He lifted his sword high and shouted a battle cry through his clenched teeth. Then he charged the circle, uncaring of who would strike the fatal blow.

Spurring his horse forward was the last he remembered.

Darkness had come suddenly, and now he realized he was still alive.

Again he heard the strange language and realized he was being spoken to. "I do not understand," he said in a voice that cracked with dryness.

"She is but telling you her name. It is Aliya," said a man speaking French. "Hold still so that she may remove the cloth from your eyes."

Miles did as he was told, and a moment later he blinked his eyes. It took another minute for his eyes to adjust to the light within the chamber, but when they did, he saw the woman, Aliya.

She was olive-skinned, with large eyes. That was all he saw of her face; the rest was hidden by a veil. Then he saw the man standing behind her, and recognition came instantly. He was tall, with a lean body encased in the strange dress of the Saracen. Hanging from the wide sash at his waist was a gleaming scimitar.

"Yes, you are alive, Frank."

"I am not a Frank, I am not French. I am of the English," Miles replied.

"All Christians are Franks to us. Are you not pleased that we spared your life?"

"I would rather know why."

The man threw his head back and laughed loudly. The laughter ended abruptly when he fixed Miles with a hard stare. "Do you know who I am?"

"Yes."

"And that does not frighten you?"

"I do not fear my own king, why should I fear you?" Miles asked in a mild voice.

"Because I could have you killed with the snap of my fingers," stated Saladin.

"And lose the ransom?"

"There will be no ransom for you."

His words shocked Miles, and it took him a moment to fully understand this. It was custom to hold captured knights for ransom; it was one way both kings financed this war. Only a personal hatred every stopped the exchange of a prisoner for ransom. Miles held back his question when he realized that he had somehow come to the attention of Saladin in a very deadly way.

Miles forced his protesting body to move. Sitting up, he ignored the lance of pain in his side. But he knew he had been hurt worse than he thought.

Saladin saw the knight wince, but kept his face expressionless. Instead, he ordered the slave girl to give Miles water mixed with a small amount of powdered hashish to ease the pain.

"You are a brave fighter, Miles of England. But I have made a promise that of all the Franks I capture, only you shall remain unransomed."

"Then kill me now." He stared at Saladin's lined face for a moment in challenge before he took the bowl the slave girl held out. Miles drank the water, ignoring its rancid taste, and a moment later the pain in his side diminished.

"Your wounds are not great, and you will recover. I have seen to their care and dressing and have been told they will heal quickly. Although I am not permitted to ransom you, your life with us will not be overly harsh."

"Any life not of my choosing is harsh."

"But it is life just the same. Death offers no opportunity for change."

Miles listened to the Moorish king, but the effect of the drug began to slow his mind, and soon it seized him fully. Saladin's words began to recede, and Miles was again enveloped in the pleasant forgetfulness of sleep.

Outside the chamber, Saladin was met by his grand vizier. The two men, accompanied by Saladin's bodyguards, walked in silence toward the audience chamber of the castle. Only when they were inside, with no other ears to listen, did Borka-al-Salu speak.

"Master of Life, what will you do with him?"

"Taunt Richard for a while."

"Would you have that done to al-Nasir?" Borka asked, naming the foremost of Saladin's fighters.

"Al-Nasir would not have been taken alive."

"This Frankish knight had no choice. He was prepared to die. You saw that for yourself."

"True."

"And you respect him highly?"

"You know that is the case."

"Then do not shame him further."

"I will think on it. Now I would be alone." Saladin

watched his chief advisor bow low and leave the tent. Sadness filled Saladin's mind. It was rare that he felt any respect for these Christian murderers, but of all the men he fought, two stood out above the rest. Richard was a mighty adversary, a worthy opponent, and a good general. And the knight he held captive was also a strong opponent, and one who held himself with honor.

But winning and ending this war was more important than any single man, and he must use this English knight to weaken his enemy. Although he was loath to place shame upon Miles's head, he knew that he must. Yet, he also promised himself that upon the war's end, he would elevate Miles from the rank of prisoner to that of honored guest, with all that went with it. But, no matter what the future brought, Saladin saw it was the will of Allah that had determined his position, and for as long as he lived, he was bound to his promise to keep Miles in his lands.

While Miles slept within the walled city of Jerusalem, recovering his strength, and Saladin debated the wisdom of his actions, Arthur waited for an audience with Richard.

It was long after the sun had dropped from the sky, the chill of the November night wrapping its tentacles over the land, when Arthur returned to the main encampment from the hills he had hidden behind. He had waited, long after the battle had been fought, trying to understand what he'd seen.

When he'd been separated from Miles, he'd tried to fight to his master's side, but two of Radstock's knights had prevented this. Then, Arthur had ridden to the highest point overlooking the battle and had seen Miles fight the overwhelming numbers of enemy. He had seen a lance bounce from Miles's head and had seen also a scimitar flash against his armor. He had watched when Miles's stricken body fell to the earth, and had stared in shock when the Saracens, instead of killing him, had lifted him from the ground and tied him to a horse.

He knew then that it would be ransom they were after. Arthur was certain that Richard would pay anything for Miles's safe return, and with that in mind, waited in the tents of Radstock for two days. But early on the third day, as he walked past Morgan of Guildswood's tent, loud voices reached out to stop him.

He listened to the drunken talk and recognized Morgan's grating words. "At last I have nothing to stop me from taking Radstock. Saladin kept his word to me. He refused the ransom negotiation from Richard."

"It is as you said he would do," came the voice of another knight whom Arthur did not recognize. But the words painted the true picture for Arthur, and in that moment he knew what must be done. An hour later he was dressed in the clothing of his station, waiting to see the king.

When he was finally called before Richard, he went to his knee and waited until Richard bade him rise. Then he stood and gazed at Richard.

"We are all in mourning of our loss. Sir Miles was the best of us," Richard said.

"Your Majesty, I ask permission to return to England and carry word of what has happened to my mistress."

"I understand your desire, but we need everyone here to fight the Saracens. Do you not want vengeance for Sir Miles?"

"I do, Majesty; that is the very reason I seek your permission. I would return to Radstock so that Lady Gwendolyn may send Sir Eldwin to avenge the insult Saladin has laid at your feet."

Richard's laugh was deep and strong. He sighed loudly and placed a large hand on Arthur's shoulder. "Do you think Sir Eldwin powerful enough to win back Sir Miles?"

Arthur looked around the tent, his eyes sweeping across the men gathered there. When they fell on Morgan's face, they stopped. Arthur spoke to the king, but his eyes never left Morgan's.

"There has been treachery set upon Sir Miles and you, Your Majesty, and I pray you let me go to the Lady Gwendolyn. It is her right to know what has happened, and Sir Miles would want Sir Eldwin to lead his knights and fight by your side."

"Well said, lad," Richard stated. Then he shrugged his massive shoulders. "Go to your mistress and tell her what has happened. It is the winter season, and I know not when we shall meet Saladin again."

Arthur did not wait; he bowed and quickly left the tent. Before he reached Radstock's tents, he was stopped by Sir Hugo.

"I liked not what you said, Boy. You spoke of treachery. Was it truth?"

"It was truth, but I cannot prove it."

"Tell me what you know," Hugo demanded.

Arthur looked at the knight, and wondered if he dared take the chance of telling him the truth. "What difference can it make to you?"

"There are too few men of Delong's ilk. We need them all. If something black was done to him, might it not happen to any of us?"

"It might," Arthur agreed, deciding that he would chance trusting this man. He told Hugo what he'd overheard, and also what he'd seen during the battle.

"It is because of the tournament!"

"No, it is because Morgan wants what my lord has. He wants the Lady Gwendolyn."

"Treachery to gain a woman? There must be more," Hugo whispered.

"There is, but I do not know everything."

"You will return with Eldwin?"

"I am sure of that. Sir Eldwin will somehow free my lord."

Hugo stared at the squire for a minute before he nodded his head. He remembered the tournament and his fight with Eldwin. He remembered, too, the strength and power of the hooded knight. "Perhaps he will. All right, Boy, I will take you myself to Acre and see that you have a ship to return by. Be ready at first light."

Arthur bowed to the knight who offered his help, and when Hugo left, hurried to the tent and packed the few things he would take back with him. He told the other knights what had transpired and told them also that he would return with Eldwin.

Then, unable to sleep, Arthur lay on the pallet inside Miles's tent, waiting for the first light of day.

Chapter Eighteen

THE CHILL WAS FULL UPON the land, and the first snow of the winter spread its soft white blanket from Wales to Radstock. But it mattered not to the three people hidden in the deep chamber beneath the foundations of the castle.

Gwendolyn worked steadily with her practice sword, advancing upon James and forcing him to defend himself and utilize all his training. Roweena stood off to the side, watching the practice, wondering what devil possessed her mistress. For a week following Gwendolyn's strange sleep, she had come to the fighting chamber to practice with James, leaving the castle to run itself.

Each day, Gwendolyn had given Roweena certain tasks to do and had warned her that none must know of them. She had done as her mistress ordered and, when each task was completed, had reported the fact.

Silence descended in the chamber, and Roweena realized the practice was over. Gwendolyn and James walked toward her, and she rose to meet them. "Tomorrow James and I ride to Bath. You must assume my role until I return."

Roweena stared uncomprehendingly at Gwendolyn. "How, mistress?"

"In a similar manner as always. You will direct the castle from my sick bed. I will be gone but a fortnight."

"So long? I don't know that I can do it that long."

"You must. And for longer if need be. Roweena, we will soon be leaving England."

"Leaving England?" she echoed, her eyes widening at the prospect.

"Miles has been captured by the Saracens. We must go to the Holy Land and free him."

Roweena had long ago given up trying to understand certain parts about her mistress, but this new revelation was almost too much to handle. She shook her head silently, unable to respond.

"Do not fear, Roweena. No one will learn of our deception." And Gwendolyn knew it would be so. In the years she had spent with Roweena, a bond had formed between the servant and the mistress, joining them together in a way few could understand. Each loved the other, and each knew the other's mannerisms perfectly.

Gwendolyn had taught Roweena to read and cypher Latin and French, and to write not only well, but in perfect imitation of her own flowing hand. Any messages that would come for her, Roweena could read, and reply to if necessary.

She had learned the running of the castle at the same time as Gwendolyn, and had been at her side for almost all the decisions regarding the lands she had ruled for her husband. Yes, Roweena could act for Gwendolyn in almost all matters.

"When do you leave?"

"Tonight," Gwendolyn stated.

That night, when the castle slept peacefully, Gwendolyn, in the guise of Eldwin, left the castle by its secret passageway and, with James, rode under the full moon toward the ancient city of Bath. Her goal was the Abbey of Bath, situated just outside the ruins of the old Roman city. She was going there to talk with Theodore, Miles's brother, to ask him to return to Radstock and care for the lands until either she and Miles returned, or he learned of their deaths.

They rode through the night and into the day. Once, when the sun broke through the clouds, Gwendolyn noted it was near noon. An hour from Bath, in a small stand of woods, Gwendolyn, with James's aid, took off her knightly trappings and put on the smooth Saxon tunic she carried in the bag attached to her saddle. When she was done, ignoring the cold, she allowed James to place a woolen mantle on her shoulders.

Bidding James to wait for her return, she mounted the

black mare and rode to Bath Abbey. Nearing the abbey, Gwendolyn saw the snow reflected on the sandstone walls and spotted a clearing, and the piles of stone that awaited the construction of yet another wing to the building.

Bath Abbey, the only cathedral for miles, was a medium-sized structure, with all its lines built on the perpendicular by the monks who had constructed the site two hundred years before. Gwendolyn knew of its history because Theodore had spoken often of it. He had also told her of the great conflicts that faced it, and he prophesied that within the decade, Bath would replace Wells, as the center of religion for both Avon and Somerset.

Gwendolyn cared nothing for the bickerings of the Church and wanted only to convince Theodore that he was needed in Radstock. With this thought firmly planted in her mind, she rode to the entrance of the abbey and dismounted.

Two monks appeared before her. "Welcome, my lady," one intoned as he looked at her and saw she was of the nobility. "How may we serve you?"

"I seek Theodore, a brother of your order. I am Gwendolyn Delong, Lady of Radstock."

"My lady, permit me to take you inside. I am Brother Charles. Brother Allain will see to your mount." With that, the first monk began walking with Gwendolyn to the ornately carved door of the abbey.

When they entered, Gwendolyn gazed at the vaulted walls and ceiling, seeing for the first time of what Theodore had spoken. The columns and arches were fanlike in their ornamentation, and the long thin windows reflected well the hard lines in which the abbey had been designed. But for all its linear design, the abbey was a thing of beauty, and Gwendolyn knew that those who had built it, and those who had come after to care for and add to it, did so with a gentle love.

"I will fetch Brother Theodore, my lady. Can I also have warm mead brought to you?"

"Thank you, Brother Charles, but I crave nothing other than to speak with Theodore."

"Please," said the monk, pointing to a long bench, "seat yourself." When Gwendolyn did as he asked, Brother Charles left her and disappeared through one of the many doors lining the interior of the church. A few minutes later, that same door opened, and Theodore walked toward her.

Rising, Gwendolyn went to him. Although he wore the dark, shapeless robes of his order, she saw his tall, lanky frame. His large eyes, the same green as Miles's, seemed to sparkle when they fell on her.

"This is a pleasure, Gwendolyn, and a surprise. What brings you here?" he asked, taking both her hands in his. Gwendolyn had almost forgotten the warm relationship they'd shared in the brief time they had lived together in Radstock.

"I must ask a favor."

"If it is within my power, it shall be yours." Theodore meant what he said. He gazed fondly at his brother's wife. He had liked her from the moment he'd met her and had felt a strong friendship grow between them. But when he looked into her eyes, he saw she was deeply troubled. "Tell me," he coaxed in a gentle voice.

"I cannot tell you all, just that Miles is in great trouble. A week ago he was taken prisoner by the Saracens, and he will remain so for the rest of his life unless he is rescued."

"A week ago you say?" Theodore tried to hide his disbelief, but knew it carried in his voice.

"I said I could not tell you all, and I know how hard it is to believe, but you must. Call it a vision, or whatever you desire, but I saw it happen. I lay in my bed for three days, unable to move, and I was carried aloft over the Holy Land. I saw a battle, and I saw Miles fall. I witnessed his capture by the Moslems."

"Even if this is the case, I do not know how to help you. I cannot go to fight in Jerusalem."

"Nor would I ask you. I am going," she whispered.

"You cannot!" A chill rushed through him, brought on by her words. He knew how strong-willed she was, and that she was capable of doing whatever she set her mind to—but she must not do this.

"I have no choice. I have come to ask for your return to Radstock, to oversee your family's lands until we return."

"If you return."

"If . . . If not, you are the only surviving member of the line. The lands will fall to you."

"I want them not," Theodore stated.

"Will you do as I ask?" Gwendolyn stared into his green eyes, her breath stilled while she waited for his response.

"When will you be leaving?"

"I do not know exactly. Soon after Christmas. Theodore?"

A bare nod of his head was his answer.

"Thank you."

"If I had refused?" But Theodore already knew the answer.

"Then I would have to leave Radstock unprotected."

"Will you stay for the evening meal?"

"I must leave. I have much to do. I thank you, my brother. We will return to you, and to Radstock." They embraced tightly, before Theodore accompanied Gwendolyn outside where Brother Allain held her horse.

Theodore stood outside long after Gwendolyn had gone, bothered not by the cold winds or his bare feet on the ground. He remembered something he had once been told by his old teacher upon first joining the priory. Again, the words of his teacher surfaced in his mind, comforting him and easing the decision he had made.

"There is a strange bond between a man and woman who love each other deeply. Perhaps it is because they share themselves so closely. There is an unselfishness that happens only rarely, but when they have joined together as man and wife, they truly seem to become almost as one."

"This always happens?" young Theodore had asked.

"This happens only rarely. It is a special gift given by our Lord, Christ, and to those who receive it, they need little else from life. I witnessed once this strange power, when I was called to the bedside of a woman I had known for years. She was taken ill, and I was called to administer the holy sanction. She lay as one dead. Her skin was the color of snow and her breathing was so shallow I had to press my ears to her mouth to feel it."

"When I asked where her husband was, for they were rarely apart, no one had seen him for three days. Then, as I began to pray for her immortal soul, I saw her eyes open to look at me."

" 'You live,' I said to her. 'No, I die,' she responded to me. I did not know what to say, her words shocked me so. 'Why?' I asked her."

" 'My Peter, he has been killed.' 'That is impossible,' I

told her. 'Two days ago, he was killed by a boar. I saw it in a dream. I will not live without him.' And saying that, this woman died in my arms."

"Because her husband died?" young Theodore questioned.

"No, because a part of her she could not live without had died. The power of love is strong. We of the church do not fully understand this, but, Theodore, do not dismiss it just because you will never know it."

The lesson had remained in the back of Theodore's mind for many years, and, he reasoned, perhaps it was because of it that he had agreed to Gwendolyn's request. But he also realized that Gwendolyn herself was partly the reason. There had always been something different about her. From the moment he'd met Gwendolyn he had sensed a power within her. It was a nameless thing. It was no physical trait; rather, it was an aura carried upon her shoulders like the mantle she had worn today. One day he hoped to find out what it was, because it was the very thing that set her apart from the ordinary. He had felt this before, with others who had been granted a strong destiny.

Eight days after leaving Bath Abbey, Gwendolyn and James stopped their horses in a secluded area of Devonshire. Dismounting, Gwendolyn motioned James to follow her into a small opening in the face of a hill.

James was surprised at the warm interior of the cave, but held his questions until Gwendolyn spoke first. He watched her take off the coif-de-maille, and then the chamois mask before she spoke. "This was the place in which I learned about myself. This cave is known only to myself, Miles, and now you. You will wait here until I return. It will not be more than two days. The buck we brought down this afternoon should see you through. Rest easy here; there is no safer place in all of England."

"Yes, my lord," James said in a low voice.

Gwendolyn smiled at his expression. "You do not approve?"

"I am a squire; it is not my place to say."

"Of what do you not approve?"

"Your grandfather will think you mad."

"That is nothing out of the ordinary."

"I would feel remiss in my oath and duty if I were not with you," James admitted at last.

"I must do this alone," Gwendolyn told him. "Bring my clothing."

An hour later, Gwendolyn, dressed again in the Saxon tunic and mantle, rode to the gate of Kildrake Castle, the home she had not seen for almost two years.

The gate opened to let her through, and by the time she had dismounted and given her horse over to a groom, Hughes was striding across the inner keep.

He stopped a foot from her, staring at Gwendolyn. "What brings you here?"

"Is it not enough for a granddaughter to seek out her family?"

"Yes," Hughes replied in a tight voice. Then he reached out to her and pulled her close. He kissed her firmly on the cheek before releasing her, only to hold her an arm's distance away and look at her closely.

"You have become even more beautiful."

"And you are the same as ever."

"No, I am starting to feel my age. I am cursed to live a long life and suffer with every cold day."

"Do not play the ancient with me; it ill suits you," Gwendolyn said half seriously. In the time since she had married Miles and left Kildrake, she saw that the years had begun to show on her grandfather. It saddened her, but she pushed aside the thought and smiled. "Perhaps we can talk inside. I must be getting as old as you, for the cold is seeping into my bones."

Hughes laughed at her words and escorted her into the walls of Kildrake Castle, calling out to the servants to have her old bedchamber prepared.

Hughes brought Gwendolyn to the small hall, the warm room where he spent many of the cold winter days. A fire burned cheerfully, and two of his dogs lay sleeping near its warmth.

When they were seated, and a servant had brought warm drinks, he turned to Gwendolyn, his sapphire eyes sparkling. "And what mischief has caused you to ride through England unescorted?"

Gwendolyn took a deep breath and, for the first time in her

life, asked her grandfather a special question. "Do you remember my mother's hardship, and my conception?" She watched her grandfather's ruddy complexion pale and waited, her breath held, until the color returned to his cheeks.

"Aye," he whispered.

"Then you know I am different from others?"

"I have always known it, Gwendolyn, but like most men, I pretended it had not happened. I dismissed everything and accepted the lot of a shamed father."

"But you know the truth?"

"I know what I must believe. Your mother was the gentlest woman I have ever known, and her life was but a shadow of what it should have been."

Gwendolyn felt his words wrench her heart, and realized suddenly how deeply he had been hurt. She wanted to reach out to him, but could not. There was still a barrier between them, a wall that had been built many years before.

"I am sorry for the pain and disappointments, but it was something that was meant to be. Do not feel that my mother's life was not a good one. It was. She was happier than you or anyone could have ever believed. Grandfather," she whispered, calling him by his true title as she had so rarely done before. "Gwyneth never once regretted what happened, and never once did she speak anything but kind words for you." Tears came to Gwendolyn unbidden, and she let them flow freely.

She saw Hughes's eyes become distant for a moment, before they fastened on hers. "I have never spoken to a soul about what happened to your mother and have never believed what was foretold. Was it the truth?"

"I do not know what the truth is. I am different than other women, yet I am the same. I feel love, desire, pain, all things that others feel. Yet there is something else within me; something so mighty that it drives me beyond what others seek. That is what is different about me."

"When you were wed to your husband, I tried to tell him of you, but I could not."

"The morning after we were wed, I told him of my birth, and of my mother and father."

"And he did not think you mad? He did not seek to annul your vows?"

"Our love is strong; it stands powerfully in the midst of doubt. No, Grandfather, he did not think me mad."

"Why have you come to tell me of these things? For if I am not mistaken, this is not the reason for your visit."

"You are not mistaken. I have come to speak with you about this, to tell you of something, and to ask your advice."

"But you had need to clarify my own feelings first?"

"Yes. What I must tell you is hard to believe. Only you, who knows about me, could understand." Gwendolyn paused, waiting for Hughes to respond. But he did not; he merely waited for Gwendolyn to continue.

"I must go to the Holy Land." Still there was no response from her grandfather. "Miles has been taken prisoner by Saladin. He is held without ransom."

"You have received word?"

"It happened a fortnight ago. I was granted a vision and witnessed the battle."

"Madness!" muttered Hughes, but his eyes did not reflect the word.

"By Christmas, Miles's squire, Arthur, will arrive by ship at Portsmouth. He will bring news of this to me. I would meet him there, and return with him to the Holy Land."

"And what would you do there? Put on maille and fight the Saracens? Your presence in Palestine would do nothing to free your husband."

"Grandfather, my presence in the Holy Land will free Miles. I will have Sir Eldwin with me. We will find a way."

"Would that it were possible. And even so, your reputation would be ruined. No woman goes with an army lest she is but a whore. I will not have you so looked upon, nor would your husband."

"My reputation is nothing without my husband! I have come to ask your advice, not to listen to your moralistic views!"

Hughes gazed at the anger-filled eyes of his granddaughter and held himself in check. For too many years he had pushed aside his memory of her, her mother, and his wife, her grandmother. All the women of Kildrake had a certain pride and carriage, and none of them had ever bent under his willful thumb. Perhaps for that reason he had always respected and loved them. Nothing they could do had ever brought real shame into his mind.

"What do you plan?"

"That is why I am here. I need your help and advice."

"First tell me about this knight of yours, Sir Eldwin."

"What do you wish to know?"

"I have heard two stories. One is that he was a ward of the Earl of Radstock, Miles's father. The other that he was a knight of Kildrake and sworn to you. Which is true?"

"Does it matter?"

"It does. A man who hides behind a mask is either good or bad. There is nothing in between."

"Sir Eldwin was of Kildrake, but you knew him not," Gwendolyn admitted.

"I know all my vassals," Hughes defended.

"Eldwin is good and you know who he is. It is for that reason he cannot reveal his identity. Trust me, Grandfather, you would not like to know the knight's true identity."

"And now you presume to know my mind?"

"I cannot help it. We are of the same blood."

"I heard of his victory over Morgan. And I heard the story of his silver-dipped sword," Hughes told her, his eyes never wavering from hers. "They say it was longer than most, and wider, too. I was told it had a plain hilt, with perfectly shaped quillons. About so wide," he said as he held his hands a foot apart.

"Yes," she whispered.

"I have seen that shape before, Gwendolyn, impressed upon the skin of your mother's belly. That is the truth, is it not?"

"Yes."

Gwendolyn saw the suspicion cover his face and knew she had to stop him before he spoke. "Will you help me?"

Hughes stared at her, trying to hold back his mind from releasing the knowledge he had suddenly found. The words of the Druid priestess, uttered almost twenty years ago, filled his mind, telling him again what he had once shut out. A moment later he nodded his head. And he saw in Gwendolyn's expression that she knew he had reasoned out the identity of Sir Eldwin.

"I do not know why this has come to pass, but I see that nothing I can say will deter you. I am against it, but I yield to your request. Here is what must be done," he said, as he outlined everything she would have to do.

Gwendolyn spent the night within the walls of Kildrake Castle, and the next day rode with her grandfather along the moors that she had loved. The feelings that they had shared between them had changed since her arrival yesterday, and when it was time to leave Kildrake, she did so with a heavy heart. She had finally found her grandfather's love, and the openness of his heart that her mother had always spoken of.

When she rode away, she carried with her a small fortune. Her grandfather had given her enough gold to outfit a contingent of knights, hire a ship, and pay the high expenses needed to avoid a slow journey. When she left England, she would sail directly to Cypress and not stop in Sicily. The journey to the Holy Land would be a swift one, because Hughes himself would make sure of that.

Hughes would meet her in Portsmouth, with more knights to join Richard's army. There, he would give the ship's captain his orders and make sure nothing amiss would happen. There were ways of dealing with the men who plied ships, especially when they carried a beautiful woman.

On the fourteenth night after she had left Radstock, Gwendolyn returned through the hidden passageway and entered her private chamber. Valkyrie's cry of greeting echoed loudly and woke Roweena from her sleep.

Roweena jumped from the bed and ran to Gwendolyn, her face both animated and fearful. "Praise be that you've returned in time."

"In time?"

"My lady, Prince John will arrive in Radstock on the morrow. He sent word ahead."

"Why?" Gwendolyn asked, taken back by this new development.

"I know not, but he will arrive tomorrow, that is for certain."

"Damn!" Gwendolyn spat. Turning to James, she began to issue orders. "The castle must be made ready for the prince."

"It is done," Roweena said. Suddenly Gwendolyn relaxed. But her mind still churned in its search for a reason for this untimely visit of Prince John.

Chapter Nineteen

WHAT COULD HE WANT? Gwendolyn asked herself the same question for the hundredth time since hearing the news. When Richard left on the crusade, he had entrusted England to be governed under the joint regency of Hugh Puiset of Durham and William Longchamp of Ely. Yet, before he had even sailed from Marseilles, he had changed his decree, naming Longchamp sole regent.

Richard had also richly gifted John with lands and earldoms, securing from him a pledge to stay away from England for three years. But nothing had come about in the way Richard had planned; instead, political intrigue was the rule of the day.

The land was torn with dissension. The nobles felt restrained by Longchamp and were almost in open rebellion of his rule. This was partially due to Longchamp's anti-English prejudices, and partially because Longchamp was holding up Arthur, the son of Richard's brother Geoffrey, as the rightful heir to England's throne.

Word of Longchamp's activities brought John's return to England. Immediately upon his arrival, he cultivated the barons and dukes to his banner, getting each of them to swear allegiance to him as rightful successor to Richard.

Gwendolyn had been following the news of John's fight with Longchamp for many months and had learned of Eleanor's decision to side with her son in this instance; although it was well-known that Richard was her favorite.

Gwendolyn wisely discerned that Eleanor's actions were but a method of keeping England from open rebellion until Richard could return home to settle the disputes and control the warring factions.

But no matter what was happening, Gwendolyn did not like the fact that John was coming to Radstock Castle. He would want fealty sworn to him, or he would take the castle as he had so many others in the past months.

Looking down from the upper battlement of Radstock Castle, Gwendolyn saw the activity in the inner keep was slowing and knew that everything would be in readiness for John's arrival. She looked eastward and saw the line of horses looming closer. They had crested the last hill and were now moving steadily toward the castle.

An hour later, Gwendolyn left her chamber in a dress befitting her station as Lady of Radstock. She waited within the inner keep until John had dismounted and then went to her knee before him.

"Rise, Lady Delong," he ordered, and Gwendolyn stood before the man whose harsh hand was felt over the length of England.

"We bid you welcome, my lord prince."

"And we accept, gladly. It has been a chilled journey, but one of necessity."

"Will you be honoring us long?" Gwendolyn did not like the way the prince was staring at her, even though she had purposely worn a modestly cut tunic. She had heard the stories of John's unhealthy appetites and did not want his hunger to stray to her.

"Only the night. I must reach Cardiff in three days."

Relieved, yet still on guard, Gwendolyn issued orders to have John's men and horses seen to. After which, Gwendolyn graciously led John into the castle, and to the chamber prepared for him.

"It must be hard, having your husband so far away," John said when he stood at the threshold of his chamber.

"Many things in life are difficult, my lord."

"'Tis true, Lady Gwendolyn. There is much I would discuss with you, but first I need relieve myself and change out of these dirty garments. We shall talk over the evening meal. Please wear something in white; the color is soothing to my eyes."

Gwendolyn left John, holding back her anger in the face of his words. She yearned to ask who he thought himself to be. This was her home, and no one, save Miles, had the right to speak to her as he had. The lust she had seen in his eyes had also angered her, but she knew she must be careful.

The great hall had been prepared, and two hours after darkness fell, the hall roared with life. Twenty of John's knights sat at the table, intermingled with twenty of Radstock's own. Platter upon platter of food was served while musicians played high upon the scaffolding. At the High Table sat only Gwendolyn and John, attended by Roweena and John's squire.

Gwendolyn, although she detested the thought, knew she had to accede to John's wishes and had worn a Norman dress with a white underskirt. The turquoise overdress had a full bodice that reached to her neck, but the dress's underskirt and long billowing sleeves were pure white. As was her custom, she wore the Saracen dagger on a golden rope. On her head she wore a simple woman's coif-de-maille that had not one jewel in it, and which blended nicely with her hair.

Since they had sat for the meal, John had continually drained goblet upon goblet of wine, and before the meal was half-done, Gwendolyn saw he was well on the way to becoming drunk.

"Why do you wear that bauble?" John asked, leaning toward her and fingering the handle of the dagger lying between her breasts.

"It was a wedding gift from my husband."

"A strange gift," John muttered, as he withdrew his hand. "It must be lonely to live without a man. Do you not find it so?" His eyes sparkled darkly when he spoke, and Gwendolyn shivered internally.

"It is lonely only when there is no love between a husband and wife, and then it matters not if they are together or apart."

"And you love your husband, and therefore are not lonely?"

"I carry him always within my mind and heart."

"But a cold bed is not a pleasant thing."

"Surely you did not travel all this way to discuss my empty bed. What is it that you have come to Radstock for?" Gwendolyn asked in an effort to change the subject.

John stared at her. His fingers ran through his short beard, and he shook his head. "Fear not, Lady Gwendolyn; you are far from what I consider desirable in a woman. Your virtue is safe with me."

"My lord, I know not what you mean. My virtue has never been questioned, nor has the ability of my knights to protect me ever been put to so foolhardy a test," Gwendolyn replied, but her eyes turned cold and challenging as she stared at him.

John shifted uncomfortably under her gaze. "It is time for the nobility of England to stand beside the man who will be the rightful heir to the throne."

"Heir? My lord, Richard is still young."

"But he is a fighter. He is unwed and childless. He will not live long. When he dies, England must have a king who is prepared to rule her properly. A king who will stay with his country and not go chasing blood and dreams."

"And you would be this king?"

"It is my right! I am the successor to the throne. Even my mother has so stated. Lady Gwendolyn, in the absence of the Earl of Radstock, I ask you to declare allegiance to me."

"My lord . . ." She had guessed Prince John might make such a demand, yet she was unprepared for this direct request and forced her mind to work quickly.

"I am but a woman. It must be Miles who gives his backing."

"He is half a world away, following a king who cares little for his lands. Nay, Lady Gwendolyn, if the earl does not survive the crusade, the lands will be yours. I will consider your pledge to me binding upon Radstock."

"My husband will return!"

"I pray so, madame, but for now, I need your support. Give me your pledge!" John's voice turned hard when he spoke, and his eyes bored into Gwendolyn's. His unvoiced threat was as clear as her earlier one had been to him.

Taking great care, Gwendolyn answered. "I can only give you my pledge conditionally, to be reaffirmed by the earl when he returns."

"I will accept that. Lady Gwendolyn, will it not be better to be ruled by a man who will live in his country, rather than one who thinks Normandy to be the capital of England?"

"Is that what you have promised the others? Do you think young Arthur would rule from Aquitaine?"

"Arthur will never rule! I have pledged that for the first time since William conquered England, England will have a king who will live in his kingdom. Is that not desirable?"

"I do not know. I am but a simple woman, not given to intrigue."

"You, Lady Gwendolyn, are far from a simple woman. I will accept your conditional pledge for my backing."

Gradually, with their business concluded, the talk turned to general things, and the tension that had flowed between them eased. Soon, John succumbed to the call of the wine, and was lost in drunken gestures that all but Gwendolyn ignored.

Gwendolyn grew more uncomfortable as the minutes turned into hours, and did her best to stay out of reach of the prince. For all his words dismissing her charms, Gwendolyn was too aware of the reputation of his strange lusts that had spread across the land.

At one point, John turned to her, his eyes red-rimmed, his lids half-closed. "Perhaps I spoke too hastily before. My bed, too, has been cold and empty for too long."

The words sent a cold chill racing along her spine, and without realizing it, her hand curled around the hilt of the Saracen dagger. John's eyes followed her move, and he threw his head back, laughing derisively.

"Do you think you could use that upon me?"

"It would not be the first time its use was called upon."

"Do not push too far, my lady, for you may need me as a friend in the days ahead. Many castles have found themselves ill-equipped to survive in these hard times."

"My lord, I have no fear of survival. Radstock is strong, and is allied with Devonshire, or had you forgotten?" she said innocently, reminding him that if he were to try and seize Radstock, her grandfather's knights would not be so easily subdued.

"I have no need of Radstock, other than its backing. And I accept your desire, though I do not understand it. Many wives while away their husband's absences in far better circumstances than you have chosen."

"You have already extracted my pledge of backing; I believe that is all you came for. Now, I find myself tiring, my lord, and pray you allow me to retire."

John dismissed her, not by standing courteously, but with a neglectful and insulting wave of his hand. He was so preoccupied with himself that he did not see the immediate reaction from the two knights sitting nearest the High Table. They were men of Radstock who had chosen their seats to be near their lady. Both men had their squires in attendance, and those squires had swords resting unseen in special niches within the great hall's stone walls.

When she left the great hall, Gwendolyn ordered the servants to continue serving the knights, and to take great care in their attitude toward John. But when she stepped outside the hall, Justin, the leader of the knights of Radstock in Eldwin's absence, came to her.

"My lady," called the knight.

Gwendolyn turned and waited for him to reach her. With an upraised eyebrow she commanded him to speak.

"We do not trust John. I have already ordered ten stations manned tonight. It would not be the first time John has tried to take a castle in this way. We heard also what he demanded of you. When he leaves the hall, I will stand guard at your chamber."

"You think this best?"

"We would be remiss in our obligation to our lord if we did not do this, Lady Gwendolyn."

"Very well," she replied. Gwendolyn was touched by her men's loyalty and smiled warmly at the knight. "The earl will know of this night and reward you suitably."

Sir Justin bowed to his mistress and returned to the hall, leaving Gwendolyn alone with the night. She gazed at the sky and thanked the powers above that the early December sky was cloudless this once, and there would be no snows to prolong Prince John's visit. There was much to do, and very little time to accomplish it all.

The walled city of Jerusalem was like none other in the known world. It was a large, sprawling complex of high stone houses, thatched and impoverished shanties, and cavelike dwellings. Yet for all its apparent dissimilarities, it was a city united for one thing—religion. The great church of the Christians still stood, overshadowed by the mosque of the Dome of the Rock, and surrounding that were the ruins of the great temple of the Jews, which had been erected hundreds of years before either.

Under Saladin, Jews, Christians, and Moslems mingled in the streets in the same manner as the buildings mingled with each other. It was both a poor city and a rich one. Saladin and his entourage occupied five of the largest stone buildings, turning them into a city within a city. In the tallest of the buildings, Saladin lived and ruled. In a smaller building, attached by a courtyard, was the residence where the emir of the Turks housed his Christian prisoner.

From Saladin's bedchamber, a window overlooked the white stoned courtyard, and Saladin had formed the habit of watching his prisoner exercise beneath him.

He had grown to like the English knight for his bravery and strength of character and had granted Miles Delong's requests to practice his knightly arts, after securing his word of honor, as a knight, that he would make no attempt to try an escape if Saladin returned his arms.

Yet he was bothered by the strangely stoic mood of his captive and yearned to find a way to set him free. But he knew Miles was the price he was paying for the information of Richard's plans, and he could not renege on his word.

Instead, he sought to win Miles's acceptance of his position by gifts of clothing, jewels, and slaves to be available for his every whim. But Saladin had not been able to break past the knight's barriers and restraints.

Shaking his head, Saladin stepped away from the window and the two men practicing their sword strokes below to attend to the matters of state that awaited him.

Miles concentrated on his wrists, making the sword he held blur through the air before it struck the curved blade of his opponent. Every day he came into this courtyard, dressed in his armor, to spend three hours wielding his sword against the Moor who had become his jousting partner. Fighting the large Moslem, sword against scimitar, was a release for his frustrations as well as a catharsis for his tortured mind. This daily duel was an escape from the imprisonment of his body and spirit, and from the walls of the city he could not leave.

From the moment of his capture, the weeks had dragged

on. Deception and treachery had brought him here, and no matter how he planned, he knew escape would be impossible. It was for that reason he had given Saladin his word that if his arms and armor were returned to him, he would give his parole to remain. Spurring that decision was the fact that between Miles and freedom were four thousand Turkish knights and warriors. Escape meant only one thing: death—and Miles Delong was not the breed of man who sought a fruitless death, when life, itself, meant hope.

And hope, for Miles, was in the shimmering form of a golden-haired woman and her silver sword. Not one night went by when Miles did not dream of Gwendolyn. The vision of her within his mind calmed him, and although it was but a dream, he knew deep in his soul that his wife, with her special powers, knew of his lot and would somehow find the means to help him.

Although Saladin treated him courteously, he was a prisoner nonetheless. He had the freedom of his rooms, and the use of this courtyard—but there were guards at every exit. He was not restrained physically and could even walk the myriad streets within the walled city, but on each side would be two of Saladin's bodyguards.

The only times Miles felt any peace within himself was when he worked with his sword, when he slept, and when he thought of Gwendolyn. Saladin had sent him slave woman after slave woman, but he desired none. His only desires were to be free to face Morgan and kill him.

Miles lowered the sword and gazed up at the gray sky. Since his capture, winter had set in over Jerusalem. It was not as cold as England's, but the constant chill and dampness infiltrated every pore of his body.

Bowing to Amir, the thick-bodied Moor who came to him daily in the courtyard, Miles sheathed his sword to signal the end of the day's workout. When the Saracen returned the bow, Miles went to the entrance of the courtyard, and through the archway. Once inside his chamber, the slave girl who had become his servant helped to undress him and then led him to the waiting bath.

This was a custom of the Moors that Miles welcomed. The hot oil-scented bath would ease his muscles and lull his mind into complacency for a short time.

After the bath, he would be massaged by one of the slaves

and then dressed. During the past five weeks, it had become a daily ritual to join Saladin in the afternoon. They would sit and talk, each learning the customs of the other, and asking questions without restraint. Usually they would do this over the Moslem game of Shesh-besh, a strange yet fascinating game using bone cubes and carved jewels on an embroidered board. The sport combined skill, strategy, and luck, and in the five weeks he had been playing it, Miles had become adept at all its maneuvers.

Miles rose from the tiles of the bath, letting the water cascade from his lean body, and then allowed the slave, Aliya, to wrap him in muslin. He went to the long cushion on the floor and lay face down upon it.

With his eyes closed, he gave himself over to Aliya's knowledgeable fingers as she spread oil on his muscles and began to massage it into his skin.

He thought about Gwendolyn, and the constant dreams he lived with. Although Saladin was content to think Miles his prisoner for life, Miles knew that Gwendolyn's visits to him when he slept were the assurance that one day he would see her again and their lives would be brought together once more. There was within him a space that she occupied, and as long as he lived, she would be a part of him.

Nightly, when he lay in his bed, he thought of her and built a mind picture. He would speak to her, call out to her, and tell her of his circumstance. Whether she heard his silent calls or not was unimportant. For Miles, speaking to her in this way was his real link with sanity.

"Turn," Aliya said, and Miles did as she requested. In the time he'd spent here, he had picked up a great deal of the Saracen tongue which enabled him to get across his wants.

Aliya's fingers were like magic on his body, easing the tightness in his muscles and soothing his conflicting thoughts. But today he sensed something different happening. Her fingers began to ease in their pressure, and changed to lilting strokes on his inner thigh. He tried to ignore her ministrations, but they were too determined.

This was not the first time a woman had tried to excite him, but it was the first time for Aliya. Nightly, Saladin had sent women to him. They offered him their lush bodies, but he had sent each away untouched.

When Saladin had asked why, he'd avoided the question,

and the ruler of the Moslem world had not pursued the subject. But Miles knew that no woman could satisfy him. There was only one he desired, and if he could not have her, he wanted no others.

Aliya fondled him gently, drawing on the arts she had been taught since childhood, but when she looked into Miles's eyes, her hand stilled.

"It is not right," she said to him.

"I am different," Miles stated.

"Yet you do not like boys, either."

"No." Saladin had even taken to sending him boy slaves, to see if that was the problem. But Miles had spurned them without even speaking.

Aliya shook her head, unable to solve the mystery of this handsome Christian knight, wishing that she could help ease his torment, as she, too, knew the futility of not owning her own life. She also wanted to help him because she had fallen in love with him, but that was only for her to know.

"You are but a child, Aliya," Miles said, knowing that she would understand little of his words, but needing to be able to speak to someone of his thoughts. He had seen her devotion grow daily and had come to accept her as a friend, looking on her with a brotherly love. "Child of another world. I do not spurn your offer, I just cannot accept it. You would think me mad if you understood my words, but it matters not. Although I touch no woman, I am with my wife nightly. I feel her comforting arms around me and sleep on the softness of her breasts. One day, if you are fortunate, you, too, will know this feeling."

Miles smiled gently at her doelike questioning gaze, and then reached out to caress her uncovered cheek. Yet, he saw within her large brown eyes a form of understanding—not of his words, but of the way he had said them.

Miles sat up, ending both the massage and his confession. He ordered Aliya to bring him his clothes. When he had begun to visit Saladin, he had been given the clothing of the Moors. But again he had protested, and Saladin, for some unknown reason, had acceded to his desire to wear the clothing of his culture and had several surcoats made for him. But Miles had made two concessions to the Arab dress. He wore the soft kid slippers of the Moslem, and when he went out of doors, in the colder days, he covered himself in the long flowing folds of the burnoose.

After he was dressed, Miles glanced at the sky outside. Evening was upon them, and the gray sky was growing dark. Without a word to Aliya, he left his chamber and went toward Saladin's.

His two guards stepped behind him and silently followed, but when he reached the caliph's quarters, the large black guard at the door stopped them.

He spoke too rapidly for Miles to understand, but when he had finished, Miles's own guard spoke in French.

"Saladin has requested you join him in the audience chamber."

Again Miles walked along the hallway. At the large entrance to the chamber, Miles heard the sound of many musical instruments.

Entering, Miles saw the audience chamber was filled with people. The sounds of music floated in the air, and slave women danced in diaphanous veils that whirled in accordance with their movements.

Saladin sat on his high chair, his large frame covered by a long, flowing robe. A keffiyah covered his head, and his olive skin glowed in the light of the burning oil lamps.

Making his way to the sultan of the Moors, Miles paid his obeisance to the seated monarch before going to the place Saladin had always reserved for him.

"You are well today?" Saladin asked.

"I am still a prisoner," Miles replied.

"So you are. Perhaps that will change."

Instantly, Miles concentrated his attention on Saladin's face. His words had been spoken lightly, but Miles sensed a deeper meaning within them. Yet, he held back his questions and waited for the king to speak.

"I have grown to like you, Miles of England. Why do you spurn all that I have offered?"

"I have not spurned your offers, Emir of the Chosen," Miles replied, using one of Saladin's many titles of respect. "I have been unable to accept them. There is a difference."

"A very slight difference. You know that I may not release you, yet you persist in clinging to some stray hope. Do you think Richard strong enough to defeat me?"

"War is itself an unknown area. The strong are not always victorious, nor are they smartest. War is directed by the caprices of fate."

"Embrace the true faith, my friend, for you speak with the wisdom of a holy man," Saladin said with only the faintest of smiles.

"Would you in my place?" Miles asked.

"But I am not. You are an enigma to me. You are brave to a fault in battle. You are strong, young, and have a superior body. Yet you practice celibacy like a holy man. Why, whenever I offer you a woman, do you turn her down?"

"Is it not my right?"

"It is not natural. Do you think when you die that your God will look kindly on you for this?"

"What I do is for myself, not for an unknown being called God. Saladin, though you be the wisest man of your land, you know not how I feel of religion. Yet, I have spent much time studying yours. The God of the Christians and of the Moslems is the same. The same even as the God of the Jews. It is only your belief of Muhammad, as the prophet, that differs from our beliefs."

"That is but the surface of it," said Borka-al-Salu, interjecting his own words.

"Exactly!" Miles stated. "Underlying this is the fact that it is but one God that all pray to."

"Our fight is much more than that." Saladin's words had a chilling effect on Miles, and Miles slowly nodded his head in agreement.

"Yes, Caliph of the Faithful, your words are true. Our fight is not one of religion, but of power. Foolish is it not?"

"And wasteful. But it has been so for over a hundred years."

With that, Saladin turned his attention to the entertainment before them. A startlingly beautiful woman was dancing, clad only in a loincloth and veil. Her body was perfectly formed, and the undulating muscles of her stomach attested to her art. She moved lithely, covering the floor in sweeping arcs of arms and hands, moving her body in perfect rhythm. For a moment, Miles was taken from the chamber he sat in and transported to another world where beauty and grace lived, and war was but a faint memory.

The music grew louder, accenting the pace of the dance,

until, with a clash of cymbals, the woman fell to the floor before Saladin, her dark eyes looking up at the king.

"Have you any woman in your land to equal the beauty of this one?" Saladin asked.

Miles gazed openly at Saladin for a moment before he spoke. When he did, his voice was heavy with emotion. "There is one, but her beauty is of a different kind."

"I would that I could see her," replied the caliph.

"If I were you, I would pray that that day will never come." Miles was suddenly aware of Saladin staring strangely at him.

"And why is that?"

"Because the woman we speak of is my wife."

"Tell me of her."

And Miles did, describing for himself, as well as Saladin, the beauty of Gwendolyn Delong. When he was done, Saladin pierced him with a stare for several long moments.

"She is the reason for your abstinence?"

"She is the reason for my life," Miles whispered.

"You English are a strange breed," Saladin said, once again turning from Miles to watch the ongoing entertainment.

Miles waited patiently, his mind still holding the earlier words Saladin had spoken, and when there was a break in the entertainment, he ventured a question. "What may change my status?"

Saladin barked a laugh and shook his head. "You do not let anyone sidetrack you, do you? One way for you to be freed is for Richard to defeat me. My spies inform me that Richard is preparing for another battle. His army is a day from Jerusalem.

"What price did you pay Morgan to be your spy?" The question was spoken in a low voice, but Miles was aware of the Moor's sudden flash of anger.

"That price was you. I have already said as much. I have no further dealings with that man!"

"If you hate him so, why do you not offer me for ransom?"

"Miles of England, I have told you on more than one occasion that I respect you. And I have also told you that my word is sacred. I cannot release you, no matter what the circumstance. Yet," Saladin whispered in a faraway voice that brought Miles's nerves to the screaming point, "there is one other way. Take up the true faith. Join with me completely, and I promise you a rich and full life. I will not ask you to fight your own. I would but have you join the highest ranks of my counsel. I respect and admire you, Miles of England, and would welcome you at my side and in my family. Join me so that you may be free."

A hush had swept across the chamber. The music had stopped, and not a single person moved. Saladin's words echoed from the stone walls, and everyone—slave, petitioners, and advisors—waited to hear the Frankish knight's answer.

Miles was aware of the great honor Saladin was offering him, but knew that anything less than freedom to do as he chose would be unthinkable.

"We are too different, you and I. Perhaps if we had met at a different time, a different place. But we are too different."

"I offer you power and wealth, and the knowledge you are not a prisoner. I have treated you as an honored guest since the moment of your capture. I do not take kindly to your arrogant and foolish dismissal of my offer!"

"Then treat me as a prisoner, not as a guest. For I have asked for nothing more!" Miles anger flared heatedly and he stood, his entire body shaking.

"Be careful, Frank," Saladin said in a low voice.

"I fear not for my life, oh Master of Deceit!" With that, Miles spun and walked away. He did not see the signal Saladin flashed to stop his bodyguard from drawing the scimitar and striking Miles dead. Saladin knew the English knight cared not what happened to him, but Saladin himself did. Honor was important. And the price he had to pay in order to keep his word to the Frankish knight who had aided him was a festering sore within his mind.

"It is as I said. You have made a bargain with the spawn of the devil," Borka-al-Salu whispered.

"Yet I must see it through. I will give our prisoner his wish. Have the Englishman prepared for battle. It will anger Richard to see his knight humiliated before him."

The grand vizier nodded his acceptance of his ruler's words, but he did not fail to see the look that Saladin tried to hide. Although he would hold Miles up to humiliation before

Richard, he knew Saladin did not like doing so. But this was a war that must be fought, and any method affording a victory must be employed.

Two days later, the battle for Jerusalem was joined. Saladin was well-prepared for the fight and, acting the astute general he was, had deployed three thousand troops to the rocky hills outside of the walled city. Richard, with his thousands of men, had planned well, too, but his plans called for a different battle.

He had planned to lay siege to the city, attacking it constantly, until Saladin would be forced to negotiate a surrender.

Richard, having received more messages from home, was chafing at his inability to end this crusade. He was needed at home if he were to maintain his kingdom. He, thus, made the fatal mistake of not being prepared for every contingency.

Before the Christian army reached the walls of Jerusalem, Saladin, leading two thousand men, met him on the hill before the walled city. They fought fiercely; arrows covered the sky like a dark blanket. Longsword and scimitar met, lance and spear found the weaknesses in the armor, and the cries of the wounded mingled with the screams of the dying.

Yet the battle went on, and Richard's army pushed forward until they were at the very gates of the city. It was then that one of the knights yelled to Richard, his sword pointing to the top of the white stone wall. Richard paused to look up, and what he saw froze him to the spot. Tied to a wooden cross suspended from the wall was Miles Delong. The Earl of Radstock was naked, his long dark hair blown about by the cold wind. A terrible rage filled Richard, his blood burning hotly, and his mind turned black with anger and humiliation for his friend. At first he thought Miles dead, but a bare second later, he saw Miles's lips move.

He then realized what the knight was mouthing. Retreat! Whirling his mount, Richard looked at the hills. In that moment he saw thousands of mounted Saracens charging toward him.

He turned back to Miles, sadness washing through him for his friend, and lifted his sword high in salute before ordering a retreat. The Christian knights fought well, but with the addition of the new Saracen cavalry, there was no chance for victory. Richard's army had been defeated, and he withdrew as quickly as possible.

Miles watched his king leave, ignoring the pain in his wrists as well as the cold winds that whipped across his body. He had done something to help Richard, although he was a prisoner.

Yet the shame of what had happened this day would spread, and it added yet another item to the long list that Morgan would one day pay for.

Chapter Twenty

A MILE OUTSIDE OF ASCALON, the site of Richard's winter encampment, three riders sped across the sandy ground. A hooded knight led two squires toward the gates of the fortified city that Richard was now using as his headquarters. As she pushed the mounts onward, Gwendolyn breathed deeply of the hot, arid air and readied herself for the next step of her plan.

It had been three months since she'd left Portsmouth. Three months of chafing at the inactivity of life on board ship. Three months of impatience to be in the Holy Land and be close to her husband.

Her journey to Palestine had been the hard undertaking she had expected. The complications of being two people had taken its toll on her, but the deception of Gwendolyn and Eldwin had been the easiest part. The hardest had been getting the ship's captain to sail in the middle of the winter and go directly to the Holy Land. The costs had been extraordinary, but a combination of King Richard's authority that Arthur had brought with him, a huge payment of gold, and the fierce threats from the Duke of Devonshire had convinced the ship's captain that sailing in winter was far more agreeable than dying on land, in a cold, damp dungeon.

To ease the minds of the curious, Gwendolyn had sent James ahead, supposedly accompanying Eldwin to Portsmouth to arrange for transportation. This way she was able to ride openly with her knights, going first to Kildrake, where her grandfather and his knights joined them on the final leg of the journey.

For most of the journey, the men of Radstock were sick from the heavy swells of the sea, and few questioned the whereabouts of Eldwin. Only Gwendolyn seemed unaffected by the journey, and all who saw her saw only her impatience and determination. And both, the knights she had brought with her, and the men who manned the ship, wondered at the sight of the Lady Delong and her golden eagle, Valkyrie, who, like its mistress, seemed unaffected by the ocean voyage.

By the time they reached Jaffa it was April. The weather had calmed, and the air had grown hot. They stayed in Jaffa only a day before leaving for Ascalon. It was in Jaffa that Gwendolyn purchased the Moorish conveyance that would protect her identity. It was a wooden-wheeled carrier, supported by two horses, and completely encased by layers of diaphanous material. All that could be seen were the shapes within it, and Roweena became Gwendolyn once again. Aiding her disguise, Valkyrie rode behind the curtains, too.

When Eldwin, with Arthur and James, rode ahead, she pushed the horses to the edge of their ability, and when the sun began to burn down fiercely, she called a halt.

In the desertlike country, with none around to see, Gwendolyn took off the mask of Eldwin, and ordered James and Arthur to stand guard. Then she drew her silver sword and sank to the sandy ground.

She closed her eyes, and moments later let the trance take her. The silver sword came alive, and its surging power flooded her every sense. Then, opening the channel in her mind, she built within it a picture of Miles. Concentrating on this, she formed a simple message and, building up a sphere of energy, she sent it surging heavenward.

A moment later the sword lost its glow and Gwendolyn opened her eyes. She knew that at that instant, Miles had heard the message: "I am here!"

After that, the three riders continued on to Ascalon to put into full effect the plan that she, James, and Arthur had devised during the long journey from England to the sandy land of Palestine.

They stopped at the gate of the city, and James called out their identification. A moment later the gate opened, and the three rode in. Sir Eldwin was met with cries of welcome, and dismounted in front of a line of knights headed by Hugo.

"We welcome you to our ranks," he declared, grasping Eldwin's gauntleted hand in his.

James stepped forward to speak for Eldwin. "My lord would speak with the king."

"And he shall," came the shout from behind the knights. Richard, wearing only his surcoat, stepped forward. Eldwin, James, and Arthur went to their knees before the king, but Richard clasped Eldwin's shoulder and ordered the knight to rise.

"I see you have heard of Miles's capture."

"As I promised, Your Majesty, I have brought Sir Eldwin," Arthur stated.

"Have you no other knights?" he asked.

This time it was James who spoke. "Twenty-five knights are coming with the Lady Gwendolyn."

"What!" roared Richard, his eyes glaring fiercely not at James or Eldwin, but at Arthur. "I gave you our permission to seek the aid of Eldwin and the other knights. I said nothing about bringing your mistress."

"Sire, we could not stop her, not even the duke was able to hold her back," whispered Arthur.

"This is madness. She does not belong here." Richard shook his head and issued orders that rooms be prepared for the Lady Delong. Only then did Richard gaze at the masked face of Eldwin. "There is much I would tell you about the earl. Come with me," he ordered.

Eldwin motioned James to join them. As they followed Richard, Arthur went to see about their quarters. Inside the king's rooms, Richard waved Eldwin to a seat. But Richard himself did not sit; instead, he paced back and forth while he explained what had befallen Miles, and the ensuing battles with Saladin. When he finished, he stared directly at Eldwin.

"And you would find a way to free the earl?"

Eldwin nodded her head and signaled James. The night before, Gwendolyn had written a missive to Richard, stating that Sir Eldwin and all the knights she had brought with her were at his disposal until the time came to free Miles.

James removed a scroll from the pouch on his side and handed it to Richard. A moment later Richard spoke again.

"I do not know how you plan to accomplish your mission,

but until you do, I will be glad to have you at my side in battle. You will take Miles's place on my right. I will also accept your mistress's wishes and make sure that no man disturbs her peace."

Eldwin rose and bowed to Richard, signifying acceptance of the king's wishes. Before she left, Richard called out again. "Tell your mistress I would join her for the evening meal." With that, Eldwin and James left and went directly to the rooms that were being prepared.

Once the servants and slaves had left them, James undressed Gwendolyn, and she breathed a sigh of relief.

"Everything is as you said it would be."

"So far, James, but we still have much to do. Arthur, what have you heard?"

Arthur detailed what he'd learned, including the Christmas battle at Jerusalem, and Miles's humiliation upon the walls. But as for Sir Morgan, he was not around.

"He will be when he hears I have arrived," she stated.

An hour later, the rest of her party arrived, and, in the privacy of the bedchamber, Roweena dressed Gwendolyn for the king's visit.

When Richard arrived, the room was ready, and a meal laid out. Gwendolyn bowed before Richard, but he pulled her quickly to her feet. "We are in private, madame, and I would be treated as a friend, not a king."

"As you desire," Gwendolyn acceded, guiding Richard to his seat.

"My heart is heavy with the loss of your husband."

"He is not dead, Sire, but a prisoner." Her flashing eyes were enough to make Richard nod his head in agreement.

"Yet he is still lost to us. I thought his squire made it clear that Saladin refuses to ransom him."

"But he is alive. As long as he breathes, there is hope."

"You are a good woman, but you should not have come. This is no place for a woman of your breeding."

"Breeding?" Gwendolyn laughed at Richard's words, but saw a frown crease his brow. "Know you not of my breeding? I am bastard born."

"As are many," Richard said quickly. "I speak not of your birth, but of your carriage and your bravery."

"I apologize, my lord."

"You are forgiven."

"Sire, when will you meet the enemy again?"

"Word is that Saladin is gathering his army for a new assault against us. I expect it to happen within the week."

"Then my arrival is timely, for Eldwin and the other knights will help you."

"That is so. Philip's French troops have all but deserted. Those who remain are but a handful. Our losses have been heavy, but I sense a victory soon."

"Eldwin and my knights are totally at your disposal until such time as we can free my husband."

"If at all."

"It will happen, Sire."

"I pray. Now, tell me what is happening in England during my absence."

Gwendolyn told him of the unrest, and of John's machinations to secure the ascension to the throne. She did not spare herself of what she had been forced to pledge, but told Richard that Miles would release her from it when he returned.

"I understand and do not hold you responsible. My brother is a greedy fool and will pay for it when I return."

By the time they finished talking, three hours had quickly passed. After Richard left, Gwendolyn retired to her bedchamber.

There, she sat on the floor, the silver sword resting in her hand, and let herself fall into the trance of knowledge. She opened her mind channel, and let the purity of the light fill her. She willed her mind free from her body and soon floated in the plane above the earth, drawing peace and comfort from the otherworldly spirits, joining them in their ceaseless wanderings within the heavens.

"Soon, my child," came the soft voice of the priestess.

"Soon, Miles," she whispered in response.

Morgan was in foul temper when he returned to Ascalon. He had been sent out three days ago by Richard to see what Saladin's army was planning. He had seen that the Moors were preparing for a battle and knew that he would be fighting again soon.

But that had only given him pleasure. Morgan loved

fighting and loved the feelings of exaltation that went with it. No, his mood had darkened after he entered the walls of Ascalon and learned of the newcomers.

Eldwin was here, and with him, Gwendolyn. Passion built within him, stimulated by the unattainable desire which had gone unsated for too many years. He had never hoped to have her so soon and felt himself grow eager to see her.

It was midday, and his first obligation was to report to Richard. When that was done, he returned to his rooms, and to the men who waited there.

"You know where she is?"

"In the north section, near Richard's chambers."

"Good. I will go there tonight."

"Three knights stand guard before her chambers. None are allowed to see her without an invitation," said one of his men.

"Do you think them enough to stop me?"

"The king has ordered that no one attend Lady Delong without her permission. All have been instructed."

"Damn her!" Morgan spat. "Give me quill and vellum."

Ten minutes later, Morgan's squire took his message across the town and handed it to one of Gwendolyn's guards.

In the meanwhile, Morgan had dismissed his men and called for a slave to bathe him. The Moorish habit of bathing after several days of riding had been taken up by many, but Morgan's reason was far different from most. He cared little for the bath, but enjoyed the hands of the slave women who washed him.

And this day was no different. The woman who entered, a Moslem slave he had bought a month before, looked at him without fright. The one thing Morgan had found different in the east was the fatalistic acceptance the women lived by. There was nothing he could do to them that would bring a protest from their mouths.

But although they were there for him, and he satisfied himself whenever he felt the urge, he missed the milky skin of the women of England.

Sitting in the tiled bath, Morgan let the girl wash him, closing his eyes when her hands began to play with his limp organ. But even as she did, thoughts of Gwendolyn rose to taunt him. He laughed harshly, and the slave girl drew away. Instantly his hand caught her wrist in a cruel grip, forcing it back to fondle the bulging sacks of skin.

Morgan was pleased with himself. Delong was a prisoner of Saladin and would never bother him again. And Gwendolyn would soon be his, too. Only one thing prevented that right now: Eldwin.

Just the thought of Eldwin brought rage surfacing madly in Morgan's mind. He would kill the faceless bastard before he was finished in Palestine. Perhaps in the coming battle. It would be easy. No one would know where the knight's death came from, but it would be done.

His thoughts brightened his mind and fed his desire. "Enough!" he yelled. Standing, he grabbed the girl's hair and drew her with him. When they were on the carpet-covered floor, he threw her down, yet did not release his hold on her hair. From her knees, she looked up at him.

His now-engorged member arched near her face, its swollen red tip throbbing angrily. Slowly, he forced her face to it and pressed it against her lips. A moment later he was engulfed in her mouth. Then both his hands were twisted in her hair, forcing her head to move back and forth in complete obeisance to his desires.

Morgan, his eyes closed, gave himself over to her, and a few moments later his loud groan of pleasure echoed in the silent bedchamber.

Yet again, as it had been since the day he'd met Gwendolyn, he saw only her body before him, only her hair, and only her lips.

"I will have you," he whispered when he withdrew, spent, from the slave girl's mouth.

Gwendolyn held the vellum at arm's distance. Just its nearness sent waves of hatred speeding through her mind. Morgan's almost unintelligible scribing was much like the man himself. But her plan was working well, and she would soon be free of him. Yet, she did not lose the edge of wariness she held him in and had not forgotten her defeat at his hand two years before.

"My lord, it is almost time," James advised as he adjusted the hauberk on her shoulders.

"Very well," she said, dropping the message onto the floor and turning to face her squire. She took the mask he held, and once it was on, bent so that James could drape the coif-de-maille over her head.

Then she turned to face the archway of the chamber to wait for her enemy's entrance. Hatred rose in terrifying waves, threatening her very ability to stand silent when he came. She had never in her life wanted anyone to die as she did Morgan, but she would wait until the proper time.

The day before, Gwendolyn had gotten his message asking for an audience with her. This morning she had sent Arthur with her reply, inviting him to join her in the privacy of her chambers.

But he would not find Gwendolyn.

"He comes," said Arthur, stepping into the chamber and going to James's side. Together, the identical twin squires stepped against the wall and waited.

Morgan came into the chamber, a smile set on his lips, but froze when he found himself face-to-face with Eldwin.

"Where is your mistress?"

Eldwin stood still, the dark slits before his eyes looking directly at Morgan.

"Answer me, you damned fool!"

"Lady Gwendolyn was forced to cancel her appointment with you," James said.

"What is the meaning of this?" Morgan's anger gripped him, and his face began to mottle with purplish blood.

Eldwin lifted a mailled hand. In it was a fighting gauntlet of steel and leather. With a blur of motion, Eldwin flung the metal-embedded glove at Morgan, striking him fully in the cheek. When the gauntlet fell to the ground, James spoke.

"You are challenged, Morgan of Guildswood. Your treachery and treason have been discovered, and Sir Eldwin demands the satisfaction of your blood in return for that of Sir Miles Delong."

Morgan ignored the pain in his cheek and did not realize the steel edge of the gauntlet had opened his flesh. He stared at Eldwin for a long silent moment.

"Accepted."

"When the sun rises, Morgan of Guildswood, Eldwin will meet you."

"Done!" Morgan spat.

A moment later, the chamber was silent again. In that silence, James and Arthur removed Gwendolyn's armor. Then Roweena entered the chamber with Gwendolyn's evening clothing. Along with her message to Morgan, she had sent another to Richard, begging an audience and writing that it was of the utmost importance.

Richard had agreed, and was to join her for the evening meal once again. Tonight he would learn of Morgan's treachery, and of the fight on the morrow.

"Impossible! Morgan has been among the bravest of fighters. Many battles would have been lost if it had not been for Morgan and his knights," Richard stated after Gwendolyn had faced him with the actuality of Morgan's deed.

"It is as I have stated, Sire. Morgan has had dealings with Saladin. He has acted the traitor in his efforts to destroy my husband."

"You were in England when this happened. How could you know of it?" Richard demanded, unyielding in the face of what he thought to be a woman's weak hysteria.

Gwendolyn drew in a deep breath and stood calmly. "Your Majesty, I did not cross the ocean to demean myself by becoming a camp follower. I came because I knew what had happened, and I could not sit helplessly by while my husband rots within Saladin's grip and Morgan laughs at us all. I have the means to free Miles, and I intend to do so. I have told you of Morgan's deed and am but warning you that on the morrow, when the sun rises, Morgan of Guildswood will meet Eldwin, and his evil life upon this earth will end!"

"You have the audacity to tell me! You ask not my permission to seek vengeance, but merely inform me of the fact?"

"My lord, as God is my witness, there is no man upon this earth who will stop me from what I do. I have spoken to you of Morgan's treachery so you will know that Eldwin does not seek the blood of a good man."

"Do not make me angrier than I am. One more word, Lady Gwendolyn, and I will send you back to England," Richard threatened, rising to his full and menacing height.

But nothing he could do or say brought the least amount of fear to Gwendolyn. "Sire," she said in a barely audible voice, "I am loyal to you, as is my husband. Do not force me to fight you, for it would ill suit you to have my blood on your hands."

Richard stared at her, and then a smile formed on his lips. "This is the second time you have stood against me. Because of this courage of yours, if for no other reason, I shall respect your wishes. But, I demand proof of Morgan's treachery."

"And you shall have it. Arthur!" Gwendolyn's voice was loud, and within a moment, the light-haired squire entered the chamber.

"Tell the king what you overheard."

Five minutes later, a mollified Richard sat heavily on a cushion. "It shall be as you have asked. I will tell my knights of Morgan's treason so that they, too, may witness his execution."

"No, Majesty, it is for me and mine to do. I want no execution. I want satisfaction. He has shamed us all, but he has hurt me the most, for it is his twisted desire for me that made him go to Saladin."

Richard stared at her, his jeweled eyes darkening as he paced the room with the feline energy that was his mark. Everything that had happened since Miles's capture flashed through his mind, and he realized just how deceived he had been by Morgan. He also remembered his hurt and humiliation for the way Saladin had held up Miles, his friend, to taunt him during their battles.

"Every move I have planned, every defeat I have suffered in the past months, has been because of Morgan. I wish that it could be my own hand that takes his lifeblood. I would watch his death and draw wisdom from it!"

"But no others," Gwendolyn begged.

"No others, if you so desire. But I would think you would want all of Christendom to be witness."

"My lord, just yourself, for no others would understand what they would see. Eldwin is different than most. He would not have the men he joins in battle be frightened of him."

"I do not understand what you say, but I shall do as you ask."

When Richard had gone, Gwendolyn sat for several long hours preparing herself for what would happen when she met Morgan. She knew anger held her in its vacillating grip, but she did not force it away; rather she let it feed her muscles and prepare her for what must be done.

It was late when she fell asleep, and when she did, she did not know that three others sat near her form, each holding a weapon and guarding her against their own fears of Morgan and his devious mind.

In the early hours before dawn, Arthur walked through a narrow street until he reached the landside gates of the small town. He and James knew just how devious Morgan could be and, after Gwendolyn had fallen asleep, they had agreed on their own plan. After the challenge to Morgan had been issued, and after their mistress had spoken to the king, Gwendolyn had sent Arthur to Morgan's abode to deliver the location where Eldwin would meet Morgan.

It would be in a grove outside the town, hidden from the eyes of the town, on the landward side of Ascalon. Arthur had argued with Gwendolyn that they should not notify Morgan of where the fight would take place, but rather, send for him in the morning.

But Gwendolyn, choosing to follow the code of chivalry she had promised to uphold as Eldwin, ordered Arthur to tell Morgan of the grove. He had done so, and although he had tried to stay near, he'd been unable to get within hearing distance. Yet, he knew Morgan well, and knew not to trust him.

Now, with but a few short hours before the duel, Arthur stood at the stone wall of the town, looking for the best place to hide.

He climbed the wall near the low tower and was hidden by the dark night, and by the black cloak he wore. He sat patiently, waiting for what he knew would happen.

An hour later his vigil was rewarded, as several men rode to the very gate near which he sat. In the lightening sky, he saw the riders wearing the coat of arms of Guildswood and knew his time on the wall had been wisely spent.

When the men were out of the town, Arthur came down from the wall and went directly to the chambers of Radstock's knights. There, he woke Justin and explained what would be happening. Twenty minutes later, Justin, with seven of his own men, rode out of Ascalon toward the small grove.

None of the men wore full armor, only maille hauberks. Each carried a longbow and each knew what must be done.

With his mind more at ease, Arthur returned to Gwendolyn's chamber and sat next to his twin brother and Roweena to continue the watch over their mistress until the first rays of sun broke across the sleeping town.

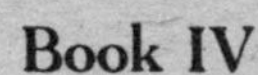

Book IV

Of the Power and Might of the Issue of Kildrake

Chapter Twenty-one

IT WAS ONE OF THOSE RARE spring days that welcomed life with both beauty and grace. The sky was clear and blue, and the air that came in from the sea was warm and fresh, bathing Ascalon with scents of salt and peace.

Within the fortressed city, life stirred to greet the day, and the town's inhabitants went about their daily duties, unaware that just outside the walls, a drama was unfolding. In a small grove, called the Oasis of the Just, Gwendolyn, in the guise of Eldwin, waited for her enemy's arrival. From the moment she had set foot in Ascalon, she had searched for the best place to meet Morgan that would be undetected by the thousands of men who followed Richard.

Arthur had spoken with several knights and had learned of a small grove which had been used by the nomadic Moors who had traded with the merchants of the town for many years before the fighting had begun.

After issuing the challenge to Morgan, Gwendolyn had sent a message to the knight, telling him that Sir Eldwin would be waiting for him in the grove, one hour after the sun had risen.

An hour before sunrise, Eldwin, leading a small procession, had gone from Ascalon to the Oasis of the Just. Two Moslem servants carried a curtained litter that supposedly held Gwendolyn, while Arthur and James rode at its side, and two of the knights of Radstock brought up the rear. When they reached the center of the grove, Eldwin, dressed in armor, walked to the middle of the grove and kneeled, the silver sword held before her in both gauntleted hands.

Roweena sat within the litter and watched her mistress walk from her. She felt strange, dressed in Gwendolyn's clothing, pretending, as she had so often in the past two years, to be the woman she served. But within her heart and mind rested a certainty that Gwendolyn was not an ordinary person, but one destined for things which Roweena herself could not understand.

While Gwendolyn kneeled away from her, Roweena parted the curtains and called the two Moslems to her, giving them the instructions she had been told to by Gwendolyn. She spoke to them through the shimmering veil which hid her features from any prying eyes, and when she closed the curtains, the two Moslems stepped into the woods and sat, hidden from view.

Arthur and James stood by the horses, allowing their mistress to be alone and to meditate as was her wont. Yet both squires could not stop their matching blue eyes from searching the trees, and wondering if Justin had been successful in stopping Morgan's men.

The sun broke above the horizon, flooding the land with golden light. Random rays of yellow light filtered through the trees, and one struck the silver blade, making it glow gently.

Gwendolyn, her eyes closed behind the chamois mask, had freed her mind to roam, content to wait for Morgan within a light trance. But suddenly she felt the sword come alive, and when she opened her eyes, she saw its length caressed by the sun.

Then, within her mind, the same warmth seemed to caress her body and remind her of the path she had followed to come here today. "*Yes, Child of Thunder, you have been guided to this spot. Remember what you have learned. Draw upon it and utilize it, for it is your most important strength. Do not forget that Morgan knows not the forces which govern him and use him for their own ends.*"

Gwendolyn accepted the soft words of the priestess within her mind and returned the warmth she had been given. Then, with the sun rising powerfully in the crystal clear sky, Eldwin rose to her full height within the center of the Oasis of the Just.

The silver sword now hung at her side. It was the only

weapon Sir Eldwin carried, the only weapon she would need. The sunlight glinted off her steel helmet, emphasizing the darkness of the chamois mask.

When Gwendolyn stood, James moved to her side. He wore the padded armor of a squire and the surcoat of Radstock. Arthur remained with the black stallion that Eldwin rode. He, too, was dressed in the colors of Radstock.

The scene was set perfectly. The curtained conveyance rested within the shadows of the trees, the shadows lending even more darkness to the curtains to protect the identity of its occupant. On top of the litter perched Valkyrie, his amber eyes never once not moving, but constantly searching the woods around him.

The two knights who had escorted the party were now stationed at the entrance of the grove facing Ascalon. There they waited for Richard and Morgan. A rider burst through the trees, and Gwendolyn watched Richard, disguised in a plain mantle, ride to where Arthur stood with the other horses. He dismounted and silently went to stand within the woods, hidden from view, but within clear sight of the open area.

Gwendolyn watched everything that was happening around her, but could not think about it. Her entire being was concentrated in her wait for Morgan. Since awakening this morning, she had not spoken. She refused the food that Roweena had prepared and let James dress her completely. Anticipation flowed through her body and mind. Anticipation that with this day's end, she would be even closer to Miles.

The echoes of hooves floated within the silent air of the grove, and Gwendolyn's nerves began to tense. Her hand tightened on the hilt of the sword, and through her maille-encased hands, she drew warmth from the blade.

When Morgan rode into the grove, Gwendolyn willed herself to see the foul black aura that surrounded him. Her breath hissed in an angry stream, and her fingers curled tighter around the silver.

Morgan was dressed in full armor, and draped on his body was sword and mace. Yet the sight did not bother Gwendolyn at all; in fact, she welcomed it. Her rage had been contained for too long, and she needed to expel its harsh force.

Morgan wore his dark surcoat, and beneath the conical helmet, his eyes bore down on Eldwin's form. He dismounted slowly, letting his squire take the horse's reins and lead him away.

"Are you prepared to meet your end? For you shall not leave this grove with breath in your body," he told Eldwin.

Gwendolyn stared at him.

"So you wish death to be met silently?"

Again Gwendolyn merely stared at him through the opening in her mask.

"Then it shall be as you desire. And, when I am finished with you and leave your body to rot, I will take your mistress for my slave!" Saying that, Morgan turned from Eldwin and started toward the curtained litter and the dark shape within.

Instantly, Arthur and James blocked his path.

Morgan stopped before them, a frown on his lips. "Lady Gwendolyn does not wish to speak with you," James said.

Moving quickly, Morgan pushed both squires out of the way, and stepped closer to the litter. "Face me, Gwendolyn!" he shouted.

Valkyrie gave vent to a warning scream as he turned to stare at Morgan. His wings were spread a full five feet, and his burning amber eyes seemed to throw flames at the knight. Morgan froze for a moment, but before he could continue, Eldwin blocked the way, the silver sword's point resting over Morgan's heart.

"You will be mine today!" Then the anger left Morgan's face and he smiled at Eldwin. "It is time."

Gwendolyn lowered the sword and nodded her head. Turning her back on him, she walked to the center of the grove. His words fed her anger, and she could barely control the trembling of her hand on the pommel of the sword. But she fought for control and won. When she faced Morgan again, her hands were steady.

When he was ten feet from Eldwin, Morgan drew his sword and grasped it in two hands. "Die!" he screamed loudly.

But he did not move. Gwendolyn saw his eyes flicker madly about, skimming through the trees. "Now!" he shouted again. "Kill him now!"

A loud thud sounded hollowly within the grove and Morgan spun. Behind him lay the unconscious body of one of his men. Again a body fell from the trees, and Morgan spun to see yet another of his men fall.

In the space of a minute, five bodies littered the ground of the grove. A moment later, the hidden knights of Radstock emerged, their longbows unstrung.

Sir Justin stopped between Morgan and Eldwin. "There are none left to win this fight, save yourself, Morgan." With that, Justin drew his sword and saluted Eldwin.

Gwendolyn closed her eyes for a moment in relief. For all her planning, she had not thought that Morgan would try to kill her in any other way than by their own fight. But she should have known better. She should have.

She watched Justin walk away and join his men. Then she stepped toward Morgan, her sword held high in challenge.

"Damn you!" Morgan roared, coming at her like a mad bull.

Gwendolyn set herself for his attack, and when he reached her, she ducked under his wild swing, letting the force of his charge carry him past her.

She waited until he turned to face her again. His face was discolored, and the dark nasal bar almost blended with his distorted features. But this time Morgan did not charge her blindly. He moved steadily at her, and she knew the fight was truly on.

Clearing her mind of everything, Gwendolyn hefted her longsword. She opened the channel in her mind and felt the sword vibrate in her hands. Then Morgan was on her, and her own sword blurred in the air, meeting his above their heads. Sparks flew from the juncture of their blades, and the clash of metal filled the trees.

Morgan moved quickly, sliding his blade into her quillons in an effort to disarm her. Gwendolyn locked her wrists, and when his blade hit the sword's crossbar, she stepped back, flicked her wrists, and neatly disengaged the other blade.

Her breathing deepened as her lungs drew life from the air in the grove. She became attuned to her body, to the smooth flowing of her blood, and the steady beating of her heart. When she moved, her breasts pressed against their bindings and her muscles quivered in anticipation of the fight's pace. Everything around her was visible, and her mind was brilliantly clear.

Then she changed her stride, spinning before Morgan in a

sudden rhythmical move, the silver blade whistling through the air in a deadly arc aimed at his head.

When Eldwin moved, Morgan instinctively readied himself for the attack. He lifted his sword, and an instant later Eldwin's blade met his, inches from his face.

In that moment, while their blades held and their faces were close together, Morgan sensed a strange power flowing from Eldwin. He sensed death and defeat, and a cold chill gripped him.

Using his animal-like strength, he pushed the other away and stepped back. He gauged his enemy while he shook away the feeling of dread. Yet it lingered in his mind until he felt something begin to seep into his thoughts and return his courage. Accepting whatever had come to his aid, Morgan roared his defiance at Eldwin and drew on his years of training. He charged Eldwin, uncaring of himself as he sought to strike a deadly blow.

Gwendolyn had watched Morgan draw back, and then heard his loud scream. When he moved toward her, she was ready. Everything was in crystal focus, and all that remained of the world was Morgan's dark bulk before her.

She held back the power of the sword, yet did not let it fade completely. She met him halfway, and their blades began a dance that blurred within the vision of the witnesses. Both knights fought passionately, attacking and defending, thrusting and deflecting.

Suddenly Morgan dropped to his knees to duck under a hard swing. Gwendolyn was carried past him by her force, and took three steps before she could regain her balance and face him.

"No!" yelled James in warning, but it was too late. Morgan had drawn his battle dagger and flung it at Eldwin, even as he stood.

The deadly blade sailed through the air faster than Gwendolyn could react. Turning from it, Gwendolyn did the only thing she could—she tried to make herself a smaller target. But she was unable to do so, and the battle dagger, highly tempered and honed to the thinness of a leaf, struck her side and penetrated the maille.

A flash of pain shot through her side, but she did not succumb to it. Moving quickly, Gwendolyn twisted back to face Morgan's new charge. She whirled her arms, and her sword blurred in the air. More sparks flew, and Morgan's fatal blow was avoided.

But the pain from the dagger was intensified by her movements. Quickly stepping back, Gwendolyn grasped the handle of the dagger and pulled it free. Her only sound was a loud grunt. Then she held the bloodied instrument before her. Rage filled her mind and she flung the blade away.

Then she attacked Morgan, letting loose the powers within her mind. The silver blade began to glow, and suddenly the dark aura surrounding Morgan deepened. His eyes seemed to sink deep into his head, and a haunting, evil laughter bubbled from his throat. "Think you the better of me?" he asked in a strange voice. The ground shook, and a fierce gust of wind shot through the grove. Valkyrie's cry shattered the air as a whirlpool of wind and earth swirled around them, cutting them off from those who witnessed the battle.

It was as if a sheet of earth had been lifted; nothing was visible outside the small circle they stood in, and no eyes, other than Morgan's and Gwendolyn's, saw what ensued.

Morgan cried out again, and his voice changed into an echoing spectre of vileness. "Defy me, will you? Kill me, will you?" he shouted. Suddenly Gwendolyn realized his words had not been voiced—his words had not assaulted her ears, but her mind. It was as if his blade had pierced into her soul.

He is the earthly embodiment of the dark powers, the priestess had told her. But she hadn't understood what she'd meant. Morgan was evil, but he was just a man. Yet now he spoke to her in her mind, and, at last, she understood. She was not facing Morgan alone, but those dark forces who used him and his body to gain what they wanted.

Instinctively, Gwendolyn knew they had not asked to join Morgan, but had taken him as their vassal. As long as Morgan's body walked the earth, she and Miles would never be safe. But was she strong enough? Could she defeat him now?

"Never!" came the voiceless challenge. Then he was on her, and Gwendolyn smelled the taint of hell he carried with him. She moved like fluid lightning, giving herself over to her instincts, reinforcing them with her sword, and calling for their aid.

The powers flowed through her mind as she called upon

the purity of the silver light to help her against the blackness that controlled Morgan.

And then it happened, and Gwendolyn sensed she was no longer alone. To her left stood a giant. His long flowing blonde hair reached midback, his massive chest rose and fell easily, and in his hand was a giant metal bludgeon that glowed with unearthly light.

She watched Morgan suddenly stop. The dark aura that had radiated around him like a noxious cloud began to waver and expand. Darkness flowed from him in a billowing cloud, and then it coalesced, forming another entity. She shivered but faced the entity that held no human shape. Dark red eyes glowed from a misshapen head. Long scaled arms ending in claws grasped a curved and blackened blade.

We meet again, Son of Thunder, came the dark thoughts into Gwendolyn's mind.

As we shall through eternity, anathema of my father, replied Gwendolyn's sire.

Gwendolyn saw her father pull himself taller and lift the giant hammer in the air. But suddenly the dark being raised a clawed hand toward the towering Norseman. She saw a blood-red flash leap from the claws and instinctively she swung her sword upward. The silver blade screamed when the force struck it. Darkness raced through her mind and pain threatened to take her life. Nothing in the world moved. Everything was frozen in the instant that the dark energy struck the sword. Yet Gwendolyn knew she must stop this attack, fighting both the force of the blow, and the consuming darkness that drank of her soul. She called on everything she had learned, building a picture within her mind of that special place she had flown to in search of Miles, where she had challenged the priestess, and the powers that created and ruled the universe. Then she forced back the darkness and pain until suddenly her mind was free.

"Filth!" screamed Morgan, breaking the frozen tableau by charging at Gwendolyn. Just then, her father, the son of thunder, drew back his arm and flung the metal hammer at the wavering shape of vileness.

Gwendolyn rolled forward, tightening her body into a ball, letting Morgan's blade go through the empty air where she had stood.

An unearthly roar shook the ground, but Gwendolyn

heard it not as she stood to face Morgan again. Then the powers that had conceived her set her free, and the silver blade shimmered with undisguised iridescence. Behind her, her ethereal father was joined in battle against his ancient race's enemy, while Gwendolyn faced her own.

Morgan's insane scream echoed in her ears, and he came at her. Gwendolyn deflected his stroke, but pain raced along her arms. Morgan was more than what he'd been earlier, and the force of his madness, combined with the powers of his vile master, lent even more strength to his arms. Gwendolyn swung her blade, calling upon it to sever Morgan's, but Morgan's unearthly ally aided him, and the blade stayed whole.

It was then that Gwendolyn let herself become one with her sword. She called not upon the priestess or otherworldly powers for her aid, but to Miles, who had trained her and had shown her the true path of a warrior. Since their first joining, Gwendolyn had known they had become as one. Now, that part of her that was Miles grew within her, and his essence and hers became one, as her body flowed with her glowing sword and she attacked Morgan mercilessly. She fought with all the expertise of her training and sensed her husband's presence within her mind, guiding her hands and arms. She fought like one possessed, backing Morgan against the wall of sand and earth his malignant master had created to veil them. Suddenly she saw an opening.

Again all the world stood still—except for Gwendolyn. Her arms moved with the speed of a striking viper. The glowing blade slid beneath Morgan's and struck his side fully. Light exploded from his maille, and the cry of protesting metal spewed loudly, overshadowed only by Morgan's own scream of defeat.

Gwendolyn freed the blade and spun, letting the sword create a glowing path of silver light shooting toward Morgan's heart. The tip of the blade touched maille, and Gwendolyn put her entire body behind it, pushing it through Morgan, until the quillons rested against the crest of Guildswood.

The earth shook again, and blood began to seep from Morgan's lips while his dark eyes stared at Sir Eldwin.

Behind her she saw her father standing over the misshapen mass of darkness. Then she turned back to Morgan and saw the life begin to leave his eyes. She bent quickly, and when her face was but inches from his, she lifted her gauntleted hand and pulled the mask up for a brief moment.

Morgan's eyes widened and his mouth opened. "No!" he screamed, and his voice shook the branches above him.

Slowly, Gwendolyn stood. She drew the silver blade from Morgan's body and watched his eyes glaze over. Then she turned and saw her father stand, the giant hammer again gripped in his hand. She looked at him for a moment and stood proudly under his caressing gaze.

We have won, she stated to him.

For the moment, daughter, he replied, his voice gentle in her mind. *But you have much left to accomplish.*

Miles.

Your husband is first. See to him.

Then his shape began to dissolve, and as it did, the whirlwind which had surrounded them ended, and Gwendolyn found herself staring into the eyes of Richard *Coeur de Lion.*

To those who had witnessed the strange events, they neither heard nor saw what had transpired within the whirling wall of sand. Yet each of them had stood tensely by, waiting to go to the aid of the two knights should they call out.

When the strange storm ended, they saw but one knight standing. Arthur and James glanced at each other with sighs of relief, while Justin and the other knights ran to the fallen body. But it was Richard who walked to Sir Eldwin.

Sir Eldwin bowed before the king and then rose to point to the slain body of Morgan.

"I have never seen the likes of what I witnessed here today. We thought you both dead and carried off by the strange desert storm. Yet you seem unaffected by it."

"He is dead!" cried Justin, who had gone to Morgan's body when Richard spoke to Gwendolyn. Sir Eldwin merely nodded.

"You have served me well today. In two days we meet Saladin. I ask you to fight at my side."

Sir Eldwin gazed at Richard through her mask and slowly and carefully knelt again. This time she held the blade of the silver sword within her hands, its pommel extended to Richard in a silent pledge of fealty.

"Join my council tonight, so that you may hear my battle plan. None will call upon you to violate your oath." With that, Richard walked to his horse and, a moment later, rode from the grove.

Silently, Eldwin walked to Morgan's body, bent, and ripped his surcoat. When she stood, she held the coat of arms of Guildswood in her mailled fist. Then she motioned to James for her horse. After mounting the stallion, she turned and stared at Valkyrie. Without a word or gesture, the golden eagle left its perch and settled on to Sir Eldwin's shoulder.

Gwendolyn spurred her mount out of the grove, and headed toward the sandy desert that stretched endlessly before her.

Half an hour later she saw a high sandy hill and urged the stallion upward to its crest. There, above the unending desert, she dismounted and removed her helmet and mask. Reaching into the neck of her armor, Gwendolyn took out a thong of leather. Carefully, she tied the ragged piece of garment she'd ripped from Morgan's surcoat and then looped the leather around Valkyrie's neck.

"Seek Miles. Give him my message," she told the eagle. Valkyrie left her shoulder and walked along her arm until he was again perched on her wrist. With a deeply drawn breath, Gwendolyn pulled back her arm and, as she had for so many years, released the golden eagle.

Valkyrie fought the pull of the earth as he followed the downward slope of the hill, his wide wings seeking currents as he skimmed along the ground. Gwendolyn drew her sword and closed her eyes. She built a picture of Miles in her mind and sent a message with her thoughts.

A moment later, Valkyrie's loud call echoed over the sandy hills of Palestine, and then he was gone.

A dry, arid breeze washed across Saladin's face as he gazed at the two hawks circling high above. Of all sports, Saladin loved hawking the best. He enjoyed and admired the grace of the large birds and had learned much of his warfare from them.

Before the sun had risen, and the desert was still cool, he, with ten of his men and his English prisoner, had ridden from their new encampment to spend the morning in sport.

Soon sport must be put aside, he realized, as the time to renew his attack against the Franks drew nearer. He had been fortunate in defeating Richard twice when the infidel forces had attacked Jerusalem, and the next few months could mean the difference between years of fighting or a suitable peace.

His battle plan was simple. Meet and defeat his enemy as many times as possible. First, take Ascalon, and then Jaffa. With no strongholds left, Richard must sue for peace, or be driven from the land. Yet Saladin recognized the fierceness of his enemy, and knew that if he drove Richard from the land, the king of the Franks would return with a larger army. He did not want this; he wanted peace.

Turning, he glanced at Miles and forced himself to think not of the future of this gallant man. Since their confrontation before the winter battle at Jerusalem, Miles had refused to accept any of Saladin's hospitalities. It hurt him, but it also reinforced the respect Saladin felt for this man.

"I understand hawking is widespread in your homeland," he ventured.

"It is," Miles replied, looking at Saladin and then up at the circling birds. "Why have you brought me here today?"

"Must I have a reason?"

"For almost a half a year I have watched you, Master of the Chosen, and never once have I seen you do something without purpose."

Saladin laughed and shook his head slowly. "You are astute, Miles of England. Yes, there is a purpose. Your king's spies are nearby. I wish them to see us sporting, not preparing for war. It lulls the enemy to think us wastrels."

"And you would have them report that I join in your sport?"

Saladin's features hardened for a moment when he looked into Miles's face. "Above all, I must rule my kingdom, and keep it whole and safe from those who would take it from me. I use you to taunt Richard, that is true, but I have no choice. It has nothing to do with my personal feelings."

Miles held Saladin's gaze for a moment before he looked up at the circling birds of prey. Since arising this morning, he had been in the grips of a strange mood. Something had disturbed his sleep, something that had reached to the very core of his mind. Throughout the ride from the oasis encampment, Miles had been unable to rid himself of the feeling. It was there, as if a warning, or perhaps, a feeling of preparation for something about to happen. Whatever it was, Miles let his instincts rule and held himself ready for whatever this day might offer.

A sudden overhead screech broke through their words, and both men looked skyward just in time to see a giant eagle diving earthward. Both of Saladin's hawks seemed to pause in midair, and then the eagle cried out again as it struck the first hawk.

Large talons sunk into the smaller body, and the birds spun in the air. A fraction of a second later, the eagle straightened its flight with the hawk securely grasped in its talons. The eagle circled the group of men and then dove at its leader. When Valkyrie was within five feet of Saladin, he released the dead hawk.

The hawk landed with a low thud at Saladin's feet. Then Valkyrie circled the group once more, before gliding to a stop on Miles's shoulder.

As soon as he'd heard Valkyrie's first scream, Miles knew who it was. He watched the giant eagle strike the hawk and smiled when he dropped the bird at Saladin's feet. When the golden eagle flew toward him, he braced himself for its landing, and when Valkyrie was settled on his shoulder, he gazed into the eagle's amber eyes.

"Hello, old friend," he whispered. Then he saw the leather strip, and the piece of cloth attached to it. Slowly, he slipped the message from Valkyrie's neck and opened it. He unrolled the cloth and was unable to hold back his laughter.

Turning slowly, he met Saladin's deep eyes and then pointed to the dead hawk. "You have been challenged," he stated. Then he threw the coat of arms of Guildswood on top of the hawk. "As has been Morgan, who is no longer of this earth."

Reacting before Saladin, Miles grasped Valkyrie with both hands and ran. As he ran, he flung the eagle upward. Valkyrie found his current quickly and flew higher, ignoring the remaining hawk as he sped to return to Gwendolyn.

Chapter Twenty-two

THE VELVET BLANKET OF THE eastern sky spread above the earth in a scintillating pattern of luminescence. The cool night air of the desert washed across two thousand Christian soldiers, lulling them to sleep with its serenity.

In their midst, Sir Eldwin sat silently. All around her, men slept as best they could while others talked in low voices, girding themselves for the morning, and the confrontation with the Saracen forces.

Gwendolyn paid no attention to the others, not even when she heard two voices raised in argument. She recognized Justin's voice and knew he was again defending Lady Delong. A smile curved her lips, but none could see it hidden behind the mask of Eldwin.

The smile brought back the memory of the past two days, when she had shocked Richard's army, and begun the spreading of tales that were a part of her plan.

It had started the day after Morgan's death, in midafternoon, when the streets of Ascalon were at their busiest and both Christians and Moslems swarmed through the bazaar, buying and selling whatever suited their needs.

Gwendolyn had appeared suddenly within one street, and all activity had ceased. Hundreds of eyes had fallen upon her and had drunk of her beauty.

She wore the costume of a Norman lady, which contained, yet bared all her charms. Her feet were encased by doeskin slippers, which were only visible when she walked. An underskirt of pale blue flowed from her waist to her toes, broken only by the pure white bodice of the Norman overdress which started at her hips, and veed to a perfect point midway down her thighs. But what attracted the most attention, and not a few remarks, was the matching vee line of the bodice's top. The white material came together in a point, a full three inches below her breasts, showing clearly the porcelain of her skin and the outline of her full breasts. The darker circles of her nipples could also be faintly seen. Her face was unveiled, as was the custom of the Christians, but she wore a white coif-de-maille which covered her hair and then flowed across her shoulders, spilling over her breasts and ensuring a slight degree of modesty without hiding any of her more than abundant charms.

The bodice was sleeveless, as the weather allowed, and the milkiness of her skin radiated under the springtime sun. For several hours, Gwendolyn walked the streets, stopping at various stalls to inspect merchandise, but she bought nothing. The only thing she acquired were stares and followers, from whom Justin and three of his men protected her.

That night, she appeared again as Eldwin and went to Richard's council meeting as she had the night before. She sat silently while the king outlined, again, his battle plan for Saladin's defeat. Yet although she listened intently, she cared little for what he desired. Her only desire—her obsession—was to free Miles. The battle between Christian and Moor meant little to her now, but those battles would serve their purpose, a purpose that was reinforced within Gwendolyn's mind.

The only note of discord came from Richard himself, speaking to Eldwin and Justin. "Tell the Lady Delong that word has reached us of her wanderings within the city. Advise her to caution, for the Moors are not beyond spiriting away beautiful women to be sold into slavery and harems."

Eldwin had not reacted, but Justin had, not with words, but with an angry scarlet flush across his face. Only Eldwin's gloved hand upon his arm constrained his reply to the king. When the council meeting had ended, and Justin and Eldwin had returned to the chambers of Radstock, it took all of Gwendolyn's self-control not to reply to Justin's heated, angry words for Richard. It was in that instant that

Gwendolyn realized the depth of love Justin held for his mistress, and understood, also, that it was not a physical love, but one of loyalty to both herself, and to the man he pledged fealty to, Miles Delong.

But not even Richard's words of caution had swerved Gwendolyn from the path she had chosen, and in the middle of the afternoon of the next day, she sallied forth again, to wander the streets and expose herself to the eyes of all.

As she walked, Arthur, who had been absent that morning, met them in the bazaar. He went to Gwendolyn and whispered urgently in her ear that one of Saladin's emissaries was meeting with Richard.

Making a quick decision, Gwendolyn ordered Justin to take her to Richard's chambers. Five minutes later, she stood before the guarded entrance while Justin spoke with a guard.

"I cannot disturb the king," the guard stated.

Gwendolyn stepped close to Justin and whispered in his ear. Then they turned, and the second the guard had relaxed, Justin whirled, pinning the knight's arms to his side and allowing Gwendolyn to enter the chamber.

When she stepped inside, she froze. Seated on cushions were Richard and the Saracen. They spoke in fluent French, and Gwendolyn understood everything being said. Suddenly Richard glanced up and saw her above him. His eyes widened for a moment.

"What are you doing here?" he demanded angrily.

Instead of bowing, Gwendolyn straightened her shoulders and stared down at Richard. "I would speak with this man."

Ignoring her insult, Richard rose and drew her aside, just far enough from the Moor so that they would not be overheard. "Lady Delong, this is not the time."

"Will it ever be? I want word of my husband." Her voice was low, and the words barely audible.

"When this meeting is over I will speak with you. Leave now before I lose my temper."

Gwendolyn stared at Richard for a moment before stalking out. She was not angry, not even the least bit agitated, for she had accomplished what she'd wanted. This emissary would carry word of the tall, light-haired woman to Saladin.

Later, when she was in her chamber, Richard came to her. His anger diminished, especially when Gwendolyn pleaded that it had been her heart which ruled her actions in her efforts to learn about Miles.

"Yet, it would be proper for you to give us an apology," Richard told her after she had explained her actions. "But I feel you are not the type to do so easily."

"Only when I am in the wrong. Until my husband is a free man, I will do whatever is necessary and will never find myself in the wrong!" Gwendolyn did not know what to expect, but Richard's smile was the last thing she thought possible.

"He is well. He is treated like an honored guest. But Saladin will never release him. He has stated that to me many times, both in negotiation, and in fight. He knows of my feelings toward Miles and holds him over my head to taunt me."

"I will have his release. Believe what I say, Your Majesty."

"I sympathize with you and I hurt with you. I love Miles as a brother even more than as a loyal subject."

"But I love him as a wife. I will win out."

Richard left, but not before he again cautioned Gwendolyn about appearing in public. "A woman as beautiful as you would rouse the desires of even Saladin himself," he told her in farewell.

Gwendolyn drew in a relieved breath after he'd gone. Ever since she'd arrived in Palestine, she had heard of Saladin's unending appetite for women—especially foreign women. Why, when he had the choice of any woman in his land, he wanted what was not available, she could not begin to guess, but it was that very peculiarity that gave her the perfect way of meeting him and freeing Miles.

When she had interrupted Richard's meeting to demand news of Miles, she had really gone to show Saladin's man her charms, so that he would tell the sultan, himself, of the Frankish woman he had seen. For that was the second step in her twofold plan to secure Miles's release.

Her original plan was to ride in the guise of Sir Eldwin, letting the Saracen army learn of the hooded knight's might. And, if Saladin continued to use Miles to taunt Richard during battle, she would do her best to reach her husband and free him. If this did not succeed, she would have her second plan ready, the plan that used Gwendolyn as bait, not Eldwin.

Yes, Gwendolyn thought, and after this battle, word would reach Saladin that this woman wanted to speak with him. "My lord," called James, interrupting Gwendolyn's thoughts and bringing her attention back to the present.

Eldwin turned to her squire and waited for him to continue. "I have sharpened your battle-axe," he said, extending the newly-honed blade for her inspection.

Gwendolyn grasped the wooden shaft of the axe and gazed at the head. She wanted to begin the battle with the axe. Only when she had reached a certain point would she unsheath her sword and call upon its powers.

Holding the axe in one gloved hand, Sir Eldwin lay back on the sleeping blanket and closed her eyes.

The sun was up, and heat washed across the desert floor in shimmering waves. Tension so heavy that one could feel it filled the space dividing the two armies. This was to be Eldwin's first battle, yet she felt as though she had been fighting her entire life. Her nerves were calm as she hefted the battle-axe in one hand and rested the rim of the shield on her mailled thigh.

Beneath her, the stallion's muscles quivered in anticipation, and Gwendolyn knew the horse was also readying itself for the coming battle. Miles had trained the stallion, and he was of a long line of war-bred horses.

Then she saw activity in the Saracen ranks and, suddenly, she saw what she had only heard about. A large cross rose in the enemy's midst, and tied to it was the body of her husband.

Rage swelled within her while she was forced to watch this display. She had thought herself prepared for it, but now realized she wasn't. Sadness washed through her, riding hard on the tail of her anger. Then she saw an armored Saracen knight ride forward, his scimitar flashing with sunlight as he sped in front of the ranks of the waiting army.

"That is their warrior of courage. He rides before the Saracens to show his bravery in challenge, and to stir the army into readiness," Sir Hugo explained to Eldwin. "The battle will start soon. Do not let the sight of Sir Miles disturb you, for that is what Saladin desires."

Gwendolyn forced herself to hold back as she watched. Then Richard was at her side. "He is alive. He is unharmed. Do not let them anger you!"

Eldwin spun to face Richard. Then, with her eyes locked on her king, she waved James forward. She pulled James's longbow from his hands and took an arrow from his quiver. With one more glance at Richard, she spurred the stallion ahead. Ten yards in front of the Christian army, Eldwin stopped the stallion.

Slowly, the hooded knight notched the arrow and drew back the bow. Following the path of the challenging Saracen, Eldwin gently released the shaft. Everyone watched the arrow fly and traced its arc, waiting, their breaths held.

A loud roar escaped from thousands of throats as the shaft struck its target at the only spot where the Saracen was vulnerable. The arrow entered the visor of the Saracen's helmet and pierced the knight's brain.

Gwendolyn watched the Saracen fall from the horse before she returned to her place in the line. Richard stared at her for a long moment before he wordlessly urged his horse back beneath the banner of England.

After Eldwin returned James's bow, she again looked across the sand dividing the armies. The dead Saracen had been taken away, and Miles, still tied to the cross, was carried to the rear of the Moslem army, where the cross was set upright in the ground.

Then Richard raised his arm and the English army began its advance. Two thousand men and horses thundered across the desert to battle the enemy.

Richard, riding behind his banner, was a stirring sight. Across from him, Saladin sat astride a white stallion, his armor glinting in the sun, a large scimitar held in his hand.

Eldwin rode at the head of her knights and was a bare ten feet from Richard's side. Her axe, attached to the maille by a slender chain, was gripped in one gauntleted hand. But as she rode forward, her eyes never once left the cross upon which Miles was attached.

As the sounds of the two armies grew louder, Gwendolyn held her gaze to the spot where the cross now stood. Behind her, wearing body armor and holding longbows, were Arthur and James. Then the trumpets sounded their final notes and the battle was joined. Gwendolyn spurred the black stallion forward, cutting across Richard's path and heading directly toward Miles. The knights of Radstock followed her, and with them they drew Richard and his own men.

Soon she was in the thick of the Saracen knights, her axe flying with deadly efficiency, and none able to get near her.

The pace of the battle filled her, and her own energy rose in response. She fought methodically, defeating time and again any who came against her. After the battle had been joined and she'd fought her way closer to the cross, she found herself facing only a single Saracen knight. As she rode to meet him, his scimitar descended. Moving by instinct, Gwendolyn urged her horse to rear, and at the same moment raised her shield to deflect the blow. The scimitar caught in the shield as her battle-axe completed its arc, and a loud scream reached her ears just as she felt the metal head of her axe bite through the armor to reach bone. A bare second passed before her opponent fell from his horse.

But the scimitar was hooked in her shield, and the Saracen held its handle in a grip of death that threatened to unseat Gwendolyn. Bending with the weight, Gwendolyn straightened her arm and let the shield and scimitar slip free. Then she hooked the battle-axe to her armor while Arthur and James reached her side to protect her during the few moments she was vulnerable.

Swiftly, Gwendolyn drew her sword. Then James shielded his twin brother while Arthur tied the Saracen's mount's reins to his saddle. Horses were an important spoil of war and not to be left behind.

Gwendolyn took stock of the situation. All around Sir Eldwin the battle progressed, reaching the stage of individual fighting rather than the mass melee of minutes ago. She glanced around quickly and saw Richard strike down a foe and charge anew into the ranks of the Saracens. Then she saw Saladin, charging across the battlefield toward the spot she now occupied.

Gwendolyn held up the silver sword and began whirling it over her head. She spurred the stallion forward, her eyes fixed upon Saladin. She needed to get by him in order to reach Miles, and, as Sir Eldwin, she was determined to do this. She reentered the battle, and with the silver sword flying in the air, she rode a straight line toward her destination. Knight after knight blocked her path, but she was in the grip of a battle fever the likes of which were unknown to her adversaries. Her arms were weightless, and her power strong. Nothing could stand before the might of her sword, and as she charged, Saracens fell to their deaths. No sword, javelin, or arrow penetrated her defense, while no man withstood her fatal strokes.

She fought on, the silver sword a deadly blur in the air, until the path between Gwendolyn and Miles was open, save for one lone Saracen. Exhilaration flashed through her mind. She had done it! She had done what had been impossible for any other; she had fought through the Saracen army. Then recognition struck her sharply. The man facing her was no ordinary knight, it was Saladin, himself! Slowly, Gwendolyn raised her sword and invoked the power of the silver blade to aid her, and when she felt it vibrate within her grasp, she realized, too, that she must not kill Saladin. She would meet and defeat him, but she could not destroy him. Then she understood what must be done. There was one path still open to her. She must capture Saladin and use him to ransom Miles, and force negotiations between the two kings.

Reining in the stallion, she stared at the Saracen leader. He sat proudly, his quilted body armor blood-stained but whole. Then she dipped her sword to him.

Saladin gazed at this new Christian knight in wonder. The man had hewed a path through his finest men, and had not once been stopped. His prowess was amazing, but it brought no fear to Saladin's heart. Yet when the knight raised his longsword in challenge, Saladin was startled. Raising the visor of his helmet, Saladin bared his face to the Christian. It was then that he saw that the knight's face was not covered by a helmet bar, but rather a leather mask. And, the emir of the Moslems also noted the replica of the large eagle embroidered above the crest of his surcoat.

Slowly, Saladin lowered his visor and raised his scimitar into the air, accepting the challenge of the knight.

Gwendolyn waited until Saladin had seen her before she

charged. But when she was halfway to him, she saw a blurred shadow fly through the air and realized that someone had unleashed a javelin at Saladin. The Moor saw it, also, and drew back his reins sharply.

The horse reared high on its back legs, and the javelin sank into the horse's flesh at the exact spot where Saladin would have been seated had he not forced his horse into the air.

A second later, Saladin was on the ground, trapped beneath the dead white stallion.

Without hesitation, Gwendolyn stopped her horse and dismounted, signaling James and Arthur to her. She ran to the trapped Moslem king and drew him from beneath the horse.

Then, with her silver sword at Saladin's throat, she waved Arthur forward and pointed to the horse he'd captured. Arthur untied the horse and brought it to Eldwin, while James guarded both Saladin and Eldwin from further attack.

Lowering the blade, Gwendolyn held Saladin's deep eyes in a long stare before motioning Saladin to the mount. When he was astride it, Eldwin mounted her black stallion. It was then that she saw her route to Miles blocked. Hundreds of Saracens had formed a blockade behind Saladin. Javelins, arrows, and scimitars were held to the ready. Yet when she gazed at Saladin, he held his hand up, restraining his men.

With a bow to Saladin, Eldwin turned the horse and rode back into the ranks of the English army, tasting the bitterness of her foiled plan, yet knowing she still had her other avenue open to her.

Saladin watched the knight leave, and within him knew that he had faced the best that Christendom had to offer. He had no doubt that had they met in battle, he would have been hard pressed to win. Yet, when he had fallen, the knight had not taken advantage. The gesture of this unknown knight affected him deeply, and he felt honored with the gift of his life. Especially since to have captured Saladin would have given the knight untold honor, riches, and fame.

Yet Saladin knew this knight represented something new. He represented a focal point which could not only unite the Christians, but charge them onward.

Why, so late in this war, has so strong a champion

emerged? With that question burning in his mind, Saladin turned his horse and began to marshal his men.

"Who is he?" Saladin asked Miles the question in a low voice, but Miles did not miss the passion within it.

"None know. Not even Richard knows who Sir Eldwin is."

"But you do!" Saladin's words were statement, not question, and needed no answer. "Before I fell, I saw his design. His . . . coat of arms. It was the same as yours, but it differed. It had a band around the shield, and above it was a golden eagle. Was it the eagle who killed my hawk?"

"I said you had been challenged."

"So it was the trainer of the eagle."

"A woman trained the eagle."

"But this knight has come because of you, not the war. This is true, is it not?"

Miles held Saladin's stare with his own. "First your hawk, then your warrior of courage was slain by Eldwin's arrow. Yes, Leader of the Faithful, Sir Eldwin is here because of me."

"Then why did he not strike me when he had the chance? The day would belong to the Christians and Richard, and it would be many years before my people could unite again."

"Release me and Eldwin will not fight you."

"I cannot. Answer my question."

"Sir Eldwin is a knight, a knight sworn to a code. If you had been upon your horse, Eldwin would have met you in battle. But you were trapped on the ground—helpless. His code does not permit him to take the life, or capture, someone who cannot defend himself."

"It is as I thought."

"Saladin . . .?"

"Yes, my friend?"

"It will be over soon. I want my freedom."

"I have not the power to grant it."

"You are making a mistake," Miles said in a low voice. There was no tone of threat, or even of pity; he was just stating a fact, and Saladin seemed to realize that.

"So said Borka-al-Salu when I gave the infidel my word. But my word is sacred."

"More sacred than the reason you fight us?"

The flickering light given off by the oil lamps illuminated Saladin's face hauntingly as he gazed into the green eyes of the English knight. He truly considered Miles a friend; yet, he was unable to reply to Miles's question, for he himself did not know the answer.

The dark sky once again glowed with a myriad of stars above the heads of Richard's army. His council was gathered about him, as other knights buried the dead who had fallen this day. Across from the English, the Moors were doing the same. Christian and Moslem, who had fought fiercely against each other, worked silently side by side to separate their dead and carry them to their encampments for burial.

Richard avoided watching this ritual as he spoke to the council. "Neither I nor Saladin has won the day. We could consider this battle a victory, but if we fight them on the morrow, we will lose even more men. We can ill afford that."

"Had Eldwin done his duty, it would be over now!" yelled William Belouise.

Eldwin turned to face the knight, her hand gripping the silver sword.

"Sir Eldwin has done nought but uphold his honor as a knight and his faith as a Christian," Richard said in a level voice. "What he did this day upon the field was to give our army and our purpose honor!"

"Honor be damned! I am tired of fighting for something that I will never see again."

The knight's words struck harshly into Gwendolyn's mind, and she was aware of the anger that filled him and many others, but she was not ashamed at what she'd done.

"I will have no further talk of this. When the bodies are buried, we return to Ascalon. I would have more time before facing Saladin again."

When the council broke up, Richard went to Eldwin's side and motioned him to follow. When they were alone, he spoke in a low voice that forced Gwendolyn to listen carefully.

"I would have agreed with Belouise if I were not king. But when the fighting was over, and I found myself alive and unwounded, I thought about you, and about Saladin. What happened to him today could happen to me in my next battle. Would that I find someone such as you to face when it happens. What you did was right, no matter what your reason."

Gwendolyn's throat constricted, and she blinked her eyes several times. Then she went upon her knee and took his hand within hers, to kiss the ring on his finger.

"Rise, Sir Eldwin, for I will not have you kneel before me on the field of battle where all men must eventually become equal. Your honor reflects upon me this day, and I would have you walk with me in friendship rather than in fealty, for I need friends more so than vassals."

Chapter Twenty-three

GWENDOLYN PACED ANGRILY in Richard's antechamber as she waited for the king to finish his business. Two weeks had passed since the battle with Saladin, and she felt herself no closer to gaining Miles's freedom than before.

She had flaunted herself daily before the inhabitants of Ascalon, yet not once had the bait been taken. Her confidence in her plans was beginning to weaken, and she needed some physical action to help her. Realizing this, she had thought of yet another step she could take against the Moslem army.

Richard's chamberlain stepped into the antechamber and nodded to Gwendolyn. "His Highness will see you now," the man said. Gwendolyn refused to feel embarrassment when the man's eyes roamed to her almost-revealed breasts; instead, she quickly swept past him.

Inside, she found Richard seated on a large Moorish cushion. She went to him and knelt.

"You must want something badly, Lady Gwendolyn."

"Sire?"

"When you demand something of me, you never humble yourself, yet when you ask of me, you are the embodiment of courtesy. Please, madame, be seated."

"Have I offended you, Sire?" Gwendolyn asked, unsure of the answer this time.

"As a man, or as a king?"

"You are both, are you not?"

"To only a few. What crisis brings you here?" he asked. The smile on his lips softened the harshness of his words, and Gwendolyn relaxed.

"I understand the negotiations are not going well."

"And?"

"I know I am but a woman, Sire . . ."

"That is all too evident," he stated bluntly.

Gwendolyn had the grace to blush before she spoke again, but when she did, her words were steady and her tone was underlined with determination.

"If I might offer a suggestion," she ventured, not giving Richard a chance to reply as she hurriedly continued. "Saladin feels no pressure to end this war. His supplies are constant and plentiful, and none oppose him save when you meet him in battle. Would not small bands of knights attacking his supply caravans speed up the process of negotiations?"

"Would that this thing were possible, and yes, you are right in your thinking, but my army dwindles. Every day men desert, with each battle I lose more and more knights, and their replacements are months away. Saladin can draw on all the resources of his nation to fight me. I cannot spare men to do as you suggest."

"Your Majesty, I would charge Eldwin with the harassment of Saladin's caravans. He would not be lost!"

"No! I need him with me. I will not take the chance of losing him."

"Is it because I am a woman that you will not accept my counsel?" Gwendolyn asked, her voice ringing tensely in the chamber.

"Lady Delong," Richard said formally, "my first counselor was a woman. I learned more from her than from any knight who lived. I respect the advice of a strong woman, and you are one of the strongest I have ever known. But what you ask is impossible."

"Sire, I came here to free my husband, not to push forth a crusade that espouses God and peace, but in reality gives vent to murder and savagery. I brought my knights with me, unpledged to this crusade, yet I gave them to you to aid you. Nothing stops me from withdrawing their support except my loyalty to you. I have already told you that nothing and no one will prevent me from accomplishing what I have come here for!"

"You threaten me?"

Gwendolyn held Richard's gaze for a silent moment before she replied, and when she did, it was in a low voice. "No, Your Majesty, I state fact."

"You would send Eldwin out against my wishes?"

"If need be."

"Damn! Do you realize I have the power to send you back to England?"

"Sire, you have the power to order me back, but unless you accompany me, you will never be certain where I am."

Richard laughed suddenly and shook his head. "You are an amazing woman, Lady Delong. Why do you persist in wearing these revealing clothes?"

"It is but the dress of my homeland."

"Stop playing your game with me. I know of your heritage, and of your feelings for things Norman. Is this some part of your plan to win back Miles?"

Gwendolyn thought about his question for a moment before she answered. Richard was not as easy to fool as most, perhaps because he was king, or perhaps because a woman's charms were not important to him.

"Yes, Your Majesty."

"You play a dangerous game. Why?"

"Will you accept the truth?"

"Only!"

"Sire, my love for my husband is strong, and until he is with me again, I cannot be a whole woman. I know of Saladin's lust for women and hope that word reaches him of me . . . for I would give myself to him, to gain Miles's release."

"You are doing this in the name of love?"

"That, and in the name of life, for Miles is my life." For the first time since she arrived in the Holy Land, tears spilled from Gwendolyn's eyes. She did not try to wipe them away, nor did she feel embarrassment at their presence. Silence followed her words, and Richard sat as quietly as did she.

"I have said many times that I do not understand this feeling between a man and a woman. I have tried, but it passes me by. Yet, I can see the truth of your words plainly."

"Then you will allow me to charge Eldwin with the mission?"

"It would be either that, or to hold him in chains, would it not?"

Gwendolyn did not answer. She waited silently.

"I will agree, on one condition."

"Sire?"

"That you do not hold yourself out for Saladin's lust."

"My lord . . ."

"We cannot spare you, Lady Gwendolyn. England has far too few women of your ilk. Do not make me use force."

"I will dress with modesty, Your Majesty," Gwendolyn replied.

But, after she had left, Richard realized that Gwendolyn had not really answered him. Dressing with modesty had not been what he'd sought. Then he smiled to himself. One small concession was better than none.

Miles soaked in the tiled bath, letting the hot water caress his body. His humiliation at being tied to the cross to taunt Richard had affected him deeply, and many times Miles had thought of ending his life. It was only the vision of Gwendolyn that stopped him.

Then, when Valkyrie had come to him, his soul had returned, and he knew that he must live. He began again to exercise daily, rebuilding his muscles, and preparing for the day that Gwendolyn would arrive.

Aliya, who had been in attendance since his first day of imprisonment, had become his friend. After the one time when she had offered herself to him, she had never done so again. And because of that, Miles accepted her friendship and love.

He spoke with her often, using her as his only means to verbalize his thoughts. He did not once think her a spy who would run to Saladin and report on him, for he saw the devotion to himself within her eyes. And as the weeks and months passed, Aliya taught him the language of the Saracens while he taught her the tongue of England. With the slow passage of time, Miles learned much of the Moslem world. He learned, too, that his relationship with Saladin was unusual. Rarely had an infidel prisoner ever been accorded the honors given to him. Never had a Christian knight been permitted the use of his sword, unless he had also embraced the Moslem religion.

And never did a week pass, when Saladin had not asked him to accept the religion of the Moors and join him. He promised great rewards and fabulous riches, but Miles steadfastly refused.

Recently, however, Saladin's requests were growing more demanding, and Miles sensed a change in him. When he spoke to Aliya, she explained Saladin's position in Moslem terms. His conscience was bothering him because he had made a bargain with a dishonorable man and was forced to hold Miles.

Saladin's release from his obligation could be achieved only by Miles accepting the Moslem religion. And Aliya had warned him that if Miles did not soon agree to Saladin's terms, the emir's conscience would force him to send Miles away, so that he would not be reminded daily of his mistake.

With those thoughts running through his mind, Miles stepped out of the tub just as Aliya entered the chamber. She ran to him, lifting a sheet of muslin and wrapping him within it. "Forgive my lateness."

"What did you learn?" he asked.

"Another caravan was attacked. The supplies were taken. It was Eldwin again."

"Thank you," Miles said. In the past month, Aliya had fallen into the habit of bringing Miles gossip from the harem baths, and since the last battle, and the arrival of the new Christian champion, Miles had asked her to get him as much information as she could.

"Patinah says that Saladin grows angrier every day. This was the fourth caravan lost. All of our warriors stand in fear of Eldwin, and rumors have risen that he is invincible. They say he is not human, but the very devil the Christians always speak of."

"I warned him."

"I did as you asked. I told Patinah to whisper into her master's ear that if he freed you, he would be free of Eldwin."

Miles smiled and then lay upon the cushions to let Aliya begin the ritual massage. Patinah was presently Saladin's chief concubine and had much access to the emir. Patinah was also Aliya's half sister.

"The women feel a change about to happen," Aliya offered.

"Many changes will happen, little sister," Miles agreed.

"And you will soon be gone."

"Not if Saladin has his way."

"I sense I will lose you and I am saddened."

Turning suddenly, Miles stared at the slave girl. He saw her eyes brimming with tears, and her young shoulders shake with contained sadness. He drew her to him and held her close. Then, in a low voice, he soothed her.

"You are a child of your land, and I am not of it. Aliya, I love you as a friend and will miss you when I have gone, for you have made my life here bearable."

A few moments later, Aliya withdrew from his arms and forced him to lie down again. She continued the massage in silence, and only when she was done did she speak again.

"There was also talk of a beautiful infidel woman in Ascalon. Her hair is said to be the color of the desert sands, and her skin as white as goat's milk. She has eyes that are taken from the sky, and is taller than most men."

Miles stared at her, waiting for more.

"Patinah says Saladin has been told of her, and has voiced a desire to see her." Aliya paused at Miles's wide smile. "When I first heard her described, I thought I knew who it was. Now I am sure. But why does she let herself be seen by so many?"

"For the very reason you speak.'

"I do not understand."

"I'm not sure I do either, but I believe in her, and in whatever she is doing."

"Your love is strong, my master."

"As is hers."

The heat rose from the desert sands in waves. The late spring sun burned down unmercifully, bleaching the earth whiter with every passing hour.

A lone rider crested a dune and then urged his horse down the far side. At the base of the dune were thirty mounted men. Each wore the long flowing robes of desert Moors, but the language they spoke was of England.

Arthur stopped his horse next to Eldwin's. "They come, but this time the caravan is guarded by fifty men."

"Should we not let it pass?" asked Justin. He was not afraid of fighting the Saracens, but knew the futility of being outnumbered.

The hooded leader shook her head and gestured to Justin. James, acting as he always did, spoke. "Lady Gwendolyn has charged Eldwin not to fight this day. We are to deliver a message to the leader of the caravan."

"But when they see us, they will attack."

"No." And saying that, James pointed to his brother, who was unfurling a banner.

The thirty knights gasped as one when they saw the painting on the cloth. It was Saladin's own markings. Then Justin laughed. He understood perfectly.

"When we are close to them, we draw our weapons and hold them at bay until the message is delivered?"

Eldwin nodded. Five minutes later the band of knights rode toward the oncoming caravan. Saladin's banner fluttered above them, and the masked knight rode in the center.

They met the caravan and the fifty Saracen knights who protected it. The Saracens, seeing the banner of their king, did not draw their weapons and before they realized what was happening, Eldwin and the knights of Radstock were within their midst. Their desert robes were flung off to reveal Christian armor, their weapons out and threatening.

But no knight struck a blow. Then the ranks parted, and Eldwin, with silver sword drawn, rode to the leader of the Saracens.

Silently, she stared at the man. Slowly, she extended a gauntleted hand and the scroll resting within it. James spoke then in French, and all knew the Saracen leader understood.

"This message is for Saladin alone. Be sure only he receives it."

Eldwin raised her sword, and the men of Radstock began to withdraw. "You are letting us proceed?" asked the Saracen leader.

"Sir Eldwin is gracious today. Begone before he changes his mind!" warned Justin.

As one, the English knights turned their mounts and raced

away from the caravan. Behind them, the Saracens watched their enemy depart, wondering why they had not attacked, and wondering even more what the message contained.

"You cannot!" pleaded Saladin's grand vizier.

"Do not tell me what I am permitted to do."

"Master, would you risk all for this mad desire?" Borka-al-Salu asked.

"I would see her for myself. I would hear what she wants of me."

"She is an infidel. It is a plot of Richard's. The message says for you to go alone to the Oasis of Prosperity. You cannot do this!"

"You have been my advisor for many years, my old friend; I would not like to replace you."

"Nor I you!" the grand vizier spat. Then he saw the darkness spread across Saladin's face and felt himself tremble. He bowed low, even as he spoke. "A thousand pardons, Master, but I think only of your safety."

"We are tired; let us drop this discussion."

"Then you will go?"

"I have no choice. It is not a desire for this woman's body that drives me. I must find out what she wants. I must learn more of this knight who sends such fear through my army."

"But if it is a trick?"

"I think not. Remember, the hooded knight delivered the message. No matter what is thought of him, I know he is a man of honor. He would not have been the bearer of this message if deceit was involved."

"And so I pray."

"*Ins'Alla,*" responded Saladin, "the will of Allah shall prevail." When he stopped speaking, a slave entered the chamber and bowed low before him. When he rose, he stared not at Saladin, but at the emir's feet as was the custom.

"The infidel is waiting."

"In a moment," Saladin replied. He turned in his seat to gaze out the window. *Time brings change* had been the saying of his early tutor. And time, he'd hoped, would bring a change in the English knight's thinking. He had given Miles time and had offered him much. But for seven months, the Englishman had spurned his offers. Today would be the last time he would hold his friendship out to the man. He would no longer accept the insults that the Frankish knight returned for his friendship and respect. Without taking his eyes from the window, he spoke. "Bring him in."

Standing before Saladin, Miles stared directly into the Moslem king's eyes.

"*Salaam,* Miles of England."

"*Salaam,* Saladin, right hand to Muhammad."

"You refused my gift of yesterday."

"There is only one gift I may accept," Miles replied.

"For over seven months you have been with us. You have learned our language, and our customs. You could be one of us, and rise to greatness alongside of me. I can make it so."

"Is this why you summoned me?" Miles asked.

"No. I would speak of your unknown knight."

"Eldwin has taken another caravan?"

"No, he has let one pass. Am I wrong in believing that the word of this Eldwin is as sacred as a deed he would perform?"

"You are not wrong." Miles gazed at Saladin, wondering what Gwendolyn had done now. No word had come from Aliya, and he knew not of what Saladin spoke.

"I have received a message, given my men by Eldwin. It is for a meeting. Should I fear for my life?"

"A meeting with Eldwin?"

"No, another."

"But it was Eldwin who carried the message?" When Saladin nodded his head, Miles said, "Then you should not fear for anything, save the day Richard defeats you."

"That day will never happen. Miles of England, we have discussed this many times. I have never fought an adversary equal to Richard, but he cannot defeat me. We are equal, I must admit, but the advantages are mine. The best he can hope for is a truce, and only when I have taken back all my territory will I agree to that."

"Then we have nothing else to speak of."

"My friend, we have much to speak of and will have years to do so. Relent, accept the true faith and become one with us."

"May I return to my chamber?"

"When I say!" roared Saladin, standing to glare at Miles. "Why do you fight me? Why do you persist in this foolishness? Why do you deny what any of my people would accept without question?"

"I am not one of your people," he said simply.

"So I have learned." Saladin stared at him meaningfully, until finally a curtain seemed to drop across his face. "Very well, I have no choice but to accept your decision. Return to your chamber and prepare yourself for what you have chosen." Saladin turned then and spoke to the grand vizier in a low voice.

Before Miles was out of the chamber, Borka-al-Salu bowed to Saladin and left through the rear exit. This time he knew better than to argue with the caliph, for Saladin was angrier than he had ever before seen. The insult the Frank had given him had finally ended the growing friendship between the two. And again, Saladin's chief advisor sensed a danger because of it.

Miles left the chamber as he was instructed, and when he walked through the hallways, he realized that his position had changed. In the instant Saladin had spoken, Miles knew he would no longer be treated as a friend. But strangely, he welcomed this change, for it served to strengthen his resolve.

An hour later, while he sat on a cushion in his chamber, four armed Saracens entered and silently collected his armor and weapons. Miles watched them, uncaring what they did, until one grasped Aliya's arm, and began to drag her away. Moving swiftly, Miles raced across the chamber and flew onto the Saracen's back, grabbing his neck in a twisting hold. Suddenly the room exploded in a whirling of rainbow colors, and blackness descended.

The end was coming. Gwendolyn knew this with a certainty that could not be denied. But *how* it ended would depend on her own special abilities. As Eldwin, she had led her knights against Saladin's supply caravans, disrupting the flow of food and equipment to Jerusalem. But those forays had only disrupted, not stopped them completely.

Yesterday's meeting with the latest caravan would be the last the Saracens saw of Eldwin and his men. The convergence of her two plans had solidified, and now there was but one path left.

She had been successful in drawing attention to herself

and had insured this success by paying two men who were devout Christian Moors. They acted as spies for Richard, and Gwendolyn had used them to send word to Saladin, through devious channels, that the Frankish woman was a beauty such as had never been seen in this land.

Word had reached her, through these spies, that Saladin had taken an interest in the stories, and rumor stated that even the women of the harem heard of Saladin's desire to see the beauty of the golden-haired woman.

That was what had prompted Gwendolyn's move to stop the caravan and deliver the message to Saladin. In the missive she had asked for a meeting and expressed her great desire to meet the monarch of the Moslem empire. She had also stated that there was a purpose to this meeting that could only be spoken of to him. If he desired to meet her and also wanted the attacks on his caravans stopped, he would come alone to the Oasis of Prosperity.

Alone! That had been the key word. For Gwendolyn's plan to succeed, Saladin must come alone. That had also been the reason she had exposed herself to the lascivious stares of the townspeople. Word of her different beauty had to reach him, to pique his interest, and to make him want to see and meet this strange woman.

When she had been satisfied that he was interested, as the spies had indeed reported, she readied her message, and, in the guise of Eldwin, delivered it.

"The horses are ready, my lady," Roweena informed her as she entered the chamber.

Gwendolyn gazed at her servant and friend and saw Roweena's face pinched by worry. "All will work out," she said, trying to ease the girl's mind.

"You are always so sure of things, but I am not. I am frightened, my lady. I am scared you will not return."

"You must believe in me—believe that I will come back."

"I will pray for you." Then Roweena forced a smile and unfurled the long riding cape she had brought. "This will hide your form from those who watch."

Gwendolyn looked at the dark hooded cape and nodded. She bent and lifted the silver sword and secured it to the sash around her abdomen before allowing Roweena to place the cape on her shoulders.

"Take care, my lady," Roweena whispered.

Gwendolyn stretched out her arm, and Valkyrie went from his perch to rest on her leather-banded wrist. Silently, Gwendolyn left the chamber and walked out into the night, confident that Roweena would prevent anyone from knowing that Gwendolyn had left Ascalon.

Outside she met James and Arthur and mounted the mare waiting for her. Together, the three riders and the large eagle rode through the silent town, and through the gate that had been opened for them. The small band rode through the day, ignoring its heat, and continued deep into the multicolored desert.

Above the riders, arcing magnificently in the sky, flew Valkyrie, leading them forward to their destiny. When the sun dropped from the western sky, the riders drew to a halt. Below them was a rocky valley, and in its center was the Oasis of Prosperity.

The oasis was an anachronism, as was much of the country. It was a small spot of beauty fighting against the relentless rolling of time that threatened to consume and make it a part of the large area of waste. Sandy, rocky desert spread for as far as the eye could see, yet centered in the valley was this lush sward of green. Tall trees spread their arms to the sky, and a proliferation of cacti, their yellow fruit contrasting to the green, welcomed all travelers with their juicy sweetness.

Yet, Gwendolyn's eyes passed over the beauty as she sought to learn if any had arrived before her. The slopes leading to the oasis were deserted, and there seemed to be no life within its green confines.

Then she gazed up at Valkyrie, who was slowly circling above. A moment later he flew over the oasis. The giant eagle circled the valley twice more, and then Gwendolyn relaxed when she saw the bird alight on top of one tree.

"It is safe," she told her squires. A half hour later, the three riders stopped within the oasis. Night had fallen, and only the illumination of the early stars lit their way. The moon would rise, but not for several hours.

When Gwendolyn was on the ground, she turned to her squires and spoke. "You remember where the cave is?"

"Could we not wait in the trees?" James asked.

"It would be too risky. You will be able to see from the cave."

James nodded his head reluctantly and then went about his duties while Arthur opened a leather bag to spread out their evening meal.

After eating, Arthur and James mounted their horses and rode away from the oasis to the small hidden cave Eldwin had found the week before. The cave overlooked the oasis and afforded a perfect view of its center, where Gwendolyn would meet Saladin. From the cave, the twins would watch, and if any others came, they would stop them with their longbows.

But James realized that if any came at night, they would come unseen. The twins kept watch for two hours, but found it to be a futile exercise, and, following their mistress's instructions, finally gave themselves over to the sleep they had been denied for two days.

Gwendolyn, beneath them, prepared herself for her meeting with Saladin. She took off the hooded cape and, ignoring the chill of the desert night, sat wearing only a simple Saxon tunic. Powerful forces played within her mind, and she gave herself over to them, as she drew the silver sword and laid it across her lap.

She sat for hours, with memories assaulting her mind. Memories of herself and Miles, of their first meeting, of their love, and of the sharing of that love with their bodies. Within her, Gwendolyn knew the ache of loneliness, and the sadness of her desires. Then came the strengthening of her will, and the forces that had guided her across the world returned to lend support to her resolve.

Then the sword began to vibrate within her hand, sending trembling surges of energy throughout her body. Her eyes snapped open in the instant her sword began to glow. The moon had risen, and the silver blade reflected the luminescence of the night's haunting sheen.

With only instinct guiding her, Gwendolyn lifted the sword before her, grasping the pommel in both hands, and holding its tip toward the face of the moon. To any who might have seen, they would have sworn a lightning bolt had been released by the moon to sail toward the center of the desert.

Gwendolyn's arms trembled within the powerful grip of the sword, as light exploded all around her. She fought it, trying to control what was happening, but could not. Then she stopped herself and gave in to the silver call, realizing that her energy and need had called forth this power, and nothing else.

The instant she submitted to it, the light calmed, and the sword hummed in harmony with her thoughts.

"Use the power, Daughter of Thunder, ride the heavens and see your desire." The calm, wordless voice of the priestess soothed her mind, and Gwendolyn accepted the old one's advice.

The gentle wrenching separation of body and mind was smooth this time, and no discord shook her thoughts. Then she entered the multifarious layers of the otherworld, to float within a crimson cloud.

"Welcome, Daughter."

Gwendolyn's mind shook, and emotions threatened her very existence. The sparkling sapphire eyes of Gwyneth Kildrake gazed lovingly at her.

Chapter Twenty-four

WITHIN THE SWIRLING ETHEREAL plane, Gwendolyn faced her mother. It was not the wavering images of the woman she had seen in the company of the old Druid priestess, but the actual and pure spirit of Gwyneth, with her beautiful features and soft glittering eyes.

"It is time for you to learn more, my daughter."

"And time for you to grow," added the Druid priestess who appeared beside Gwyneth. "You have used your powers wisely, Child of Thunder, and have striven to reach your destiny. Look!" she commanded with a wave of her hand. The crimson cloud parted, and Gwendolyn gazed upon a kaleidoscopic scene that tore at her imagination.

It was a changing, fermenting vision which turned her mind into a mass of confused thoughts. When the realization of what she saw struck her, tears fell from her bodiless eyes. Years passed before her, hundreds of them. She watched Devonshire and Radstock change. She witnessed battles and death and plague. She saw lives become meaningless existences, their only purpose to serve the cruel needs of others.

She saw wars and machines that defied description lay waste to the beautiful and bountiful earth; and then she witnessed the end. Throughout the land, horrid inventions of death rained. Volcanic clouds of unknown magnitude spewed across the face of the earth, and almost all life ceased to exist.

"No!" she screamed, denying what she saw.

"It is the path mankind has chosen long before your birth, and one that we must follow."

"Then why am I here? Why do I exist? For what you have shown me proves only the futility of life!"

"No, Daughter of Thunder," said the old one. But Gwendolyn no longer listened to her mentor; the horrors she witnessed were too strong in her soul. Then she felt the most gentle caress she had ever known. A soft, lingering caress of love and devotion rippled through her mind. Turning, she looked into the shimmering pools of her mother's eyes.

"Look now, Gwendolyn, and see what your purpose is."

Gwendolyn gazed again through the crimson veil and saw a small tunnel within the earth open. Although they were much changed and deformed, she recognized the hills of Radstock and saw that the opening was the very tunnel that led from the training pit Miles had built for her.

The land surrounding it was strange, with unknown foliage and vegetation. Intuitively, she knew that the terrible weapons which had destroyed her home had wrought these changes to land and life.

Then she was startled from her thoughts when two figures emerged from the tunnel. Both rode strange beasts that barely resembled horses and both wore glistening armor that resembled a shining second skin.

When the two rode out of the tunnel's mouth, they stopped to look around. Suddenly a scream ripped through the air, and a golden eagle flew from the bowels of the earth.

Gwendolyn's first thought was of Valkyrie. But she noticed the eagle's wings reflecting light in an unnatural way. A moment later she saw the bird was not a living thing, but something made of metal. *How could it fly?* she wondered.

The two riders, acting in concert, removed their helmets. Gwendolyn cried out voicelessly and again felt Gwyneth's soothing caress, for before her, she saw duplicates of herself and Miles.

"No," whispered the old one, "look closely."

Gwendolyn did. The woman was as tall as she, with long hair of gold and silver, and if Gwendolyn had not known better, she would have thought herself to be looking at her reflection within a still pool. But then she saw the difference. The woman's eyes were the sea-green of Miles's own. Then she looked at the man who wore the face of her husband. His eyes were different, too; his eyes were the blue of a morning sky—his eyes were Gwendolyn's.

"I don't understand," she whispered. She cried out again when the woman drew a sword. "My father's sword!"

"It belongs to the issue of Kildrake, who will rule the earth and all upon it in the generations to come," intoned the Druid priestess. She waved her arm, and the picture dissolved.

"You have been blessed, Gwendolyn, daughter of Gwyneth, and cursed. For what you have seen is a thousand years distant. A thousand years of darkness and death to survive. You have been chosen and blessed, yet that blessing is a curse, for you and your issue are what stands between life and darkness for all."

"Why?" she whispered.

"There is no answer to satisfy your question. Ask me not, for only the future can respond. But know you well, that you have proven yourself able. You not only defeated the puppet of darkness, but aided your father, as well. In defeating Morgan, and that which controlled him, you have set yourself free to continue your life, and also lifted the earthly bonds which held the son of thunder at bay."

"And Miles?"

"We cannot control the destiny of all. Morgan's deceit was guided by darkness; we knew of the possibilities, but not of the actualities. That is why we prepared you. Saladin is but a man, as is Richard. You have the sword of your father. That is the legacy we have given you. Our time on this plane is done, and we must leave you forever."

"No!"

"It is as it has been ordained. We have taught you and guided you. We have given you knowledge and understanding. You are the beginning, you are the chosen. You have defeated the power of darkness for now, but it shall return. You and your line must be vigilant, for you are now the guardians. Ask not for more; accept not less. Now is your time to live and take control of your existence. You have the sword and the power to wield it. One day, in the far future, you will watch over your issue, as we have done over you, and see the world led back to sanity."

"But Miles?" Gwendolyn asked, her mind growing heavy with the weight of sadness and loss.

"You must secure him and free him. There are no powers to aid you, only yourself, your mind, and your heritage. We bid you farewell, Gwendolyn, Daughter of Thunder."

"Wait!" Gwendolyn commanded. The power of the thought, hurled from her with the force of her father's hammer, captured both her mother and the old one in its grasp. Only once before had Gwendolyn dared use the strength of her mind against her mentor. Now she knew she must use it again, for there was one more thing that must be done before she would allow them to leave her.

"I understand what you have said and accept it. I am the chosen and am ready to fulfill the destiny given me. I yield to your wishes and accept that which I cannot deny. But before you leave forever, I would ask of something."

"If it is within my power," replied the old one, and Gwendolyn felt the satisfaction and pleasure of her mentor's thoughts. "Yes, my child, you are strong and have become what I declared to all, twenty years ago. But hurry, for we weaken with each moment and must leave to find our own peace."

"You have said that I will no longer have your aid, but my sword will be my power."

"And your might."

"Will it be my guide through the heavens?"

Sadness spread throughout her mind, a sadness reflected from the minds of her mother and the old one. "When your earthly body dies, you will ride the heavens again. Until then, rely you must on our first earthly link."

"Then let me see my husband as he is now," Gwendolyn asked, knowing it would be the last time she could do so, and accepting the decision and its finality.

The old one waved her hand. Again the crimson cloud parted. Gwendolyn's ethereal embodiment floated through the opening, and she found herself within a walled chamber.

She gazed at Miles asleep upon the cushions and saw, also, the blood-soaked cloth that bound his head. She hovered above him and slowly let herself cover his earthly body with her spiritual one.

"He has hurt you needlessly, my love," she whispered to his mind, "but I shall ease the pain. I am coming for you soon, Miles, and we will be together. Remember." With a final caress of her lips upon his, she returned to the crimson plane and the two who awaited her.

"I shall free him," she promised.

"Be not oversure of your actions. Be as cautious as you are brave. Be as wise as you are loving," intoned the old one, in a final benediction to her pupil.

Their voices grew dim and their bodies wavered. Suddenly, Gwendolyn was caught in the whirlpool of the crimson cloud swirling around her. Then she was again sitting within the desert oasis. Lowering her sword, she gazed up at the sky.

A glittering ball of fire flashed across the sky, leaving behind it a bright trail of lingering light against the black heavens. She saw the ball suddenly split into three flaming arrows which rose upward together until they disappeared from sight. Within their bright spectre, Gwendolyn was sure she saw the forms of her father, mother, and the old Druid priestess, making their final ascent into the vast body of the universe. "Good-bye," she whispered.

Before lowering the sword completely, she had one more thing to do. Slowly, fighting the weariness that her just-ended journey had brought on, she raised the sword high. She formed a picture of Miles, and the chamber he was imprisoned within, in her mind. The sword sang with power, and Gwendolyn directed the healing purity of the light toward Miles. She guided its force to his head and expanded the channel within her mind.

Only when that was done, did she return to herself, and to the cool air blowing down from the valley's walls.

She sheathed the sword, lay down upon the cape, and closed her eyes. Valkyrie would wake her before the sun rose, and she would prepare herself for meeting Saladin.

Miles woke slowly, and for the first time in three days, felt no pain in his head. When he had returned to his chamber after Saladin's dismissal, he remembered attacking the guard, and then blackness had come. He'd wavered in and out of consciousness, aware only of the few times Aliya had attended him, washing his face with cool water and bandaging his head. Most of the time, he had thought himself dying.

When Aliya had cleansed his wound, he'd heard her gasp

of despair and knew that he'd been hurt badly. But this morning it was as if he'd never been touched. He closed his eyes and invoked the memory of his dream. He'd dreamed of his wife, and of the softness of her lips on his. He'd drawn comfort from her and had willed himself to be with her.

He remembered vividly the pure white light that had encased him. The gentle warmth which had entered his body and filled him with peace. He had dreamed of Gwendolyn after that and knew he would live to see her again. Suddenly, Miles heard footsteps entering the chamber, but he kept his eyes closed and feigned sleep.

Aliya came in, accompanied by one guard. The man stood at the entranceway with his arms crossed, but did not follow the young slave to Miles's side.

Aliya knelt beside Miles and gazed at him just as he opened his eyes. Her indrawn breath went unnoticed by the guard, as she stared at his open and unglazed eyes. "You are better," she whispered in a relieved voice.

"I—"

"Say nothing!" she ordered. First she wiped his face and then she stood. Turning to the guard, she spoke. "He has not woken."

Grunting, the guard left the chamber to take his post in the hallway. When he was gone, Aliya knelt again at Miles's side. "There are two guards in the hall, and two more in the courtyard," she whispered. "Thank Allah you are better."

Carefully, she unwound the bandage, and when she had finished, another indrawn breath echoed in the room. "I . . . it is impossible. The wound is healed. How?"

"Was it very bad?"

"The physician thought you would die. The guard split your scalp and you bled for many hours. How is this possible?"

"Aliya, none must know of this. My wife came to me last night and healed me."

Aliya closed her eyes at his words, trying to understand what he said, but she could not.

Seeing this written in her face, Miles spoke quickly. "What has happened since I was brought here?"

"I am sorry, Master. You are now a prisoner truly. None are allowed to see or talk to you. No one may visit this chamber except myself, and I am allowed only twice a day to bring you food and cleanse your wounds."

"As it should be. Aliya, I am a prisoner, not your master. Do not compromise yourself for me, for I shall be gone soon."

"It is said that if you live, Saladin will send you to the farthest corner of his land, to be a slave in the poorest of places."

"What else is said?"

"That Saladin left last night to meet the Frank woman he has heard of. He rides to meet your wife."

"I warned him; I tried," whispered Miles.

"I still do not understand."

"There is no need. Aliya, soon I will be gone. Remember me with kindness."

"There is no other way to remember you, Master."

"There is one other way." Miles turned and reached out to touch the wall. There, he pried away a small stone and took out what he had hidden many months before. He had found it beneath a cushion when he'd first arrived in Jerusalem and had secreted it away, hoping that he could use it to help free himself. When he learned the impossibility of this, he'd put it out of his mind. But now he knew what its use could be.

When he turned back to Aliya, he opened his palm. Within it rested a large, perfectly shaped blood-red ruby. "It is yours," he told her. "To buy your freedom."

"I . . ." But Aliya could not speak. Her eyes filled with tears, and she slowly shook her head. "Put it back, Master, for none may purchase their freedom from Saladin. I am as much a prisoner as you. Only his whim may free me."

"Then take it and purchase something for me. Purchase a dagger small enough for me to hide."

"That I will do, but there will be much left over."

"Use if as you deem best, for it is yours."

Silently, Aliya tore a clean strip of cloth and bandaged Miles's healed wound. "Do not let them know you are well," she cautioned before she left.

And then Miles was alone, but he knew it would not be for much longer.

* * *

Gwendolyn woke to Valkyrie's gentle call. Sitting up, she realized she had slept deeply and had awoken refreshed. Yet within her, she knew she had changed deeply. The sky around her was beginning to lighten, and painted bands of purple and pink glowed softly on the horizon, lending a soothing shade to the colored sands of the desert.

"Hunt, my friend," Gwendolyn told Valkyrie. The eagle called softly again before dropping from the tree and expanding his wings to catch the current. Moments later he was soaring high above the oasis, his sharp eyes looking for life within the sand-and-rock valley.

Gwendolyn breathed deeply of the morning air while she tried to sort out her emotions. She was saddened by the knowledge that her mentor was gone; it was a loss that would last through her life. But she was aware, also, that the old one and her mother had given her a vision of what would be, and what could be, if she was strong enough to take that which was set before her. She sensed also there was one more test before her. And this testing was the most important. Without Miles, there was no future.

Gwendolyn went to the old well and drew up some of its cool water. She rinsed her face and began her preparations for meeting Saladin. She went to the leather bags that her squires had taken from the horses and lifted the bold Norman dress.

Removing her tunic, Gwendolyn put on the first layer of her most sensual costume. Ten minutes later she was in the revealing Norman dress that had gained her so much notoriety. She then shook the dirt from her riding cape and put it on.

When all her preparations were complete, she sat on the soft ground, the sword hidden beneath the folds of the cape, to wait in silence for Saladin.

Above her, Valkyrie returned to his perch in the tall palm, content with his meal, and ready to resume his duties as Gwendolyn's sentry.

On the far side of the valley, Saladin reined in the white stallion and glanced toward the oasis. His eyes swept the area carefully before he turned to the men who followed.

"Wait here," he commanded. Without a backward glance, he spurred the stallion onward. His mind seethed with questions, and today he would get his answers. He wanted to meet this woman of whom so many had spoken. He wanted to know why she sought him, and what she wanted from him. But above it all, was his unquenchable thirst for beauty. A thirst which almost matched his desire to rid his land of the infidels forever.

Moments later, he entered the green pasture of the oasis and saw the back of a robed figure. He stopped the horse and dismounted. Drawing his scimitar, he advanced cautiously toward the person.

Gwendolyn heard Valkyrie's warning and rose to her feet just as she heard the horse's hoofbeats. She stood with her back to Saladin's arrival and called upon her reserves to aid her in this confrontation, urging the powers of her sword to enhance her image. She listened carefully, bringing all her senses to bear, and when she heard the whisper of his scimitar leave its sheath, she gripped her sword tighter.

When she sensed him to be very close, she spoke in French. "You do not need your weapon." But she did not turn to face him.

"That remains to be seen," he replied.

"Look above you and be reminded of the challenge I issued when I arrived in this land."

Carefully, Saladin raised his eyes and saw the giant golden eagle on the branch above. When his eyes met the amber ones of the eagle, the giant bird of prey cried out and spread its wings to the fullest. Saladin saw the might of the eagle, and saw, too, the long, sharp talons of death.

In the instant Gwendolyn knew his eyes were on Valkyrie, she whirled, flinging the cape back and calling on the power of her sword. The blade sang in her hands and whistled loudly as it cut through the air.

Saladin saw her move and brought his scimitar up, but he was unprepared to do anything except try to deflect her blow. The woman's sword met his own, and the cry of tortured metal sounded; then his scimitar was ripped from his hands and flew across the oasis, to land ten feet from where he stood.

Gwendolyn lowered her blade and stared at the king of the Moslem nation. "I said there would be no need of weapons; now I have made it a fact." So stating, Gwendolyn sheathed her sword and took a deep breath, aware that Saladin was studying her intently.

Saladin had never before seen a woman such as Gwendolyn, and he had seen women from every country in the world. Franks, with their white skin; blacks, with their shining ebony beauty; dark-skinned Easterners from the lands of the rain forests; and yellow-skinned maidens from the depths of the Orient were commonplace to him, littering the harems within all his palaces; but, this woman was like no other he had ever seen. Her beauty radiated all around her. Her hair shone beneath the newly risen sun, and glowed with the power of silver and gold. Her skin was the purest white he had ever seen, and her eyes were like the rarest jewels in the world. Her height only accented her beauty, and the superb form barely contained within the clothing she wore was in perfect proportion to the rest of her. In that moment, Saladin knew that nothing less than full possession of this creature would satisfy him.

"You surprise me," he finally said.

"I surprise many."

"One does not expect a woman of your beauty to have the ability of a warrior."

"That has been a mistake made by many."

Saladin ignored her words, and the dangerously low tone she had spoken in. His entire being was focused on her beauty. "Why have you called me here?"

"Why did you not respond to my challenge?"

"Your challenge?"

"I sent my eagle with my challenge. I know he delivered it."

"Your eagle destroyed one of my prized hawks. There are few like he in the land."

"Did you thank Allah that he killed no others?" Gwendolyn asked, aware of the magic that her body, changed by the unseen glow of the sword, had on him.

"I could not challenge a bird," Saladin stated.

"You were a coward! You chose to ignore this challenge. You had but to ask your prisoner, Miles Delong, Earl of Radstock, where to send your answer."

"Do not anger me; do not risk your beautiful life. You have challenged me and you have asked for this meeting,"

Saladin said, finally pulling his mind free of her charms, and chasing away the anger her words had brought on.

"Your anger bothers me not at all. For I have already granted you your life once."

Saladin was taken aback by this statement and stared openly at her. "You?"

"Sir Eldwin granted you your life. Sir Eldwin is my knight. He lives only for me and responds only to my wishes."

"What is it that you want of me?" Saladin asked, growing impatient with the meeting's direction.

"A bargain."

Saladin laughed and shook his head. "You know nothing of my land, or the way of my people. You cannot bargain with me. I am the ruler of these lands; it is I who commands, and I who offers bargains. And, you are a woman. Bargains are made by men. Women are but possessions."

"Do you not find me desirable?" Gwendolyn asked, unbothered by his words.

Saladin paused before he spoke. Something in her tone warned him to be careful, and he scrutinized her carefully. "No man alive could deny your beauty."

"Then you will listen to what I propose?"

"I will listen."

"I propose this!" Gwendolyn stepped back and outlined her body with her hands, tracing the curves of her breasts, waist, and hips under Saladin's gaze. "I offer you myself. I give you my body to do with as you will."

"That is but half a bargain. What is the rest?"

"A life," Gwendolyn stated simply.

Saladin blinked at her words with a lack of comprehension. "A life?"

"I will become yours when you release Miles Delong."

Saladin shook his head slowly. "You must find another thing for which to bargain; Miles Delong will never be released."

"You have yet to ask my name, but I shall tell you anyway. I am called Lady Gwendolyn Delong. If you desire me, free my husband!" Gwendolyn demanded.

"You are his wife." The words seemed torn from his lips, and Gwendolyn saw his face turn pale. She waited silently until the color returned to his skin, as the forgotten memory of Miles's description of his wife came back to him. "Now I understand. It was not for Christianity that he refused me, but for you. No, I will not release him. My word is sacred and I must keep it as such." Within his mind, Saladin fought for control. New truths had been revealed this day, and new desires had been born.

"Then you leave me no other choice. Again, I challenge you!"

"I have never met a woman like you before. You set my blood on fire, and I would take you here and now. It is not your sword, nor your eagle, that stops me. It is something more powerful. It is my respect for your husband and his strength. Leave now! Go while you may, before I change my mind."

Rage swept through Gwendolyn, making her nerves grow taut and her muscles tremble. She glared fiercely at the Moor, and her voice reverberated lowly. "Hear me well, King of the Saracen. I have traveled far to secure the life of my husband. I care little for your war, your land, or your rotting body! Be warned! If you force me, I shall destroy it all!"

"It would give me pleasure to tame and control you. Your place is forgotten. Never speak to me like this, never!" Saladin's rage grew hotly within him and threatened to make him attack the woman.

"How else should I speak to a coward?" Gwendolyn whispered. She saw Saladin's face change, and even as he moved, her sword was free and pointing at his heart.

"No person has ever called me a coward and lived. You have done so twice. I will accept any challenge you offer, as long as you are part of the spoils, for I promise you that you will be my slave."

"Morgan is dead. Only his memory in your mind keeps your oath alive. I challenge you to produce your most fearsome warrior—the best the Moslem land has. I ask for single combat. My knight, Eldwin, against your fighter. If Eldwin is victorious, Miles is free and your obligation to Morgan ended. If Eldwin is defeated, I am yours to enslave, a ransom payment for Miles."

Saladin's barking laugh echoed loudly. "In either

event your husband is free. That seems a contradiction."

"No contradiction exists. You will still have a Delong as a prisoner."

"Do you think your husband would agree to this if he knew you offered yourself to me?"

"He would."

"You are so certain your knight will win?"

"Do you fear that, too?" Gwendolyn retorted with a smile.

Saladin suppressed his anger and returned the woman's smile. "I accept upon two conditions: first, that your husband agrees; second, that this fight be set to my rules."

A warning flashed in Gwendolyn's mind, but she was forced to ignore it. She was too close to her goal, and could not back down now. "Agreed."

"You do have faith in your knight. The rules are simple. The fight will take place on foot, not on horseback. The champions will wear no armor on their bodies. Their only protection will be their abilities as fighters. Scimitar against sword. Man against man."

"Again, I agree."

"I would have you present to witness this, for I will have you in my harem that night."

"I will be there, to ride away with my husband."

With that, Gwendolyn sheathed her sword and called out to Valkyrie. The eagle responded with a loud, clear note and left the branch he was perched on. He spread his wings and glided gracefully towards Gwendolyn, where she stood with her arm outstretched.

"In two days, I will send Valkyrie, my friend, to you. You will attach a message about his neck, stating the place we are to meet, and when."

Gwendolyn turned abruptly away and mounted the mare. Without a backward glance, she rode toward the cave where James and Arthur awaited.

Saladin stood still for a long time after she was gone from the oasis before he turned and retrieved his scimitar. Then he gave himself over to his laughter. He had outmaneuvered the woman and he allowed himself to feel the satisfaction of his victory. His honor would be upheld, and he would not have to break his word.

He had not offered his oath to the woman, and she had not

called upon him to swear to what he had agreed, but merely accepted what he proposed. To Saladin, as to all the men of the Moslem world, a sacred oath—one that could not be broken—must not only be sworn to the seeker of it, but to Allah, the compassionate, and Muhammad, his prophet.

When the challenge was over, no matter which champion was victorious, Saladin knew he would have a new slave in his bed.

Chapter Twenty-five

THE REALITY OF THE PAST days held a tenacious grip on Gwendolyn's mind. The confrontation with Saladin, and the lingering doubts about his agreement were only a part of what disturbed her. She could not rid her mind of the visions she had been granted; of the strange and horrible future that awaited mankind.

What could man possibly do to make this world so different? And what could Miles's and her children do to save it? The guidance she had been given by the Druid priestess, her mother, and her father was gone; and with it, her ability to commune with them and learn more.

She felt deserted and alone for the first time in her life and almost wished she had never glimpsed the strange powers that ruled the universe.

But even as these thoughts bombarded her consciousness, she realized that with the loss of her otherworldly guidance, she must learn to depend more upon herself than ever before. She still had the sword, and with it, its far-reaching powers. But whatever other knowledge she would gain, would be because she had sought and learned it, with her heart and mind.

In the morning, she had released Valkyrie and bid him go to Miles and Saladin. She wanted this final encounter to come so that she could either return home with Miles or end whatever dreams had been prophesied; for Gwendolyn had already accepted the fact that if she were to lose this fight, she would not become Saladin's slave. Once she knew Miles was free, she would no longer continue her life.

Even as she thought this, she felt a strange hum pass through her. Turning quickly, she saw the silver sword glowing. She went to it and lifted it, wondering what had caused the sword to come to life unbidden. When she held it in her hand, the humming eased, her mind calmed, and her confidence returned.

And so another new experience befell Gwendolyn. She sat for an hour, holding the blade in a trance of healing she had been unaware of invoking.

She had desperately wanted to return to the crimson plane, to be able to see her husband, and to make certain her healing had restored his life and vitality. But she would be denied that ability while she lived upon the earth.

Deep in her trance, the words of the old one returned to her, and with them came even more understanding. *Until then, rely you must, on our first earthly link*. In the sadness of her loss, and in her need to visit Miles, Gwendolyn had forgotten those last words.

Within the trance nothing else existed, and she focused her considerable energy to deciphering the priestess's words. She went back in time, bringing out memories of her earliest years. She lived again in the castle of her stepfather and searched through the years for some hint of an ethereal link, but found none. She followed her life, and her move to Devonshire. She relived the weeks, months, and years of her path to maturity.

She remembered the first time she learned of her father and the silver sword. But the sword had only given her the barest glimmer of what she would become. No, the sword had not been the link. She remembered her mother's death, and then remembered finding Valkyrie, and nursing him back to health shortly after Gwyneth's passing.

In the trance, her mind absorbed with her task, Gwendolyn was again fourteen and riding on the moors of Devon in the early spring. She released the golden eagle, returning to it its freedom. But Valkyrie had not accepted the gift. He had flown back to her and stayed with her, never once leaving her side unless she told it to.

Unless she spoke to Valkyrie! The sword glowed brightly within the chamber, but Gwendolyn saw it not. She concentrated and saw the golden eagle. She remembered every time she had spoken to her friend, and how he had always done what she'd asked. She had never questioned this before, just accepting it in the way she had so many of the things in her life.

It had to be Valkyrie; there was no other possibility. Slowly and carefully, Gwendolyn formed a mental picture of the giant eagle, trying with all her might to establish contact with him.

The sword vibrated in her hands, and even in her trance, she knew the chamber glowed with bright light. Then she felt a strangeness within her mind, an alienness she'd never known before. But she could not understand this thing and forced herself to delve deeper.

Then she was seeing the desert below her, far, far beneath her as she had never before. The smallest stone could be seen perfectly, and the colors of the sands were enhanced and magnified with crystal clarity.

Then Gwendolyn knew. She was seeing through the eyes of Valkyrie. He had been her link! Valkyrie had been sent to her to watch over her by the powers who guided her. The sadness and loss that had left such emptiness within her began to ease as the knowledge that she was not alone came to her aid.

She gladly lost herself to the desert she viewed through Valkyrie's eyes and journeyed with the giant eagle to Jerusalem, and to Miles.

The call to prayer echoed through the streets of Jerusalem, and Miles listened to it in the solitude of his chamber. Nothing had changed since he'd awoken the morning after Gwendolyn had healed him. Aliya came twice daily, and the guards ignored him, thinking him to be dying. But with each visit, Aliya brought more news.

The night before, Aliya had delivered more than news; she had brought Miles a small, yet deadly sharp dagger. It now rested beneath the cushion nearest his head, waiting for him to call upon its use.

Then in the morning, Aliya had come with more news. Information that boded ill times ahead. Since Saladin's return from his meeting with Gwendolyn, he seemed to have become obsessed with her. Aliya said the rumors in the harem were heated, and that Saladin took no woman to his bed. All he spoke of was Gwendolyn, and of the day he would possess her.

"But he is in the heart of a dilemma," Aliya had said.

"Explain."

"Saladin is a true Moslem. He is a devout believer in Allah and Muhammad, his prophet. Muhammad has decreed that none of the faithful may commit adultery. Saladin is bound by this law, and although he is an honorable man, and a good leader, he is also a true son of the desert. There are none more devious than our race," she had added in a trembling voice.

Miles had listened, but could not comprehend what she had been trying to say.

"He may not bring your wife to his bed unless you pronounce the words of divorce."

"This I may not do, for my religion prohibits the act," Miles had explained.

"I know this, as does the emir. Therefore, you must die before he can have your wife."

"He would not do that," Miles had argued, but Aliya had shaken her head violently.

"He would and he will! He is all-powerful. You must try to escape."

"Aliya, until the challenge is done, he cannot do away with me."

"Who would tell your wife? Who would warn her that Saladin would have her no matter what the cost?"

"She would know of my death in the instant it happened," Miles had whispered to Aliya.

"Take precautions, Master, for death lurks everywhere for you," Aliya had warned.

For the rest of the day Miles had thought upon her words and realized they held some truth. But there was nothing he could do about it, unless he could speak to Saladin himself and tell him of the futility of his plans.

The call to prayer ended, and Miles pushed the thoughts from his mind. Somehow, he would find a way to thwart Saladin.

At the entrance to his chamber, his two guards knelt on their prayer rugs, facing east, which placed their backs toward the chamber entrance. While they prayed, the large, dour guard on the left opened a pouch and tossed it inside the entrance. Even as he called upon Allah in prayer, he heard a slithering movement behind him and smiled. He would be greatly rewarded this day for taking such a wise initiative. He had heard of Saladin's problem, and of the emir's desires.

Miles sat up and stretched his arms over his head. Aliya would be here soon. She always came within a few moments after the evening prayers. But when he lowered his arms, he froze.

Four feet from him was the flat head and narrow eyes of a pit viper. The snake's head was a foot above the ground, its long tongue flicking constantly in Miles's direction. Moving slowly, he lowered his arm and began to search under the cushion. As he did, the snake hissed loudly in warning. He saw its head go back, and its dark body coil. He froze again, and so did the deadly reptile.

Miles willed his body to obey him and, as sweat streamed down his face, he moved his hand imperceptibly toward the dagger. His eyes locked on the snake's, and he watched every movement of his new adversary.

Then he touched the cold steel of the dagger and grasped it firmly. He knew he would have only one chance, and that was a slim one.

Taking a slow, deep breath, Miles readied himself. As he drew the dagger out, the viper hissed again and rose higher. The long coiled body arched, and Miles flung himself from the cushions, his dagger held outward.

In that instant, several things happened at once. He heard a woman's loud scream of fright, and an unidentifiable sound of rushing air as the viper launched itself at Miles.

The viper moved with lightning speed, but before it reached him, Miles saw a flash cross in front of him, and heard the loud war cry of Valkyrie. The eagle caught the viper within its talons and began a dance of death with its deadliest of enemies.

The snake was no match for Valkyrie's deadly beak and within seconds, the viper's head was severed from its body. Miles's breathing was harsh and his heart pounded. Then he saw Aliya, her dark almond-shaped eyes wide with fear, staring at the dead snake.

Before Miles could stand and go to her, the two guards

entered with drawn scimitars. The largest saw the dead snake and the golden eagle who stood near it. He yelled in rage at his foiled attempt and charged toward Valkyrie.

Reacting quickly, Miles turned the dagger in his hand and, in one smooth movement, flung it at the guard. The blade entered the man's throat, and his bubbling cry was cut off by the death that claimed him. His scimitar clattered loudly on the chamber floor, landing next to the golden eagle he had tried to kill. The other guard broke free from his trance just as Miles reached the scimitar. He lifted it and faced the man.

For the first time since his imprisonment, Miles faced a Saracen and was prepared to kill him. The guard circled his prisoner warily, looking for the right opening. Then he charged. Miles deflected his blow easily, but the sound of their fight drew the guards from the courtyard, and when they saw what was happening, they, too, drew their weapons.

Aliya was still held in the powerful grip of fear, but when Miles and the other guard met, she broke free and ran from the room. Love, not fear, lent speed to her feet. Love made her do what all else would have feared. She rushed past the two guards at the entrance of Saladin's audience chamber and flung herself at the emir's feet.

"They will kill him!" she cried. "Your guards will kill Miles!"

Saladin stared at the slave for a moment before he stood. "Speak! What are you saying?"

"A viper was sent to kill your prisoner! The snake is dead and now he battles your guards."

"Bring her!" he yelled, as he ran from his chamber to the one Miles was imprisoned in. The woman was mad. He had given no orders for Miles's death. He had merely discussed several possibilities.

Miles was hard pressed to defend himself against the three Saracens, yet he fought on. He battled the two in front while trying to stop the third from getting behind. His scimitar blurred with reflected light from the oil lamps, and his feet carried him in a dance that confused his opponents. Ducking under a wild blow, Miles parried another before spinning to thrust at the third man. A shout of pain was his reward, but the man did not go down.

Then the three attacked him as one, and Miles was backed

against the wall. He thrust at one man, just as another screamed. Valkyrie had joined the fray, his talons digging into the defenseless back of one guard. The man screamed and spun, trying to dislodge the eagle, but Valkyrie's talons were deeply imbedded in his flesh. His terrified cries of pain broke the concentration of the other two, and Miles took advantage of this.

With a sweeping stroke of the scimitar, he broke through one guard's defense, the shining blade drinking of the man's lifeblood. Then he faced but one. The guard attacked him in a frenzy that Miles met with equality.

Saladin burst into the chamber and stopped dead. The sight before him shook him to his core. A giant eagle fought one guard; two others lay dead in pools of their own blood, while Miles and yet another guard fought.

"Hold!" he yelled in a powerful voice, but it was lost on the two men who battled.

Drawing his scimitar, Saladin moved forward. With one mighty swing, he killed the man who the eagle fought. With his next, he laid open the back of the last guard. The man stumbled back, pain and shock on his face as he stared at his king.

"Pig!" screamed Saladin. His scimitar flashed again, and the guard's head parted company with his body. Then Saladin turned to Miles, who held his scimitar in readiness.

Carefully, Saladin lowered his blade and stared at Miles. "I see Allah has returned you from the dead."

"And I see you have tried to change that today."

"Me?" Saladin whispered.

Miles lowered his scimitar and slowly shook his head. "You are a great ruler, Saladin, and you bear many titles upon your head, but above it is the true one, oh Master of Deceit. Do not try to hide your deed from me!" Miles spat, turning and pointing to the body of the viper.

"It is no secret I want you dead. I had offered you everything I could, to make you my friend, and to give you a life worthy of that title. But you spurned me. Yet, I would not bring death to you this way—not with the bite of a snake."

"You say this is not your doing?"

"It is not. My respect for you does not permit me to end

your life this way. When the time comes, you shall die as a warrior."

"*If* that time comes. You must still meet Eldwin."

Saladin stared at Miles for a moment before he turned. Behind him were a dozen people. Borka-al-Salu held Aliya in a tight grasp.

"Release her; she has done well this day. Have this chamber cleansed," he said, turning to Aliya. Then he turned back to Miles. "Come with me and bring the eagle."

Miles bent and offered Valkyrie his wrist. The eagle stepped onto it, but did not close his talons over Miles's bare skin. Miles lifted his arm and secured Valkyrie with his free hand, before following Saladin from the chamber.

When they were within the audience chamber, Saladin sat, motioning Miles to the seat he had occupied before gaining Saladin's disfavor. Then Saladin called to one of his scribes, and the man came forward with parchment and quill.

"Take them," he directed Miles. Miles put Valkyrie on the floor next to him and took the writing materials. "Tell your wife that my champion will meet her at the place we call the Arena of the Souls."

When Miles finished, the scribe took back the parchment and drew a map beneath Miles's writing. None present concerned themselves or noticed that Valkyrie watched the drawing of the map with total concentration.

When it was done and the parchment tied in a scroll, Miles took it and, using a leather thong, attached it around Valkyrie's neck.

They then left the audience chamber and ascended to the roof of Saladin's residence. There, among the flowers his slaves tended so carefully, Saladin watched Miles release the golden eagle into the night sky.

"I am truly sorry, for we could have had a friendship that would last a lifetime," Saladin said to Miles as he waved the guards forward. "Return him to his chamber. Let nothing happen to him, or the horror of your deaths will be spoken of for generations to come."

"My lady!" cried Roweena, as she tried to wake Gwendolyn. She had come into her mistress's rooms just after the sun had set and found Gwendolyn sitting on the floor. The silver sword rested in her lap, and her face was the color of death. She saw only the barest rise and fall of Gwendolyn's breasts and had called out to her several times.

When Gwendolyn did not respond, Roweena ran out in search of James. When she found him, she urged him to follow her, saying that Gwendolyn had taken ill.

They burst into the chamber, and Roweena had cried out again to Gwendolyn. But James had stopped her and pulled her away. "She is in a trance. She will wake," he told her. But Roweena just stared at the woman she was devoted to and prayed that James's words were true.

Finally, while she watched over Gwendolyn, she saw the color return to her face and her breathing grow deeper. A moment later Gwendolyn's eyelids fluttered, and Roweena sobbed loudly.

Gwendolyn's first sight was Roweena's red-rimmed eyes; then she saw James. "Get your brother; we leave in the morning," she stated. "James," she called, stopping him before he left, "after you talk with Arthur, go to the king; tell him I must speak with him tonight."

James nodded and quickly left. When he was gone, Gwendolyn glanced at Roweena again. "What is wrong with you?" she asked.

Roweena shook her head slowly and stood. "I feared for your life," she admitted.

"And I feared for another's. You are a true friend, Roweena, and I thank you for that."

"What happens in the morning? Will you leave me behind again to hide your disappearance?"

"No. You have an important role to play. I will explain while I dress; there is much to do this night."

While Roweena dressed Gwendolyn, she listened intently to what her mistress said. They would ride out of Ascalon the next morning and head into the desert to a place far from any Christian stronghold. Once they were near, Roweena would dress as if she were Gwendolyn and would wear a veil and a tightly woven gold coif to hide her dark hair. She would stay hidden behind the curtains of the conveyance and speak to no one.

By the time Gwendolyn was dressed and ready to leave, Arthur and James appeared.

"Richard bids you join him for the evening meal."

"Good." Gwendolyn smiled gently at the news. "Have the horse-drawn litter prepared. Put my armor in it and bring a sword for Sir Miles."

Arthur's wide smile warmed Gwendolyn's heart, and tears pooled within her eyes. "Soon," she whispered. "James, Valkyrie will return before the first light. Be ready for him."

After all her orders had been issued, Gwendolyn left her rooms and went to the king's residence. Richard would not take kindly to what she had to tell him, but it must be done.

Entering Richard's quarters, she felt relief that he was alone. She would not have to wait until an opportunity presented itself to speak with him. Richard was gracious, and only after she was seated at the table, and the meal begun, did he question her reason for this audience.

"I seek your permission to go into the desert."

"What nonsense are you proposing now?" Richard asked tersely. He had not forgotten their last anger-filled confrontation, nor the way she had gained what she sought.

"Majesty, I am going after my husband."

Richard shook his head sadly. He truly liked Gwendolyn Delong and hated to see what was happening to her. "Madame, I must ask you to leave the world of dreams you live in and face reality. Miles will never be released. And I think now is the time for your return to England."

"Your Majesty, I cannot."

"Lady Gwendolyn, I order you to do this, out of the love I bear your husband, and the respect I hold for you."

"Sire—"

"No! I have made my decision. I have let you talk me into certain things and have given in to your desires. Your love for your husband is strong and stands as an example to all of us, but it must become a memory now."

"It is too late to stop what I must do."

"Nothing is too late. Explain yourself," Richard commanded patiently.

"I have spoken with Saladin," she said in a low voice. She gazed openly at him, waiting for his reaction.

"You have what!" he shouted.

"I have met with Saladin and have arranged a challenge."

"You are insane, or I am dreaming. When did this happen?"

"Four days ago."

"You were abed, ill."

"No, Sire, I was in the desert. There I met Saladin and challenged him. He has agreed to my challenge. His best knight will face Sir Eldwin. If Eldwin wins, Miles goes free."

"If he loses?" Richard whispered.

"Miles will still ride at your side."

"Do not play word games with me, madame, but answer my question."

"If Eldwin loses," Gwendolyn said in a level voice, "my person shall be the price of ransom for my husband."

"What have you done? You have made a bargain with hell."

"I have done what was necessary," Gwendolyn stated calmly.

"You have gone against my wishes. You have met with the enemy behind my back, and worse, no matter the outcome of this challenge, England will be the loser. Do you think Saladin would release your husband if Eldwin wins? He would be a fool. Two of my strongest, most valuable men would be in his grasp. He will never release them, or you! I forbid this to happen!"

"It is too late."

"Madame, neither you nor Sir Eldwin shall leave the gates of Ascalon."

"Would you hold me prisoner?"

"If need be."

Gwendolyn held Richard's glare and waited until the anger diminished in his eyes before speaking again. "Eldwin has already left Ascalon. He waits for me in the desert. If I do not arrive when I am supposed to, he will continue on anyway."

"Then he will do so alone. Go to your quarters and prepare for your return to England."

"Why?" Gwendolyn whispered.

"Because I am your king, and because you have acted against my authority. I pray that you remember Eldwin's unquestioned devotion to you and your husband, for you have sent him to his end."

"You cannot do this to me," Gwendolyn pleaded in an emotion-filled voice.

"Lady Delong, I have given you much and have let you have your way in many things because I admired your bravery and strength. But now I see I was mistaken. Your actions are those of a woman who knows not the ways of war, or of the thoughts of men, but acts only out of selfish motivation."

Gwendolyn rose slowly and stared at Richard. She felt no hatred for him; rather, she felt a shallow pity. "As England's king, you could have been the greatest of them all, for the people look up to you and worship you. Instead, you chose to turn your back on your land in quest of glory. In generations to come, much will be said of you as a fighter, but nothing will be said of you as the leader of your people."

"Madame!" Richard roared as he, too, stood to face her.

"Banish me if you will, Your Majesty, but know you this. I live for but one thing, my husband. Your self-serving quest for glory may have lost him to me, but as long as I have breath in my body, and there is life within Miles, I shall live only to be rejoined with him. Look after your lands, Richard *Coeur de Lion,* for wisdom must be combined with your lionly strength if you are to rule as a true king!"

"I regret this outburst from you, madame. Leave me before the restraints of my temper fail."

Gwendolyn walked from the chamber, her own anger making her muscles tremble. She had expected Richard to react badly, but not as he had. She had thought he would argue with her, but give in when she told him that Eldwin had already left the city. Now, she must yet again defy his orders, for the one thing she had forgotten was that besides being king, he was a man. Her defiance of his orders had dealt his ego a blow, and that was Richard's biggest weakness as a king. His ego made him reach toward goals best left unfound. His ego, and the desires to make himself great, had been the cause of Miles's imprisonment, and the very reason for her being here now.

Her first action upon returning to her quarters was to send for Sir Justin. When he arrived, he found Gwendolyn pacing nervously about the chamber.

"My lady?" he asked when he entered.

"Sir Justin, I know of your loyalty to myself and Sir Miles. I would ask a favor of you."

"There is nothing I would not do," the knight responded gallantly.

Gwendolyn laughed for the first time that night and smiled warmly at Justin. "You are chivalrous to a fault, but I have asked only one man for a boon without first telling him of it. I would not do that to another. Justin, I have just left Richard, and he has ordered me back to England."

"He would not."

"He has. I am prepared to defy him. I am leaving Ascalon on the morrow—"

"I will have our men ready to accompany you."

"No. What I must ask of you is more difficult. More difficult than even fighting the Saracens. Richard may try to prevent my leaving. I ask that you, and the men of Radstock, see to my safe passage from the city and prevent any whom Richard sends after me from reaching us."

"I will speak to our men. They will not take kindly to Richard's orders to you."

"He is their king."

"But our first duty is to the earl, and you."

"Justin, what I tell you next must not be repeated. I leave tomorrow to go to Miles. Eldwin is waiting for me. There is a chance to free the earl."

"My lady, I am sworn to Radstock, and not to this crusade. If I must stand against my king, then so be it."

"It may not be necessary. Richard may not stop me, but I would be prepared."

"I will do my best, my lady." Bowing, Justin left the chambers to gather his men.

Chapter Twenty-six

"GOOD," GWENDOLYN DEclared after she glanced at Roweena and saw the signal her servant was giving her. Gwendolyn had asked Roweena to do one special thing, and to make sure the twins would not see it. It was done.

"How many are outside?" This question was directed at James. Through the long night, Gwendolyn, Arthur, James, and Roweena had gone ahead with their preparations. Dawn would arrive within the hour, and Gwendolyn fully expected to be gone before the sun broke over the horizon.

During the night, Richard had sent two men to guard the exits from Gwendolyn's quarters. Arthur had watched where the men had set themselves and had checked frequently to make sure they were still there.

Gwendolyn wore a simple tunic, with high kid boots she had purchased the day before in the market. James attached the silver sword to the sash around her slim waist, and Roweena draped the hooded mantle over her shoulders. Gwendolyn was ready.

"The litter is prepared?" she asked again.

"It waits in the courtyard," Arthur replied.

"Roweena, wait by the conveyance for us. Act as if you are inspecting it and getting ready to leave." When Roweena left the room, and went into the courtyard, Gwendolyn gazed at the twin squires. "Everything must be done as I have instructed. No man can be injured." With that, Gwendolyn turned and led the squires out.

Ascalon, in the hour before dawn, slept peacefully. Gwendolyn left the curved archway and stepped into the stone street, breathing in the cool salt-scented air. In a matter of hours she would be deep into the desert, and she wanted to remember the smell and taste of Ascalon.

"Hold!"

Gwendolyn spun to face the first guard. "Are you speaking to me?" she asked, favoring the man with an icy stare.

"Go back inside, my lady. It is the king's orders."

"I have business to attend to," she replied, turning from him and quickly walking away.

"Halt!" said the second guard. He now barred her path to freedom. With one guard in front and one behind, Gwendolyn turned so that both would be close together and facing her.

"We cannot let you pass. Return to your quarters, my lady," the first guard repeated.

"Would you force me?" she asked.

The guards glanced at each other and then back at Gwendolyn. "If we must," said the second guard.

"You have made a grave mistake," whispered Arthur. His dagger was at one knight's throat, while James's was at the other's. Although the knights wore light maille, their necks were exposed.

"Don't do this," warned one of the guards.

"When you are found, tell Richard he gave me no choice. Tell him that when I return, I shall face him and accept whatever punishment he decrees. But for now, inside with you!"

The twins' knife points guided the knights into the stone chamber that Gwendolyn had slept in. There, James and Arthur bound the two knights securely.

Five minutes later Gwendolyn and James rode side by side, while Arthur rode the seat of the wheeled conveyance, guiding the horse-drawn wagon toward the eastern gate of Ascalon.

Silence followed their trail, and as they rode, Gwendolyn continually looked for signs of Justin and the men of Radstock. Then they were at the gate. Gwendolyn reined in the powerful stallion a dozen yards from the gate.

Ten men stood before the gate, barring her exit. At their head was Sir Hugo.

"Madame, please return to your quarters."

"I must refuse. Step aside, Sir Hugo," Gwendolyn ordered. Her eyes locked with his, and she suddenly remembered the brave knight whom she had fought in the spring tournament. She remembered, too, his low words to Eldwin, and the joining of their hands before the crowds.

Something in the way he looked at her told Gwendolyn that he did not like what he was doing, but as Richard's mercenary he had little choice. "Go back," he whispered.

"Step aside," Gwendolyn replied.

Hugo shook his head sadly, and with both hands, motioned his men forward. Gwendolyn slipped her hand inside the mantle and grasped the sword's pommel when the men came toward them. Just as she started to draw the sword, several loud thumps sounded, and Gwendolyn's arm froze. Justin and the men had arrived. They dropped from the walls above Hugo's men, and with quiet efficiency, subdued the other knights quickly.

Moments later, Justin stepped toward Gwendolyn. He, and all his men, wore coif-de-maille and cloth masks. None of Richard's men would be able to speak of who had attacked them. None, save possibly Hugo, who was held between two of Radstock's masked knights.

"God speed, my lady. None will follow until daylight."

"I thank you with the full depth of my heart," Gwendolyn said and reached out to take Justin's gauntleted hand. "My husband shall know of your loyalty."

"Just return with him," Justin asked.

"Be watchful until our return. Richard will be angered."

Releasing his hand, Gwendolyn rode to where her men held Hugo. "Your word as a knight that you will not raise the cry until we are well gone."

"My lady, do not defy the king—for your husband's sake and for his memory."

"Sir Hugo, it is for my husband's sake I do just that, and to ensure that Miles Delong does not become a memory, for a memory is not life! Your word, or must I have these men silence you with the hilt of a sword?"

"Be warned; Richard will not easily forget this."

"Hugo, you once pledged that should you be needed, you would freely join Eldwin and serve him. That is what is asked of you this day."

Hugo stared at her. She saw the memory of that spring day two years ago surface in his mind as his eyes grew wide and searched her face intensely. He had made that pledge on the tournament field. None should have known of it. None could have. Eldwin had been sworn to silence, and Lady Gwendolyn had not been present.

"Can it be?" he asked in a husky whisper.

"Life brings many new ideas, my friend; forget that not."

"You have my word," he promised. "Go now whilst you may."

Gwendolyn nodded her head and then turned to Justin. "After the gates are closed, return to your quarters. Thank you." With a wave of her hand, Gwendolyn signaled her small party forward. The gates opened slowly, and the small band rode through and into the still, dark night.

The evening call to prayer echoed hauntingly through the streets of Jerusalem. Everything stopped as a multitude of people began to walk toward the mosque. Those who could not go unrolled their prayer rugs and set them upon the ground.

Miles, standing again within Saladin's roof garden, glanced down at the people who prayed. He was waiting for Saladin and wondering what the ruler of the faithful wanted with him.

A few moments later, the city returned to life, and the activity in the streets grew loud again. Behind him, he heard footsteps and turned to face Saladin.

"We leave in the morning."

"Why did you agree to this challenge?"

"Because it was necessary. Miles, I have a large nation to govern, and this war taxes both myself, and my people. I must take whatever advantages are offered."

"So you would lie to my wife, yet keep your word to a dead man?"

"It is more complicated than that. You are one of the few warriors who my armies fear. You are strong, and when you fight, it is with your brain as well as your body. That is what makes you dangerous. This other knight of yours, Eldwin, fights in the same manner. The two of you are worth ten dozen of Richard's others. Those who watch you, follow you. When victory looms close for me, you and Eldwin have the ability to rally your men around you and continue the fight. Neither of you can be allowed to face my armies again. I must end this war."

"Yet, as a king, as the highest authority in your world, you have no need of deceit." Miles shook his head when he spoke to Saladin, letting his emotions fill his voice.

"Deceit can at times be as strong a weapon as the sword."

"And like the sword, its edge can strike the wielder as well as the opponent," Miles warned.

"I have not asked you here to speak of this," Saladin said as he walked past Miles to stare at the city spread out around him. "I offer you one more opportunity. Join me, accept the true faith and all it means. If you do this, I will spare the life of Eldwin and I will see you and your wife reunited."

"You would give up your desire to have her?" Miles asked.

"Is that so hard to understand? Yes, she is beautiful—more so than any Frankish woman I have known. I will not lie to you. I desire her as I have never before desired a woman. But I will see that desire go unsated, you have my word, if you will embrace Muhammad, and join me as a brother and friend."

Tension filled the air around them, and the silence grew deeper. The most powerful man in the Eastern world had once again humbled himself before Miles. Miles knew it had not been easy; however, what Miles had to do was no easier.

"I have known many friendships in my life. Usually they were based on who I was. I have had two brothers. One has died, and one has given his heart and mind to his God, so I am without. Since I have grown to know you, Saladin, King of the Moors, I have known what friendship can be. I accept you as a friend, as a brother, within my heart and mind, but I cannot do that which you ask, and it hurts me deeply."

Saladin faced Miles, his dark eyes glinting with moisture. He nodded slowly. "I knew this is what you would say, but I had no choice but to ask. They say love between men is a sin, yet my love for you is anything but. I shall remember always what could have been. And you, Miles of England, must remember, too, that what I do now, I do because I must."

"That is where we shall never agree," Miles said. "Saladin, what you plan is a mistake. I have tried to warn you. I ask you in the name of the friendship and brotherly love we cannot share together to give up this idea of yours. It will not be as you think."

"Miles, when the sun rises the day after tomorrow, all will go as I think. When the fight is over, no matter who the victor, you shall be a memory of what could have been. I offered you life and I offered you your wife, yet you persist in clinging to your madness. I have an obligation to my people. I must be true to them, no matter how I do this."

"And I have an obligation to myself. In the name of your God, in the name of Allah the compassionate, do not continue this insanity. I give you my parole. Neither myself nor Eldwin will raise arms against the Moslem world if you release me now. Go to Richard, negotiate and achieve the peace you crave."

"Where did you get the dagger that you used to kill my guard?" Saladin asked suddenly.

Miles glared at him. Once again, a curtain had fallen across Saladin's face, and the man who professed such deep love, had turned as cold as stone.

"I will remember you, Miles of England."

Suddenly two guards were at his side, called there by an unseen signal of Saladin's. The emir turned away from Miles as he was taken from the garden. When the air was once again peaceful, Saladin spoke in a low voice.

"What do you think?" he asked.

"May I speak freely?"

"You are my chief advisor. You are the grand vizier of all Moslems. The power you wield is second only to mine. Speak."

"I have consulted the Magi, I have looked at the stars. I have thought deeply upon this. Do as the Frank asks. Accept his parole."

"What have the stars said to you?"

"They say that desire withheld is a blessing. Desire unrestrained turns to sickness and disease."

"They speak in riddles. Son of my father's brother, do you advise me to give in to Richard?"

"No. You shall be victorious; it has been written in the stars for a thousand years. The world has never before witnessed a leader such as you. The Franks will not defeat us."

"Then what do you speak of?"

"Of honor. Release the Frank."

"Borka-al-Salu, I value your word, but this I may never do."

While Saladin and the grand vizier spoke on the roof, Miles was returned to his chamber. Within it Aliya waited. But, unlike the time before the assassination attempt, a guard always remained in the room.

Aliya faced Miles, and he saw the tears in her eyes. She knew that he would be leaving tomorrow and, despite his words of confidence, she knew, too, that he would be dead in two days. But the love she held for him was strong, and she would help him. When he stepped into the chamber, she flung herself at him, one arm going around his back, while the other dipped into her waistband. She cried loudly of her loss even as she secreted another dagger into his hands.

Miles, taken by surprise, clutched the blade tightly. A moment later Aliya released him and blocked the guard's view while Miles sat on the cushions, and hid the blade beneath them.

"I love you," she whispered to him. "I will remember you always." Then she was gone. For a long time after, Miles stared at the space she had been in, memorizing her form, and the soft beauty of her face. Aliya had made his life within Jerusalem bearable, and the love he felt for her was a good one. He would have loved a sister no less and he would miss her greatly.

Valkyrie's call brought Gwendolyn awake instantly. She sat up, throwing off her cover quickly, and grasping the sword. The first bands of purple and pink were on the eastern horizon, and she saw that the day would soon be here.

It was the day she had been born for. The day she was to meet destiny. She was sitting in the center of a small valley that was ringed with high dunes. The Arena of Souls was aptly named. It looked like a depression within the desert. A perfect circle of brown and coral sand. It was a fitting place for Eldwin to meet the challenge.

Gwendolyn lifted her sword and looked at the sleeping forms surrounding her. Roweena slept within the comfort of a quilted covering, while Arthur and James slept upon mantles spread on the sandy earth. The fire they had lighted the night before was gone; the horses were tied together twenty feet away.

They had ridden from Ascalon two days before and had stopped the first night in an oasis halfway to the Arena of Souls. Arthur, James, and she had alternated watches so that they could get some sleep, and be rested for the next leg of the journey. Throughout the ride, Valkyrie had flown ahead, returning occasionally without warnings of danger.

The night before, they had arrived at the Arena of Souls, and Gwendolyn had released Valkyrie to scout all around the area. When he had returned, they made camp in the center of the valley so that if any approached they would have ample warning.

"Now, my friend," Gwendolyn whispered to Valkyrie. Closing her eyes, she called upon the sword and drew an image of the eagle in her mind. Even as the giant bird's wings pushed the air across her face, the sword came to life in her hands, and she touched the alienness of Valkyrie's mind. Then she was seeing the earth grow small as Valkyrie rose. Although the sky was not yet light, she could see clearly. Valkyrie circled above the small encampment, and Gwendolyn could see herself and the silver sword. The glow cast from the blade pulsated around her, enveloping her within its field. Then the first edge of the sun rose above the dunes, and a ray of sunlight struck the sword. Gwendolyn saw herself glow with a soft yellow light that covered not only her body, but the three others who slept nearby.

Find them. Her command to Valkyrie was but her thoughts. The golden eagle suddenly dove toward the desert floor, and Gwendolyn's breath caught at the speed. The sands of the arena grew larger, as she flew above her own head. Valkyrie turned and rose effortlessly, catching current after current until he was a mile above the earth. Yet even that high, Gwendolyn could see everything perfectly.

In the distance was another encampment. Gwendolyn knew that Saladin would be near. She had needed to know how far away he was, and how much time she would have to get ready. Now she knew. The camp was coming to life under the rising sun. There were twenty tents spread out below Valkyrie, and Gwendolyn counted at least a hundred men.

Find Miles, she directed. Valkyrie descended swiftly and flew above the encampment. Gwendolyn saw everything, but could not find Miles. The eagle circled the camp, and Gwendolyn saw that many of the Saracen knights were looking at the eagle.

Suddenly Saladin emerged from a tent and followed a man's pointing finger. Valkyrie circled a second time in his effort to find Miles. Then Miles came out of a tent. His arms were free, but a chain was around his waist. Valkyrie gave vent to a chilling scream, and Miles looked up with a smile on his face.

Valkyrie rolled in the air and dove toward Miles's head. The guard who was next to him fell to the ground, but Miles did not move. Valkyrie passed three inches above Miles, his hair fluttering with the eagle's passing.

Valkyrie rolled again and circled above the Saracens. Suddenly Gwendolyn saw one of the knights raise a double-curved bow, already notched with a shaft. She screamed her warning to Valkyrie, but the eagle was in a fixed current. She saw Miles move, his hand dipping into his surcoat. Everything happened with the speed of light. Miles's arm shot outward, and Valkyrie caught another current, twisting his body, and drawing in his wings.

A dagger flew through the air, striking the bowman's arm and drawing a scream of pain. The shaft missed its mark and Valkyrie extended his wings again.

Everything happened swiftly. Yet, Gwendolyn, far away, saw it all. She watched as Miles's guard stood and yanked on her husband's chains. She sat frozen, unable to help, when the guard took the free end of the chain, and using it like a whip, struck it across Miles's back.

But Valkyrie heard her anguish, and even as the guard drew back the chain again, he dove, his two-inch talons extended fully. He struck the guard's neck, but did not try to hold. Instead, his talons raked upwards along the man's neck and head, but he did not slow his flight. A heartbeat later, Valkyrie was poised in the air, ready to dive again.

Gwendolyn stopped him with a powerful thought as she saw Saladin help Miles from the ground. The injured guard was held by two others, and Saladin nodded to Valkyrie.

The giant eagle screamed once, and then Gwendolyn called him back. A moment later, the sword's glow departed, and Gwendolyn opened her eyes. Her breathing was forced and ragged, as if she'd already faced her enemy and had fought him physically. But she forced what she witnessed from her mind and put down the sword.

Descending slowly, Valkyrie came to rest on the pommel of the sword. His amber eyes locked on Gwendolyn's. *Thank you, my friend.*

Pandemonium reigned in Saladin's camp for several moments after the eagle had gone. The bowman was being held by two others, as Saladin had ordered, and the guard who had whipped Miles with the chain was lying on the ground staring at the emir. Two of Saladin's bodyguards held their scimitars at the hapless man's throat while Saladin supported Miles.

"You are like a magician," Saladin said, with a shake of his head. "But instead of drawing jewels from the air, you find daggers to fling at my men."

Miles stared silently at Saladin.

"I believe I must thank your eagle. For if it were not for him, I feel that blade would have sought yet another target." Saladin held Miles's gaze and smiled at him. "Where did you get this one?"

"Does it matter?"

"I would hear it from your lips."

"So that I may condemn one of your people to death?"

"My word to you that it shall not happen."

"Your word?" The sarcasm within Miles's voice struck Saladin harshly.

"As Allah is my witness, and Muhammad his prophet, nothing shall befall the one who gave you the blade."

"Your word is meaningless. You plan to kill me this day. I will not have you do the same to the one who helped me."

"I admire you. No harm shall come to Aliya."

"You do not know she was the one who aided me."

"There is no one else who would dare. You inspire love and loyalty, Miles of England. I would not destroy anyone who acted because of that, no matter how misguided."

"You are a man of many contradictions," Miles admitted.

"No, Miles, that is where you are wrong. I have nothing to contradict. What I say is law. What I do is right. I am the ruler of all I survey, and what I do, I do with the guidance of Allah."

"If my blade had reached the target it was meant for, would you still feel the same?"

Saladin laughed loudly and shook his head. "Would I not be dead? How could I punish her then?"

"You amaze me," Miles said. "And what happens now?"

"Everything," Saladin declared. He turned and signaled two men forward, speaking so rapidly that Miles could not understand what he said. A few minutes later a cart was brought to them. The knights whom Saladin had spoken to grabbed Miles and carried him to it. Three other men came to them, chains and manacles in their hands.

Then Miles knew what would happen. He twisted his face to Saladin and stared at him, hatred pouring from his eyes.

"It must be this way," Saladin said with finality.

Two men held Miles while he fought against them, but he was no match for the five knights. Several minutes later they were done, and Miles was suspended within the cart. His wrists were manacled tightly, and he hung on outstretched arms from a beam above his head. His ankles were likewise manacled and his legs were spread. The chains holding them were attached to another beam on the base of the cart.

When he was secured, Saladin looked at him hanging between four lengths of chain. "The dagger would have done you no good, Miles. Be happy you found a use for it before it was too late."

Then Saladin clapped his hands. Miles watched, ignoring the pain in his wrists, as the crowd surrounding Saladin parted. Walking down the center of the parted crowd was the largest Saracen knight Miles had ever seen. He wore only the split voluminous pants of his race, with a deep blue sash securing them. His chest was a myriad of well-defined muscles, and his shoulders were wide spread and powerful. The knight's neck was as thick as a small tree, and his shaven head gleamed under the morning sun. In his hand he held a large scimitar, its curved length looking sharp and dangerous.

"This is al-Nasir. He is our mightiest knight. He has never been defeated in war, or in the arena. Do you think your puny champion will defeat him?" asked Saladin.

Miles studied al-Nasir. He was indeed the largest man he had ever seen. Miles remembered, too, having seen this knight on the battlefield several times, but he was always on the far side, and they had never met. Instead of answering Saladin, Miles merely smiled.

"Very well, we shall see." Turning abruptly, Saladin spoke to the grand vizier. "Have the fifty men I have chosen follow when we crest the dunes. Have them wait for the signal. They are not to be seen until then."

"As you wish, Master of Life," Borka-al-Salu whispered.

"When you have given my orders, I would have you drive the wagon. Only you, I, and the prisoner shall enter the Arena of Souls."

"Is that wise?"

"It is the only way. We do not want to chase away the Frank knight and the woman. They must believe the bargain to be as they see."

Borka-al-Salu nodded slowly, but he could not force away the feeling of wrongness from his mind. He prayed to his God, but knew that his prayers would be wasted. No matter what Saladin had said, the emir wanted the two knights dead, and the woman in his harem.

"It is time," Gwendolyn stated. Her three companions stood silently. Roweena lifted a jewel-encrusted coif and veil and placed it on her head. She hoped the fine mesh would hide her features so that her image would not give Gwendolyn away. Then she placed the golden rope that held Gwendolyn's Saracen dagger over the maille so that the rope would hold the veil in place. The dagger's tip rested in the center of her breasts.

While she did this, James, acting as Gwendolyn's squire again, removed her tunic. Gwendolyn stood naked in the center of the Arena of Souls and accepted the heated rays of the sun on her body. Then James held out the only two pieces of clothing she would wear beneath her surcoat. The padded breast bindings and loincloth. She allowed him to put on the breast binds and then turned to give him easy access to secure it. "Tighter," she said when he closed it the first time. "No one must see the outline of my breasts beneath the surcoat." A moment later she was satisfied. James then strapped the loincloth around her hips and secured it tightly.

"The boots," she said. James lifted one of the kid boots and held it for Gwendolyn to step into. The boots were important. She must stay disguised, and her legs and feet might give her away. She was permitted no armor, but nothing was said of coverings for feet, legs, and hands.

When both boots were on, and secured above her knees, she nodded again. Arthur joined James, and together they began to wrap Gwendolyn's arms in thin lengths of cloth, binding her skin efficiently, and hiding its porcelain luster. She would wear no gloves, but her arms, hands, and fingers would be bound and somewhat protected by the strips.

"A coif-de-maille?" James asked.

"No armor."

"It is wrong," Arthur stated when he handed James Gwendolyn's surcoat. Together, they held it up so that Gwendolyn could step under it. When it was settled on her shoulders, and her arms were free, she smiled at the twins.

"You have done so much more than was ever expected. You have proven yourselves to be special. Today marks a change in our lives. James, before you place the mask over my head, give me my sword."

James did as he was bid, and when she was holding the blade, she looked first at James, and then at Arthur. "James, son of Harold, squire of Eldwin, kneel. Arthur," she called as she gazed at the other blonde-haired squire. "Arthur, son of Harold, squire of Miles, Earl of Radstock, kneel."

When the twins were kneeling before her, she stepped back. Closing her eyes, she invoked the power of the sword and raised it high. A bolt of light shot from the tip of the silver blade, spreading outward, covering them like a cloud. The blade was still glowing when she lowered it over their heads.

"By the powers given me as a knight of England, by Miles, Earl of Radstock, and by the hand of Richard I, King of England, I do hereby formally dub you a knight of the realm," she said as she lowered the blade and touched James with the triple dubbing of knighthood. Then she stepped before Arthur. "And you, Arthur," she said, slowly touching his shoulders solemnly with the sword and repeating the words she had spoken to James.

"I charge you both to uphold the code of chivalry, and give you the knightly rights and responsibilities to bear arms and mete justice. In the name of England, King Richard, and God, rise, Sir James of Radstock. Rise, Sir Arthur of Radstock."

The twins rose slowly, their eyes wide and staring. "When this day is done, and if you have need, my husband will reaffirm my actions. Roweena," she called.

Roweena came forward. In her arms were the two long objects she had secreted in the conveyance the night they had left Ascalon and had kept hidden from James and Arthur until this very moment. The twins gasped as one when they saw the swords. "Use them wisely and treat them well," Gwendolyn intoned. The two newly knighted twins took their new swords and held them reverently in their hands. Then, acting as one, they knelt again and held the swords upward.

"We pledge our oath to you, Sir Eldwin, Lord Protector of Radstock, and to Sir Miles, and the Lady Gwendolyn."

"Rise, my knights," Gwendolyn whispered. "The mask."

A moment later, James adjusted the mask of Eldwin and secured it. When he stepped back, his throat constricted painfully. He knew that this day would be the last day he would assist the knight he loved so dearly.

Gwendolyn sheathed her father's sword and, as Valkyrie called loudly, she turned to watch as Saladin appeared in the distance.

Chapter Twenty-seven

GWENDOLYN STOOD MOTIONless as Saladin descended into the Arena of Souls. He rode his large white stallion, and behind him was another knight. Behind that knight appeared a cart, and a stab of anger burned into Gwendolyn's mind when she saw Miles suspended by chains within it.

Turning, she walked back to the conveyance. She had spoken to Roweena yesterday and told her exactly what to do and say. When Gwendolyn reached the curtained litter, she saw an image within it and could make out the low sheen of the golden coif. Roweena would suffice if Saladin did not force his way inside. James and Arthur had been ordered to prevent that, and she knew they would.

But she wanted to leave nothing to chance and had still another idea. She did not know if this idea would succeed, but she grasped the sword and closed her eyes. She invoked its power and sensed it stir within her hands. Building an image of herself in her mind, she pictured herself in the litter and asked that all who gazed at it believe she was truly inside. Then she lowered the sword and nodded to the twin knights.

They moved the litter toward the edge of the field and, when it was set, they took their places in front of the curtains, their swords drawn in protection.

Then Gwendolyn turned to await Saladin and his champion. While she waited, she turned her outrage for Miles's treatment into a white-hot fury that would control her hands and the sword they would soon wield.

As they came nearer, Gwendolyn studied her adversary. He was large, and even on horseback she saw he would stand well above her. His arms were corded with layer upon layer of muscle, and his broad shoulders would add to the strength of his blows. He was naked from the waist up. His skin glowed with a fine sheen of perspiration.

Then they were there. Saladin dismounted and stepped in front of Sir Eldwin. "You are ready?" he asked.

Gwendolyn nodded.

Saladin walked past Eldwin and stopped a few feet in front of the litter. Both James and Arthur stood stiffly, but their swords moved swiftly, crossing in a blur to block Saladin's goal.

He laughed as he watched them. "Our bargain is met. Prepare to join me shortly!"

The form behind the curtains shifted, but no response issued forth.

"Will you not speak to me? Will you not show yourself? Open the curtain! The contest will not start until I see your face!"

Slowly, a slender hand reached out and parted the curtain. Saladin stared at the golden-veiled woman, trying to pierce the mistiness of the threads. A moment later the curtain fell back in place, and Saladin turned to face Eldwin. "Your mistress tempts me with her veil. I shall enjoy removing it in a short while."

For an answer, Gwendolyn held out her arm. Valkyrie left his perch on the litter and glided over to her. She stared at Saladin for a moment through the slits in the chamois mask and then gave Valkyrie his command with a thought. She flung him skyward, his loud call shattering the day. Then he circled above them. Gwendolyn's guard was on patrol.

"Look now at your master, Knight of England. Look at how he is held to mockery. You must defeat al-Nasir before you gain your master's release. Are you ready?"

Gwendolyn glanced at Miles and saw him hold his head up proudly. A shadowy smile graced his lips, and his green eyes shone with love.

Sir Eldwin bowed formally to Saladin before striding to the center of the arena-like valley where al-Nasir stood in waiting. She noted well the overlong scimitar in his hands. Behind him, sticking up from the ground, were javelin and battle-axe; the peculiar battle-axe of the Saracens, with its sharp-tipped back edge, and razor-honed assault blade.

At her own spot rested only the battle-axe which Miles had had made for her. "My champion chooses the weapon of the fight, you must do the same. You have no javelin, only the axe. You may use your sword or axe against the javelin. Is that understood?" Saladin asked.

Gwendolyn bent and picked up the battle-axe. She hefted it and swung it in her cross pattern. That was her answer. Then she turned to al-Nasir and waited.

Gwendolyn had known since the moment she issued this challenge that she would be put to her ultimate test. It would take more than her silver sword to win this contest, and she sensed it would be she, not the blade, that determined the outcome.

Perspiration coated her face beneath the mask, as it did her entire body. The heat of the day was strong, and Gwendolyn gave thanks for the strips of cloth binding her hands.

Al-Nasir stared openly at her. Then he smiled. Turning, he pulled his axe free of the earth and grasped its long handle in his hands. Gwendolyn saw the muscles of his shoulders knot when he swung the axe. But even as he moved toward her, she inspected him minutely. The slippers he wore were curved near the toes and they were as thin as a second skin. They would find purchase no matter where he stepped. His muscles rippled under his olive skin, tanned crisp by his life in this land.

Sir Eldwin drew herself tall and bowed at the Saracen knight. Al-Nasir paused for a moment as he watched her, then, he, too, nodded his head. When he lifted it, he screamed and charged.

Gwendolyn was ready. When the man swung at her, she moved, neatly sidestepping the blow. The large axe whistled by her, missing her shoulder by two feet, and the battle was on.

They circled each other warily, neither making an advance. Four eyes watched, and four legs moved in rhythm performing a strange dance that was both graceful and deadly.

Gwendolyn let her mind float freely, choosing to let instinct and training guide her movements. She blended together all the parts of her mind and, as she had done when fighting Morgan, called upon that area of herself that was Miles.

Then she moved, using the training he had taught her, and jumped straight at al-Nasir. Before she reached him, she tucked her head and dove to the ground, the battle-axe's handle drawn against her stomach while she rolled in a perfect somersault past him. She was on her feet then, and the deadly blade of the axe whooshed through the air.

Al-Nasir had been ready for her attack, but was unprepared for what Eldwin did. He had barely turned and raised his axe when she struck. The blade of Eldwin's axe caught al-Nasir's in the center of the handle, shattering it within his grasp.

Gwendolyn recovered quickly, but not fast enough to stop the Saracen from sprinting away. Before she could go after him, he held the javelin in his hand, another wide smile spread across his face as he gave vent to a loud, haunting laugh.

Al-Nasir swung the javelin around and grasped it with both hands. *"Ins'Alla,"* he screamed, charging toward Eldwin.

Gwendolyn set herself for the charge. Her breathing was heavy, her blood pounding in her head. She had never faced a lance on foot and never without a shield. She did not have time to draw her sword, and had to depend on the axe. She watched the tip of the javelin come nearer. Then she looked into al-Nasir's eyes. She saw blood and death written within them, but she held her fear back.

Then he lunged across the final few feet. Gwendolyn spun, whipping the axe in an upward arc. The impact of the axe on the javelin sent shivers of pain lancing through her hands, but she ignored them.

The lance had not broken, but al-Nasir had been carried far beyond her in his mad charge. He shook his head like an angry bull and spun to face Eldwin. This time his eyes locked with hers, and she saw the fighting madness which held him. He bellowed angrily, set his shoulders, and charged at her again.

Gwendolyn stood still, knowing that she could not battle him with the lance. Just when he was on her, she ducked and rolled beneath the javelin's tip, her axe swinging not at the lance, but at the Saracen's unprotected legs.

She felt the axe bite into al-Nasir's calf and saw the man trip and fall. But he was on his feet in a second, and Gwendolyn stared, unbelieving, at him. The axe should have severed his leg, yet he stood.

Al-Nasir laughed loudly and flung away the javelin. Then he tore the material of his pants at the spot Gwendolyn's axe had struck, exposing a mailled leg to her eyes.

"Fool!" he spat. Then he ran back to where he'd left the scimitar and lifted it in the air.

Gwendolyn stared at her enemy. All the warnings she had given herself had meant nothing. Saladin had lied to her. His champion was armored. His legs had been protected by armor, and she had been denied the victory she had fairly gained.

Eldwin turned to Saladin. She saw he, too, smiled broadly. She shook her head at him and then drew the silver sword. She called upon its aid, but also held its power in abeyance. She was more determined than ever to win by her own hand.

Yet, she accepted the warmth that vibrated through her and joined in with its eternal call to battle. Her arms grew light, and the strength of the sun no longer bothered her. Her breathing grew steady, and she tasted the sweet air filling her lungs. She could feel every grain of sand beneath her feet and hear every sound that floated in the air.

Al-Nasir's breathing was loud, and his step was cautious. She gazed at him intently, her sword held before her in both hands. She crouched in an offense position, yet waited for her opponent to come at her.

Her eyes were locked on his, waiting.

Then he moved, the giant scimitar lifting in a blur as he rushed her. Gwendolyn did not move. Her arms rose in a fluid movement, carrying the sword high. Al-Nasir's blade descended and struck the silver sword.

The sounds of the blades exploded, and for an instant of eternity, both fighters were poised motionless together. Then Gwendolyn, again letting her instincts control her actions, swiveled under the blades. As she did, she drew her sword down. The moment it was free, she sidestepped and let the Saracen's weight carry him past her. Before al-Nasir could recover, Gwendolyn lunged forward. The tip of her sword bit into the sinewy muscle of his left arm.

Al-Nasir roared as he turned and, once again, faced Eldwin. He ignored the blood seeping from his arm and attacked her, calling to his God to guide him. His scimitar flashed in the sun, and the sounds of their battle grew loud in the Arena of Souls.

Saladin watched intensely as they fought. He saw his champion lose his axe and then watched as his fighting rage made him careless with the javelin. When the Frank's axe failed to hurt al-Nasir, Saladin permitted himself a laugh of indulgence. But when he held Eldwin's gaze, his smile froze on his lips. Although he could not see the knight's eyes, he felt the accusation of what Eldwin had just discovered.

For the first time, Saladin's conscience bothered him with the truth of his deceit. But that was wiped from his mind when the two met with blades. Throughout his life, he had never before witnessed a duel such as this. He had never seen a man move as swiftly as did the Frank. The long Frankish sword was like lightning in the knight's hands, forcing al-Nasir to battle time and again, yet never letting him get close.

When Eldwin's stroke drew blood, Saladin sensed the knight's own victory growing near. When the two champions came together again, Saladin turned to the grand vizier and nodded.

Borka-al-Salu took a deep breath. He lifted the bow that rested by his feet and grasped the arrow that lay next to it. But, as he watched the two men battle, he left his seat on the wagon and went to Saladin.

"It is wrong. You are making a fatal mistake. Please, Oh Guardian of the People, do not do this."

"Send the signal!" Saladin roared, his eyes never leaving the two warriors who battled under the grueling sun.

Gwendolyn fell back under the Saracen's assault. Not because he was beating her, but because she wanted to lull him. He fought passionately and, gripped within his fanatical madness, she knew he would give no quarter.

She stopped suddenly, planting her feet in the sandy soil, and countered his thrust. Then she whirled the sword over her head once, and the blade sang in the air. Its whistling path could not be followed, but its end could. The silver blade met the scimitar and forced it back.

Again and again, Gwendolyn attacked al-Nasir. Now it was her turn to press on, and she did so unmercifully. Still she did not call for the aid of the sword's power. She flowed like a spirit, blending with the blade as she attacked him. The sound of metal upon metal rang clearly, and with her heightened battle senses, she heard al-Nasir struggling to catch his breath.

Then she whirled unexpectedly, and the silver sword blurred in the air. The whistle of its passing sounded more like an arrow shaft. When it met the Saracen scimitar, the world exploded in sound.

Suddenly, al-Nasir tripped and fell backward, his scimitar held only in one hand. In an instant, the tip of the silver sword was at the Saracen's throat, penetrating the first layer of skin.

Al-Nasir stared up at the masked knight and waited for his death.

Gwendolyn turned, but held the sword against her fallen enemy as she stared at Saladin. She watched Saladin bow to her and hold his hands outstretched in the sign of peace.

Gwendolyn drew a deep breath and took the sword from al-Nasir's skin. She took a step slowly toward Miles and saw his eyes widen and his mouth open. Without hesitation, she grasped the sword in both hands and called for its power, even as she turned blindly, swinging the long blade in a fast arc.

Sparks exploded when her blade cut through al-Nasir's scimitar. His scream of rage was cut off when the glowing blade paused in midair and returned to take the gift it had only moments ago given. When Gwendolyn turned back to face Saladin, her silver sword was coated with the lifeblood of Saladin's greatest warrior.

Then she saw the other man with Saladin and watched helplessly as he released a shaft into the air. *Signal!* her mind screamed. Instantly, she willed herself into rapport with Valkyrie and saw fifty mounted Saracen knights spur their horses on.

Withdrawing from Valkyrie's vantage point, Gwendolyn stared at the high dunes surrounding the Arena of Souls. Then she saw Saladin draw his scimitar and face her.

Instead of accepting the challenge, Gwendolyn ran to the black stallion who was waiting patiently. Unhindered by the weight of maille, Gwendolyn was able to leap onto the stallion's back.

She kicked the horse's flanks, urging him forward. Then she held the sword high, withdrew the restraints from her mind, and channeled her energy into the blade. Light flared around her, and an ethereal glow filled the arena, freezing everything and everyone as it did.

Then she was at the cart. The silver sword flashed four times, cutting through the chains that bound Miles as if they were but silken cords. She waited until Miles was able to stand in the cart. When she saw his smile of love, she kicked the stallion forward again.

She rode toward the oncoming wave of Saracens and stopped. Closing her eyes, she willed the power of the sword to magnify, and when she felt the blade vibrate powerfully in her hands, she unleashed its might within the Arena of Souls.

Light erupted everywhere, shooting from the silver blade, rushing up from the dry sands of the desert floor. The dunes exploded with bands of silver and white, and the charging Saracens drew to a halt before the power they rode within.

Gwendolyn knew that nothing would make them come forward this day. Satisfied, she whirled the stallion around and rode toward Saladin.

The ruler of the Moslem world stood bravely before Sir Eldwin, his scimitar ready to do battle, his hands as steady as his eyes. But before the masked knight reached Saladin, the black stallion stopped, and Eldwin dismounted.

The blade still glowed as Gwendolyn neared her enemy, but she stopped ten feet from him and lowered the sword. She freed one hand from the pommel, and with her eyes locked on Saladin's, lifted her hand.

She grasped the chamois edge of the mask, and with excruciating slowness, began to withdraw it from her head. A moment later it was free, and with a shake of her head, Gwendolyn unleashed her long hair.

"Would you break our agreement, Saladin, King of the Moors? Would you try to win this day in any method, and then dare to share a bed with me?"

Saladin stared at the vision before him. His eyes told him

the truth, but he could not believe them. No woman could best al-Nasir. No woman could have pulled him from beneath the horse that had fallen on him in battle. No woman could have stood up under the onslaught of his legions. But his eyes continued to stare at the wheat-and-silver hair of Gwendolyn Delong.

"Do not look as if you see a ghost. I am no Saracen jinni, come to take you to hell. I am but a woman in search of my husband. Yet, Saladin, despite your treachery and lies, you have gained a victory this day. Today was the last battle of Sir Eldwin. Neither I nor my husband will have more of your hypocritical bloodbaths, called for in the name of a God who you, as well as the Christians, say is a God of love and peace. No more will I or mine fight for such an unworthy cause. The Frank devil, as your people call me, has died this day. Salaam, Saladin. Remember this day, and what you have witnessed. Think carefully before you give your word to someone and think doubly when you make a promise of duplicity!"

Gwendolyn moved quickly while Saladin stood paralyzed, her words ringing over and over in his ears. Miles was on the ground now, walking toward his wife. They met, and Miles Delong caught Gwendolyn to him, lifting her from her feet, and spinning her in a circle.

Their embrace left the rest of the world behind. Their lips met for the first time in two years, and Gwendolyn became whole again. The empty place within her heart filled, and she knew that this was only the beginning of the destiny she had been born to follow: that in the years to come, she and Miles would rise to greatness, and in the centuries that followed, their issue would ensure the continuance of a destiny that had been decreed when the earth was being formed, and the silver blade had been forged.

When Gwendolyn and Miles parted, they turned to face Saladin again. What they saw caught them unprepared. Saladin was kneeling, his head bowed before Gwendolyn.

Then Gwendolyn heard the voice of the old one echo in her mind. *Throughout the breadth of the land, greatness will follow, and kin[illegible]ill bow low before the issue of Kildrake.*

Of Significance

On August fifth, seven thousand Moslem warriors led by Saladin attacked Richard *Coeur de Lion*. The Christian knights battled heroically, and held off wave after wave of Saracens. At the proper moment, Richard led his mounted knights in a charge against Saladin. There were only fifteen knights who followed Richard, but they were mighty fighters, inspired by the mightiest of English kings.

Richard and his men fought gallantly, wreaking havoc through the width of the Saracen line. Richard was like a man possessed, going to the aid of any knight who needed his help, while battling the Saracens in deadly combat. Then, suddenly, Richard's horse was killed from under him, and he was on the ground, facing the wrath of the entire Saracen army.

Before a fatal blow could be landed, a Moslem knight galloped through, stopping before Richard, and offering him the reins of a fine stallion. When Richard was mounted, the Saracen spoke.

"The horse has been sent by Saladin, who knows the truth of chivalry."

Richard rewarded the Saracen knight and then returned to the battle.

One month later, a five-year treaty was signed by Richard *Coeur de Lion*, and Saladin.

Who is to know? Who is to judge why Saladin, when victory over Richard was ensured, held back his forces and gave the gift of life to the only man he had never been able to completely defeat? Could he have been remembering a time when another knight had done the same for him? Could he have been remembering long flowing hair the color of wheat and moonlight?

But all of that is fantasy.

Isn't it?

David Wind
Spring Valley, N.Y.

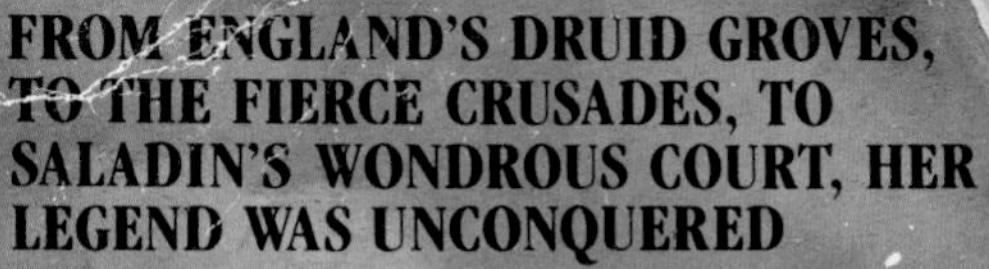

FROM ENGLAND'S DRUID GROVES, TO THE FIERCE CRUSADES, TO SALADIN'S WONDROUS COURT, HER LEGEND WAS UNCONQUERED

In the days of King Richard the Lion-Heart, the beauteous Gwendolyn was born. . . conceived in the twilight Druid mists, at the shimmering Pool of Pendragon.

As prophesied, she grew into golden womanhood, luminous in grace and power. When England's mightiest knight taught her the arts of war, she taught him the arts of passion, and their love burst into flame. But a jealous knight vowed to destroy them both. Only their deaths would quell his rage. . . only their union, destined by the gods, would forge the lifeblood of a new and timeless age.

ISBN 0-671-46973-8